Ain't No Mountain

Acclaim for Sharon Ewell Foster

"Foster is one of the brightest lights in Christian fiction. She takes us to places that our hearts sometimes fear to tread, and she rewards us with wonderfully complex characters who live with us long after the story ends."
> —Angela Benson, author of
> *Telling the Tale: The African-American Writer's Guide*

"Sharon Ewell Foster writes with boldness and sensitivity. Her believable characters easily find their way into my heart and stay there as friends."
> —Alice Gray, creator of
> the STORIES FOR THE HEART series

"Foster introduces a vibrant new voice to inspirational fiction, offering wisdom and insights that are deep, rich, and honest."
> —Liz Curtis Higgs, bestselling author of
> *Bad Girls of the Bible*

"Foster's prose is often evocative and eloquent."
> —*Publishers Weekly*

"To read a book by Sharon Ewell Foster is to have had an inside look at the heart and mind of God."
> —Regina Gail Malloy, Heaven 600 Radio

"Foster is an author who allows God to use her through her novels. . . . With every page, readers are left feeling inspired and hopeful with the knowledge that through God, all things are possible."
> —Lisa R. Hammack, Ebony Eyes Book Club

"Foster's characters are unforgetable; full of life and unhesitatingly charming. . . ."
> —Kweisi Mfume, President and CEO, NAACP

Ain't No Mountain

BETHANYHOUSE
MINNEAPOLIS, MINNESOTA

Ain't No Mountain
Copyright © 2004
Sharon Ewell Foster

Cover design by Koechel Peterson & Associates

Published by Bethany House Publishers
11400 Hampshire Avenue South
Bloomington, Minnesota 55438
www.bethanyhouse.com

Bethany House Publishers is a Division of
Baker Book House Company, Grand Rapids, Michigan.

Printed in the United States of America

ISBN 0-7642-2885-4 (Trade paper)
ISBN 0-7642-2911-7 (Large Print)

Library of Congress Cataloging-in-Publication Data
Foster, Sharon Ewell.

Library of Congress Cataloging-in-Publication Data

Foster, Sharon Ewell.
    Ain't no mountain / by Sharon Ewell Foster.
      p. cm.
    ISBN 0-7642-2885-4 (pbk.) —ISBN 0-7642-2911-7 (large-print pbk.)
      1. Women—North Carolina—Fiction. 2. African American women—Fiction.
  3. North Carolina—Fiction. I. Title.
    PS3556.O7724A74   2004
    813'.6—dc22   2004001021

Dedication

God, I lift this book to you. No doubt, it is flawed, like me—but I have tried to deliver what I heard you speaking to me. If there is failure, lay it at my feet. But cover it, please, with your power and your love. You make us perfect; make it perfect. May the words of my pen and the meditation of my heart be acceptable in your sight.

This book is for all the imperfect people; they are the ones to whom I am sent. God loves you, right now. I wrote this book because He wanted you to know that—He loves you first.

The LORD is merciful and gracious, slow to anger, and plenteous in mercy. He will not always chide: neither will he keep his anger for ever. He hath not dealt with us after our sins; nor rewarded us according to our iniquities.—Psalm 103:8–10 KJV

The LORD is compassionate and gracious, slow to anger, abounding in love. He will not always accuse, nor will he harbor his anger forever; he does not treat us as our sins deserve or repay us according to our iniquities.—Psalm 103:8–10 NIV

God is sheer mercy and grace; not easily angered, he's rich in love. He doesn't endlessly nag and scold, nor hold grudges forever. He doesn't treat us as our sins deserve, nor pay us back in full for our wrongs.—Psalm 103:8–10 THE MESSAGE

We love because he first loved us.—1 John 4:19 NIV

"The unexamined life is not worth living."—Socrates

Acknowledgments

Thank you to my son, Chase (who is the model for the prince in this book); to my daughter, Lanea, who is a beautiful princess in her own right; to my lovely, compassionate cousin, LaJuana, and to my wise, compassionate friend, Ervin. You each gave me friendship, wise counsel, and unconditional love. I would have collapsed without you.

Thank you to Rev. Dr. Walter Scott Thomas, Senior Pastor of New Psalmist Baptist Church. Thank you for giving us wise, challenging, and life-giving words. Thank you to Rev. Dr. Ron Williams, Senior Pastor of Pleasant Grove Church, for hearing my confessions and giving me wise counsel. Thank you to Don Milam of Destiny Image Publishing, and writer-reconcilers Deni Williamson, and Dave and Neta Jackson, for praying for me, worrying about me, and writing books that get me into trouble. Thank you, Bishop Oby, Miss Portia, Little Portia, Elder Maynor, and all the Starks clan.

Thank you to everyone I've forgotten to thank. I'm sleepy, y'all. Forgive me.

Thank you, posthumously, to John Steinbeck (There is no better Christian fiction author, you all. Really. Read *East of Eden, The Grapes of Wrath* and *Of Mice and Men*—his word-wrestling with Christian themes is masterful.) and to the living Toni Morrison for forcing me to be better. Thank you to Maya Angelou and Jesse Jackson for challenging me to never stop speaking truth, and for inspiring me to attempt to do it with individual style.

Thank you to Kweisi Mfume for endorsing my work—though you still don't know me. Thank you to all the folks at Bethany and Multnomah. May God bless you abundantly.

Thank you to all my loyal and devoted readers. Thank you for your prayers, support and kindnesses.

Thank you to Baltimore for loving me and pressing me to your bosom. This is my song of love to you.

Thank you, God, for choosing me and loving me first. Thank you, Jesus, for showing me and teaching me the way.

Cast of Characters

Mary—the urban princess
Her friends . . .
- *Naomi* "the hair girl"
- *Latrice* "the nail girl"
- *Thelma* "the eye girl"

Her protégées . . .
- *Cat*
- *Pamela*
- *Agnes*

Puddin—the Hip-Hop God Mama and wife
Her husband . . .
- *Joe*

Her Comfort Circle sisters . . .
- *Othella* and *Minnie*

Moor—the African prince
His friends . . .
- *Blue*
- *Brighty*
- *Ali*

Out-of-town guests:
- *Meemaw*
- *Garvin*
- *Mr. Green*

1

Mary

The ringing telephone startled Mary awake. Her chest was heaving, her skin was clammy, and her white T-shirt clung to her shoulders and chest. She pushed the yellow sheets away from her face and tried to find quick safety in the old flowered wallpaper. As she lifted the phone from the cradle, she reminded herself that it was daylight. She forced herself up from nightmare panic to listen to the call. Once she answered, she wished she had stayed asleep and tried not to listen.

"Hello, Mary? It's me, Garvin."

It was her cousin from North Carolina—the D.C. party-girl turned married, saved mommy—calling way too early about nothing in particular. Always a dead giveaway. Garvin was calling, mostly, to be in her business.

Mary gave short answers: "Mm hmm" and "okay." Her breathing settled as her mind spoke to her lungs. It was just a dream, she repeated under her breath. What happened before the call was all a dream, the dream she'd been having every night for a while now. But what was happening now—this phone call—unfortunately was real and just part of the nightmare of her daily routine.

Okay, so maybe she didn't get a phone call every day, but it seemed that way. It felt like every day someone believed him or herself elected to tell Mary how to live her life.

Mary waited and pretended to listen to Garvin. She knew that sooner or later the conversation was going to come around to one thing—the same thing Garvin and everyone else seemed compelled to talk about.

Sex.

There, she said it. It was a new millennium, and it didn't seem like it should be such a big deal. But it was. In fact, somehow, it seemed like a bigger deal now. Years ago, no one seemed much concerned about her purity. She didn't remember any messages in church about it. There were plenty of messages about not getting pregnant, but none about abstaining from sex. No words about being virtuous—virtue was for other people. People from the wrong side of the historical tracks didn't get to have virtue. *Honey, don't have a baby before you get married! It will ruin your life!* But no one seemed to care. Or, they seemed to take for granted that as she came of age, she would also come of knowledge.

Now, everyone seemed to want to talk about sex. And whether or not she was having any. More to the point, it seemed that Garvin and almost everyone else Mary knew spent all their waking hours reminding her that she shouldn't be having any. Like the whole world should care? She was convinced that she was holding the interest of, and providing entertainment for, the entire free world. It felt like there was an anti-sex committee that took turns calling her.

Just wait. You've got plenty of time. Keep your eyes on the prize.

It's not that sex was even on her mind. Well, not most of the time.

She was busy. Her life was fine. But who were they all kidding anyway? Prince Charming wasn't beating down her door or the doors of any of the other single women she knew.

"Uh huh," she said while Garvin's voice droned on in her ear.

The truth was she was sick of all the friendly, concerned, unsolicited advice. Mary was particularly sick of the advice from people who *had* love, who *had* marriage; women who woke up in the morning after sleeping in the arms of their loving husbands, but who felt the need to preach to her, to tell her, *"Wait on the Lord!*

Wait until you marry." Or, they quoted Bible verses at her. *"'Whoso findeth a wife findeth a good thing!' Let him find you, baby."* Or, *"Seek ye first the kingdom of God'"* or *"The apostle Paul was single, you know."* Or the worst of all, *"Be single and be satisfied!"*

"Wait until you're married"—all from people who suddenly got amnesia when they got married and forgot that they hadn't waited. *"Let the man find you!"* from the same women who knew they chased their own men down and even flew from city to city so they could be seen on the front rows of churches in front of single pastors they weren't *supposed* to be chasing. *"Be single and be satisfied"* from married people who didn't have to be satisfied with being single. *"The apostle Paul was single and look what he did"* from the same married people who fed singles out of a long-handled spoon at church because they were single and wouldn't let them serve in certain positions in the church because they were single. Single. Not human, not saved. Single.

When they weren't calling her, the anti-sex committee, they were watching. When they were shaking their hands at her. Even in her sleep she could see their hands. Sometimes the hands were wringing and pleading, sometimes they were wagging and nagging, and other times they were pointing and accusing. Even though she wasn't doing anything, the hands always signaled that she was. They filled her with guilt and doubt.

All this was unsolicited advice—advice about not breaking the *Eleventh Commandment:* Thou shalt not be thinking about a man, wanting a husband, and definitely not thinking about *sex* or *romance* in any way. This was advice from people who at the same time seemed to feel free to break the other Ten Commandments willy-nilly. They could have other gods before God—like making money, watching television, shopping, or seeking status and titles. They could steal by not paying tithes or by taking office supplies from work. They could kill by gossiping—saying mean and slanderous things about one another or about the preacher or even people they didn't know. Their own commandment breaking seemed harmless to them. *"The Lord knows it's just how I am, chile."* However, they seemed dedicated to making sure that she and all other singles didn't transgress in any way—that they didn't break the Eleventh Commandment.

"I understand." She spoke and nodded as though she was really listening to Garvin. "Mm hmm."

Besides, it was hard to believe that the God of the whole universe—with all the wars, famine, and tragedy in the world—was so interested in whether she was sleeping around or not. It was all Mary could do to hold her tongue as she listened to Garvin drone on and on.

Mary had been to every singles conference. She went to church. She focused on the greater plan for her life. She kept busy caring for the needs of others. She had a hobby. She practiced going to the movies and out to dinner alone—even though it made her feel silly. But the truth was, she still felt alone. And there were no signs of a prince looking for her or even waiting to be found. Of course, he didn't have to be a prince. At this point, the neighborhood mailman was starting to look pretty good.

Get off my back and out of my business! That's what she wanted to yell at Garvin. That's what she wanted to tell every uptight, nosy person who showered her with unwanted concern. But she didn't. *Love is patient, love is kind, even . . . to people who are getting on your last nerve!* Mary just tried not to listen.

When an opportunity appeared, she quickly said good-bye to her cousin, escaped from the phone, and slipped out of her bed. She carefully avoided looking in the mirror on her dresser as she stepped past her computer, through the doorway to her bathroom, and into the shower.

Everything was as it had always been—the same pink translucent shower curtain, the same pink tiles on the wall, the same pink rubber fish pasted to the bottom of the tub to keep her from slipping. All of it, each piece, reminded her of her granny. The bathroom things, the house, and some pictures were just about all that

Mary had left of her grandmother.

When her granny was dying, Mary had stood by the front door waiting for her uncle to come. She didn't know him—her mother's brother, her granny's son—but she needed someone. So, just before Granny had slipped away, she had waited by the door for him, waited for him to come and tell her that everything would be all right. It was strange what had happened instead. Instead of coming wrapped in love, he had been clothed in a strange kind of jealousy.

He made certain that everyone knew that she—Mary's granny—had belonged to him and no one else—not to his niece Mary or other relatives. She belonged to him. Her friends were his alone. Granny's things were his alone—even underwear, hair combs, and floral scented powder. His behavior was most peculiar. He was not so attentive in life, but in death he was consumed with controlling each detail.

Even the grief was his alone. The suffering he gave to Mary, but the grief was his alone. He got to put on the show. He got the comfort. Mary got the death. She got to determine when the last breath was breathed. She got the nights and days of death rattles, while he entertained the friends that used to be hers and Granny's— the friends that were now only his. "She's not suffering at all," he told them, while in the other room Mary watched Granny grimacing in pain and struggling to breathe—her eyes, her face, saying she felt alone.

When it was all over, he told her to take whatever she wanted. "Go through her things. She would want you to have them," he said. Then like Tolkien's Gollum, jealousy and greed overcame him, and he wanted everything back. He wanted it all so badly that he even threatened Mary, accused her of stealing, and said he would call the police. He wanted it all—all the things, all the memories— except for the suffering. He generously gave that away.

From her pink shower, Mary looked toward the light coming through the bathroom window. Just before the memories could begin to drown her, she turned her face into the falls raining from the showerhead.

When she was finished washing, she stepped from the shower, got the courage to look in the mirror on her dresser, and sighed. Her hair was too short, dull, and black. She exercised, but her hips were too full. She looked down, straight to her feet. Something was missing! She was too small on the top. Seek the Kingdom and all else would be added? It looked like some of her *added* stuff must be on back order. And what had happened to her flowing hair, hair like the girls in the music videos? Girls who didn't look like *they* were seeking anything but good times and mo' money seemed to be getting all the good stuff while *she* was busy seeking. They were getting everything, including the handsome princes.

"Be happy with who you are, baby. God didn't make no mistakes." Mary could hear her grandmother's voice speaking to her. *"The man that's looking for you will recognize you when he comes. Trouble is, women are always making themselves look like someone else and the man can't find or recognize the one that is his meet, the one that is fit for him, the one his heart's been searching for."* Mary smiled. Granny felt so near. *"Just keep dancing in the skin you're in. Wait on the Lord. He's got a good plan."* It had been easier to be satisfied with her grandmother cheering her on to victory.

Mary looked at her hands and wanted to hide them. Besides her words of comfort, Mary treasured the memory of her granny's hands, hands that had been smooth, steady, and strong. She used them to work hard, but her nails were always well shaped, and the skin smooth. They were feminine hands—working hands, but still feminine. Mary clenched her own hands, and then opened them wide to inspect them. Her nails were bitten and the cuticles torn. The skin, though, was smooth and brown and the water beading there was lovely until she took the towel and wiped the drops away.

After drying off and dressing, Mary reached into her dresser drawer. She stooped to feel toward the very back. When the tips of her fingers touched the cool surface of a box at the very back, she closed her fingers about it and dragged it from the darkness of the drawer into the light and set it on the dresser.

She carefully lifted the lid. Before it was completely opened, the heavy, sweet scent of the perfume escaped. There was a citrusy warmth to the aroma. Mary drew two fingers over the surface of the solid perfume, and then held her fingers to her nose. It was cool in the room, but the scent always had the same effect. In the cool of the room, or wherever she was, the fragrance carried her to the hot, humid, sensuous, jazzy streets of New Orleans.

Just the few days away there, after she lost her granny, had saved her life. She smelled the scent each day now. The smell reminded her of her plane ride to New Orleans, the hotel, and of the days and nights in the exotic city. She had felt more alive in New Orleans. The city seemed to snatch her back from following Granny into death. The city made her glad to be alive.

Mary rubbed her fingers on the veins that pulsed in her neck and at her temples, behind her ears, on her wrists, behind her knees, and on her breastbone until she could no longer smell her memories or loneliness. Instead she was transported to streets with horse-drawn carriages, shops with beautiful red, green, and blue cut-glass vases and goblets of amber-colored glass, and sidewalk cafés heavy with the smell of seafood and deep-fried, pillow-shaped confections drowned in powdered sugar—donut-like treats called beignets.

The smell took her back to a place where men flirted incessantly with her, called her *chère* and told her she was beautiful. In New Orleans, Mary had been alone, but not lonely.

She closed the engraved box and, looking left and right as though to make sure no one spied on her, slid her secret treasure back into its hiding place.

Mary stepped out of her front door onto her row house stoop and looked down the block at the tiny sloped and manicured lawns. All the brick fronts of the houses looked the same—two windows and a door with a cast-iron rail next to the steps. A stranger might have found the sameness odd, but to her, the predictability was comforting.

Patches of flowers dotted the edges of the stairways and seemed to get smaller the farther she looked, until way down Old Frederick Road, the flowers looked like pink, white, and yellow pastel dots. That was if she looked to the right. If she looked to the left, though, boards covered the windows of dilapidated red brick buildings—apartments that had once been people's homes. It was a working-class neighborhood. People took pride in their homes. Yet the abandoned apartment buildings sat like something dead in the middle of the life of the street. Instead of flowers, there were clusters of navy blue–suited policemen on the lawns—a daily presence, she supposed, to keep the abandoned public housing from becoming home to drug dealers, users, and squatters.

City life.

Mary thought as she always thought when she looked at the projects. They knew the end from the beginning. They must have known. If the psychologists and sociologists knew all along that rats in cages—or in boxes next to boxes on boxes—would kill their neighbor, friend, and brother rats—then, certainly, city planners, sociologists, psychologists, and government officials knew that men crowded in boxes on boxes next to boxes would each one kill his neighbor, his brother, his friend, himself. How could they not have known?

Like most people, Mary didn't want to think about it. So she looked the other way and headed for the bus.

As she walked along Old Frederick she noticed Sister Puddin and Brother Joe's car missing and wondered when they would be back home.

2

Puddin

Puddin held her breath.

White powder flew from her hand all over her clothes. *They should hand out masks in these places.* It was a health hazard. She noticed the mask hanging around the neck of the technician sitting across from her. Maybe the issue was providing them for the customers.

Puddin adjusted her sitting position. The arms of the chair were getting to know her hips just a little too well. The technician across from her—Nona, she had said her name was—talked ninety miles an hour.

"Can you believe that?" Nona talked on, ponytail jiggling as she wagged her head.

Puddin tried to hold her breath against the alcohol and other chemical smells of the process. *Is it really worth all this?* To take her mind off the whining, grinding sounds, Puddin looked around the small room. Cream-colored walls, gray industrial carpet, large framed posters of manicured nails every four feet or so—she could have been anywhere. There were little white and black manicure stations throughout the room—one chair on each side, a light on a retractable arm, a cord hanging from a drill, and an assortment of nail polishes—pink, taupe, red, blue, green, gold. Most of the technicians, except for Nona and two others, were Asian—most likely immigrants, Puddin could tell from their conversation.

She could have been at home in Baltimore just as easily as Atlanta. Well, it really wasn't Atlanta. It was—well, she couldn't remember the name of the town, but it was just outside of Atlanta.

The hotel rate was better, and the roadside advertisements said there was cable TV and a VCR in each room.

"It's just as good, if not better," Joe had said, pointing at the billboard as they cruised down the highway in their silver gray Town Car. "We stay just outside the city, and we won't have to fight the rush-hour traffic when we leave in the morning. We'll be just that much closer to home."

Joe had laughed his "hee-hee" laugh. The tone of his voice, the smile on his face, and the way he nodded his head had been as though he had made a serious executive decision.

Puddin hadn't nodded, hadn't done anything. He was driving; she was riding. Besides, a smart woman knew it paid to let her man feel good—even if it was just about choosing hotels.

"And I know you want to get home. You got the Comfort Circle and what not. And I got a meeting with the men. . . ." Joe nodded as he spoke. "We got a couple of new fellas, one of them I hear is from somewhere in Africa, I think. Not to mention that I can't wait to get back and hear the preacher preach."

The grinding sound turned to a sharp whine, and Puddin turned her attention away from thoughts of Joe, back to her own nails.

Nona the nail technician flipped her wavy weave and kept right on talking and right on grinding. She was so mad, she was almost spitting. "If I catch the so and sos that did it, you can believe I'm going to beat them black and blue!"

Puddin tried to nod, tried to give Nona some positive feedback. But Nona was cutting it just a little too close to the edge—to the edge of Puddin's cuticle. It was hard for Puddin not to flinch when she felt the warning flash of heat that usually came just before the cuticle went up in flames.

Nona held Puddin's hand, filing the acrylic tip into an oval shape with a file tip on a drill bit. "They egged my door! I mean they actually threw eggs at my door! When I got home, there was yellow slime sliding down my door!" Nona frowned. "Jealousy is all it is!" Nona lifted the drill in the air and waved it like she was directing a choir. "I don't bother nobody. I try to live in peace. When I buy beer, I buy them beer. . . . I used to, but not anymore. Not now. They just jealous. Jealous I got this shop." She pointed around the room with the humming drill. "I got nice customers." Nona smiled patronizingly at Puddin, and then at a girl in braids sitting with her baby boy on the red sofa just to the right of them. The little boy gnawed on a blue pacifier.

Puddin nodded at Nona, then followed with her eyes as Nona motioned with her head toward the young girl. Puddin smiled at the girl in braids, thinking that she could not have been more than sixteen.

Nona squeezed Puddin's chocolate brown hand tighter and directed the drill toward her fingers like a mad scientist. "I got plenty of good customers," she said.

Puddin had had enough. She came to be pampered, not terrified, and she didn't think she wanted to be one of those *good* customers anymore. "Not for long! You keep wielding that drill the way you're doing, and I'm out of here!" That's what she intended to say before the bell tinkled and the front door opened.

In walked another young girl wearing a baseball cap and holding the hand of a baby girl.

Nona nodded at the girl and told her to take a seat on the couch where the first young girl and her toddler son waited.

Nona kept talking, obviously not realizing that Puddin was close to pulling the plug on the whole operation. "What I should do—" Nona had progressed to the ring finger on Puddin's second hand "—is stand out in the middle of the street and just call them out. They wanna fight—" Nona lifted the drill, shrugged, and put one hand on her hip "—they can bring it on! I don't want them thinking I'm scared of them!"

Stay calm. I just have to make it through two more nails. Puddin hoped that her grimace masqueraded as a smile. No point in arguing with Nona—not while she had the drill. No point in playing mother to someone she didn't even know. No point in telling Nona that she didn't have anything to prove, that fighting with her neighbors wasn't going to solve anything. Puddin stayed quiet.

"No," Nona said, as though she had been reading Puddin's mind, "that's just what they want me to do. And I don't have time for that. I could end up losing everything I have over some foolishness. Nope, instead, soon as I get done with your hands—" Nona raised an eyebrow, paused dramatically, before announcing "—I'm gone call the police." The technician sighed, knowing that what she threatened was almost the cultural equivalent of saying she was going to drop the atomic bomb.

Puddin nodded, looked around the room again, and let her thoughts drift back to Joe. She imagined him checking the television to see what games were on . . . or he might be fiddling with the VCR.

"There it is," he had said as soon as he saw the machine sitting on top of the television. "Just like the sign said—a VCR in every room." He quickly set the luggage down and patted the machine.

"You should get your nails done," he had told her as soon as they settled in the hotel room. He looked so earnest. The heat and struggling with the bags made his face flushed and his freckles more prominent against his fair skin and kinky sandy-colored hair.

She looked at her hands and sighed. It was just one more thing to do. She wanted to rest. "Joe, I can just wait until I get home." Puddin touched her hands to her black hair, poking strands back into place. "I need to get my hair done, and I can just wait and get it all done at one time. I'm too tired."

He put his arm around her shoulders. "But, see, the thing is, getting your nails done will help you relax, see?" He smiled down at her.

It would be nice, maybe, if she were at home. But she didn't like going to new places, meeting strangers. You never knew what was going to happen. "Joe, I don't know anybody here. I don't even know where a shop is. And I sure don't feel like looking."

Still athletic in his late fifties, Joe had hopped on the phone and called the front desk. "There's one right down the street," he said with pride when he got through wheeling and dealing on the phone. New places and new people never bothered him. Every place was home. "Baby, my sweet chocolate Puddin," he said with a wink, "I think you really ought to do it. It will be good for you."

His face morphed from earnest husband to beaming, innocent choirboy. He walked to her, lifted her—all of her—from her feet and spun her around. He kissed her lips and then kissed the palm of one of her hands.

Puddin fought not to get caught up in the breathlessness of it all. Joe wasn't fooling anyone. She knew him. She knew what he was up to; he was trying to get her out of the room. Puddin had hoped that the vacation, the trip home to visit his relatives in Dallas at a family get-together, would change things—but obviously it hadn't. He had been so pleased to see everyone, especially his aunt Evangelina, who made the trip to Texas all the way from North Carolina. But even seeing her hadn't done any good.

Puddin knew he was trying to get rid of her, even if it meant that he had to spring for the price of a manicure, with his cheap self. He was willing to do whatever he had to do to spend some time alone communing with his other love.

It had gotten to be a regular thing with him. It was getting more regular, more common, more obvious all the time.

"For real, baby." He took one of her hands in his. "You know I like to see you looking pretty. And ain't no expense too great to keep my baby looking good."

Who did Joe think he was kidding? If there was a cheaper man alive, she didn't know him.

"There's nothing I won't do to keep my woman satisfied." Joe began to sing and do Temptations moves. "Ain't no mountain high—"

She snatched her hand away. "Cut it out, Joe."

"Come on, sugar." He kept dancing.

"You're doing the wrong moves anyway. Wrong group."

"But I'm dancing for you, baby."

Right. Did she look like she just fell off the turnip truck? Puddin sucked in her breath and was just about to wind herself up and tell him something when Joe grabbed his cap and began to hustle her out the door.

"Come on, baby. It's right down the street. It will take the edge off." He kissed the tip of her ear. "You can even get a pedicure."

Joe was desperate.

While they drove, he talked nonstop. Puddin knew it was to keep her from getting in a word. "See?" Joe pointed. "There's McDonald's, Wendy's, Wal-Mart—it's just like home."

He turned the car into an old strip mall. Carefully, he inched the car over cracked asphalt and around potholes that looked like craters from a meteor shower or a small arms blast. Joe was right; it was looking more like home all the time.

"I'll be back to get you in a couple of hours," he had said after hustling her inside the shop. She had stood in front of the door, looking forlorn, like a kid dropped off at daycare. Joe readjusted his baseball cap and almost scampered to the car, which he'd left running by the curb.

Joe wasn't fooling anybody. She knew *what* he was up to—she just couldn't figure out *why* after thirty happy years of marriage. She sighed. They had been away from home for two weeks. He hadn't been able to get a minute away from her or the family. So now he was making his move. It was why he had gotten off the road and stopped early. It was why he picked the hotel he had—he had to make sure it had cable or, even more importantly, a VCR. It was the same reason he had hustled her off to get her nails done, even if he had to foot the bill for a manicure and pedicure at a strange shop in a strange town.

Joe was right, though; there was nothing strange about the shop—except for why she was there. He had it all figured out. But what he probably hadn't figured on was the tongue-lashing he was going to get when she got back to the room. *You're not fooling anyone, Joe, with your tired self.* That's what she would tell him. She wasn't going to back down this time. This would be the last time she was going to be inconvenienced because of his nasty little secret.

Puddin sighed, adjusted her seat, and looked around the room again. Nona the nail technician finally stopped grinding and reached for a baby food jar without a label. The jar was full of what looked to be olive oil or cooking oil. Nona used a watercolor paintbrush and slapped oil on each of Puddin's fingers.

Pointing with the oily paintbrush toward some sinks at the back of the room, Nona smiled. "Just about done. You can go wash your hands and pick out your nail polish col—" Nona stopped mid-word, poised like a guard dog on alert.

Puddin's eyes followed as Nona's head swiveled toward the young girls sitting on the sofa.

"So, what's your daddy's name?" the second girl sitting on the sofa—the one wearing the baseball cap—said to the first girl's toddler.

The little boy pulled the well-worn pacifier out of his mouth with a smacking sound. "Ricky," the little boy said, dragging out both syllables.

The girl with the baseball cap looked the first girl—the one with the braids—squarely in the eye. "Ricky my baby's daddy too."

Nona flinched as though she had been slapped. "Uh oh," she whispered to Puddin. "Baby mama drama."

Puddin tried to look nonchalant. She'd left Baltimore for a vacation; yet here she was smack dab in the middle of *drame des mamans des enfants*—at least that's how she thought it should be translated, if her high school French was worth anything.

Nona pretended to be engaged in conversation with Puddin, but kept her rounded eyes locked on the girls. She stage-whispered to Puddin, "You be ready to get up out of here if something jumps off." Nona's eyes narrowed to slits and her teeth clenched together while she spoke. "Last week, two girls got to fightin' up in here.

They had the nerve to pull out their cell phones and call their families. Next thing you know, they were all outside—family members and all—in the parking lot bangin'." Puddin looked out at the potholes while she listened to Nona. "Fists were flying, braids and tracks were laying all over the place." Nona shook her head. "A few broken nails too."

While Puddin imagined the twisted hair corpses, Nona seemed to turn one eye on her while keeping the other on the two girls. "We had to call the police." Nona said the last word once more with a mixture of revulsion and incredulity. She squeezed Puddin's hand again. "Uh oh," she said.

Puddin turned back to the girls. The first girl, the one with the braids, was standing. "Ricky ain't none of your baby's daddy," she said.

The second girl stood to her feet, yelling as she did the snake with her neck, "Yes, he is!" She grabbed her baby's hand.

The first girl grabbed her baby's hand.

Nona dropped Puddin's hand and jumped to her feet. "Wait a minute, y'all!"

Puddin jumped out of the way just before the manicure station—oil and a rainbow of nail enamel colors flying through the air—crashed to the carpet in front of her.

Joe was going to hear about this! She wasn't going to back down from telling him this time. It was going to cost way more than the price of a pedicure and manicure to get him out of this one!

3

Mary

Sometimes she felt like the cost of her coming here was too high. No doubt about it, Mary was always grateful, climbing the hill, that it wasn't snowing, that it wasn't raining. The afternoon sun peeked in and out of the overhanging tree branches as she walked up the concrete walkway. It seemed strange, each time she crested the hill, to see the large, modern church. It was tucked out of view from the street and— except for the sign that faced Old Frederick Road and the throngs of people that drove and walked up and down the driveway on Sunday mornings and Thursday nights—people could pass the entrance to the church grounds and never know that New Worshippers Baptist Church was there.

She stood in front of the glass doors and then looked up to the steeple. It was like a new mountain rising where all around it buildings were falling, crumbling, being boarded and bulldozed—like a horn rising from the earth's smooth surface.

Mary pushed a glass door open and entered the lobby. She checked her watch, and then walked more quickly.

Tuesday afternoon things were quiet at New Worshippers. Not just quiet, but filled with the supernatural hush that sits in places where many souls have been in worship and prayer. The vestibule was empty, so it was easy to see that the carpet was dusty rose and the doors were stained teakwood. Silence was not the way most people experienced New Worshippers. On Sundays more than eight thousand people sang, danced, wept, worshipped, prayed, and jumped before the Lord. It was exciting just thinking about it— thinking about the poor people, the young people, the old people, the doctors, the lawyers, the teachers, the prostitutes that all gathered together on Sunday to hear and learn. On other days, like this Tuesday, the presence that hovered was still powerful, but quiet, contemplative, and even scholarly.

Walking down the hall, Mary stopped to push the elevator button for the ride down to the classrooms on a lower floor. She shifted the bag on her shoulder from right to left, then patted it. She sighed and hoped she was ready for what was ahead of her.

She paused outside of Room Thirty-One and ran one hand over her hair. She laid a hand on her stomach in hope that it would stop flip-flopping, and then stepped inside the room. It was this feeling, the anxiety and all the drama, that sometimes made her wonder if it was worth it all.

This is silly. It *was* silly. After a day of interacting with grown folks, here she was—a grown woman—panicked by some kids. Mary looked at the three girls sitting in front of her.

One of them, Cat, the one who always gave her the most trouble, pushed her dark glamour girl sunglasses down and peered over them at Mary and then back at her matching rhinestone-encrusted watch. "Just eleven minutes late, if my watch is right. Which it is."

As Mary unpacked, the girl began to nod her head, rapping softly to herself. "So you can hate, or hail the Queen. But it don't matter . . ." Cat was New Worshippers' answer to Lil' Kim. She cut her rap short, uncrossed her legs and took her feet down from the chair on which they rested so that the spike heels of her brown ankle boots rested on the floor. She leaned forward to check for scuffs on the very pointy toes. She tugged nonchalantly at the hem of her short blue jean skirt, then picked up her purse and began to dig through it. "Just let me know when you're ready."

Cat pulled a tube of green apple–scented lip-gloss from her bag and, checking in the mirror she held, ran the application wand over her full lips until they shimmered. Her hands looked soft, like little girl hands, but her nails were long, hooked, and painted a shiny hot pink with what looked to be gold zebra stripes. She closed the tube and checked her eyelashes and the mole near her mouth with her portable mirror. When she seemed satisfied, Cat put her things away and fluffed the huge cloud of wavy strawberry-blonde hair that floated around her honey-colored face and drifted down her shoulders.

Mary watched the girls—especially Cat—as she continued unloading books from her shoulder bag and asked herself for the thirtieth—no, the one hundredth—time why she would let a sixteen-year-old intimidate her—even if Cat *did* look closer to thirty.

Mary took a couple of deep breaths. She was not about to get gray hair over three schoolgirls. They didn't have jobs. They didn't pay bills. They didn't have to rush here after work. They probably didn't have driver's licenses—their mothers were probably shuttling them. She was giving up her free time—not that she had anything else to do—volunteering with them, mentoring them.

Mostly, she was spending her hard-earned money trying to find books, magazines, or anything that would keep their attention. "I got some new books for us to try out." She hated the way her voice always sounded when she spoke to them, as though she was trying to placate them, as though she hoped they would be her friends. Like when she was in elementary school. *Please play with me at recess time, okay? Let me stand by you in line, okay?*

Cat yawned. "Yeah. I see." She looked at her watch again. "Do you think we'll be starting anytime soon?"

"Cat, give me a break, okay?" The words popped from Mary's mouth before she even realized she was speaking. Cat was right about her being late, but she didn't have to be so messy about it. Between the buses and work, she was usually late, which didn't help things get started on the right foot. The truth was, Mary spent most of her days, in between the times she met with the young ladies, trying to decide if it was worth it. If there was any point. Maybe it was better to do nothing than it was to do less than her best, to leave herself open to the criticism of three sixteen-year-olds.

One of the others spoke up. "None of us has been here that long, Cat. So cut it out, okay?"

Mary appreciated the reassuring look that Pamela gave her as she spoke. Pamela sat at the long table they shared, next to Cat, directly in front of Mary. Part of what was intriguing about the three girls was how different they were. Pamela was as reserved as Cat was flamboyant. The girl looked like she could have stepped out of an ad for the Gap or Old Navy. She wore the perfect shirt, the perfect sweater tied in the perfect knot at her neck, the perfect khaki pants, and the perfect matching shoes. Her skin color and hair were dark enough and her hair texture kinky enough that it was pretty certain that she was black. But there was just enough room—she was just light enough and her hair just straight enough—to cause some doubt . . . exactly the kind of person that was popular in television and magazine ads now. She looked like a trouble-free teenager.

Pamela shrugged and looked at Cat. "You don't always have to give her a hard time." Her soft, unblemished hands hardly ever moved when she spoke.

Cat dug in her purse again and pulled out a round, bright red lollipop. She unwrapped it and popped it in her mouth. "You're right," she said in between slurps. "You're right. And she doesn't always have to be late, either."

Pamela looked at Cat. "I'm sure she has a good reason. Sometimes my mom and I are late. We have to drive from a long way to get here. You live right here in the city, Cat. So you don't have to deal with traffic or whatever. Maybe Miss Mary lives in the 'burbs, too." She twisted a lock of hair on her finger. "Whatever the reason, she's here. And I'm sure she has a good reason why she's late."

Mary was silent as they spoke. It was strange, almost surreal, to listen to the two of them talk about her as though she was not in the room, as though she didn't matter or didn't have a voice. Mary continued laying books on the table. There was no way she and any of her friends would have spoken that way about any adult when she was a child—at least, not and lived. "*Girl, don't butt in to grown people's conversations!*" "*Children should be seen and not heard!*" "*Keep talking, child, and I will knock you into next week!*" Things had definitely changed.

Two empty chairs away, Agnes quietly observed it all. She hunched forward in her seat, her back curved like a turtle. Her blue eyes seemed guarded, and her gaze jumped from person to person. It was obvious that, like most days, she was taking it all in. She hardly ever said anything unless directly spoken to—this conversation was no different. She pulled at a hank of dark blonde, almost brown, hair and pushed it back into the scrunchee that held part of her hair in a ponytail. The rest of it lay on the back of her navy blue polyester pullover.

Pamela kept speaking. "It's easy for you and Agnes to get here."

Cat popped the sucker from her mouth and laughed. "It's not easy for Agnes to get here. The girl just gets here fast!" Cat cackled. "Shoot, Agnes runs soon as she gets off the bus so those clowns that get off the bus at her stop don't beat her down before she gets here." Cat winked at Agnes, who hunched forward more and winced. "Right, Aggie?" Cat's short laugh was cynical.

Agnes's pale skin blushed pink. She bent even further forward over the table. "Whatever," she mumbled while chewing at what was left of her nails.

Pamela shook her head full of black, crinkly curls. "Why do you have to pick on her?"

Cat laughed louder. "I'm not picking on her." She leaned forward to look at Agnes. "I'm not picking on you, am I, Aggie?" Cat settled back in her seat. "I'm just telling the truth. Aggie knows the 'hood can be a dangerous place. I'm not the one chasing her. I'm just telling the truth. I don't care that she's white, or whatever she is. You don't see me messing with her."

"Well, I don't see you trying to help her, either." Pamela pressed her hands on the table in front of her. "Why don't you help her? It just makes me sick to see it, and to see people laugh about it." She looked pointedly at Cat. "It wasn't funny when it was happening to us, when people were picking on us, and it's not funny when it happens to anybody else."

Cat shrugged her shoulders, looked at Mary, and raised her hand. "Are we going to get started soon? *Please!* Anything so she don't start preaching to me about racism, reparations, reconciliation, or whatever the *r* word is for the day. I ain't killed no white people or took their jobs, so I don't want to hear it. I'm not responsible. I'm just telling you what I see other people do. Besides that, Aggie ain't white—not all the way, anyway."

Pamela huffed. "Cat, you are so rude!"

Cat checked the bracelets on her wrists. "Look, Pam-e-la, life is life. Life is hard. Okay? I didn't make it; I just live it. I didn't make Aggie's mama do whatever creeping she did to turn Aggie out looking like she does. I didn't make her family—even though most of them are kind of light skinned—try to pretend like something funny didn't jump off there. Okay? Ain't nobody crazy. Look at her. Somebody was doing a little sumthin-sumthin somewhere. It wasn't me. Okay? I'm just telling it like it is. I'm just keeping it real. Okay?" She licked her sucker.

Mary cleared her throat and opened her teacher's guide. "Okay, now that we've gotten our greetings and expressions of goodwill out of the way, let's look over the new books and then talk about what we're going to cover." The three girls looked very different, but they could have been squabbling sisters. She didn't know whether to stop the bickering or let them work it out. Mary wasn't sure about anything; she only knew she was trying. "Agnes, why don't you open up for us in prayer." After the brief prayer, Mary took her seat. "Okay, let's look over the chapters and the tapes that go with them."

Cat sighed dramatically. "Here we go again. The same old, same old." She rolled her eyes.

Mary tried not to let her frustration show on her face. "How do you know it's the same old thing, Cat? We haven't even gone over the material."

"I can look at the cover and tell. Look at these people." She pointed at the people on the cover. "You know they don't know nothing about real life. They've never even *been* to the 'hood. They have those fake shiny smiles and pinstripe polo shirts. They don't know anything about real life; they're hiding from real life. Why can't we talk about things we're dealing with here and now? Why can't we talk about something from real life? Why can't we be real?"

Pamela pouted and turned to Cat. "Real? You mean something like . . . racism?" It was obvious she was still smarting over Cat's earlier remark.

"Whatever, Pam. You know what I mean." Cat looked back at Mary. "Why can't we talk about real life? People are dying on the streets. I've got other stuff I could be doing with my time other than looking at this whack stuff." The book made a slamming sound when it dropped on the table.

Mary's face felt warm and she could feel her jaws tightening. Every time, she spent the night before telling herself it wasn't going to happen. She'd told herself the same thing last night. But every week it happened anyway. She could feel her patience slipping. "Look, Cat, we have this same discussion every time. I don't know what it is you want from me. I just got these new books. What more do you want?"

Agnes tilted her head so that she was staring at the floor. Pamela shrugged her shoulders with frustration. "Do we have to go through this again?"

Cat pushed her chair back from the table. "Maybe I'm crazy, but if I have to be here, I want to learn something that's gone help me." She lifted the student book in the air, then let it fall again to the table. "This stuff is nothing but mush."

Pamela pointed her finger at the book. "I don't like this stuff, either, but it is what it is. Why does it have to be this way every time? Why do we have to argue every time? Why can't you just get along?"

Agnes looked briefly at Mary and then bowed her head. Mary

wanted to join her, to be invisible, to not hear the argument, to not be responsible or present.

"Look, the boy who used to sit next to me in math class is dead from AIDS. The girl that used to sit next to me got shot by mistake." Cat was animated, using the lollipop in her hand to emphasize her words. "Three girls in my homeroom have babies. The rest of us don't—but it's not because we ain't got no man, if you know what I mean." Cat smirked and then resumed speaking. "Two boys got arrested for selling drugs. The police came and got them at school. I've been seeing crack vials and people laying on the ground stabbed and shot every since I been going to school." Cat was leaning forward, sincere, involved. The cynicism had disappeared from her face.

Mary tried to imagine Cat as a younger child walking through what must have felt like a war zone. She couldn't imagine it, didn't want to imagine it. Nothing like that happened on her street—same city, but a world away.

Cat was still talking. "People keep trying to talk to us about Dick and Jane, and 'Just say no,' like this stuff is not happening around us. Like we live in this fakey, pretend world." She shook her head. "We need something real, something that's gone tell us how to deal and how to survive. " She pointed at the student guide. "All these books want to talk about it is not missing your curfew."

Mary took a deep breath. "They write these lessons for everybody, Cat. I know it's tough for you, but all young people aren't living the same kind of life." She nodded toward Pamela.

Pamela shook her head. "Uh huh. I get tired of Cat fussing about it, and I hate to admit it, but she's right. It doesn't matter where you are. We're dealing with the same things where I live. We've got security guard snipers walking around on the roof of my school carrying guns, ready to shoot in case anything jumps off—in case any fights break out or a kid comes to school with a gun to kill everybody. And that's not in the 'hood, that's in the county. People are killing each other in the malls." She shoved her body further back into her seat. "What is that about? And nobody, especially in the places that should be helping us, wants to talk about it."

Cat nodded. "That's what I'm talking about. It's everywhere."

Pamela sighed. "And sometimes I thought it was just us, you know, I mean—black people. My parents got divorced, and I didn't see us having the happy, perfect life I was reading about in the books in the church we were going to in the suburbs. The church was all white people, you know? It looked like they were the ones having happy lives. Like their lives were perfect. It was just *us* with troubles."

Mary looked at Pamela's face, at the sadness and the confusion she saw there, and wondered if the girl's mother saw it. She wondered if Pamela poured out her heart and shared her fears with her mother like she was sharing them now.

"And all the books about chastity and purity that I read were written by white people, and so I thought it was just us. But then I looked around at all the stuff going on. Really. It's the same everywhere—it's just easier to hide it when you have money and when you're in control." Pamela bit her bottom lip and looked between Mary, Cat, and Agnes. She glanced up and then down, shame in her eyes. "If you want to know the truth, little girls where I live— like girls in grade school—are having oral sex with boys and kissing other girls and not calling it sex and just thinking they're having fun. And some of the homeschool kids are just as bad."

Cat's cold laugh interrupted Pamela. "No, it ain't just black people with problems. Aggie is proof of that." She pointed at the girl. "She's the only person in her family that looks like that. They all got the same mama, same nose as hers, same lips. But Aggie here is the only one with blue eyes and blonde hair, and ain't no white man living in the house with them. Her mama ain't married to no white man. Somebody been dippin' and trippin'. Not to mention that all these light-skinned black people—all over the city, all over the country—got here some kind of way. I mean, let's be for real."

Mary thought of all the conversations she had overheard

through the years, about upstanding citizens who crept to the other side of the tracks when it was dark. Stories of respected men who forced themselves on their maids, while waging wars of terror to protect the purity of their own wives and daughters. Men who kept up the illusion of their goodness, their righteousness, by only exposing their *badness* among people who had no voice, no power. She thought of those conversations and the light-skinned babies, babies called yellow, called red—babies who grew up to be grandmothers and grandfathers like her own granny—who were living reminders of the hypocrisy of centuries-old systems of double standards. Mary wanted Cat to be wrong, but Agnes wasn't the only undeniable proof.

Mary looked at each of the girls. She tried not to be shocked, at least not to *look* shocked. She wanted them to know she was sincere, but she didn't want to hear about any of it. She didn't want to hear any of it.

She didn't want to hear about little girls, mothers' babies—that horrible things had crept in unseen while adults were on guard. She didn't want to hear that something evil had crept in while adults were earning money to build safer places to guard their babies, her babies—they were her children too. . . . While walls were built to keep others out evil had crept in. . . . Or maybe the builders carried the evil in with them behind the safe walls. *Maybe we carried it in.*

God, don't let this be. Don't let it have gone this far with our children. God, we've spent years, our lives—generations—trying to circle the wagons and keep them safe. God, I hear what they're saying but I don't want this to be—not our babies, not my babies. . . . Maybe someone else's—I'm willing to sacrifice other people's children, to leave them outside for evil to devour, but not these . . . not my own.

Mary spoke to the girls, tried to put on a happy face while she prayed silently. "Look, I understand. It wasn't that long ago that I was your age." She smiled and knew it was a weak thing to do, to try to make a joke or defuse the truth or passion of what the girls were saying with a weak smile and joke. "Well, maybe a little longer than I want to say." Her voice sounded patronizing and foolish. None of the girls smiled back. "The thing is, it's not just important to cover the material—I paid for these books myself." She hoped that they heard her—she paid for the books *herself.* She hoped that they could hear in that that she cared. "What's important is not just what's covered, but it's also important that it's presented in a manner that's appropriate for your ages." She coughed and tried to clear the boulder out of her throat. What she was saying even sounded lame to her. "It's appropriate to speak to you in a way that encourages wholesome lifestyles, in a way that's edifying."

The room was silent. Mary tried to think of the right thing to say. *We want to tell you a little truth—but not all of it—in a way that won't drag you too soon into the mud that we've walked in, in a way that doesn't force you to leave the safety of where you are too soon. We're trying to protect you, you know, from what we've learned—from what has given us gray hair that we have to dye and permanent frowns on our faces. We don't want you wallowing in pig troughs. We don't want to teach you those things. We want to keep you innocent. We want to keep hearing that little child sound, that trusting sound in your voices as long as we can. But we know, it's too late already. . . . In our hearts, we know it's too late. . . .* That's what Mary wanted to say—it was the honest thing to say—but she said nothing. She thought about the parents objecting, about the church ladies disapproving, and said nothing.

"You know the reason I keep coming back, Miss Mary?" Agnes's voice startled Mary back from her thoughts. The girl looked from underneath the hair that hung in her eyes.

Pamela and Cat leaned forward and stared at the third girl. They seemed as surprised as Mary felt to hear the reclusive girl speak.

"I don't know what edifying means. But you know the reason I keep getting off the bus and running here trying to stay away from people that are chasing me?"

Mary could see that the other two girls were frozen like she was.

They had been together for almost a year, and Agnes had never done much more than grunt. Now her eyes were wide, and her face was reddening. She sat up a little taller.

There were tears in her eyes. She frowned and shook her head. Her hands, red where the nails had been bitten and pink around the cuticles, gripped the edge of the table, then the arms of her chair. Agnes rubbed her knees, and then jerked at her jacket zipper. "Based on what I got now, I might as well take some pills or draw a tub of warm water, get a blade, and get it over with." Her eyes were open wider, clearer than Mary had ever seen them.

The other two girls stared at Agnes. Cat pulled the lollipop from her mouth as she listened.

"I keep putting up with people calling me white trash, calling me 'swirl,' trying to jack me up, because I came here one Sunday and I heard one sentence that kept me from killing myself. And now I keep coming, hoping to hear one more sentence to keep me alive."

Cat nodded at Agnes and her face softened so that she looked like a little girl. "I don't mean to come off like I do all the time, Aggie. But I get tired of it, you know? All the fake stuff." Agnes shrugged, then Cat looked back at Mary. "It's like people in church spend so much time arguing over what to wear or what not to wear, over whether the dinners for the fundraiser will be chicken or fish, whether to sing fast new songs or old slow ones, like that's important. But my mama's been leaving me home alone and I been doing all kinds of stuff to feed myself since I was a little kid."

Cat's voice sounded fragile. She blinked back tears from her eyes. Mary wasn't sure what it meant. It was hard to imagine that Cat could be vulnerable.

"And everything I been doing, I know she has too. Shoot, I've probably done stuff even she's never done. We do what we got to do to survive. There ain't nothing you can say that I ain't heard. So people in these books worrying about hurting my ears are wasting their time." Cat shook her head. "Scare me away from hell? Shoot,

I already live there." She pointed at the book, then touched it and flipped the pages. "Appropriate for my age? I probably know things and have done things you will never know."

Mary could feel herself blushing as Cat spoke. "You know why I keep coming back? Because one day it came to me, it was like God spoke to me that I could tell Him the truth. What I need to talk about or ask questions about might be too much for church ladies to handle, but everything I ever done, the Lord already knows. He's not ticked about it, people are. But in my heart, I keep hearing Him tell me not to worry about the people."

Pamela sighed. "It's the same where I am. People pretend that it's not, but it is. Everything's supposed to be perfect, but I know it's not. People just hide their sins and deny to themselves that they're sinning. And it's not just divorce and stuff like that. It's like they want to pretend that having money and living away from the city makes it all go away. But it doesn't. It's there anyway. They want to pretend they don't have problems, but they do."

Cat looked at her so directly, Mary wanted to look away. But she forced herself to meet Cat's gaze as the girl spoke. "The reason I keep getting mad is that I'm waiting for something real, for some-body to talk about the real stuff in my life. God keeps telling me that everything I've done, people in the Bible have already been through it. So I keep waiting for the day when we gone talk about the stuff *those* people went through, because we never talk about them. The real rough-life people like me. That's what I'm asking for. That's what I keep waiting for."

Mary looked at the books and all the tapes lying on the table before her. She looked at her lesson plan and opened her book to the first reference. She felt Cat, Pamela, and Agnes watching her, their eyes focused on her like spotlights. She raised her head to look at them. She couldn't do it, not anymore.

Mary closed the book. She wanted to leave. Let someone else do it. They weren't her children. She didn't even *have* children.

She looked at the three girls. *God, what am I doing here?* There had to be a better way.

4

Puddin

The trees rushed by, the car appeared to be swallowing the blacktop road in front of it, and Puddin recounted the story. It was like a dime-store novel. Maybe she should write the book. "Somebody grabbed the babies, and it seems like it ended as fast as it started. They got the girls out of there, then I was seated back in the chair getting two coats of Outrageous Red Number Five." She held up her nails to show them off. "She threw in the gold stripes for nothing."

Joe touched her fingertips, then quickly turned his eyes back to the road. "They look good." He stole glances and smiled at her the way he used to when they were young, like he couldn't get enough of looking at her. She touched her hair. His looks always made her feel like there was no one more beautiful. "Nothing's too good for my baby," he said.

"It was nice to be able to do it. It would be nice to do things like that—getting my hair done, going shopping, and stuff like that all the time." Puddin turned slightly in the seat to face Joe. "We don't have to pinch pennies, you know? I told you, I could just get a little part-time job and—"

Joe's chest swelled as though someone had suddenly pumped a tank of air into it. "No wife of mine is going to be working while I sit at home."

She pressed the issue. "Well, then you could get one—"

"And I've worked enough years for the man. I'm not giving him any more of my life or time. We just have to tighten our belts."

Puddin sighed and sat back in her seat. "Well, my belt is so tight it's looped around my body a couple of times and I'm out of notches."

"Puddin!" Joe said her name in that way he used that meant he was through with the conversation—not yelling, just through. "We're doing all right. We got a roof over our heads. Ain't neither one of us missed no meals. We got a car, we're on this vacation." He reached out and patted her hand. "Have a little faith, baby. Things are gone work out all right."

Puddin sniffed and pulled her hand away. "I got faith. This is not about faith, Joe. This is about . . . never mind." She closed her mouth, then opened it to speak again and shook her head. "Never mind," she said.

Joe turned the dial on the radio station to a golden oldies station. "Don't worry, Puddin. I'm working on something. Everything is gone be all right."

Puddin turned her face toward the passenger window and rolled her eyes. Yes, Joe was working on something all right. She knew what he was working on—carrying bootleg videotapes into his "reading room," as he called it, at the house. Puddin wasn't sure how many more days she could take watching him sneak into the house hiding videotapes in brown paper bags behind his back. Once in his reading room, he would lock the door. When she complained, the answer was always pretty much the same.

"A man's entitled to his privacy. I worked hard to buy us this house and to buy you everything you wanted. I don't follow you around and knock on the door when you have it locked."

"I don't lock the door," she would tell him.

"Well, if you did, I wouldn't knock." His face would look pitiful. *"What? Don't you trust me?"* That's the way it always went, and the answer was, it *was* getting so she didn't trust him.

Joe touched her on the shoulder. "I'm sorry about all you went through back there." His eyes were round with sympathy. "It's a crazy world."

Puddin took a deep breath. There was no point in arguing. It wasn't going to change anything. They were on vacation; they could save the fighting until they got home. She made the choice that long-married people make all the time—she chose not to fight. She cleared her throat and her head and began talking to him about the young girls at the nail shop instead. "Crazy? That's putting it mild. I don't understand it, Joe. Girls fighting over boys, and babies having babies. And the way the girl said it, like she was talking about shoe sizes, about the weather or something. 'My baby's daddy is your baby's daddy.'" She shook her head. "The insanity of it all!" Puddin pulled her skirt around her knees like something might get on the tail end of it if she wasn't careful. "I never heard of such a thing."

Joe chuckled. "I wouldn't go that far, baby. There have been men fighting over women and women fighting over men since I can remember." He tilted his head. "Maybe it just seems funny because they're younger and we're getting older." He shrugged. "Or maybe it's just they do it out in the open, and we want them to be shame."

"Well, I don't think it's right, Joe. They aren't fighting over husbands or anything. Not that that's right, but this *sure* isn't right."

Joe turned on the blinker and switched lanes. "Oh, I'm not saying it's right. I'm just trying to be honest. I look at it and I just think some of our generation's drama has spilled on them. We did stuff wrong, too. We still doing wrong, but we don't want to admit it."

Puddin's heart fluttered and her face got a little warm—probably just a hot flash. She reached in her purse for a tissue and wiped away the moisture on her top lip and on her brow, and the memory that tried to touch her. "But something is different."

Joe passed a car and switched back to the right-hand lane. "Yeah, you're right. It used to be people were fighting for love. Now, who knows what they're fighting for." He shook his head. "They think they're fighting for love, fighting over romance. But it's been a long time since men and women knew what real romance, what real love, was."

Joe began to rock back and forth, toward and away from the steering wheel, the way he did when he was agitated. He looked so young and full of passion. Puddin could feel her heart fluttering as he spoke. "You can't blame the young folks. They don't know no better. Parents don't talk about it anymore, if they ever did—like they're afraid to believe love really ever existed. You know, like the more educated and sophisticated we are, the less we believe in love. We don't need it. At least that's what we say. We can see how real love in somebody's life can make them glow, or bring them back to life, but we just ignore that evidence. 'Cause it's supposed to be foolish and weak to believe in love." He shook his head. "It's a cynical world. And if they're going by TV or movies, they'll think sex is romance."

He rocked a little harder. Puddin could feel herself turning toward him as he spoke, like an invisible hand, or more likely, her heart moved her. "Now, what people call love, what they call romance, or even what they call sex is cold-hearted like a bank exchange. People are afraid, and even children have been disappointed too many times." Joe shook his head. "Loving and putting your heart on the line to be loved is scary, it's hard. So people tell themselves love doesn't exist. They settle for loveless lives, loveless relationships and marriages, not realizing that they're living in the very pain they were trying to run from all along."

Puddin touched his arm, and then reached her hand to touch the side of his face. Joe kept his eyes on the road, but leaned his face into her hand's caress as he continued. "We're afraid to trust, so our children are afraid to trust. That's what we've taught them. We look at them and shake our heads, but what we're really looking at is a reflection of us. We have given up on love for something fake, cold, hard, and ugly. But we're trying to pretend it's real. We're being short-changed . . . all being short-changed."

She laid her hand on his. When he was passionate about something, when the truth moved in him, he couldn't help speaking about it. She loved him for it. "Love is patient, love is kind. . . .

They don't know anything about that. Maybe you're right, Joe. Maybe we have failed them. It's a shame, too, because there was a day when people knew there wasn't much finer treasure on earth than the love between a man and a woman."

He stole a glance at her. His voice was husky. "You're right, baby. What most people have now is just counterfeit love. Even the saints . . . we're desperate for love. . . . But we're like everybody else—settling for something less. We're standing in lines trying to buy the feeling, but running from the real thing because it's hard work and we're afraid. So, instead we buy books or music that give us that feeling. And we keep doing it, even though it doesn't satisfy." Joe shook his head. "Why, I was just watching a videotape. . . ." Joe's voice trailed off to nothing.

The moment fizzled.

"Someday I'm gone write a book about it."

Right. Joe write a book? That would take too much energy. It would require him doing something more than watching videos. It was all talk, and it all came back to the same thing. She knew he didn't want to talk about it. Puddin pulled her hand away from Joe's face and looked out the window. Romance? Love? He had a lot of nerve. Joe wasn't fooling anybody. She stared at the stark blue sky and white puffy clouds. Traveling down the highway, away from the city, the sky was so beautiful; it was hard to trust if it was real.

If Joe was having romance right now, it was with the cable television stations he spent most of his time with, and a few videotapes that he was courting behind closed doors.

When they were young, he was a wild, red thing—all muscles, smiles, and tenderness, but he was wild. Now, sometimes since he'd gotten caught up in church—she hated to even think it—but sometimes she was sorry he had gotten saved. Before, he was like a wild red bull charging through life, and she had wished then that he were more peaceful, more sedate. *Be careful what you pray for, because you might get it.*

Now, he had changed.

Now Joe could tell everybody else what was wrong with them, but he didn't recognize his own faults. She loved him, but she didn't know how much more she could take. He could quote the Bible to everyone else, but he had forgotten the verse that said "rejoice in the wife of your youth. . . ." Now, instead of her fiery red bull, she had a Scripture-spouting hypocrite. And she wasn't sure if she could live with that—or if she even wanted to. Puddin turned her head, looked out the window, and let the broken white highway lines pull her home.

5

Moor

Cooking was the closest, right now, that he could get to home. Moor bent his head over the stove. The heat from the pot he stirred, and the spiciness of the mixture, warmed his face and, temporarily, cleared his nose. It was almost like being home— almost. Chunks of hard-cooked beef floated in tomato sauce and lime juice mixed with hot peppers and curry powder, but he pretended that it was fish stew cooked in his grandmother's twenty-year-old clay pot. In a bowl nearby was a spicy bean paste. It was the best he could do. It was the black-eyed beans, or peas as the Americans called them, that he could not seem to get right.

If his grandmother were present, she would have laughed. *"Funny that such an educated man, such a large, strong man cannot conquer a little, tiny bean!"* As tiny as they were, it was the beans that made him scratch his head—how to boil them to just the right softness, to mash them and strain off the husks, so that the paste was smooth. He could never get it quite right.

He had been cooking since rising early that morning. He dipped his wooden spoon in the pot, blew the steam away, and tasted. It was the right heat, but still something was missing. When he spoke to his grandmother again, he would have to ask her, to see if she could ferret out the missing ingredient. Of course, if his nose were not always so stuffy with the change of climate and all, it would be easier; he might be able to solve the mystery himself. He took another taste and shook his head. Until his nose cleared or his grandmother gave him a word, it would have to do.

Moor lifted an eyebrow. It was as close to home as he would taste for some time.

He closed the lid on the first pot and then opened the lid of the one next to it to admire his rice. No matter what else he got wrong, his rice was masterful. It was always perfect. He smiled, nodded, then laughed as he thought of what his grandmother would say to see him.

"No one would believe to see such a tall, broad-shouldered man bent over such small pots." He imagined her tiny body, still strong though she was very old. Mostly he remembered her smile—three front teeth missing—but still it was a beautiful sight to see. It was, after all, not the teeth that made a smile. *"Who would believe such a man of the town would use his great arms not to build an obi for his family or to hunt, but to cook rice."* She would shake her head. *"Big men now do women's work. It is a crazy mixed-up world!"*

He closed the lid and stood looking around the small flat. It was nothing like home, nothing like his family place in southern Africa. In some ways, it was the same—many people huddled together in a town, many homes together in a small space. But hardly anyone there had his own place where he lived alone. Families, male workers, or female friends lived together in groups. It was strange to him the way people wanted to live alone here—to be separate.

Sometimes an abandoned car or a homeless person's stare would remind him of the poverty there, in Africa. In many ways, this place was better—the carpet, the lighting, all the niceties and city conveniences; there was something to be said for U.S. cities. But what Lesotho lacked in amenities, it made up for in family and togetherness. At least it seemed that way to him.

In Lesotho, an independent country within the borders of South Africa, he could still look out the window and see a tree or mountains that told a story of long ago before white men came, before things changed. Some days the sky was so clear blue, the sun so bright, the clouds velvety white, while the mountains—

sometimes indigo, sometimes purple, and other times black—stretched to reach them, that it was medicine for a soul to stare hour upon hour. And the night sky was so dark and the sky so full of stars that it made the heart ache.

He drifted in thoughts of home. Maybe it was the natural, intentional beauty of his homeland that made people there more sure that there was a God who loved them, a God who worked miracles. Such beauty did not happen on its own.

At home one could still look out across the grasslands and see wildflowers that looked like torch flames in the distance. Still, here and there, and in the mountains there were *rondeles* with thatched roofs—small, round huts painted in bright colors, with vivid patterns to rival nature. The bright colors were also visual medicine against the poverty that ran through the land. There was enough beauty that people trained themselves to look beyond the galvanized tin roofs of the shanties in which many of them dwelled.

Moor looked out the window over the stove. There was no point in entertaining so many memories of home. A man had to do what he was called to do, and he had learned quickly that homesickness could fell the strongest of men, could leave them lying on benches with empty bottles in their hands, or waking up in strange places with strange women.

He would be in the United States for eighteen months while he trained in banking and economic systems—six months in Baltimore, twelve months in California. It was too long a time away to be mourning for his home so far away, too long a time to let loneliness sing to him. He had settled in his mind that he would be alone the eighteen months, with few companions. There was too short a time; there would be no time to find a woman, a wife. He would have to wait until he went back home. The important thing was to get the training so that he could go back home and help his people. There was no point in even thinking of a wife. It was too short a time.

His grandmother would have laughed at his thoughts, again.

"Who can say what is too short or too long? Such things are known only to God, who sits on high. 'A man's mind plans his way,' the Holy Book says." He could see her shaking her gray head. *"See, of course, my grandson, that this wise book says 'a man's mind.' It is a waste to think these thoughts. Women are wise, of course, and know better than to make such plans."*

He turned away from the window. She knew many things, his grandmother. However, on this point, he was certain. Women were led by their hearts, even his grandmother. But there were times when sacrifices had to be made, when a man had to do what a man had to do. A wife, a family, a home would all have to wait. There was much work to be done, and sometimes doing was a solitary thing.

He lifted the lid on the pot to smell again. It almost took him home.

6

Mary

Mary stepped off the Number One bus, crossed the busy
street, and walked over the cobblestones to meet her
friends in Phillips Seafood Restaurant at the Inner
Harbor. The smell of good food made her relax. She slid into the
booth next to Thelma, across from Latrice and Naomi.

They had met while attending Morgan State University and had
remained good friends. More than friends, they were sisters.

"Girl, where have you been?" Latrice fluttered her fingers as she
looked at her watch. "We have been waiting here forever." Latrice
picked up a piece of shrimp and dipped it in cocktail sauce. "We
had to get a little something"—she waved the shrimp in the air—
"just so we wouldn't starve to death, okay?" It was on already; each
one of them outdoing the other with banter and teasing—the kind
of humor found only among the closest of friends, only among sis-
ter-girls.

Thelma winked—her blue contacts, contrasted with her mocha
skin, still startled Mary—and pointed at Latrice's sagging tricep that
jiggled as she ate. "And you know some of us are just an inch from
starvation."

Latrice fired back while the others laughed. "Don't be hating
across the table, okay? Someday, if you're lucky, when you grow up,
you will develop some of this that I already got!"

Thelma smiled and shook her head. "We were about to give up
and order."

Latrice clicked the tips of her nails together as she dipped them into a small bowl of water nearby, then smiled at Mary. "Girl, where were you?"

Naomi tossed her blonde hair and pursed her dark lips. "You know where she was—she was on the b-u-s bus. We sitting in here waiting and starving while she rolling all over town on Maryland Transit Authority's finest." She shook her head. "You *have* to get a car, Mary. It's ridiculous, girl. It's not just impacting you. We could have fainted away up in here waiting for you."

Mary smirked. "Somehow, I doubt it." The verbal game they played with each other was about hyperbole, about satirical wit and quick comebacks. Said to a stranger, the words could mean war, but between friends, it was all humor.

Latrice pointed and waved one perfect, brightly decorated nail at Mary. "I just don't understand it. You got that house your grand-mamma left you. If it was me, I would borrow some money against that thing so fast and get me a car, a condo, and a—"

Thelma raised an eyebrow and then reached across the table to pinch Latrice.

"Ow! What?" Latrice waved her hands in the air and pouted. "I'm just telling the truth!" She looked at Mary. "You know I love you. And you know I loved your grandmamma, and I haven't said anything—"

Thelma gave Latrice a piercing look. "I don't think you ought to be saying anything *now*, either."

Latrice brushed Thelma's comment away with a gesture of her hand. "Well, I think different. It's been over five years." She looked from Thelma back to Mary. Mary felt a conversation coming on that she really didn't want to have. "It's time to pick yourself up and move on, Mary girl. Your grandmamma wouldn't have wanted you to just waste away. You can't go to the grave with her. You might try to look like it, but you ain't dead yet." Inwardly, Mary winced. She still wasn't ready to talk about it. It wasn't the comment about her appearance that stung, it was the *move on, move forward* part. It hit a little too close to home.

Outwardly, she forced herself to look calm. It was part of the game; to hold back laughing as long as you could when things were funny, to hold back crying when they vexed or hurt. And the thing was, these were her sisters. They were four women who would have died for each other, four women who had already proven that they would be there for each other when times were hard. They had been there to hold each other when there were tears, to lend money when the eviction notice was on the door, and to laugh and celebrate when times were good. They had history. And even more rare, they were sisters who would find a way—even through jokes and barbs—to say the hard, honest things that needed to be said.

Naomi elbowed Latrice and then used a hand to brush the hair out of her eyes. "She ain't dead yet? Latrice, you don't care *what* comes out of your mouth." She shook her head and tossed her hair. "Girl, if you don't hush, I'm gone knock you out of this booth."

Latrice picked up a fork and pointed it at Naomi. "I don't think so, Miss Thing, Miss Goldilocks. You and whose mama?" Both of them began to giggle like schoolgirls.

Thelma turned her most stern and motherly gaze on Naomi and Latrice. But the two kept right on talking. "They are so ghetto. Why do we even take them out?" she said loudly while looking across the table at them, but speaking to Mary.

"Knock me out of the booth? Not before you come rolling out of it with me, girlfriend." Latrice play-jabbed at the air, making karate sound effects. "I don't know karate, but I know how to ka-fork you!"

Mary smiled. Watching the two of them clown was usually the highlight of their meetings. There was nothing like hanging out with your real girls. They kept her grounded when she thought she was about to fall off the edge.

Thelma, the sensible one, weighed into the fray. "Okay! Cut it out, you two, before they kick us out of here. I swear, you two are just like two elementary schoolchildren."

Naomi tossed her hair. "And you think you are our teacher, Miss Crab Apple."

Mary wouldn't let herself laugh out loud. She didn't want to encourage Latrice and Naomi, but she couldn't help but smile. They had been performing these roles for years—Naomi and Latrice as silly children, while Thelma played the mother.

Mary looked around the restaurant. Some people, looking at the four of them, would understand—they were four women enjoying themselves and decompressing. Others would have found it difficult to believe that Mary was a government employee, that Thelma was a schoolteacher in the county, that Naomi was a dentist with a fabulous home in Bel Air, and that Latrice was a successful art dealer who lived in upscale Columbia. Some looking in from the outside would have misjudged them.

While the ancient song that sang in the veins of most of the people judging told them to blend in, to conform, in order to survive, the old, old song that Mary and her friends heard told them to be proud of, even fierce about, being who they were. It was the only way to survive.

These girlfriends, these sisters of hers, weren't imposters. They didn't change their language, their pronunciation, their enunciation, so that people wouldn't know where they came from. To them, being successful didn't mean they could never laugh out loud or that they could only wear gray or black suits. All four of them knew the King's English and used it well when appropriate, but being successful didn't mean they couldn't get together and speak in the rhythms that flowed from their hearts.

There are people—successful people, saved people—who change their hair, their walk, their clothes, their associations and friends, so that people won't know they were raised on the wrong side of the tracks, the wrong side of sin. They never speak too loudly. They never laugh loudly; they titter and cover their mouths. They don't draw attention to themselves. They don't wear loud clothes. They don't laugh loud or long or do anything that arouses passion—like eating spicy foods or listening to foot-tapping music—because they are afraid something will seep, or spill, or explode out of them. They are afraid someone will recognize who they are, afraid someone will see that they are flawed and frail.

They don't dance. They smother themselves until they are almost lifeless. Then they set about smothering life in other people—afraid that if life is discovered here or there, if someone sees a shoulder shaking or a hip moving, they will see that life in *others* and then recognize *them*.

They make life miserable for others, these imposters. They make success, salvation look dreadful, these imposters. But these girl-friends, these sisters, were not imposters.

Thelma rubbed one of Mary's hands. Even in college she had been more like a mother to the other three. Only then Thelma's eyes were brown—not the almost turquoise blue that the contacts made them. "Latrice is crazy," Thelma said matter-of-factly.

Latrice wagged a finger at Thelma. "Wait a minute now, Mother Superior!"

Thelma gave her the eye, then turned back to Mary. "Latrice is crazy, but she's still right. You have been in kind of a funk since your grandmother passed. And we didn't want to say anything. We know how close the two of you were. And we're sensible women." She looked around the table. "Everyone needs time to grieve."

What is this, pick on Mary week? Mary tried to keep her breathing even, tried to not let them see her getting anxious. *Do we have to go there?* Why didn't she just tell them to back off, it was none of their business? She didn't have to listen to this.

Thelma was still talking. "But it's time now, you know? We thought things were going to get better when you joined the church—you know, when you got saved."

Naomi nodded, and her hair bounced. Naomi always said if you were going to get a weave, spend money and buy long hair that moved—hers was the proof. "You *need* a relationship with the Lord.

We all do. Ain't nothing sweeter than Jesus." Naomi's smile was compassionate and sincere.

Latrice moved her hands back and forth as though she were praise dancing. "I know that's right. Mm hmm! I love to get my shout on!"

Thelma's gaze was direct and her voice very even and calm. "But, Mary, you are in a rut, you know?"

Latrice snapped her fingers. "Girl, you have got to fix yourself up!" She held out her hands, as if to display. "Get your nails done. Your nails is lookin' rough!"

Naomi flicked a hand at Latrice's nails. "Latrice, girl, other people's lives don't revolve around their nails just because yours does."

Mary knew why she didn't just tell them to mind their own business, why she didn't get up and leave. It was because she knew they were right. It had been long enough. They were right; she had let herself go. She looked at her neglected hands. As much as it hurt, she knew that they were telling the truth. They were speaking words she had thought and ignored. Besides that, while they were doing the emotional surgery, they also made her laugh.

Latrice spread her fingers wide and flashed them around the table. "Baby, these nails and these hands have brought grown men to their knees. Humph! I've had men fight their way across the room—" she pantomimed their actions "—to meet me just because of these nails, okay? Don't hate the player, baby. Hate the game! *Ha, ha.*"

Thelma put on her first-day-of-school-I'm-the-new-teacher-taking-authority voice. "Latrice, this is not about you. Remember, we are trying to help Mary. We'll work on you next week."

Latrice pursed her lips, folded her hands on the table—nails up—and looked away, mumbling to herself, but just loud enough to be heard. "I'm just trying to help, offer some suggestions, give some pointers, share my beauty secrets with my friend—my *secrets*. People pay good money for what I'm giving away to you all for free!

But you don't appreciate it. Don't have to talk to me like I'm some child. Like I'm crazy."

Mary smiled, though her feelings were still hurting.

Thelma gave Latrice the eye again, then continued talking. "Like I was saying, we're happy about you joining the church, especially when you got that group of young ladies to teach, or mentor."

Naomi shook her head full of shoulder-length golden curls and picked up a shrimp. "Better you than me, honey. I give it to you. I can't be bothered with no children that are not my own." She stopped for a second, as though she was thinking, and then plowed on. "Especially some mouthy teenage girls. Oo-oo-oo, they are *too* fast and they think they know everything. Girl, I admire you for taking it on. If it was me, I know somebody already would have been laid out on the floor—and it sure wouldn't be me." Naomi saluted Mary with the shrimp. "Honey, my hat is off to you."

Latrice snapped her fingers. "You mean your wig is off to her, don't you?" All three said *ooohhhh* at the same time. It was a barb comedian Don Rickles would have been proud of. They held their breath, waiting for the comeback.

Naomi tossed her hair again, then rolled her neck, smiling. "First of all, it ain't a wig. Second of all, don't let me get on you about your old played-out press-on nails. Okay?" The comeback was worthy—there was nothing Latrice was more sensitive about than her nails—and Naomi's status in the game was redeemed. She gently brushed the hair back from her face. "What I'm saying," she continued to Mary, "is that I commend you for even trying to work with some teenagers, you know?"

Latrice reached for another shrimp and spoke between bites. "You got that right. I give you props on that one." She beamed across the table at Mary. "Not to mention that we all know that the church is a good place to meet a man!" In the midst of all the joking and jabs, Mary knew her friends were very naturally using a tried-and-true feedback technique: *tell the client what needs improvement, but also remember to commend her on something she's doing well.*

Thelma nodded. "I thought—girl, I take that back—I *hoped* that while you were being a role model for the young ladies, that, you know, you might try to fix yourself up a little, but . . ."

Latrice sucked cocktail sauce off another shrimp. "I'll tell you what you *need* to do. Number one, like I said before, you need to take out a loan on that house your grandmamma left you and get you a car. Then, number two—" she held up two shiny fingers—"you need to get you a man!" She jiggled her shoulders—a short shimmy. "Then after that, you don't have to worry about number three, 'cause a good man is the cure for everything, baby! Humph! Somebody call the doctor!" She clicked her nails in the water bowl on the table, then wiped them on her white linen napkin. She lifted two fingers and touched them to her cheek. "You see this pretty skin? I can write you out a simple prescription: M-A-N!" Mary couldn't help smiling. Her friends were worthy of a sitcom.

Naomi fluffed her hair and then nudged Latrice. "Girl, you know you right. You can tell a woman that ain't got no man." She fluffed her hair again. "Her hair looking bad, wearing just any kind of old clothes." Naomi looked pointedly at Mary. "Looking all old-fashioned." She shook her head. "Mary, girl, a man will bring you out. Give you peace of mind. He'll make you blossom, put a little bloom on your cheeks."

Mary sighed and laughed, against her will, at the merciless teasing.

Latrice nodded her agreement. "That's the truth."

Mary rolled her eyes. It worked for them, but she wasn't so sure. . . .

Thelma leaned closer to Mary, as though to comfort her, and then weighed into the conversation. "You know your grandmother wouldn't want you to be alone."

Mary willed the muscles in her face not to tighten, and held her eyes steady so that the lids would not flutter. Why was everyone so worried about her love life—or lack thereof? It was enough to talk about a makeover, but she wasn't so convinced about a relationship.

Do not overload the client with feedback. Remember, she can only process one or two things at a time.

Had they all gotten together and decided this was going to be the week they all took turns stirring in the pot of her personal life? First, her cousin Garvin, and now the three of them. Mary tried to keep frustration off her face, but she could feel one eyebrow rising and her teeth beginning to clinch. *Get it together, Mary. These are your friends, your girls. They're just trying to help. They're just a little concerned is all.* Her facial muscles still weren't relaxing.

Latrice tapped her on the hand. "Now, don't get all bunched up, girl. You know we love you. Don't get all uptight. We're just talking to you because we love you."

It was true—they loved her, but Mary couldn't sit quietly any longer. She would at least tackle the safer subject. She sniffed the perfume scent on her wrist before she began talking. The perfume's smell comforted her. She needed a sniff of New Orleans to help calm her. "I don't care what you all say. I'm not about to mortgage my granny's house—my house—for a car."

Naomi tossed her hair. "That wasn't me that said that. That was Latrice."

Latrice leveled a narrow gaze at Naomi. "Girl, I can't believe you would put me out there like that. Left me all out in the wind."

Mary kept talking. She could hear her voice sounding more and more defensive with each word. This was not how you played the game. "I'm saving money. When I have enough saved to make a good down payment, I will get a car. Until then, I'll be walking and catching the bus. Plenty of people ride the bus—on purpose. If you all can't wait for me to get places on the bus—if I'm making you late—"

Naomi shook her head, hair flying. "Oh, girl, don't get all worked up. My goodness!"

She had lost her cool, so they knew they had touched a sore spot. Mary pursed her lips, frustrated with herself. She had shown her hand. They knew she was protesting too much—she knew she was protesting too much—that what she was really worked up about was not the house or a car, but something more.

Thelma nodded. Her eyes were round with sincerity. "Okay, so you don't get a car today. That's okay." Thelma patted Mary's shoulder as though to calm her down. "But, I do think—and I almost hate to say it—but I do think Latrice is right about the man."

Her mouth dropped open before Mary could think to control it. They had hit the spot.

Thelma kept patting. "Not like Latrice, I mean, you don't need an army of men." Some zinging humor to soften the blow.

Latrice leaned forward in the booth and pressed her hands flat on the tabletop. "Wait a minute, now!" She began to rise in mock indignation.

Thelma ignored her. "But, a woman *does* need a man in her life." Her voice lowered into a therapist's comforting monotone. "Even the Bible says it's not good for a man to be alone."

Naomi shook her mane victoriously. "And what's good for the goose is good for the gander, baby!" She thought for a moment. "Or what's bad for the goose, is also bad . . . you know what I mean."

Mary smirked at Naomi's dumb blonde—store-bought blonde must also qualify—act while she thought back on her telephone conversation with Garvin. "You won't believe this, but just yesterday, my cousin called me trying to tell me what would fix my life. And, funny, but she said just the opposite of you. Instead of telling me to get a man, she sang me the be-single-and-satisfied song."

Naomi twisted a lock of her hair around her ring finger. "She's married, right? Of course she is. Of course she did. All the married women at church say the same thing to single women. 'Be happy to be single. Don't rush to get married. Don't be in a hurry to get in a relationship.'"

Latrice clapped her hands together and put on a mocking voice. "'That's right, baby. This is the best time of your life!'" She dropped her hands. "They ain't foolin nobody. They know it ain't but a few men in the church, and they want to make sure you ain't stealing theirs!" She hooked her nails liked tiger claws. They all laughed as she growled.

Naomi let go the curl and patted it back into place. "Mm hmm. They want you to forget that they knocked you down, a year ago, trying to beat you to the only eligible man in church—you know, the one they married 'cause they got to him first."

Mary laughed. It was good to talk to other sisters who understood.

Thelma laughed. "You know as well as I do, Mary, that they are all hypocritical. Besides," she turned her gaze intently on Mary, "God made us. He put these desires in us; at least He put them in me. Lord knows I have prayed about it, and if He wanted to take the desire away, He could have at any time." She looked at the women and lowered her voice. "Not to mention, it's not 1950 anymore. It's a little old-fashioned to think that any man worth having—with all the women willing to give it up to just anybody—is going to wait around for a ring." She shrugged her shoulders. "Besides, we're big girls, we're wise women—we know what we're doing. I mean, we know the right man, the right one. . . . It's not like we're being promiscuous or anything." Thelma looked at Latrice. "At least most of us, anyway." It was obvious she couldn't resist pitching one Latrice's way.

Mary looked back and forth at her friends. It was so strange to hear the conversation that had been in her head earlier, since her conversation with her cousin Garvin, now played out among her friends. She felt even stranger as she listened to the words that tumbled from her lips. "It's not easy, and I know lots of people are hypocrites about it. But I'm trying to teach the girls that I work with to be . . . and I'm trying to be, you know, a godly woman . . . a woman that loves God."

"Wait a minute, Mary! What are you trying to say?" Latrice spoke up. "I'm a godly woman. I love the Lord." She waved her hand in the air. "I'm saved, sanctified, Holy Ghost-filled, fire-baptized, with the evidence of speaking in tongues. Just what are you trying to say, Mary?"

Thelma shushed Latrice. "Calm down, now, girl. You don't have to play your denomination card. She didn't mean anything. Did you, Mary?"

Latrice's nails flew through the air like sparks, like brightly colored fireworks. "I hate that, though! People trying to tell me—trying to be holier-than-thou—that I don't love the Lord! I love God, okay? I was saved before you ever thought about it, Mary. I been going to church since I was a little girl. I hate that. I can't stand people judging me. They telling me I bet not be with a man, but it's okay for them to run around and gossip and cheat and lie, and talk mean to people. I hate that. . . ." She shook her head. "Especially when it comes from a real friend."

Naomi used her hand to brush her hair back from her face. "That's right, Mary. Do you remember when you were the main one telling us your cute little stories about you and the latest man of the day? So don't be so high and mighty, 'cause your behind is going to judgment just like the rest of us. Besides that, it ain't *murder*. It ain't *selling drugs*. It ain't *stealing*." She tossed her hair again and tears filled her eyes. "I don't know why I'm getting so emotional about this anyway. I love God, okay? And I know God loves me, okay? I usher at church, and I'm always there. Some of the main ones talking about what I ought to do, and what I ought *not* do, they are never around when there's some work to be done. They're not dependable or faithful. What about that?"

Mary sympathized with them. She understood; their thoughts were her thoughts. Still . . .

Thelma looked at Mary matter-of-factly. "We are all saved women here, Mary. But we've got to be realistic. Prince Charming is unavailable to take our calls. If we're waiting for that, we're going to shrivel up and die. The point is not whether we love God. It's about reality. Those kinds of relationships—the man bringing roses, paying for candlelit dinners, throwing his cloak so you can step over a puddle—they don't exist anymore. The older women criticizing don't have to deal with that reality. As Miss Tina Turner says, 'What's Love Got to Do With It?' There is no happily ever after anymore—if there ever was. There's no doubt that we love God, that we love the Lord. But we have to be sensible. The Lord knows that. He knows our hearts. People forget that—that God judges the heart. And He's the only One fit to judge."

Latrice nodded. "That's right. They can't tell me *nothing* about my relationship with God. When I pray to Him, He answers, and I can feel it, okay? I know I'm a blessed woman, okay? So don't tell me that God doesn't love me or that I don't love God because I get some romance, a little touch, every now and then, okay?"

Mary reached over to touch Naomi's hand. She hadn't meant for things to get so serious; she hadn't meant to touch their sore spots. They had just gotten through touching hers; she knew how it felt. "I'm sorry, Naomi." She looked at Latrice. "You all know that I'm not trying to hurt your feelings. We're friends, okay? You know I love you. I'm not judging you. How can I judge? You know I'm your girl." She shrugged. "Truth be told, I'm trying to figure it out myself. It's hard for me to believe that it's such a big deal to God. Even though I do have to admit that every time somebody brings it up, I get a guilty feeling. Then I think, why am I feeling guilty if it's not a big deal?" She shook her head. "Plus, you all know this whole thing about being pure and being abstinent is a whole new thing. Nobody at church was talking about it years ago."

Latrice nodded. "I know that's right! They were just saying, *'Make sure you don't bring no babies home!'*"

"Now, everything's changing, and I'm not sure how I feel about it, you know? Nobody wants to give up anything they've been doing that makes them feel good."

Latrice waved her hands. "Girl, you about to start preaching up in here!"

Mary nodded. "While they're telling me to give up my thing, why don't they give up theirs?"

Naomi flung her hair. "That's right! Get that big pole of wood out of their own eye before they start messing with mine!"

"Girl, don't you make me shout up in here! These people in Phillips ain't ready for it!" Latrice hunched her shoulders and started singing, "Sweep around your own front door, before you try to sweep around mine. . . ."

Mary laughed, relieved that the mood had changed. She nodded and chuckled, until a memory sobered her. "But then I look at the girls. The children are living on the edge. You all just don't know. And I wonder if what we do, or don't do, and how we live, if it has anything to do with them." She looked around the booth at her three friends. "I don't know. And truth be told, when my cousin brought it up to me the other day, I was thinking the same thing that you all are saying. What business is it of hers? What business is it of the church people what I do with my body? A bunch of dried-up, uptight people trying to tell me not to enjoy what they wish they had. You know? People that think being a Christian means you've got to be frowning and unhappy." She smiled, hoping they would smile too. "I was about to get worked up myself listening to her. I was about to tell her off, but then I thought of something."

Mary looked at Thelma, Latrice, and Naomi, and chuckled. "What was I going to argue for? I don't even *have* a man. And no telling when the next time will be that I get one. Why was I going to argue over a man I don't have? Then I had to laugh at my own self." Her smile broadened. "I don't know the answers. Maybe it's God's way of helping me to be *single and satisfied* whether I want to or not."

The four of them were quiet for a moment. Suddenly Naomi laughed out loud. "No, it's not God. It's that bad hairdo you're wearing that's keeping you single!" Her comment broke the ice. They were back to the game. No more serious talk—just girlfriends sharing and making each other laugh.

Latrice reached across the table and held up one of Mary's hands. "No, no, honey! You got to get something done to these nails and cuticles. Don't no man want hangnails scratching up his hands, let alone his back."

"Latrice, you are so common!" Thelma clucked over them like a mother hen. "No, Mary, you need to try some of these contacts." She pointed at her eyes, and then to her chest. "And a little store-bought enhancement never hurt anybody."

Naomi shook her hair like a black, blonde eighties Farrah Fawcett. "That's right, girl. Stick with us, girl. We gone hook a sister up!"

The four friends placed their orders and dined by candlelight. Mary, from time to time, in between eating and laughing, sniffed her wrists. There was nothing like friendship. But even among friends, the scent and the recollections that floated on the fragrance comforted her and helped her cope. She looked at the plate before her, lifted her fork, and savored a mouthful of buttered lobster. Whatever she didn't understand, whatever she had to go through, of one thing she was certain: friendship, good food, and good memories always made it taste better.

7

Puddin

Puddin *stared down* at the food in front of her. It would be nice, sometimes, to eat something different. It was chicken all the time. Fried chicken. Stewed chicken. Barbecued chicken. Chicken soup. Chicken fricassee. Chicken gumbo. Chicken sandwiches. Chicken strips. Chicken nuggets. She and Joe had even had chicken spaghetti.

She looked at the baked chicken thigh on the end of the long-handled fork she held in her hand. Forrest Gump might as well be joining them for dinner. Joe had done what he planned: he had retired early. But retirement wasn't a victory over "the man" if they had to have poultry—yard bird—every doggone evening. There had to be a better way—just a little part-time something or other—so they could let the chicken have a rest.

God bless the children of Israel! She was never going to make any more comments about how they got sick of eating manna when they were in the wilderness. She was sure sick of chicken! Puddin dropped the piece of chicken she held onto a serving platter in the middle of the dining room table, then peeked at her watch before she skewered the next piece in the metal baking pan.

She looked up when she heard the key turn in the lock. The kitchen door, on the side of the house, swung open, and she heard Joe's familiar footfalls. Without seeing him, she could imagine him moving through the yellow-painted kitchen.

"Hey, baby girl."

"Hey," she replied when he poked his head inside the dining room doorway, while she kept stacking chicken on the serving plate.

He winked, then withdrew into the kitchen.

Something had to give. Not only were they beginning to grow pinfeathers, but she didn't have money to go out with her friends or buy herself something nice from time to time. Well, she was fed up. Tonight was going to be the night. She was going to fill her husband up with mashed potatoes, green beans, corn bread—and chicken— lots of chicken. Then, after he was full, they were going to have a little chat about chicken, the man, and a part-time job. Joe could stay in his little dark, locked room if he wanted to, but—

Joe walked into the dining room, his eyes bright and full of cheer. Almost immediately, he was across the room, one of his arms wrapped around her back, enfolding her. Embracing her, he kissed her on the mouth. Not a Sunday-morning kiss, not an on-the-way- to-work kiss, but a full, wet kiss like when they were first married.

Puddin giggled and wiggled, uncomfortable that she was embar- rassed and breathless. She giggled again. She felt and knew she sounded like a schoolgirl.

Joe massaged the round of her spine and then kissed her again. He winked. "Something sure does smell good." Joe kissed her neck and nibbled her ear.

Puddin felt her face get warm. "It's just dinner. Just chicken. Just plain old chicken." It was ridiculous. Here she was a fifty- something-year-old woman, *twitterpated* and out of breath.

Joe kept his eyes glued to hers. "Doesn't look plain to me. Looks all warm, brown, and spicy." He glanced at the platter of chicken and then back at her.

Puddin laughed. She actually felt dizzy. It was silly. She tried to push him away. "What's got into you, Joe?" She felt fifteen and couldn't for the life of her figure out how to look nonchalant.

Joe kept his one arm tight around her waist. "Can't a man appreciate his wife? Can't a man be happy to come home to the woman he loves? Can't a man like chicken?" He kissed the tip of her nose. "Or better yet, sweet chocolate pudding?" He pinched her waist.

She tried to wiggle free. His pinching made her uncomfortable. She didn't like his fingers touching her "problem areas," as the magazines called them.

Joe smiled and kissed her again. "I'm a man that knows what he likes. I like chocolate puddin', and I like a lot of it. The more the merrier!"

"Joe!" She looked around as though someone might be watching them. He could always embarrass her so easily. Puddin pushed against her husband again and freed herself. "Boy, you better stop it!" She stepped quickly away from him, almost dancing around the table, just beyond his reach, still trying to fork chicken onto the platter.

He followed after her. "Boy? Now I'm a boy?" He pulled at the bow that tied her apron in the back. It fell open.

"Stop it, Joe! I mean it, now!" She felt silly. She clutched the pan of chicken to herself for protection. It was silly to giggle so over your own husband, your own husband of so many years.

Unencumbered by a pan of chicken, Joe quickly moved up behind her and recaptured her. He pulled her closer. "Can't a man love his wife? What's wrong with a little romance?" He rubbed his lips against the back of her hair, against the back of her neck, and then breathed deeply. "I love you, Puddin. I still love the very scent of you."

She gripped the pan tighter. Puddin felt her knees weaken and was afraid she would let the chicken fall. He nuzzled her hair once more. "That's the problem. Nobody believes in romance anymore. Nobody believes in true love. People don't even know what love is." Joe loosened his grip and used his hand to loosen her grip on the pan—her shield. When he had finally wrestled it from her and set it on the table, he turned her to face him and encircled her waist again.

"Romance is the way I feel about you." He gave her a peck on the forehead. "It's been thirty years, but when I look at you, I still see the same sweet girl I married. My sweet chocolate puddin'.

"People think that romance is that first spark they feel. But romance is that I still see fire in your eyes after all these years." He laughed. "Romance is that when I got a cold and you rub Vicks VapoRub on my chest, it don't just cure the cold, it fans the flames!"

She hit him on the arm. "Joe, you are so silly."

He nuzzled her ear. "No, I'm serious. True love is the way you make me feel like a man, the way I'm a better person when I'm around you. True love is that you always believe in me, that when I look in your eyes, I still see that I'm your hero. That's true love, baby. That's romance. That after all these years," he kissed her gently and then winked, "you're still making chicken for me."

She was about to protest, to tell him that she didn't think chicken and romance were synonymous, but he kissed her before she could complain. Puddin turned to gooey mush. She threw both of her arms around Joe's neck and buried her face in his chest. She allowed herself to surrender to the loss of control, to the moment. She whispered to him. "Put both of your arms around me."

Joe laughed shortly and abruptly pulled away. "In a minute."

Surprise made her laugh too. "In a minute?" She stepped closer to him and wrapped her arms around his waist. "It wasn't *in a minute* just a second ago. Don't get scared now." She giggled again.

Joe pulled away again. "After we eat. We've got plenty of time."

"Joe?" That's when she noticed that one arm, throughout the chicken dance, had remained behind his back. "What's behind your back, Joe?"

He grinned. Puddin was almost sure she saw canary feathers sticking from the sides of his mouth. "Nothing, girl. Let me just run to my reading room and I'll be right back." He sidestepped her.

The flushed warmth on Puddin's face was turning to angry heat and burning embarrassment. She was ashamed to have let him make such a fool of her. *Am I still, after all these years, so desperate for love? How many times do I have to be embarrassed before I stop letting Joe make a fool of me?*

He had bamboozled her, but she didn't have to let him off the hook so easily. "I said, what is that in your hand, Joe?" She knew what it was. Of course she did. It was so obvious, so sleazy—videotapes in a brown paper bag. She knew what they were; she wasn't born yesterday. But she needed him to admit it. If he was going to do it, he should be man enough to stand flat-footed and own up to it.

The mealy-mouthed, cheating hypocrisy—that was why she was beginning not to like him. Joe was always in church, helping the pastor, doing this and doing that. He was always running his mouth about other people's sins and faults; he ought to at least admit to his own. Covering up the tapes with a brown paper bag didn't change what they were. "Joe, I mean it. Tell me what you have in the bag, Joe."

He stood in the doorway of his reading room, turned to face her, took a deep breath, and said, "Nothing, baby."

Puddin sucked in so much air, she was sure she saw the carpet pulling up from the floor. It took all her fruit—patience, mercy, meekness, and all the rest—not to pop him one good one upside his head. She could feel her shoulders tightening and her hands balling into fists. She was a peaceful woman, but she wasn't about to stand here and let him disrespect her to her face. Puddin wasn't sure if what was welling up inside her was more anger or humiliation. It was bad enough for him to bring that brown paper sack–wrapped filth into their home—her home. It was bad enough for him to make a fool of her, to use the love he knew she felt for him to distract and deceive her. But the worst thing of all was the lying. He was even lying to himself.

Joe still had a little smile on his face. How could he be smiling? He didn't care; that's how he could smile about it. It was obvious that he didn't care how he was making her feel, or how he was making himself look.

He put his hand on the door to close it, still smiling. He shrugged. "Give me just a few minutes, baby. Ten minutes or so, and I'll be right out. What I'm doing is good for both of us." He winked. "We'll spend some quality time this evening."

"Joe, don't you—"

Click. He closed the door.

Just like that, he closed the door. *Click.* Funny how one small sound like that could change a whole relationship. He was closing the door on them—on who they were. He was fooling himself, but she was taking off the blinders. *A few minutes?* It never took a few minutes, but with the damage that one small sound had made, it could have been a lifetime.

Suddenly, it was hard to see. Her eyes filled with tears; a few of them slid down her cheeks. Puddin crossed the room. She lifted her hand to knock on the door—no, to beat on the door. She sighed softly and let her hand drop to her side. She backed away and walked to the dining room table. What was the point? He was only going to lie, and she didn't want to hear any more lies. There was no more fight left in her.

Puddin picked up the fork and attempted to put the rest of the chicken on the platter, but it all felt wrong. Dirty.

Pornography.

She had seen women on talk shows crying about their husbands being addicted to computer porn. Wasting all of the families' hard-earned money. Bringing shame on them. Until now, though, she didn't know why they cried.

She sat in a chair at the table and poked with the fork at the last piece of chicken in the pan. She laid the fork aside and covered her face with her hands.

Maybe if she had insisted that he get a part-time job, or if she'd paid more attention to him—maybe if she'd watched for earlier signs, she would have seen that his self-esteem was suffering, that he felt like less of a man after retiring. Not earning money, not being able to afford all the niceties that were common when he was working was getting to him. He needed to escape to a fantasy world where he was powerful and desirable, she guessed. It was really bad for his ego; he must be feeling really bad about himself. He had to be if he was willing to do something this bad in front of her.

Wait a minute!

She stopped herself, uncovered her face, and wiped her tears.

Wait one cotton-picking minute!

That's what she was always doing—making excuses for him. *Poor Joe.* Covering for him. The truth was that he was a hypocrite. He stood in front of other men telling them to love their wives, but here he was disrespecting his own behind closed doors and expecting her to be silent about it—to cover for him.

Right now, he was choosing to be with other women—albeit fantasy women—in front of her face. He might as well be bringing the women in the front door and sitting them at the table. He might as well be making them a chicken sandwich, for goodness' sakes. Didn't he know how it made her feel? She was his wife of thirty years, but evidently that wasn't good enough . . . or maybe . . . Maybe it had been too long.

Puddin reached her hand to touch the places around her hairline where she knew there were gray hairs. She tried to keep them covered, but still they were there. She laid her hand on her chest. Lots of people said she was still a beautiful woman. When she fixed herself up, she could still turn a head or two. But there was no doubt about it. Gravity was winning the war.

Maybe Joe just wanted something younger or different. Were the women on the tapes blondes? Were they Asian? Were they thinner, or younger? Was their skin lighter than hers? Were they those young women dressed like schoolgirls that they advertised on television late at night—girls that made him feel young? Or was it just that there was too much temptation for a man in today's world? Would any woman do? Puddin touched her hair again. Maybe she was just no longer enough.

Joe wasn't on the Internet. She looked past the reading room to the room that held their computer. He rarely opened the door. In fact, he hardly ever used their computer. If he wanted to send email to friends, he tapped her to do it. She glared at his reading room door. No, her husband didn't cross the digital divide to do his dirt. He kept things conventional, nothing technical for him. He did his dirt the down-home, old-fashioned way. He stuck to what he knew—videotapes. If there was eight-track pornography, he probably would have that too.

Puddin hung her head again and her breathing slowed. She closed her eyes. She could just pack her bags and leave.

For better or for worse. The words of her marriage vows came back to her. This was the worst.

In sickness and in health.

If it wasn't the worst, it was definitely sickness. The truth was, she wasn't going anywhere. Puddin lifted her head. Besides that, if she left, no doubt some chippy would just come in, settle in her place, and probably lead Joe into an even greater life of sin and shame.

For richer or for poorer.

And why should she suffer? Puddin looked around the room—the framed pictures on the wall, the years of photographs, the flowers and memories. She had made their house a home. Why should she give up what was hers? He had the problem. He had the issues.

Puddin sighed again. He had the problem, but the shame was hers to bear. It was her burden to keep his secret among friends, family, and at the church. It was her shame that he wanted someone younger, someone different.

She pursed her lips. Not that he was still some dream lover. He *had* been—she had to tell the truth—he had been fine as wine, as people used to say when they were young. She still thought he was fine—Puddin could feel herself pouting—but that called for her ignoring the added weight around his middle and the pooch that had replaced his board-flat stomach.

Why couldn't he do the same for her? Why couldn't he overlook the changes?

Puddin stood up suddenly, knocking the fork to the floor. She had never wanted another man, but two could play this game. If he wanted to throw away thirty years of love down the tubes, then let him.

She began a long, slow walk down the hall to the computer room. If he could spend his time searching the cable channels, looking for videos of "hotties," so could she. He was not going to get out of this without feeling a little of the sting, a little of the heat, himself. If he could find a playmate on the VCR, she would find a boy-toy on the Internet. It wasn't romance, but what was good for the goose was good for the gander. She set her mouth in a determined line.

Using the hem of her apron, she wiped the tears from her face. She wasn't going to give him the satisfaction of seeing her cry. She retied the apron strings, then continued walking slowly toward her fate—toward the computer room—as though it were a death march. All the while she softly hummed, "Anything you can do, I can do better. , , ,"

8

Moor

Moor *adjusted his backpack* as he walked from his place on Old Frederick to Baltimore Annapolis Turnpike. He walked down the street, having learned the ways of city walking—which had little to do with walking, but rather more with disguising the intent of his heart. His eyes rarely met anyone directly, his face was set firmly. His shoulders were poised like a leopard's, as though at any moment he might pounce.

He crossed the street, navigating through traffic, after passing St. Joseph's Church. Just beyond the barbershop, before the corner takeout restaurant—windows covered with grease, broken worn tiles on the floor, an ageless grill, and vats of rolling boiling fat, three fried chicken wings with hot sauce between two slices of white bread, two pieces of fried white fish with hot sauce between two slices of white bread, a greasy hamburger patty with cheese between two slices of white bread, and lines of hungry people—he turned down a concrete pathway that led to an alleyway. At the alley he turned right, sidestepping green, brown, and clear broken glass bottles and blowing pieces of paper that danced over the concrete and over the alley pavement. He slowed when he heard Blue's voice and stopped at the table in front of the old man.

Instead of spots of rust on the table legs, there were spots of silver peeking through the rust. What was left of the brown vinyl tabletop was ripped, gashed, and scratched. What had once been off-white stuffing now bled dark gray from the edges of the table's wounds. The table sat just beyond the edge of the alley on a strip of browning grass outside the fence that enclosed a house that backed to the alley.

The balding man leaned his back against the fence. An empty pipe hung from the side of Blue's mouth. Dressed in a black, frayed suit coat, the old man's stomach stretched the cream colored jersey he wore and pressed up to the edge of the table. He leaned back in his chair as if resting on a throne. He took the pipe from his mouth and nodding his head toward the old man sitting next to him, pointed to Moor. "Well, look who it is. The prince hisself. What you know good, your highness?"

Moor bowed. "How are you, my wise fathers?"

"Pretty good, if I say so myself," Brighty, the second old man answered.

Day after day, the men sat at their table in the alley holding court, commenting on current events, spouting proverbs for living like modern-day Solomons. They weren't loitering any more than men who meet in coffee shops each day to chew the fat with their friends are loitering. They weren't homeless. They had family and friends and beds on which they slept. They were free men who had worked a long day, or a lifetime, and one of the privileges of their liberty was to be able to relax and rest from their labor in each other's company. Outsiders often mistook them for common folk, or even parasites. Only those who looked with pure hearts saw their value. They were unacknowledged royalty—except around the neighborhood—and, sometimes, the thrones of such royalty could be found on street corners, front steps, or—as in Blue's and Brighty's case—at an old table in an alleyway behind Blue's home.

Blue adjusted the suit coat he wore and pointed again at Moor. "What's that on your back, there, Prince? You studying even on Saturdays now?"

"No, my wise fathers. When you visit a wise man, it is good to bring gifts."

Brighty slapped his hands together. "Watch out there, now! Ain't no doubt about it, young fella—you got a good head on your shoulders. You hear that, Blue? Gifts. That's how you get in good."

"Oh, yeah, he's an honorable fella, all right. That's how I met him, you know? I was coming home from taking care of some business I had with a woman—"

"What business you got with a woman, Blue? Who you trying to fool? Man, Shriveled-Up is your middle name!" The two old men revved up the biting, never-ending game of the dozens that they had been playing since they were boys. They played the game of verbal jousting—which is to arguing and verbal abuse what fencing is to swordfighting—not to draw blood but for sport and entertainment, as a way of learning the skills of oral offense and defense in times of peace. It was an elegant and refined game and those who understood it laughed at the two old men, knowing that they loved each other. Those who knew the game knew that Brighty and Blue were particularly skilled.

"See, Brighty, if I thought you were worth the time, why then I would say something about it. I would engage you in some conversation. But since we know what you just said is nonsense, I'm going to proceed on telling my story. So, like I said, I was coming home after taking care of business"—the way Blue's tongue slid around the word *business* was especially comical—it was like the *z* sound had been left behind—"when a young thug accosted me and demanded my wallet. He looked particularly desperate." Blue paused dramatically. "In fact, the Negro was looking crazy!"

"He must have been desperate, or crazy, or at least from another neighborhood, 'cause everybody around here know you ain't got no money," Brighty said. He slapped his knee, laughing at his own joke, at the flash of his blade.

Blue ignored Brighty's comments, but went on telling him the story. "If my mind hadn't been on my earlier business, I would have been prepared to handle the young thug myself."

"Um hum."

"But as it was, I was caught unawares."

"Underwears?" Brighty cackled again.

Blue pressed on. "I wasn't prepared, you see, and thought this might be my undoing, you know? Until a big black angel, speaking in another tongue, came sweeping down on the young punk and threw him to the ground. Barehanded. That big black angel was this African prince standing right here in front of us."

Brighty bowed from his seated position. "You all been friends every since. Now, here he is bearing gifts."

Blue nodded. "Come on over here then. Court's in session. Let us see what you got."

Moor walked to the table, lifted the backpack from his shoulders, and unzipped the bag. He removed a blue paper tablecloth, shook it, and threw it over the table.

Blue took the pipe from his mouth and used it to point. "What's this? What you up to, boy?" Only royalty could call a prince boy. Moor knew it was a sign of their kinship and affection.

"Just a little something to eat. A small repast for two great men such as yourselves. It is good sometimes for great men to eat together."

Brighty began to wipe his hands on the front of his grayed clothing. "Repast? They sure do teach you to talk fancy in Africa, there, Prince." He scratched his head. "Repast," he said again.

"Stop talking, Brighty, and let the man do what he came to do." Blue tried to peek into the bag. "You always stopping progress at the wrong time."

Moor laughed as he began to unload the containers from his backpack, plastic containers of the dishes he had prepared—the rice, bean paste, and beef with tomato sauce—onto the table. The old men, his friends, stopped talking and leaned closer to see.

Brighty fumbled in the pocket of his stained, worn jeans and put on his very thick glasses. He removed them, wiped them on the plaid shirt he wore that hung open over his dingy undershirt with holes and runs. He replaced them and pushed them up the bridge of his nose. "What you got there, young fella?" He squinted, then looked in one of the containers again.

Blue leaned forward in his chair, and Brighty began to smack his lips together in anticipation. Moor pulled paper plates from the bag, pleased that the two old men were intrigued.

Brighty leaned from side to side, taking it all in. "You cooked all this for us? How you have time to cook all this for us?"

Blue frowned at Brighty. "Stop smackin', Brighty, for goodness sakes! You always smackin' your lips. You was smackin' when you was a boy in primary school. I thought you would have got over it by now." His frown deepened. "It ain't right a man smackin' so much." He waved his hand and adjusted the grimy Ravens skullcap on his head. "You giving this young man the wrong impression about the whole city. You embarrassing the whole city of Baltimore in front of the prince. Show a little class."

"I am not a prince. I am not royalty like you two, my fathers." Moor hoped to sidetrack the elders' brotherly arguing with his comment—most likely not. In any case, their bickering did not bother him. He knew it was a language spoken between brothers and between those who are like brothers. It was not real. Their behavior no more represented real anger or displeasure with one another than the phony smiles of socialites represented real love and affection.

Brighty seemed to ignore Blue's recriminations. "That's what you say—that you not a prince. But you living mighty high on the hog. Look at all this." He pointed at the food. "Look. And you feeding us, too."

"I was cooking for myself when I thought of my two wise fathers. Besides, food shared always tastes better."

Brighty laughed and pointed at Blue. "Look who drooling now."

"Shut up, old man." Blue pulled his jacket close around him.

Brighty flexed his arms. "Old man? Who you calling old?"

Moor continued talking as though he did not hear the argument. "It was my pleasure to share what I have with two men of peace, such as yourselves. A man may not have much, but when it is shared, somehow it looks like more. Cooking is lonely unless one thinks of the ones with whom it is to be shared."

Blue lifted the corner of one of the lids as though Moor was moving too slowly. "Cooking? What's all this? You mean to tell me that men do all the cooking where you come from?"

Moor chuckled as he set out napkins and plastic forks. "Of course not, my fathers. But it is there as it is here—a man must eat."

Brighty nodded. "I know that's right!"

Sticking plastic spoons in the containers, Moor showed how to serve the food. "Sauce over the rice, and bean paste as you like. It is made with black-eyed beans."

Blue shoveled rice from the container onto his plate. "Black-eyed beans? I ain't never heard of no black-eyed beans. You mean peas, don'tcha?"

"Peas here, but beans where I come from."

Brighty waved his fork as he spoke, like a pointer. "And you come from South Africa, right? Like where apartheid is from? Like where you have to have a pass and permission to walk around or the white folks will put you in jail?"

Blue smirked. "Sounds like Baltimore to me."

"Oh, now, Blue, B-More ain't never been that bad. Baltimore was always a free city. Wasn't no slavery here."

"What you talking about, man? Free in name only. You know it was places we couldn't go downtown. On Howard Street, it wasn't that long ago that we couldn't go in the stores to try on clothes or buy furniture, even. Couldn't go to the Riverside swimming pool— no black people, no Jews. You know the schools was segregated. Wasn't but one high school where black folks could go in the whole state. White folks pretended like it was all free and equal, but we all knew. And it wasn't that long ago. No, sir."

Brighty nodded at Moor and laughed. "Yeah, he may look to be a couple of centuries old, but he's telling the truth. It was going on right here in Baltimore in the sixties. Of course, they talking about some of that same stuff now. Stopping folks standing on the corners and they got to have identification or they breaking the law." Brighty frowned and shook his head. "They say they doing it to cut down on crime, but I don't know. It don't leave a good taste in my mouth. I remember too much."

"Like I said, South Africa, South Baltimore—it's all starting to look the same to me. So, like I was saying, you from South Africa?"

"No, my wise fathers. I am from Lesotho. It is in southern Africa. We lost some of our land to the men who settled South Africa. But by the hand of God's mercy we have remained free. We are very poor. But a poor man free is still richer than a slave wearing someone else's clothes, is he not?"

"I know that's right!" Brighty ladled sauce and beef onto his plate. "You did all this this morning? How you have time for all this?"

"Just the rice this morning. The rest are leftovers. I told you, I must eat."

Blue laughed and elbowed Brighty. "What you need is a woman." The two old men nodded and laughed in agreement.

Moor pointed at the food, hoping to distract them, though it was not likely to divert his elderly friends—it was a discussion they had over and over again. "I don't need a woman just to cook. I can cook for myself. Besides, I have no time for a woman."

Brighty nodded. "Well, maybe so. It's not worth it to have a woman just to cook. They can be lots of trouble. You got to provide for them." He wiped tomato sauce from his mouth with the back of his hand, then wiped it on the front of his shirt. "A woman want to tell you what to wear, how to wear it, and even when to bathe."

Blue frowned and reared away from Brighty. "Come to think of it, maybe it's *you* we need to be getting a wife. And from the smell of things, we need to get on it right now. Look at you. Look at your clothes. You a mess, man."

"Oh, forget you, Blue! Ain't nobody got time to be listening to you! If I get married, a war a break out in the neighborhood. Probably all over the city. Might even be all over the whole Mid-Atlantic region—women fighting with each other over me. They couldn't handle me getting married and not being available. But we was talking about this young man here's cooking." Brighty gobbled a piece of meat after deflecting Blue's verbal pass.

Moor lowered his head so that the two men would not see him smile. He visited them, in great part, for conversations like these— conversations that reminded him of home, of men laughing and joshing with one another. He visited them because they did his heart good. He judged not what they wore or where they sat, but who they were inside. He looked up. "It is no big thing, my fathers. This morning when I rose to pray and study, and I thought to cook, I thought also to bring this to you."

Brighty talked in between wolfing bites. "You mean to tell us you studying and praying in the mornings, too? You didn't tell us you was a preacher. But I kind of thought something like that all along."

He couldn't help smiling. "I am not a preacher, wise one. But if God is God, does it make sense to only speak with Him or hear from Him once a week, or once a year? It does not sound like wisdom to me to neglect God, my wise father, the One who gives all blessings. The Bible says we are to study to show ourselves approved of God. So, I rise up early to meet Him and to study. It is no great thing. It is, in fact, a good thing about being without a wife. I have plenty of time to study, to pray, and to hear from God."

Brighty nodded in agreement. "I know that's right. When you married, you can't hear, you can't talk, and you sure can't get a word in edgewise."

Blue looked at Moor and pursed his lips. "Like he would know about living with a woman, anyway." He jerked his head toward Brighty. "'Course, some men don't never stop talking, either."

Brighty halted his white plastic fork in midair. "What you trying to say?"

"Oh, don't get huffed up. I'm still trying to have a little conversation with the prince." Blue looked at Moor as though he were looking over the rim of some eyeglasses. "So, you said you was cooking, and studying, and . . ."

"As I said, I got up early this morning—"

"Early? How early is early?" Brighty examined the food on his fork. "Good rice," he said absently.

"Usually four-thirty or five in the morning. Sometimes earlier."

Brighty choked momentarily. He gulped water from one of the paper cups Moor had provided. "Four-thirty! On your own?"

The two old men looked at each other.

"Yes, wise men. It is good to rise early, to pray, to hear the voice of God. The earth is still, and one can hear God easily."

Blue raised an eyebrow. "You trying to tell me you can't hear from God at six? You got to hear from Him at four in the morning?"

Brighty waved away Blue's question. "You say you hear from God? You talk to God?"

"Yes, my father."

"Like in the movies? Like in *The Ten Commandments?*"

Moor knew that the men were teasing him, but also asking questions for which they wanted sincere answers. "No, He speaks to my heart." He laid a hand on his chest. "Sometimes, there is just a knowing in my heart. But it is good to rise early to meet with Him."

Blue crossed his legs. His foot dangled. "Yeah, I hear all that you saying. But what you calling early, ain't nothing but night in disguise." Brighty laughed along with him.

"It is good to rise up early—"

"You may be fooling yourself, but you ain't fooling these two gray heads. I bet you going to bed late, too."

"Sometimes." Moor shrugged. "Many times."

Blue turned to look at Brighty. "That joker ain't fooling nobody. He just lonely." They both laughed. He turned his gaze on Moor. "You need a woman. Fast."

"In the Bible, the apostle Paul said it's better for a man to be alone."

Brighty scratched his head. "You sure you not a preacher?"

Blue pursed his lips. "Well, I know a little bit of Bible, too. Somebody in there said it ain't good for a man to be alone."

The food Moor swallowed became a large rock as it traveled down his throat. "God. God said it speaking about the first man, Adam."

Blue looked pleased. "I'm sure that Paul is a mighty important fella, but not more than God, and I'd say my cards is trumping yours, right now." He gestured with his fork. "Besides, you ain't got to marry—just spend a little time, have a little company, a little romance." The old man winked his eye.

Moor ate his food calmly, determined not to let the old man see that he was getting his goat. "I don't think it is a good thing, my father."

"Come on, now, Prince. Live a little. You in America now."

"I'm trying to live a righteous life, my fathers."

"I'm trying to live a righteous life.'" Blue mocked Moor's words and his accent. "What you mean by that? You trying to tell me something you ain't trying to tell me? You sure you ain't a minister?"

"As I said, I am trying to live a righteous life. And there are so many dying in my homeland. AIDS is marching across the land, and we must do everything to stop it."

Brighty's hand froze on the way to his mouth. "AIDS? What you talking about, young brother? If that's what you worried about, then we need to have a conversation or two. You done missed out on a thing or three. It's a few things I could tell you about preventin' them kind of diseases."

"I'm only saying, my wise fathers, that I thought at first that it—that fear—was the reason I was choosing to live as I live. But then I realized I was missing the opportunity to be intimate with God."

Blue set his plate down on the table. "Live as you live?

Intimate . . . with God? Man, what you talking about?" He looked at Brighty. "Things are way worse than we thought. We gone have to swing into action right away."

"What I mean, my fathers, is that I have chosen to walk alone . . . at least for now. And when I say intimate, I do not mean the intimate of which I believe you speak." Moor cleared his throat. "No, I mean I was missing the opportunity to draw close—to talk to God, to listen to what He spoke to me without distractions."

Brighty, his mouth full of food, nudged Blue. "There he go—talking about talking to God again."

"Why is that so strange, my fathers? Our forefathers in Africa, in Israel, and even here spoke to God, and He spoke back to them centuries ago. Why should it not be with us as it was with our fathers?"

"Brighty, let the man go on with his story." Blue wagged his fork in the air. "If you ain't drooling, you getting the whole story clear off course. Now, just let the man go on." He paused dramatically. "Please! We got to hear him out."

9

Mary

Come on, girl!" Thelma led the way, blue eyes flashing, while Latrice and Naomi walked arm in arm with Mary, almost dragging her over the ground.

"You all are going to kill me!" Mary thought she could hear the rough granite sidewalks calling out for its next sacrifice of a knee or an elbow.

Latrice laughed and waved her free hand in the air. Her nails were painted gold with what appeared to be ground diamonds on each tip. "Honey, we are going to get you there, get your nails done, and change your life. You hear me what I'm saying?"

The other three women joined in laughing.

Naomi tossed her blonde hair. Most of it was pulled into a free flowing ponytail atop her head. Tendrils curled in front of her ears and around her forehead. "And while they're doing your nails, we're going to get your hair *did* and then add on, or sew on, whatever it is that the Good Lord didn't see fit to give you!" She shook her hair. "Some new color—auburn or caramel—and a few tracks, and you'll be on your way."

They had her locked in place between them. Mary wanted to break and run. It was as though she was on her way to a roast and she was the pig.

Thelma's laugh sounded maniacal. "And after that, we're going to get you some contacts. And while they're putting your order together," she cackled, "we're going down to Cathedral and Mulberry to Cedric's of Hollywood. We're going to get you a little something to further enhance your beauty, if you know what I mean!" She winked.

They passed a street vendor. Mary was desperate for a diversion. "What about a snow cone, you all? You know I can't pass up a snow cone. We need to get this—this must be the last of the season." Everyone knew that you could tell the seasons in Baltimore by the appearance and disappearance of snow cones.

Naomi giggled. "Nice try, but no prize, sweetie. We are on a mission. We can't stop. We *won't* stop. Not even for sweet syrup on ice."

Traffic was everywhere, horns were blowing. Mary didn't know if she was yelling to be heard over the din or because she was panicking. "Look, you all, I like the way I look. I like the way I am."

Thelma turned, raised an eyebrow, and threw up a hand. Everyone stopped on a dime. "Are you telling me that you don't want a man? Are you telling me that you're happy being *alone* and *single*? Are you telling me you have lost your mind?"

Mary began to feel dizzy, as though the skewer was in and she was being turned over the flames. She didn't know if she would ever be able to enjoy barbecue again. "Well . . ."

Thelma put one sensible hand on her hip and raised her school-teacher eyebrow even higher. "Well, nothing. If you *want* something different, my sister, you're going to have to *do* something different. Keep doing what you're doing, and you're going to keep getting what you're getting."

Latrice nodded her head and snapped a finger. "Mm hmm! That's right, sister-girl. But since you're feeling so levelheaded, since you need something more scientific—since a sister's advice is not good enough for you—let's look at the empirical evidence. Let's take a poll." The stern look she put on her face resembled Thelma, some newsman, or a pollster. She asked solemnly, "Who amongst us got a lot of men?" Latrice waved both of her hands. Thelma and Naomi looked at each other.

Thelma cleared her throat. "Okay, who among us has at least

one man?" All three women raised their hands. Mary dropped her head. The fix was in; she was the only one without a hand raised.

Latrice nodded. "Just as I hypothesized. Now—who don't?" Thelma, Latrice, and Naomi looked at Mary.

Naomi grabbed Mary's hand and raised it for her. "Don't be shame. If you gone be an old maid, do it with style! Do it with conviction!"

Mary dropped her head. She didn't know whether to laugh or run. "Come on, you all. Give me a break."

Latrice pretended to dust her hands together. "Looks like the verdict is in to me. Need I say more?"

Naomi tossed her hair. "You got my vote. You convinced me. I'm satisfied."

Thelma turned and looked at the sign on the building in front of her. "Here we are, ladies." Thelma's hands were on Mary's shoulders, steering her toward the doors. "A new life awaits you, my dear. Full speed ahead!"

While the technicians clipped, curled, and painted—Mary, Thelma, Naomi, and Latrice stood huddled nearby watching the transformation.

Everything but the plants in the upscale downtown salon was the palest, most tasteful pink. The sofas were plump and soft; the carpet was deep and plush. All the windows were covered with chiffon window treatments so that no client was seen until she was reborn. The price for the transformation was as expensive as the salon looked, but it was all worth it.

Thelma sighed. "Ladies, this could change her whole life. Take a good look—this might be the last we see of Mousy Mary."

Latrice, her hands glued to her hips, nodded. "Now all we gotta do is get girlfriend to let go of that perfume—that stuff is deadly."

Naomi pulled at her ponytail. "You ain't kiddin'. That's probably the first thing we should have done."

Latrice waved a hand in the air. "It ain't nothing but a thang.

I'll tell her. I can handle it." She began to walk toward where Mary was seated. She would have made it, but Thelma grabbed her arm. "Wait a minute, Latrice. You know we can't do that." She dropped Latrice's arm and shook her head. "One thing at a time. We don't want her to have a nervous breakdown. That perfume is some kind of safety blanket to her. You know that."

Latrice snorted. "Safety blanket? That stuff she's wearing will stop every brother in his tracks at fifty paces."

"Sh-sh! We don't want her to hear." Thelma held a finger to her lips.

Naomi brushed the hair out of her eyes and whispered, "Not only will it ward off men, that stuff will kill every cockroach in a fifty-mile radius. Mary is going to put Orkin out of business!"

Thelma raised an eyebrow. "Come on, you all. It's not that bad."

Latrice returned her hands to her hips. "No, it's not that bad. It's just that a little goes a long way, and I don't think she's ever used a little."

Naomi's ponytail bobbed and bounced as she spoke. "Not since she came back from New Orleans with it. You know, it's only love that we stay around her. Sometimes I just want to scream, 'Girl, wash that stuff off!'"

Latrice waved a hand in the air. "Well, I think we should tell her. It's ridiculous." She began walking, but Thelma grabbed her again.

"We can't tell her. It will hurt her feelings," Thelma pleaded.

Latrice shook her head. "Oh, like not having a man don't hurt her feelings? Well I tell you what, next time you know something that might do me some good that you keeping secret, just hurt my feelings, okay? I'd rather hear it from my friends than from my ene-mies. I think it's better for love to tell you the truth."

Thelma looked at Latrice and Naomi. "Come on, you all. Not now, anyway. Let's just get this done first. It was hard enough getting her here. We'll work on the other another time."

Latrice waved her hand in disgust. "All right, teacher, but don't come crying to me later!"

Naomi brushed her hair aside. "We'll see."

10

Moor

Moor *squatted* on the ground, resting his plate on one knee. Except for the sounds of traffic and planes flying overhead, and the intermittent sounds of radios coming from passing cars, he might have been at home in Lesotho. "You see, my fathers, when I talk of intimacy, I am not talking of the casual dance that men and women do." The two old men laughed and nudged each other. "You know the dance, eh?" Moor winked at them.

Brighty slapped his knee. "Know the dance? I been a dance instructor."

Even Blue laughed. "Oh, get out of here, man, telling them tall tales."

"We all know the dance, eh? It is the same here, in my country, and the world over. We are strong men. We are warriors, yes? We conquer lands and sail seas—" he looked around—"or at least our own backyards. There is little that we cannot do." He lifted his plate. "We can even cook for ourselves. And when we need women, it is only to dance, eh? A dance here and there—a physical release— and we are satisfied."

Brighty and Blue, somewhere in the conversation, lost decades so that they were now bright-eyed young boys sharing secret talks about women and sex.

"We do not *need* women, we tell ourselves; yet it is women we are talking about over and over again. As it is in Baltimore, so it is in my village.

"We get the woman and we dance, thinking that is all we

SHARON EWELL FOSTER

want—that after we have danced, after we have made love to them, we will be satisfied. But we are never satisfied. So, we go from woman to woman looking for what is missing, for surely it is something missing in the woman and not in the way we approach the dance." Moor shrugged. "Such is the way of men. When I was sad, when something was wrong, I did not talk to God; I ran to a drink or to the arms of a woman for the comfort she could give."

Brighty slapped his knee. "Well, that's the truth. And ain't that what women want? They always saying"—he mocked a woman's voice—"'Let me make you feel better. . . . Tell me what's the matter. You never tell me what's on your mind.'"

All three men nodded. Brighty and Blue snickered like schoolboys as Moor continued.

"It's true, my fathers. But I didn't go to them to talk, if you know what I mean. I didn't want love. I didn't talk of love. In fact, I must tell you, wise men, there was as little talk as I could possibly manage."

The men agreed and grinned. "I know that's right."

"It made me feel better. You know how we are as men. So, after the woman has danced away the feeling, I put my anger or my sorrow away in a box. 'My body is satisfied, and this anger is finished,' I would say to myself, and then quickly leave the woman before she could begin talking about problems, love, babies, or any of the other things women talk about."

Blue sighed. "It sound like the same thing all over the world—women gabbing. I was kind of hoping it was just here. You ain't doing nothing but telling the truth, there, Prince. Women always want to talk, talk, talk. 'Let's talk about it, honey.'" He shook his head in disgust. "Just bringing it back up *again*. The thing is over. Why can't they let it die?"

Brighty took a sip from his cup. "Let it die."

"But let me put a question to you, wise men. Because we box it up and put it away, is the problem truly solved, or will it come back to bite us?"

Blue and Brighty looked at each other, eyebrows raised.

"I only ask the question, my fathers. You are wise men; you know these things much more than I. So I ask you, if you put a snake in a box, is the snake truly gone, or does he sit there waiting for the lid to open so he can bite you?"

Blue and Brighty looked at each other, one with eyebrows raised and the other with eyebrows knit together.

"Don't trouble your heads. It is just a question. Such is the way of men." Moor adjusted his seat and then continued. "One day though, sitting alone, my heart was troubled. When I was worried, I would go to my friends to talk with them, or to my fathers to talk with them. I did not talk to the women and I did not talk to God, not like I am sitting here with you now. I only danced with the women. And God? I was not treating Him like a friend. I was talking to men who knew little more than me, but never talking to the One who knows everything.

"Such has been the way of men. So, I began to seek my Holy Father and to spend time with Him. As I prayed and read the Bible, I began to see that these ways of mine are the ways of men. Such was the way with our father David and so it was with his son Solomon and even with David's first son, Amnon."

Brighty set his plate on the table and leaned forward until his chin rested on one palm. "You mean David, like in the Bible? The David that killed the giant Goliath? I knew he had a son Solomon, but I didn't know he had no other son."

Moor laughed. "Yes, he had many sons."

"Well, I'll be."

Blue set his plate down. "Why don't you hush, Brighty, and let the man tell his story. For goodness sakes! How many times . . . ? If you ain't drooling, you buttin' in." Moor could tell that they were losing heart for the game; their attention shifted to his story.

Moor adjusted his position to one where he could sit for hours. "Yes, my wise fathers, David had many sons, which is not rare for a man who has many wives."

"Many wives? I thought it wasn't no woman but that woman Bathsheba. That woman he stole from the other man."

"No my wise fathers, there were many others. You see, David, the man who would be king, before he was king he was a boy shepherd. Now a shepherd's work is solitary. Like a paperboy or a long distance runner, he works alone. His friends are the wind and the sky. In his time alone, David learned the voice of God, and he became known to God, so that as a brave boy he was chosen to be king."

The two old men leaned forward, listening closely to the tale. "He learned God, this boy David, and God learned him, but I believe this boy was rejected by his family and was alone so long, he never learned to truly trust a woman or talk openly to his family." Moor told them about David's friend Jonathan, the son of his predecessor, King Saul. "Jonathan loved David like a brother." They listened closely as he told them the story of King Saul's murderous jealousy and Jonathan's attempts to save David. "Jonathan loved David and expressed that love, but I believe it was long before David could acknowledge his brotherly love for Jonathan. It seems to me, that is, how this man David was. His heart loved his family, but when I study I do not see that he could openly express that love. This man David longed for his beautiful son Absalom, but it seems to me he only cried out his love when his son died."

The men talked about men they knew who could not love openly. "We didn't tell other men we loved them when we was growing up," Blue said. "That was too sissified."

"Not even daddies said that kind of thing," Brighty agreed. "And it was just as sissified to say it to a woman."

Moor nodded. "And as it was with him, so it is now with men today. Like men today—though not like you, my wise fathers, to be sure—these men can wage wars, but run wild and fast from the smallest thing of the heart. They love, but cannot speak it."

The two old men nodded at each other. Their eyes were round

and bright. Their plates rested untouched on the table while he spoke.

"What God taught David, this man David did not have the power to teach to his wives, or to his children. He left beautiful words behind for God, beautiful words for us to read, but it does not seem to me that he was able to express that love to those closest to him. It is clear, my wise fathers, that he had problems with women. It is clear this man David had problems with his family. If what I believe is true, my fathers—and I am not a pastor—it might help us understand the sickness in his first son Amnon. David could not show them love and he could not show Amnon love.

"This man David felt love, and trusted God enough to speak that love to Him. Maybe it was rejection by his own earthly father and brothers—but it does not seem that it was easy for this man to speak love to those he loved most." Moor looked at his hands and then back at his friends. "What good fruit can love unspoken bear?"

Moor told them the story of Amnon and of his heart sickness. "Just like now, if a father does not talk to his son, evil men stand watching, waiting to entrap the lad." He told them how a scheming cousin, knowing of Amnon's sickness—of Amnon's desire for his own beautiful sister—planted a foul plan, a plan of rape, in the young man's mind. "This wicked cousin fools Amnon—" Moor leaned toward the men—"and isn't it a pity that all over the world sometimes the most wicked people are people in our families? And it is only right; wicked people must have families, too."

He frowned and nodded, then leaned back and continued with his story. "Of course, this is to be expected—bad fruit falls from a bad tree, and wicked counsel comes from wicked men." Moor told Brighty and Blue the story of how the two cousins plotted to fool King David and to lure the virgin girl, Tamar, to her brother's bedside.

Brighty took a swig of water. "You talking about his sister? He talking about having . . . doing . . . you know, raping his own sister? His own flesh and blood?"

Blue frowned. "That's in the Bible? In the Holy B-I-B-L-E? The one they teach in vacation Bible school?"

"Yes, it is in the Holy Book, my fathers."

"I ain't never read nothing like that."

"It is there, my fathers. Incest, rape, betrayal, ages ago. And so it is that Solomon, Amnon's younger brother later writes to us in the Bible that there is nothing new under the sun. There is no new sickness—just the sickness unhealed from ages past."

Blue frowned and spat on the ground. "A brother with his sister? That's just downright nasty."

"It is nasty business indeed, my wise father. So, this foolish man, Amnon, tricks his beautiful sister. Looking upon her beauty must have made him feel better when he was feeling heartsick. So, like men even today, he must think that if he can do the dance with her he will feel better. A dance with the beautiful woman will make him feel better. But he was wrong. No outward touch is medicine for a sick, sick heart, eh, my fathers?"

Brighty and Blue were still, their eyes were focused on Moor, their heads tilted toward him to hear better. They looked as though they had been transported from the alley to an ancient village where griots told stories and passed on wisdom. Moor's words hypnotized them.

"Tamar brings Amnon food and goodness to nurture him. He only knows how to take from her, to even steal from her, but not how to give. So he rapes her." Blue and Brighty frowned and shook their heads.

"You sure this in the Bible? It don't sound like something church people would want to hear about or talk about to me." Brighty shook his head again. "If it wasn't you telling me, Prince, I wouldn't believe it."

"Don't sound like people God would want anything to do nothing with." Blue frowned. "Sounds like trash to me. How people like that get to be princes and stuff?"

Moor nodded and sat silent for a moment. "It is the thing about

God, that He loves us right or wrong. He does not easily throw us away. He is even willing to give crowns to those who are weak and to put treasure inside of trash."

He sighed and then continued with his story, telling them of Amnon's behavior after the rape of his sister Tamar. "Now, even the sight of her—the sight that used to make him feel better—now sickens him. She is a reminder of the wicked, filthy thing he has done. This girl Tamar is a symbol of his depravity."

He told them of Tamar's shame after her half-brother refused to marry her and threw her from his home. "He has now spread his sickness to his sister Tamar. This woman entered her brother's presence well, and now she leaves with no gift from him but shame and contraction of his heart disease." He told them of how the crime against the girl went unpunished. Moor kicked at the gravel with one of his feet and shook his head.

"As it was with Tamar, so it is today. The child who has been wounded is a walking story of the sickness in the family, so that child is hushed away. That child, like this sister Tamar, has done no wrong, but she is trouble for the family. 'Hush!' this child is told."

He shrugged. "Perhaps Tamar's family thought, 'This girl and her trouble will ruin our reputation.' Maybe they thought, 'If people know, they will think this man Amnon is a bad fellow, and he is not so bad.' Maybe they thought, 'If this girl talks, her brother Amnon will have to be killed.'"

Brighty and Blue were quiet, and Moor wondered what memories the story might have stirred in them. "Maybe the father, busy King David, just did not want to be bothered—it was too much trouble to sort out in a lifetime. Or it could be this father felt too guilty over his own sins to struggle with the son's." Moor shook his head. "And where is the cousin, now that he has ruined the family? He is probably out telling lies and spreading the story of the family's shame. It was just a big mess!" He waved a hand in the air.

He continued the tale, describing the reaction of Tamar's brother Absalom to the rape. "Though it breaks her heart, and this girl Tamar was crazy with grief, she was told to keep her mouth shut. So the sickness and the shame in her heart spread to Absalom, who added to her sickness his own anger."

Blue shuddered. "Man, that is craziness! It about makes me sick to my stomach." He pushed his plate aside.

Brighty nodded in agreement. "And you telling me they didn't do nothing about it?" He rubbed a hand over his gray hair.

"Nothing. As it was then, so it is today." Moor thought of stories he had heard through the years, gossip that spread from village to village, newspaper accounts of horrible family crimes. "Years passed, my fathers, and eventually this man Absalom in his anger kills his half-brother Amnon. His anger is like the snake in the box, eh? Waiting for its chance to bite." Moor recounted the story of Absalom's banishment. "Still there was no talk, no healing for the heart, not for any heart. The pain sits waiting in a box like that snake. So that years go by, and this man Absalom gets sicker and sicker in his heart until he sought the very life of his father. It seems to me, that this man Abasalom is like his father, he does not know how to speak the pain he feels to those closest to him and cannot heal his heart."

Blue rocked in his chair. "That is one sad story."

Moor nodded. "It was not until this man-boy Absalom died that I am able to see David, his king father, could cry out his love for him." Moor shook his head. "A day too late to love."

Brighty slapped his hand down on the table. "It's enough to make you want to kill them all."

Moor sighed. "It must weary the heart of our Father to see us this way still after so many, many years. Sons repeating the patterns of their fathers generation to generation, unable to change, until sons kill fathers, and fathers kill sons, and daughters weep that their fathers and brothers use them in shame."

"My goodness," Blue said.

Moor's voice was soft in his ears. "The truth is, I would want to kill such men. Generation after generation?" He shook his head, and then his voice softened even more. "But that is the easy way. That is looking with men's eyes. God, our Father, sees the heart— His ways are above ours. This same man, David—this broken, noble king, this man with a repentant spirit—God calls him a man after His own heart."

Brighty shook his head. "I don't understand that. Not at all."

Moor shrugged. "It is a mystery. David was a murderer and an adulterer, but God made him king, a singer, and poet. We only love and honor men if they are perfect. God sees our brokenness and calls us whole, He *makes* our way perfect. He picks cowards and makes them brave. He chooses thieves and makes them treasurers. Even when we are wrong, He loves us. While men want to reject us and kill us, God wants to love us and make us whole. It is a mystery, but it is good news. He loves us so much that He sent His only begotten Son—though we deserve death, like these men—to teach us new ways, to break the pattern, to teach us to speak, and to give hope to those who would choose to listen to Him."

Moor thought of his homeland, of his family, and remembered his own shame, the past behavior that he wished he could undo. He wanted to cover it up and hide it away—to let his friends go on believing that he was perfect. It was easier to point fingers at others—at Amnon, Absalom, and David—than to uncover his own scars.

He looked at his friends. He did not want to make the story personal, but it was only when it was personal that it could touch a friend's heart. So he took a deep breath and continued. "We want to kill men and throw them away if we think they do wrong. So Abasalom wanted to kill his father. But if this man Abasalom had killed his father, we would not have King David's psalms to comfort us and teach us as they have for thousands of years. If men who do wrong were thrown away, I would not be here." He nodded at Blue and Brighty. "You see, we think it is detestable that a brother would be so wicked as to use his half-sister as Amnon used Tamar. We would never do such a wicked thing, we say to ourselves. But our

God is Father to us and also to all of our sisters. When we use them just to make our bodies feel better so that we do not have to deal with the sickness in our hearts, we abuse our sisters as Amnon abused his sister Tamar. Like our brother Amnon, we are not healed by these encounters. Instead we spread this sickness and shame to our sisters." Moor took a deep breath. "But, unlike David, God does not sit by silent. He sends His Son to restore these daughters and sons. It is the heart of God to see none lost.

"Talking with God, listening to Jesus, can heal our hearts, my wise fathers. I know because I have been transformed. The love that is given to us heals us and changes us. Because of Jesus, we have opportunity to be more than warriors, to learn to walk the earth as He did—setting up kingdoms, tearing down kingdoms—but still finding time and having courage to speak love to the needs of a woman's heart." Moor could feel passion swelling his chest. He did not mean to preach to his friends, but he did mean to tell them the truth. "Maybe our own fathers on earth could not teach us, maybe our father David could not teach us, but our Heavenly Father can. He teaches us to not only take from women, but to be strong enough and trusting enough to receive and to nourish them in return."

Blue scratched his chin. Both men still listened closely to Moor, listening as men will only listen to another man who they have first called friend, as they will only listen to a man who has sat with them and called them brother.

So Moor continued. "Wise men, Our heavenly Father, through His Son, has given us the choice to live lives not only as strong men, but also to love and be loved, even as He loved. There is hope, and His name is Jesus Christ." He sighed. "I have tried many things to cover my own guilt and shame. But there is no other medicine I know that can take away both the stain and the guilt and make the heartbroken whole." They sat quietly for a while. Moor wondered if he had said too much.

Blue sat back in his seat. "You sure you ain't a preacher? I'm sure feeling like I been to church."

Brighty snickered. "Who you fooling, Blue? How would you know what it feel like to be in church?" His joke broke the tension.

Moor shook his head at Blue. "I am just a man—not even a man as great as yourselves. There is brokenness in my family. Many women have been shamed. I have played my part in it—and I do not want to carry this thing to another generation. So it is that I spend time alone with the Father and the Son, listening to the Spirit of God and studying. I want to be healed. I do not want to spread any sickness. I choose not to be afraid to learn to speak from my heart. I choose, instead, to learn about women not from my own earthly father, but to follow the One who learned to love so well that the Bible says the women followed after Him."

Moor breathed deeply. He looked at his plate, not certain now if he wanted to finish his food. He was not sure what to say to the two older men, worried he had overstepped his bounds—that they had grown weary of his talk.

Brighty shook his head. "I been teasing my friend Blue, here. But I'm impressed. To think all that is in the Bible."

"What up?"

Moor turned and looked back at the young man who had spoken. The young man appeared to be in his early twenties. He wore a green army fatigue jacket that was at least three sizes too big for his thin body. His legs were lost in his jeans and his head full of matted blonde dreadlocks that—except for two or three that had escaped—were stuffed inside of a large red, green, and black crocheted cap on top of his head. "You all look like all your peeps have died. Why so serious?"

Blue and Brighty brightened. It was the white boy they called Ali.

11

Mary

When *Mary stepped out* of Thelma's Honda, she was a new woman. She had seen it all in the mirror at the beauty shop. Where there were no nails, there were now lilac colored, hand-painted, acrylic tips that glittered with one carefully placed rhinestone on each ring finger. Her hair was not only freshly relaxed, straightened, it was lightened to a honey blonde. *"Just to make it clear to the men that you are a woman who wants to have more fun,"* Naomi had said with a giggle. Mary's own hair, that reached her chin before the makeover, now cascaded in golden waves over her shoulders and down her back. Her eyebrows were severely arched, and she now looked at the world through hazel green eyes. And in the bag in her hand were some of the finest, plumpest, most enhancing, most lush undergarments Cedric's had to offer. Just holding the bag, she felt different.

Thelma tilted her head, looked Mary from head to toe, and then nodded her approval. "You're ready, now, little sister. You've got to take your destiny in your own hands." She smiled. "You've got the look, now you've just got to find the man. You've got the bait, now we've just got to find the fish," she added with another nod.

When Mary finally got inside her home, she sat down and took a moment to breathe after the whirlwind her well-meaning friends had caused. Mary sniffed her wrists as she sat on the side of the bed, stared in the mirror, and tried to reconcile the image in front of her with who she really was. It was hard to believe that the green-eyed, blonde-haired woman was she. She looked different, but her heart didn't feel any different.

"You've got an assignment," Thelma had reminded her earlier. "You've made the outside changes, now you've got to connect with some brothers! Really! You can do it!" Her expression had spoken encouragement. "Just open your eyes." Thelma had opened her own blue eyes wider, to provide a literal example. "There are men every-where—at work, at the library, at the grocery store, and we know that church is ripe for the picking." She had that teacher look in her eyes. "You're a new person. You've got to be aggressive. When you see a man you like, walk up to him. Introduce yourself. Invite him out."

Mary was certain that her face must have been painted with skepticism.

"Okay, well, invite him out to lunch, Mary. Lunch is safe. Don't worry. It'll be easy." Thelma's expression had been warm and re-assuring. Away from the others, Thelma's schoolteacher manner had almost convinced Mary she could do it. *Almost*. Because, now, alone on the bed, Mary could feel her confidence waning.

She sniffed her wrist again. Nothing about what she was seeing or what she was feeling felt safe. *"It'll be easy."* It certainly didn't feel like it was going to be easy. She sighed and closed her eyes for a moment. She would give it a try.

Mary took one last look, then she walked across the room and turned on her computer to check her email. She didn't look like herself, she didn't know where all this was taking her, but she would give it a try. She would give it a try. Something within her said so.

12

Moor

Brighty shook his head in Ali's direction. "Look at you. The only white Black Muslim in the city. Boy, when you gone figure out who you are?"

While Ali fixed his plate, they recounted the story of Amnon and Tamar. "It really all started because we figured we got to get this brother here," Brighty pointed at Moor, "a woman. He fixed all this food and he's waking up early and going to bed late. Too much time on his hands. We got to talking that it's not good for a man to be alone."

Ali plopped down on the grass with his plate and nodded as though he understood. "How are we going to do that?"

Blue laughed. "We talking about getting him a real woman. A wife. A *sister*. You don't know nothing about that, nothing about no black woman."

Ali looked up from his plate and squared his thin shoulders. "I got a woman, man. You old dogs fooling yourselves."

Brighty winked at Blue. "What? Some skinny little girl from the suburbs? Some blind young girl that don't know no better?"

Ali took a bite and smiled. "No, man. I keep trying to tell you old dudes." He laughed, then ignored the old men—he knew the game—and spoke to Moor. "So, what kind of woman are you into?"

Moor shook his head and waved his hand, hoping the conversation would go away. "I told them there was no time to find a wife."

He was happy when Brighty interrupted. "Now, the kind of

woman I like is a woman that can cook. Don't talk too much, but one that can make a skillet talk."

Blue shook his head and rolled his eyes. "That's all you think about is your stomach. Always food on your mind. And it shows, too—look at your gut." He pointed at Brighty's T-shirt, striped with sauce. "No, the kind of woman you want, Prince, is one with a little spice, one that ain't afraid to say what's on her mind, to speak her piece. That's what I like, a woman that can hold her own."

"Hold her own what?" Brighty waved his hand in front of Blue, negating his comments. "Prince, don't listen to this old fool. What you need is a woman that looks good, can cook, and got a little something in her pocket. You a fairly nice-looking young man . . . a little dark for my taste—"

Blue pushed Brighty's hand out of the way. "What is that supposed to mean? A man ain't handsome if he ain't light-skinned, if he ain't high yellow?"

Moor shrugged his shoulders. "What is high yellow?"

Blue spat on the ground again, and frowned at Brighty. "High yellow! You old Negroes need to let that old slavery talk go, and stop puttin' it into the heads of young people. This boy didn't come all the way over here from Africa to have you put foolishness in his head." He waved his hand in Ali's direction. "And this boy here sure don't need to hear it. Look at him. He's confused enough as it is."

Ali shook his head and chuckled. "Aw, man."

Brighty pushed Blue's hand out of the way. "I ain't puttin' nonsense in his head. And keep your hands to yourself; otherwise you'll draw back a nub."

Ali laughed and rocked from side to side, as though he was watching cartoons.

"Well, next you'll be telling him about good hair."

Moor touched his hand to his head. He was enjoying this game. It was keeping the two old men off his trail. "Good hair?"

Brighty folded his arms. "Good hair."

"What is 'good hair,' my wise father? Strong hair? Dark hair?"

Blue grabbed his hands together and shook them in the air. "See, here we go." He placed his hands on top of his head and turned it side to side as though he was in distress.

Brighty feigned innocence. "I didn't start it. You did. You said good hair."

"No, *you* started it. *'You a little dark for my taste.'*" He mocked Brighty. "Remember? That's what you said. I don't know what you doing with a taste in men anyway." The conversation was escalating and getting louder with every exchange.

Ali giggled between bites, occasionally adding commentary like "oh man!" "wow!" and "no way!"

Weighed down by his dirty shirt, Brighty struggled to his feet. "Don't make me have to hit you in your pie chopper, Blue! I hate to knock out the few real teeth you got left. We been friends for a long time, but don't be casting asper . . . asper . . . doubts about my manhood. You wish you were half the man I am, you gray-haired old fossil!"

Ali laughed as Brighty balled his fist and began to move it in a circular motion. This game of dirty dozens was two seconds from becoming a world-class boxing event.

Ali and Moor were laughing so hard, they looked like they were having trouble catching their breath.

Blue put both hands on the table for leverage. "Well, you soda pop-bottle-eyeglass-wearing, old so and so—" he managed to half stand—"if you feel like you can take me, then come on!"

Moor pressed one hand to his aching stomach and half rose to his feet. He waved his other hand in Blue and Brighty's direction. "Wise men! Wise men! Let us not fight. Let us reason together. Besides if you fight, the food will get cold while you battle, and Ali and I will starve. There is an African proverb that applies here: When elephants fight, they say it is the grass that gets trampled." Moor continued laughing as he settled back into his seat.

Blue flopped back onto his throne. "You better be glad the prince asked me to stop and take it easy on you. Otherwise . . ." He wheezed and threatened. "Just stop trying to fill his head full of garbage."

Brighty shook his head. "You can't tell me what to do. He asked, so I'm gone tell him anyway," he said like a rebellious child. He focused on Moor. "Good hair is straight hair, you know, like white people's. It can be curly or wavy, but it's got to be straight and not kinky."

Moor nodded. "I understand. So, Ali's hair is good hair."

Brighty waved his hands and frowned. "Naw! What Ali got there on his head is a mess. He done messed his good hair up. I'm surprised that ain't nothing living up in there."

"Aw, lay off, old man." Ali laughed. "I like my hair. I worked hard to get it this way. I paid somebody to lock it for me."

Blue snapped forward and joined in the fray. "You paid somebody to make a fool of you is what you did, son. As much as I hate to, I have to agree with Brighty about that. And just know, we not trying to hurt your feelings. We like you, or we wouldn't even bother to tell you."

Ali smiled at the old men and rubbed his head. "It's all good."

Moor laughed. It was all very confusing. "Ali's hair is straight. So, why is not good hair?"

Brighty looked at Moor as though he should have understood, as though it were something any child would grasp. "You see, Ali's hair is naturally straight, which do make it good. But now he got it all twisted, and twirled, and knotted up, and now—it's *bad!*"

Moor set his plate to the side and wrapped his arms around his knees. "Now I think I see, my father. To be good hair, hair must be straight."

Brighty beamed. "You got it!"

"So, my father, if a sister gets her hair straightened, that is also good hair?"

Brighty's eyes appeared to be the size of saucers. "My goodness no! No, that's not good hair. It can be pretty hair, but it ain't *good* hair. Good hair got to be from the root. It's got to be natural."

"But, Ali's hair—"

Blue shook his hands in the air. "See! I told you not to get him all confused with this nonsense!" His cheeks puffed as though he were about to blow. "You two sound like Abbott and Costello—you got your own 'who's on first' routine. And what we're really supposed to be talking about is finding a wife for the prince."

Brighty looked at Moor and nodded. "So, what kind of woman do you like?"

Moor felt uncomfortable. He had hoped the hair routine would keep the men distracted. He looked at his feet, then at the sky, hoping the two old men would move on to something else.

Blue was determined. "Ain't no point in trying to pretend like you don't hear us, Prince. What kind of woman do you like?"

Moor tried to keep the discomfort he felt out of his voice. "I'm not ready, my fathers, and there is no time to find a wife—"

Blue interrupted. "We heard all that before. 'I ain't lonely. . . . I'm okay alone. . . . I can wake up when it's dark and study.' We heard all the excuses—just tell us what kind of woman you like."

Moor's face was warm and Ali was laughing. He felt like an embarrassed child. He didn't need a wife. He wasn't lonely. He was fine alone.

Brighty looked at him like a patient father. "It ain't that hard, Prince. Just spit it out."

There was no point in putting it off. The old men were not going to accept no answer, they were not going to listen to his excuses. He cleared his throat. "All right, I will tell you." He looked at the two old men. "The men in my family, we like a certain kind of woman. No matter what we do, it is the kind of woman we like. Other men in my family have tried to marry other kinds of women, but no matter how nice the woman is, no matter how she can cook, if she is not this certain kind of woman, it never works out."

Blue shook his head. "Will you just spit it out, boy?"

Ali laughed like he was happy to be off the hot seat. "You might as well tell them, man. They're not going to let it go."

Moor took a big drink of water, then looked back at the old men. "Of course, she must love God—"

Brighty slapped his knee, exasperated. "We already knew that. How is any other kind of woman gone put up with being in church all the time?"

Blue laid a hand on Brighty's shoulder. "Calm down now, Brighty. Let the man get it out." He looked back at Moor. "So, what kind of woman is it that the men in your family like?"

Moor felt trapped. There was no way out of it. "We don't like a woman with funny-colored hair or eyes, or any of those things . . . just natural. . . ."

Ali leaned forward. "Actually, I think the more natural a sister is, the more beautiful she is. The darker the skin, man, the more natural her hair. . . ." Ali closed his mouth around the words as though he had closed his lips around something delectable. "The blacker the berry, the sweeter the juice! A woman like that makes me weak in the knees."

Blue knocked his cup over. "What you know about weak in the knees, boy? You a computer geek, and we play at letting you hang with us. But if you take my advice, you'll leave these sisters alone." He sniffed while he wiped at the water he'd spilled with a napkin. "They got a little too much going on for a boy like you. These ain't suburban girls around here, you know."

Brighty nodded. "That's right! They'll have your head spinning. You'll be running home to Mama with your tail between your legs, or coming back here asking us to help you put the fire out." Brighty pointed a crooked, wrinkled finger at Ali. "Now, we took a shine to you, and we let you come hang with us, but don't get confused. Now hush and let the prince speak. Go on, Prince."

Moor had hoped that the conversation would turn, but when it didn't, he stumbled on. "The men in my family, we like a certain kind of woman. Like the men in the Bible—Abraham, Isaac, and Jacob—we like a certain kind of woman."

Blue nodded, "We know that—but what kind of woman?"

There was no way to avoid it. "The men in my family, they like a fat wife!"

"A fat wife!" Blue and Brighty said it at the same time.

Moor shrugged his shoulders. "We cannot help ourselves. It is what we like. We think a fat wife is beautiful. Not too much on the top, but still a fat wife."

"A fat wife." Brighty muttered the words to himself. "Do tell."

"Well." Blue sat back in his chair. "Ain't nothing wrong with that. Each man is entitled to his own opinion. My own wife was a little thick, you know."

Moor sighed. The grilling was over. "That's what we like. A fat wife—no funny hair or funny eyes—a nice smile is good, but a regular woman."

Ali chimed in. "I like a nice smile in a sister, too."

Brighty gave a warning look to Ali. "Boy, we keep trying to tell you, you talking about playing out of your league."

Blue pursed his lips. "That's right, Ali. One of these sisters will have you trapped up, tripped up, and tied up before you know it! You'll learn."

Moor closed his eyes to listen to the men spar and jest with one another. He could enjoy it now that the hot seat had shifted back to Ali. Except for the language, it was true; he could have been at home, listening to men there talk about the things men must talk about everywhere.

"Blue, you ain't telling the boy nothing but the truth." Brighty turned back to Ali. "She'll have you walking around singing the blues while she got her pockets full of your money. Ain't no doubt about it."

"You got that right, Bright."

"This is good, man." Ali laughed, sounding as though he were enjoying it all. "So, you old dogs think I'ma get played. Besides that, what makes you think I don't already have a woman?"

Moor opened his eyes just as Blue spoke. "Yeah. Yeah. Yeah. We know—you already said you got a girl, but we talking about a sister."

"Me too." Ali wagged his head triumphantly.

Blue pulled his neck back like a turtle. "A sister?"

Ali nodded.

"From around here?"

Ali nodded.

"You kiddin'? You playin'—I know you are?!"

Ali smirked and shook his head in response.

Brighty slapped his hand to his forehead. "That does it! Prince!" He looked at Moor. "It's done got serious. We on a mission. We can't let you go down like this. I don't care if you just here for four days. Even our white suburban, Black Muslim got a sister. Ali has tasted brown sugar!"

"I'm just a Muslim, you guys, not—"

Brighty waved his hand. "That don't matter now, Ali. You got to help us! We got to find this man a wife!"

13

Puddin

Puddin *looked at the clock:* 5:00 A.M. She had tossed and turned all night. Well, tossed as much as she could almost hanging off the edge of the bed. And the nerve, Joe had come out of the reading room trying to cuddle with her again—his regular dessert after another night of chicken and movies. When she pushed him away, he laughed as though it was a game, as though she was playing hard to get.

When they had finally gone to bed, he kept trying to steal kisses, but she fended him off.

"You aren't really mad at me, are you?" He had the nerve to look hurt. It was just like a man. "I was just in the room for a little while."

Was he crazy? She turned her back. How much insult did he expect her to tolerate?

For better or for worse . . .

She had pounded her fist into the pillow. It didn't bend or break, just muffled and absorbed the blows. "I'm not a pillow, God," Puddin had whispered. How much did God expect her to tolerate? "You're supposed to take care of me."

She didn't feel much like bending. She looked over at Joe breathing peacefully on his side of the bed. What she really felt like doing was clocking him one good one. She looked away from him and toward the ceiling. "Lord, if you want me to stay with this man . . . this man you gave me, who has obviously lost his mind . . . you are going to have to turn him around. I can't live with this. You are going to have to change him and get him right. I mean it, God."

Joe snored softly while she continued praying. "Lord, I need peace, and you are going to have to help me." The Lord must have heard because it seemed she had fallen asleep almost instantaneously. Now it was five, and she was wide-awake.

Puddin looked at her husband. Even with his mouth open and his legs going in two different directions, the feelings that had been with her for over thirty years were still there. *He is such a good man. He loves me. He would walk through fire for me.*

The words she had spoken to him so many times were on the tip of her tongue, threatening to spill into his ear—*Whither thou goest, I will go. . . .* She could feel her heart swelling with love and her hand reached to touch his cheek as she had so many times before.

She snatched her hand back. It was her heart talking, her heart making her want to reach for him. And she couldn't trust her heart now. She had to use her head. Puddin turned away slowly, so as not to disturb him, and slipped quietly from the bed.

She held her breath, and her feet made no noise on the carpet as she felt her way down the hall in the dark. The other day, sitting in front of the computer before dinner, after Joe had gone in the reading room, she hadn't been able to bring herself to make the move. To raise a finger, to click the button that would take her into any of the sites she had found—*Boys! Boys! Boys!* She hadn't done it earlier, but she was poised again, to do it now.

She tiptoed into the room, and in the dark, felt for the button to turn the machine on. Earlier, she had been thinking of all the times she had met with her two friends Sister Othella and Sister Minnie.

The three of them made up the bulk, at least the reliable part, of the Comfort Circle. They helped people in their time of need, during funerals, when the storms of life were knocking down their doors. The three of them often met for lunch, or for meetings that turned into girlfriend sessions. They shared precious private moments where they were able to encourage each other, help each other grow, and sometimes they shared secrets.

When Othella and Minnie had told their husbands' secrets—complained about a little drinking, or gambling, or chores that had gone undone, or any number of other major and minor offenses—she had had nothing to share. "He's cheap," she remembered saying on several occasions. "Joe's real cheap."

"Cheap? Cheap? That's the best you can come up with?" Her two friends would chime in together. "Girl, if that's all I had to complain about, I wouldn't complain."

"It's not easy living with a cheap man. He's watching every dime, every nickel, every penny. You don't know Joe. You have to account for every little thing."

"Hush, Puddin," they would tell her. "Girl, you just don't know." Then they would go on to tell their stories, and sometimes she could not help feeling a little guilty about how good God had been to her.

Both Othella and Minnie agreed that their husbands were good, God-fearing men, they just had some flaws. None big enough to leave them, but sure big enough to work a sister's nerves every now and then. Both women had even caught their husbands giving the once over to attractive ladies from time to time. *"Right in the church, honey. Trying to take a peek on the sly. Like I don't know him. Mm hmm."* She couldn't remember now whether it had been Othella or Minnie talking. *"That's right, girl. I whacked him right there, right in the middle of nine-thirty service. Your response has to be swift and deliberate to be effective."* Again, nothing really major, just mostly good, solid minor-league stuff. Just enough that Sister Othella and Sister Minnie regularly wore grace around their shoulders, if not halos on their heads.

"Your husband is like a saint, Puddin," they would tell her. "Girl, you ought to be thanking the Lord!"

She stared at the computer screen glowing in the dark. All that—the days of thinking Joe was perfect—was then, and this was now. Now when she got together with her friends, she would have something to confess—that is, if shame didn't choke her first. Maybe the best thing to do was to just keep it to herself.

Puddin stared at the monitor as though she were in a trance. She raised her index finger. Retaliation. Her reaction, as her friends said, had to be swift and strong. It would only take one small movement to connect by computer to all the men, all the boy-toys, all the male eye-candy she could ever have dreamed of. She held her finger paused in midair, ready to end life as she had known it. She wasn't about to just walk on the wild side, she was about to become one of its boldest residents. Her finger lowered and . . .

A pop-up appeared.

It covered the icon—the link between her and lots of exciting men—she was about to click. "Doggone it!" she hissed. She was sick of the irritating unsolicited advertisements. When it came time to renew, they were going to switch to another Internet service provider.

The red pop-up with spiked or serrated edges blinked, jumped, glowed—it did everything but grab her by the collar. *Stupid advertisements!* Puddin hated them so much; she didn't even read them. *Stupid pop-ups!* The flashing icon would not be denied. It was stupid. She looked at the electric blue letters in the center.

DO U NEED A JOB?

CLICK HERE

Did she need a job? No, at 5:00 A.M. what she needed was a computer screen with no unwanted ads. What she needed was a man who hadn't lost his mind. What she needed was some peace. She thought of a few more needs before she comprehended the words she had just read.

DO U NEED A JOB?

CLICK HERE

"Do I need a job?" She asked herself the question out loud. Sure, she needed a job. Not only was her husband a philanderer, he was also cheap. . . .

"And yet I show you a more excellent way . . ." A word of Scripture came to her.

Puddin dropped her hand. Maybe there was a better way. Maybe this was a better answer. She didn't need to soil herself just because Joe was rolling in filth. She didn't have to become what she hated. He had his dirty little secret. She could have hers, well not dirty, but a secret of her own. Puddin clicked on the icon. Suddenly she was at a website for the Charm City News, an online newspaper. One ad caught her eye.

WANT TO WORK FROM HOME IN YOUR SPARE TIME?

She clicked the link that took her to the complete advertisement.

Become part of the Charm City News Team. Attention to detail, computer literacy, and Internet access will make you the ideal candidate for this job. Part time. Salary negotiable. Principles only need apply.

Puddin clicked on a button that said APPLY HERE. An email form appeared. She filled it out, expressed interest, and hit SEND.

Become part of the Charm City News Team. Maybe God was speaking to her. This might be the answer. It was time to stop putting her life on hold. She imagined herself sitting at an old Royal typewriter pounding out a front-page story. She had given thirty years of her life to this man, and look where it had gotten her. No, not *Boys! Boys! Boys!* Instead, she would follow in the footsteps of nineteenth-century woman journalist Ida B. Wells! Puddin's heart began to flip-flop. She would write editorials about injustice, poverty, living fabulously at fifty—and the shame of pornography—that would blaze a freedom trail for women and men everywhere. . . . She would be like Sojourner Truth or Harriet Tubman!

Puddin yawned, and the chair rollers groaned over the rubber floor mat as she pushed back her seat and began to power down the computer. This was just the beginning. She was going to do something special, something meaningful—she could feel it. *Thank you, God.* It made sense that the solution for the shame and injustice in her own life was to offer her own shame as a sacrifice, and to work to gain restoration and justice for people everywhere! As she walked down the hall and slipped into her bed, she was certain she could hear the strains of "The Battle Hymn of the Republic" softly playing.

14

Mary

The trip to work on the bus *was* a trip, and all the way, Mary had to keep reminding herself why people were stealing peeks, gawking, or just shoveling her a whole load of attitude. Nothing felt really different, and unless she was looking in the mirror, she was the same old Mary. That's not how it was playing on the bus, though. Men moved aside to let her step up on the bus before them. One man even gave her his seat. And the running dialogue in her head—*Is it the hair? The eyes? Is it just normal and I'm being too sensitive? Has it been this way all along and I just wasn't sensitive enough?*—was making her tired.

By the time she walked in the post office—not the front door with the counters and the stamps, and the friendly posters, but the back door beyond the chain-link fence, with the time sheets, the posted safety and health warnings, the rolling canvas tubs of mail, the scanning machines, the shelves and boxes, and nowadays sometimes people in rubber gloves and face masks that made it look like some sort of weird operating room for sick mail—she was ready to don dark shades and a wide-brimmed hat.

The men all paused, or at least most of them did. She tried to act as though it didn't make her uncomfortable, as though it happened all the time. They didn't ask for dates. Most of them didn't say anything. They just stared. It was mostly just her hair, eyes, and nails—mostly—but some also seemed to use the opportunity to check out the rest of what she was offering. She passed by a security guard, one she had noticed particularly in the past because there was nothing about him that made her feel secure—neither his thick glasses, his very slow gait, nor the creaking sound she thought she heard when he moved.

He held up a thumb. "All right, now, baby. Work it, honey!" He made a kissing sound at her, and Mary felt revulsion rising from her stomach to become panic in her chest. She ran-walked to her workstation to get away from him.

The women, however, treated the change as though she had declared war, or as though she had signed up to fight on the other side. They rolled their eyes and did not speak to her, but around her. "You couldn't pay me to wear a weave," one of them said to the woman working next to her. Of course, she said it just loud enough for Mary to overhear.

"Me neither," the co-worker replied. "They look too phony and make you look like too much like a strumpet for me. I don't want no man trying to date me just for what he thinks I might have or might give him. If you know what I mean."

The first woman answered, "That's right. And if who I am ain't good enough, then they ain't good enough for me. The man that tries to get up in my space needs to know that I ain't no Jezebel!"

The second woman talked over her shoulder while she shoved mail into the boxes. "There's no way a child of God could look that way. The Spirit wouldn't let her. A woman looking like that, it ain't no doubt what's on her mind, and it sure ain't Jesus—no matter what she say. I don't care how many Bibles she carrying. Just like I always said. Ain't nothing but a bunch of hypocrites."

There was no rest in the bathroom. Mary tried to escape there, pausing to smell her wrist, to smell the perfume that comforted her, as she walked through the door. When she walked to the row of sinks and began to wash her hands, she noticed a woman staring at her.

"Girl, look at your eyes!"

Mary forced herself to smile and hoped to hear something positive. The woman moved closer to the mirror to see, then turned Mary's shoulders—ignoring the trail of soap and warm water Mary was dripping—so that Mary faced her.

"Do those things hurt? Does everything look green?" The woman tilted her head left and then right. "I don't think I would wear those. I don't think they're right for your skin color. I think it's going just a little too far. Make you look all washed out." The woman squinted as though she were looking through a lens. She made a big circle with her hands. "It's too much, you know? Just one thing would have been enough, but all this is overload. It cries out for attention—just a huge flag waving and saying low self-esteem!" The woman smiled, squinted, shrugged her shoulders, and tossed her own shoulder-length, caramel-streaked hair. "I hope you don't mind my saying," she said brightly. "I just like to tell the truth." The happy woman bounced out the door.

No, I don't mind. It's just what I needed, a big dollop of depression to get things perking this morning. Nothing had changed about her, but everyone else seemed to have changed *about her*.

The next woman was more straight to the point. "Hi," was all she said. In a flash she reached her hand around the back of Mary's head and up the nape until her fingers touched a track. "That's what I thought. I didn't think it was yours." And before Mary could answer, she was gone.

By lunchtime, Mary was ready to go, to quit, to retire. Instead, she walked to the courtyard of the building. There were enough people that she could get lost and pretend no one was staring. She walked around the fountain, only stopping to stare at a couple of teenagers huddled together.

One of them had purple hair. *Purple hair.* Mary looked when she thought the two of them were not looking at her, and wondered where the *you've-gone-too-far-now* line was. Was there ever any permanent and fixed spot? How many times had she judged someone too harshly, not really knowing them, but thinking their outsides were yelling something their insides might never have intended to say? How many times had she assumed things about people based on what she thought she saw? And she wondered, which one of us it was that determined which colors were too Jezebel and which were modest enough? Where were the people that decided what was too much, what made something improper or unseemly? And what about people in other cultures?

No doubt, she had made decisions about people based on what they looked like—everybody did. Words she had been studying from the book of James came to her.

"*. . . if there should come into your assembly a man with gold rings, in fine apparel, and there should also come in a poor man in filthy clothes*"—or a man in a business suit and a teenager in raggedy fatigues "*and you pay attention to the one wearing the fine clothes and say to him, 'You sit here in a good place . . .'*" It happened all the time. Even in church the beautiful, properly dressed people got the best seats. Even in church people turned up their noses. "*. . . and say to the poor man, 'You stand there,' or 'Sit here at my footstool . . .'*" It happened all the time, and now it was happening to her. "*Have you not shown partiality among yourselves, and become judges with evil thoughts?*" Hardly anyone ever preached from James, and she knew why! Brother James cut straight to the chase. *Judges with evil thoughts?* She thought of the girls she mentored—Pamela, and Agnes, and Cat—as she watched the purple-haired teenager. People were judging them, her girls—especially Cat. *She* had judged the girl instead of listening to what she had to say. And she knew people judged Thelma, Naomi, and Latrice. Now she was getting to see how it felt.

Okay, God, I get it. Whoever said He didn't have a sense humor? Mary laughed as she thought about her morning. Who were the judges? Who were the people that made the rules? The people that made the rules—today they were all at her job.

After lunch, by the time work was over, she was ready to go, ready to throw in the towel, the weave, the contacts, and everything else.

When she stepped into Room Thirty-One the next day, no one said anything. The bus ride to work had been a little easier. She had just decided she would ignore all the stares and comments. But that was work. All the way up the hill, and stepping into New Worshippers, she had waited for the chorus to begin—perhaps a group of spirits, angels, or long-dead saints that would tell her to leave the building, leave the church grounds. *No blonde-haired, funny-eyed, fake-nail-wearing harlots allowed!* But no one said anything—not much, anyway—not even when she entered the room. Except Agnes looked up. That was a big thing, Agnes looking up.

Pamela coughed several times, her eyes round.

Cat sat back and smiled. "So, Miss Mary, what's the deal?" she asked.

It was too much to ask, to think that Cat would let her completely off the hook. "Nothing."

"Nothin'? Don't look like nothin' to me. To tell the truth, it looks like somethin'. It definitely looks like somethin'." She touched her own hair. "Yeah, it's somethin', all right. We could be sisters."

She didn't have to explain to them. It didn't concern them. "I just decided to try something different."

Cat growled. "You decided to get you a man?" She rolled her shoulders like a stretching feline.

"It's nothing, okay? I just decided to make a change." She hadn't thought about Cat when Thelma, Latrice, and Naomi were dragging her down the street. Maybe she would have fought harder. Then again, maybe not. It wasn't life or death. If she waited for a perfect moment to try something different, to make a change—to do it when everyone thought she should, when everyone else was comfortable, when no one needed her to be who she had been to him or her—she was never going to make a change.

She began to pull new Bibles out of her book bag. "Speaking of changes, I thought about what you ladies were saying last week. So no more study guides. No more devotionals—at least for a while. In each Bible, I've put some tabs. I've marked off some stories about young women in the Bible—Tamar, Mary of Bethany, and others. I want you to read the stories and then you teach me. Each one of you has an assignment. You tell me who you are in the Bible and what lessons *you* have to teach *me*. It hasn't worked out so well, my teaching you. Maybe you have something to say to me. And my ears are ready to hear."

Mary turned the knob on the bedroom lamp to dim the light. The yellow furnishings took on a duskier, sandier hue. "I listed myself with a computer dating service." Snuggling further under the covers, the phone pressed to her ear, Mary waited to hear Latrice's approval. "I got online as soon as I got back from my meeting with the girls."

Latrice guffawed. "We said get *serious*, not *desperate*. Girl, what is on your mind? All that tight weave must be getting to you. See, you should have listened to Latrice. I love Thelma and Naomi, but they don't know what they're talking about. The nails were enough. That's all I use and, girl, I got more men than you can shake a stick at. Shoot, I need a stick to beat the men off." Latrice giggled. "All that dye will ruin your mind. And those contacts . . . you see how red Thelma's eyes get sometimes. Ain't no telling what those things are doing to her eyes. You just forget about all that and let Mama Latrice steer you in the right direction. We'll have a man on your arm in no time.

"Besides, girl, I know you've seen all the stories on the news about all the loonies that get to people through the computer—chat rooms, dating services, whatever. I don't even deal with computers. What kind of way is that to meet a man? No, we are just going to try the good old-fashioned approach. Besides that, I got somebody I want you to meet."

Mary wasn't sure, at first, if Latrice's laughter was more excited or deranged, but soon decided it was the latter. She imagined her friend's nails flashing while she cackled like one of the witches in *Macbeth* stirring a cauldron. "Girl, have I got a man for you! This brother will wine you and dine you." Mary wrote down the number. "He's expecting your call. And you make sure you call me and give me the 4-1-1 when it's over. And I want to hear it all, you hear me? Every last little itty-bitty drop!"

15

Puddin

Puddin *paused,* then walked past the door of Joe's reading room. He was getting bolder and bolder. His addiction was taking over; his time in the room was longer each day. He was spending more time procuring the tapes—who knew where he was getting them from—bringing them home in brown paper bags. He was watching them almost every waking moment. At least he still had the decency to keep the volume low as he viewed them so that all she could hear was an occasional unintelligible female voice.

She was through crying. Now Puddin used the time—his reading time—to keep searching the Internet. There were tons and tons of jobs out there, and she was determined to find one. What Joe didn't know wouldn't hurt him. The pop-up and the advertisement for the job at the Charm City News had inspired her. She spent so much time online now that she was late starting their meals, if she started them at all.

Joe looked puzzled when the kitchen was dark, but he was smart enough not to say anything. She wanted him to say something, she hoped he would say something, so they could get right to the root of the problem. But there was still enough of who he really was— or who he used to be—that he would just quietly go out and bring them back a chicken box, a couple of burgers, or a few fish sandwiches. He never challenged her. That was how it was with sin—it felt good when you were doing it, she supposed, but it kept you bound and imprisoned to circumstances you never expected, unable to speak.

So Puddin spent hours at the computer screen sending out

email and resumes. There had been no responses to any of them yet. But it felt good not to be taking it all lying down. Each computer search she made, each piece of email she sent, reaffirmed for her that she was strong, that she was not going to let what was going on with Joe defeat her. It reminded her that she still had power. She didn't have to rely on anyone.

Pressing the POWER button brought the screen to life. It was hard to imagine electrical impulses—plusses and minuses of information—that raced through wires and computer components at blinding speed, impulses that could change her life.

Screen after screen passed by. When she finally reached her email, there was a reply waiting from the Charm City News—a reply that might change her whole life, that might turn things around for Joe and her.

She fumbled with the keys, rushing to read the reply. When she opened it, it read

Interview scheduled
10 A.M. Room 312, Rose Building
1001 Lombard Street
Position: PT ad checker

Ad checker? She reread the last line again. How did *ad checker* relate to being an exciting part of the Charm City News Team? The picture she had seen in her mind—the one that had shown her shoulder-to-shoulder with Ida B. Wells and Harriet Tubman fighting for truth and against injustice with a typewriter, ink, and paper—quickly dissolved. Instead, she saw herself sitting alone at a desk in front of a growing mound of white, yellow, pink, and blue order slips.

She pointed with her mouse to delete the email. It was not what she had imagined.

Still . . .

Just before she clicked the response into oblivion, she paused. Maybe a job, any job—a home-based job—would be a help. It might provide a secret stash of cash that would buy her *lullies* and treats—a secret cache that only she could control—a little something tucked away that would free her if things kept getting worse . . . if Joe kept spending more time in the reading room.

She stared at the interview appointment. What would she wear? What would they pay? What was the point? Joe didn't want her to work. How would she keep him from knowing?

Puddin turned her head in the direction of the reading room. Her face crinkled with disgust, then she turned back to the computer. She pointed the cursor to PRINT and clicked. Who cared if Joe knew anyway? What was he going to do about it? What moral high ground did he stand on to be able to tell her to do, or not to do, anything?

The printer clicked and groaned into action. Puddin removed the printed sheet from the machine. She would take it with her and share it with the ladies from the Comfort Circle.

The women of the Comfort Circle met in Room Seventeen on the third Tuesday of each month at ten-thirty. It gave them time to get breakfast, wash the dishes, and go to the post office or take care of any other pressing errands they might have. The room location and the time also gave them some privacy—some girls' time—so they could let their hair down, take their wigs off, and set their corns free—just whatever a woman had to do to speak freely.

Sister Othella touched the back of her head, like she always did, to make sure her French roll was still in place. "I just think that woman is way too young to be teaching those girls." She pursed her lips. "I don't know how long she's been saved. How can she lead them the right way when she don't know where she's going her own self?"

Sister Minnie laid one hand on her chest and nodded in agreement. "And she wears so much perfume." She wrinkled her nose. "I can't hardly breathe around her."

Sister Othella waved a hand in front of her nose. "Ain't that the truth." She looked from side to side—though there were only three of them in the room. "I'm not the one to tell the preacher how to run his church, but if you ask me, I wouldn't put so much responsibility in that young woman's hands." She sniffed. "She's trying to lead them, but who knows what she's doing her own self?"

Sister Minnie rolled her eyes. "And she's single, too."

"That's what I'm talking about," Sister Othella said. "She's got that look about her. You know—like she's still got a wild taste in her mouth. There's plenty of good, upstanding married women that could mentor those girls."

Puddin tried to be quiet, but she couldn't any longer. She kind of liked Mary. She had known her grandmother, and had known the girl casually from the neighborhood. "Well, I know her a little bit. Her name's Mary, and I think she's a pretty nice girl. I don't think we need to worry—"

"No, you never think we need to worry about anything or anybody!" Sister Othella raised an eyebrow. "You are always—just like the pastor and some other people I know—giving people too much credit, until it blows up in your face. You should see how she's looking now. Have you seen her? Blonde hair, funny-colored eyes, shiny nails." She frowned and her mouth resembled a bass. She waved a hand in the region beneath her neck, pointing at her chest. "And we know that all that she's packin' ain't hers. No, sir, Lord!"

"It sure ain't!" Sister Minnie chimed in. "I tried to like her before, even with the perfume, but she has gone too far. We tryin' to teach the girls to wait, to stay pure. How she gone teach them that? She ain't nothing but a walking advertisement for the devil, for sin. Ain't nothing but a Jezebel!"

Sister Othella nodded her head. "You give people enough rope, and they will hang they own selves. You give them enough time and they will show their true colors. If you not careful, they will have you going along, just as blind, believing they one way, and the next thing you know, they somebody else."

Puddin tried to swallow the lump in her throat. Her insides felt like she had just hit her elbow on a sharp edge. That's what she had been doing—believing Joe was one way, when he really was another. Sister Othella didn't know she was standing right on top of the truth in the middle of Puddin's own home. She was going to keep her mouth closed, though. Her and Joe's problems should stay in their home.

Sister Minnie waved a hand in the air. "Lord knows that's right. You can't trust nobody. You just keep on believing and believing and they will walk all over you. Make a fool of you."

Puddin could feel tears welling up in her eyes. This was the Comfort Circle. It was the time to discuss church matters, not her broken heart.

Sister Othella sat up straight in her chair. "You are always giving people too much credit, Sister Puddin." She patted Puddin on the arm. "You so tenderhearted. You just watch and see. Trust people willy-nilly like that and it will just lead to you getting your heart broken."

Before she knew it, Puddin was choking on her tears. She laid her head in her arms and bawled like a baby. She wanted to keep Joe's secret, but she just couldn't hold back anymore. She needed to cry.

Sister Othella began to whisper to her as if she was speaking to a whimpering child. "I'm sorry, Sister Puddin. I didn't mean to hurt your feelings." She wrung her hands. "Sometimes I just speak so harsh to people. My husband tells me that. 'Othella, you got to learn to speak nicer to people.' That's what he tells me. You know I don't mean no harm. But that woman, all that hair, and those things," she motioned underneath her neck again, "she is going to ruin the children and this church if somebody don't take steps to keep an eye on her. But I don't mean to hurt your feelings. You know that."

Sister Minnie pressed her hands to her cheeks. "You know Sister Othella don't mean no harm."

"It's not you!" Puddin managed to squeeze out. Then the dam broke, and the story she didn't want to tell gushed from her and filled the meeting room. She told Sister Othella and Sister Minnie the whole truth about Joe.

"You can't trust a man! You can't trust a man! You can't trust a man! Lord, have mercy!" Sister Othella's silver-tinted curls, the ones that crowned the top of her French roll, jiggled when she shook her head. "Why that no good, trifling . . . Excuse me, Sister Puddin. I don't mean to talk about your husband, or disrespect you. But my goodness!" She picked up a piece of paper and began to fan herself. "You can't trust them! And here Brother Joe is—and him almost a deacon, too—acting a fool. Joe know that he is too old to be getting crazy now. This is the time when things should be sweet for you." She shook her head. "When I think about how hard you have worked to build a happy home. . . ." She began to fan again. "Who would have thought? Almost a deacon in the church . . ."

Puddin blew her nose into the tissue Sister Othella handed her. There was nothing for her to say. As soon as the Comfort Circle heard what was going on—about the tapes, the brown bags, and the indignity of it all—they locked the meeting room door and put their arms around her. Puddin just let it all hang out. She cried so hard she was grabbing for snatches of air, like a little kid after a spanking.

Sister Minnie patted her shoulder. "Don't you hold back, now. That's what we're here for—to provide comfort in times like these."

Sister Othella whispered so closely that her breath tickled Puddin's ear. "And you don't have to worry about a thing. It will stop right here and go no further." She hugged Puddin. "Your secret is safe with us. Just let it all out, sugar."

Puddin did. And she even remembered to tell them about the chicken.

"You must be so disappointed!" The way Sister Minnie said *disappointed* was like she was trying to get the word to go uphill against its will. "Oo-oo! And the embarrassment of it all! You must feel like a stranger in your own home, child. Like when you walking in your own living room, you walking through filth." Puddin raised her head in time to see Sister Minnie pass a look to Sister Othella. "Almost a deacon." She shook her head. "What if someone saw him coming out of one of those places with one of those brown bags in his hand? Can you just imagine the filthy things they must do and talk about in those places? *Pornography!* I don't even want to say such a word in church. Why, it could cause some weak person to backslide. Why, it could be the cause of all the men in the church backsliding! It ain't enough they got to deal with harlots all painted up like that woman we was just talking about! But now they got the example of a leader—one they thought they could trust and respect—who has now given hisself over to the nasty life—set right before their eyes. The church could be ruined!"

Sister Othella had a terrible look on her face, as though something bitter was all over her tongue. "You are so right, Sister Minnie. The whole church could be lost."

Puddin took the extra tissue Sister Othella offered her. "Now, you know I'm not the one to even talk about divorce. But when a man is disrespecting you like that good-for-nothing man is disrespecting you, he might as well be dead. And when a man is dead, a woman is free. But I don't even want to talk about it. Now ain't the time. Mercy, mercy, me!"

Puddin didn't have to answer. She just cried some more. It was so good to be with people that understood. There were times when she had thought Sister Othella and Sister Minnie were a little too severe, and sometimes they gossiped too much. But she was grateful for the shoulder that they offered her now.

Sister Othella's voice sounded as though she were about to cry. "I'm telling you, I don't know what I would do if my husband was acting a fool. I don't think I could take it as well as you. I think I might—well, I just don't want to say here in the church what it is that I might do." She waved a hand in the air. "But what was that woman's name a few years ago? You know the one. With the husband, the knife, and the convenience store." She sliced her hand through the air. "I don't even want to talk about it! Don't even get it in your mind!" She clamped her hands over Puddin's ears. "Mercy!"

That was when Puddin told them about the job interview. She took the printout from her purse and laid it on the table in front of them. "I don't know what to do. Joe doesn't want me to work, now that he's retired, and I don't want to disrespect him."

Sister Othella and Sister Minnie, between the two of them, sucked in enough air to create a vacuum in the room. Sister Othella spoke first. "Disrespect him? Listen to yourself. You are talking crazy, right now, Sister Puddin. It seems like to me R-E-S-P-E-C-T, as Miss Aretha Franklin would surely tell you, is a two-way street. And I ain't seen no traffic coming your way."

Sister Minnie laid a comforting hand on Puddin's arm. "It's just wisdom, Sister Puddin, to do something for yourself. You got to. Who knows? If he's *this* crazy now, no telling what he might do in a little while. You got to think about yourself. Thank goodness there ain't no children involved."

Puddin could feel the river of tears beginning to flow again. It all felt so hopeless, so wrong.

Sister Minnie continued patting her arm. "Me and Othella been working for years. There's nothing wrong with a woman having a little change of her own. It helps a man keep his mind in order when he knows you got a little job, a little something of your own."

Sister Othella nodded. "That's right, Sister Minnie." Her eyes were round with sympathy. "Maybe if you'd been working all along, your husband might not have . . ."

Puddin's eyes were burning. Her nose and top lip almost felt raw. She wanted to stop crying. But maybe Sister Othella was right. Maybe if she hadn't stayed home and put so much pressure on Joe . . . what if things had been different? What if she had worked? People had told her for years that she should be working.

"Well, let's not think about it now. No point in crying over spilt milk." Sister Othella seemed to be reading her mind. "I say you get yourself dressed up, go down there, and get you that job. It sounds like Brother Joe is so busy with his filth, he won't even know the difference anyway. And if he does find out, he'll just have to weigh your keeping a little secret against his great big old nasty sin. And if push comes to shove, you know you can move in with me or Sister Minnie . . . until you get on your feet."

Sister Minnie nodded. "We got your back. You can lean on us. Brother Joe may think he's got everything in hand, but he about to find out what he got is a tiger by the tail!"

Sister Othella looked at the ceiling. "Lord, who would have thought? Lord, who can be trusted?"

16

Moor

Moor *looked up* to check the clouds. It was a gray morning. "Hey, Prince!"

He turned to see his two old friends beckoning him from across the street. It was early, and dirty paper and smashed cigarette packages clung to the pavement still wet from the previous night's rain.

Wind flapped the tail of his trench coat around his legs. The smell of wet newspaper, the musk of wet grass and earth, were making it difficult to breathe; and the only other thought he had room for, other than breathing, was the work ahead of him. He had no time to play with his wise fathers now.

"I cannot talk now, wise men. It is morning and I must work." He pointed down the street. "See. My bus comes. I have important work to do." His mind was on economics—micro and macro—and world systems. He didn't have time to fool around. He needed to be thinking about the people in his country and how he could apply what he was learning to help them—not foolishness about women.

Blue hollered over the sound of the traffic. "What we trying to do is important too, and we ain't got no time to waste! We ain't playin around!" Blue shook his finger and then pointed. "We trying to help you!"

"I've told you there is not enough time." There wasn't enough time, and he wasn't ready.

Stooped with age and hunched against the dampness, the two old men stomped their feet against the morning chill and continued to wave their hands and jerk their heads at Moor like boy

135

conspirators. Brighty yelled this time. "Come on, man! Work can miss you for a day. You supposed to be a preacher. Have some faith! If God can part the Red Sea, I know He can find you a woman in Baltimore—even if you are a little on the dark side."

Blue elbowed Brighty in the ribs. "Don't start up that routine again!"

Moor shook his head. He would not let himself laugh. Laughter would only encourage them.

Blue, obviously acting out for Moor's pleasure, yelled at Brighty, again, loud enough for Moor to hear. "I ain't playing with you!"

Moor pretended not to see them. He would not let himself be drawn into the game. He was not a boy; he could not ditch school. He had work to do. He had responsibilities. There were people at home counting on him. He was relieved when the bus pulled up before Brighty and Blue could cross the street, before they could lure him away.

"Good-bye, my fathers!" Moor hollered to his friends, stepped up on the bus that rolled to a stop in front of him, and thanked God for His perfect timing.

Blue and Brighty were still sitting at the table in the alley—their elbows on the table and their chins resting on their hands—though the morning grew late.

The sun had evaporated most of the dampness, and the early budding warmth of the late August dog days peaked over the roofs of the houses. Weather was like a woman, Blue thought—hot one minute, cold the next, with no reason or explanation.

The two old men had earlier shed their heavier coats, and now just wore the shirts and frayed suit coats that were customary as they sat at their table holding court. The young man Ali, his backpack slung over one shoulder, sat on a cinder block nearby.

"We got to do something. I ain't kidding. I'm not gone be able to rest until we work this out for the prince." Blue scratched his head.

"Yeah, we got to do something." Brighty folded his arms across his chest. "When Ali here, the other evening, said he had a woman, that did it for me."

"Come on, you guys. Give me a break." Ali scratched at one of his locks.

Blue shrugged. "It's just the ever-loving truth. The day *you* can get a woman, and a *sister*, well we ought to be able to get a woman for *anybody*. It ought to be easy to fix up the prince. He's tall, he ain't bad looking, and he's pretty smart. And after the way he walloped that young thug that tried to rob me, we know he's brave. . . . And we know women like that."

Brighty leaned forward in his chair. "What you know about women, Blue? With your old self. But I do agree with you. It seem like to me it ought to be easy, too. And all he wants is a kind of fat, brown-skinned girl."

Blue flicked his hands in Brighty's direction as though there were something nasty and sticky on them, like dirty tissue paper stuck to a shoe. "Why you always got to bring up color, Brighty? Why's that always got to be an issue with you? For goodness' sakes! This ain't about you, anyway—it's about the prince."

Brighty waved the other old man's gesture away. "I ain't stuttin' you now, Blue. I ain't got time to argue with you. If you and Ali and the prince like chocolate, well, that's your pleasure. I ain't keeping you from it. Why you got to bother with me about mine?"

" 'Cause it's just prejudice. You prejudice against your own kind, you old fool. It's just a throwback to the slavery days."

Brighty narrowed one eye. "Are we gone have a geography lesson, or history, or whatever? Or we gone find a woman for the prince?" He rapped his knuckles on the table, and the pitch of his voice rose to emphasize each word. "You and I can slug our differences out later! You know you ain't ready to take me on—and we just don't have the time right now."

Ali's head turned from side to side, watching each man. "You guys are too much. All this is wasted in the alley. You guys should be on stage." He laughed and tugged at his backpack. "Are you sure you're not brothers? Me and my kid brother argue this way."

Brighty kept talking to Blue. "You said it yourself. We are here about the prince. We got business to attend to now. It ought to be easy, if you can just keep your mind focused. Why can't you stay on track?" He frowned and pulled at his coat. "Besides, I didn't make it up. The prince said it hisself, right here, the other night, when we was talking." He looked in Ali's direction.

Ali nodded.

Brighty huffed a few times, as though he was trying to calm himself down, as though he was trying to give a patient explanation to a child. "See what I'm saying? The prince said"— Brighty began to mock Moor's voice and accent—"'If I should want a wife, she should be the kind of woman like the men in my family like. No funny hair. No funny eyes . . .'"

Ali joined in with him. "'I want a fat wife!'" they said together. Ali snorted and bobbed his head up and down. "Yeah, man!"

Brighty looked at Blue and shook his head like years of frustration pressed on him, as though he was hoping that Blue *finally* got it, and then turned to the younger man. "Tell me this, Ali, does she have all her teeth? I mean something's got to be wrong with her. Your girlfriend, I mean."

Ali chuckled. "She's fine as wine, old man." He bobbed his head. "There's just a little more to this boy than you ever gave me credit for."

Brighty swiveled suddenly in his chair. "Credit? Credit?" His missing teeth made the word sound more *credick*. "Luck is more like it," he continued. "Or she blind, crippled, crazy—something's wrong!"

Blue pressed his hands to the top of his head and then shook them toward heaven. He kept his eyes there for a second or two, not sure what help he was looking for, or from where. He sighed, then looked back at Brighty and Ali. "Come on, now, you two. We got to get serious. The two of you can take up this small potatoes stuff at another time. Right now, we got to figure this out about the prince, now. We got to find him somebody." Blue knew his voice sounded as desperate as he felt.

Brighty rubbed grizzled hairs on his face. "All right, Blue. All right. Don't catch a stitch. We thinking." He scratched his head. "Where we gone look?"

Blue stuck a finger in his ear and wiggled it, hoping to stop the itching. His ears always seemed to itch when he was worried. When his wife was alive, she used to tell him, *Stop worrying, Blue. I know you worryin' cause you diggin' in your ears.* He couldn't help it. "We can try everywhere. The grocery store. The bus stop—"

"The bus stop? What you talking about, Blue? If a woman is at the bus stop, that mean she ain't got no car. What a man want with a woman that ain't got no car?"

Blue frowned at Brighty while he pulled at his ear again. "What you talking about, Brighty? You ain't got no car and the prince still take up time with *you.*" He looked at what was on his finger and wiped it on his pants. "This is serious, now. We can't rule out nothing. We can even try the church."

Ali sat back on the cinder block and then tilted his head.

Brighty's eyebrows rose almost to reach his scalp. "How we gone try church?"

"Well, it seems like a good place to try, Brighty. He goes there all the time."

"He may be *going* there all the time, but he ain't found no woman there. It seem like to me that ought to be the place where the Lord get involved. Seem like He ought to take care of that particular place. That's what it seem like to me. I don't know nothing about church." Brighty hunched his shoulders.

"Well, you know they say God helps those who help themselves. We may have to help out a little. One of us may even have to go there."

Ali and Brighty looked at each other. Brighty shook his head. "I don't know who that's gone be. All them women and hats and shouting, or else they dead and putting you to sleep. I ain't got nothing to wear. I can't go."

Ali lifted his hands in the air. "I can't go. I'm a Muslim."

Blue could feel his chest puffing up and getting tight, both at the same time. *Exasperation!* That's what he was feeling. "Look, now, you two. This is one for all and all for one. If one goes, we all going." He'd only gone a couple of times with his wife, just to please her. But, if going to church was what it was going to take to get Prince a wife, to make him happy, then that's what they were going to do. Blue knew the prince said he was okay, but he knew the signs of loneliness—the sleeplessness, the anxiety. The prince was right, it was good to be alone sometimes—but just for a season . . . and some men's seasons were shorter than others.

He closed one eye and focused the other on Ali. "And don't shake your head, boy. You ain't fooling nobody. Your mama ain't raised no Black Muslim—"

"I keep telling you guys—"

Blue and Brighty couldn't miss the opportunity to chuckle—not even in a crisis. Blue waved his arm like a hatchet. "Ain't nobody got time to hear all that, Ali. If one go, we all go. That's that. So if I was you, I would be praying that the Lord step in and send somebody. If somebody don't come along, the three of us gone have to go to church. And that's something to worry about." He pouted. "'Cause if the three of us step up in church, no doubt about it; lightning is sure to strike."

Brighty hopped up from his seat as though the first flash of electricity had just zapped him. "Well, I'm gone try the grocery store, then." Brighty winked. "I got a few contacts up in there."

"All right, Brighty! Now, you talking. I guess I'll try the buses and such." Blue took a deep breath. They were about to get down to business. "What about you, Ali?"

"Look, you guys, I'm busy. I've got school to think about. The semester's just starting."

Brighty thumped his chest. "Ali, what kind of black man are

you? We talking about a brother in need of your help, and all you can do is whine. *I'm* going to the grocery store. Why can't you help out? I guess since *you* got a woman, you don't care about nobody else. See, you used your connections in the 'hood with us to get you in, now you don't have time." Brighty began to wag his head and whine. "We gone end up in church for sure." He stomped his foot.

Ali shook his arms over his head. "Okay. Okay. I suppose I could try the library."

Blue nodded. "Now, that's the way we do it! That's the way to hustle. That's the way to stick together. That's how the Ravens got to the Super Bowl. And that's how we gone get the prince a chunky chocolate girl!"

17

Puddin

Puddin *eased herself* and her chocolate suit into the upholstered chair after first checking in with the receptionist. It was one of those narrow, modern chairs, done in a modern color that *popped* and lit up the room. It was one of those chairs that seemed to go out of its way to remind whoever sat in it that he or she needed to give up the carbs and spend more time running the treadmill and riding the bike. The chair looked firm, but the longer Puddin sat in it, the lower she sank, and the higher the hem of the straight skirt of her business suit began to rise.

She'd dug the outfit out of a box packed away in the back of her closet.

"You can't wear a church suit to an interview," Sister Othella had told her. *"They won't understand. Nobody in the workplace wears a tangerine or lime suit with sequins on the shoulders. They just won't get it."*

"No, they won't," Sister Minnie had said. *"You have to wear something more muted, something with less color, so they will take you seriously. Black is good. And don't wear a hat or gloves to town—they'll know you're from the sixties. . . . And for goodness' sakes, don't wear a hat!"*

Puddin pulled at the material gaping around the brown buttons that matched her suit. It had taken a whole lot of exhaling to get into the thing. She looked at the pictures on the wall and pretended she didn't notice that she was revealing way more of herself than she had ever intended.

Maybe she shouldn't have come. She was going to look like an old fool—well, a middle-aged fool, skirt all hiked up and wrinkled—in front of these confident and *young* people. Even their conversation was short and snappy. Sweat broke out around her hairline. *Oh great! Here comes summer!* She pressed the back of her hand to her forehead, hoping she looked calmer than she felt.

She'd probably flunk the test.

Everything was computers, now; there wasn't a typewriter to be seen or heard. Puddin looked at her hands and heard the memory of her teacher's voice over the clack of thirty sets of typewriter keys. *"When you go for a typing job, they will test you. Don't worry—you are prepared."* She used a computer at home, but no one was checking her speed there. The last typing test she'd had was on one of the Royal manual typewriters they used in high school. *"Make sure your nails are clean and clipped. Keep your eyes on the document,"* her typing teacher had counseled all the girls. Her teacher would have disapproved of her oval-shaped nails, even though the color was a neutral, frosted shade of taupe. That was more years ago than Puddin cared to remember. She was out of practice, out of uniform, and she wasn't sure about taking a timed speed test—especially on a computer.

"Eleanore Jenkins."

Puddin looked up. No one called her that. No one called her Eleanore. She was always Puddin. She jostled and fought to rise demurely from the chair that had spent the last twenty minutes trying to eat her skirt and swallow her dignity. Once she was on her feet, she waved her fingers. "Here I am." She followed the receptionist's directions and tried to mimic the young woman's sultry walk, then waited in the conference room.

The table was made of some synthetic black material. All the colors in the room were . . . *edgy*, no pastels, but deeper, startling colors. Two walls were mostly windows. There was a large round mirror on the wall facing her.

A young man slouched into the room. He was young enough to be her nephew. His worn, faded jeans sagged in the back like his diaper was crying out to be changed. His glasses were perched on the end of his nose. In one hand he held a leather-bound notebook. The other hand combed incessantly through his long brown hair. He slumped into a chair across from her.

"Bob," he said and thrust his hand across the table to her. His hand was soft, the shake brief and unconcerned. He pulled her application from the folder, studied it, then nodded and smiled. "Ever worked for a newspaper before?"

An answer raced through Puddin's mind. *I've written for the church newsletter. I've taken several creative writing courses, and a journalism course in college. I didn't finish college, but I did well in the course.* Instead she simply answered, "No." There was no point. If she was supposed to get the job, she would. If not, oh well.

"Ever worked from your home?"

Had she ever worked from her home? *Why, yes. For more than twenty years I've been the chief executive officer of my own firm, responsible for day-to-day operations, budgeting, resource management, facilities management, personnel matters, employee incentives, vacuuming, chicken cooking, and dishwashing. Why, I've even dabbled in interior design.* "Well," was all she answered. It was pointless. She had paid for parking, bought pantyhose that were at this very moment cutting into the tops of her thighs, and dug her way out of a chair only to be told she wasn't qualified. Great.

"How soon could you start?" Bob flipped his hair again.

"Right away." There was no way he was going to hire her.

Bob gave her a superficial smile. His lips turned up, slightly, on the corners, but there was no light in his eyes. "Could you wait right here for a moment?"

No, she couldn't wait. She was leaving. She had a chicken that needed to be introduced to some potatoes and a flame. "Of course I'll wait. I don't mind."

When the door closed, Puddin stared out a window at a pigeon hopping on the ledge. He was smart. He was doing what pigeons do; he wasn't trying to complicate his life. Here she was—when she should have been at home, feet up, cooling it—begging a child for a job. She should have stayed home. She thought of her stockings again—no, *felt* her stockings—and the money she'd spent getting the too-tight suit cleaned.

She didn't hear him reenter the room. "Mrs. Jenkins?"

"Yes." Her heart fluttered and she swiveled in her chair to look at him. Maybe there was a chance.

He smiled. "I'm sorry," he said as he closed the door behind him. "I appreciate you taking the time to come down here for this interview." He turned around in his seat so that his back was to her. "The job you applied for has already been filled."

Right. He appreciated her coming, all right. He appreciated it so much that he wasn't even willing to show her basic common courtesy. He could have at least dismissed her face to face.

Bob kept talking with his back to her. "So, I checked with my partner to see what else was available." He swiveled around. He shrugged. "Not much."

Well, that was that. Joe would keep doing what he was doing, and she would keep doing what she had been doing. In the meantime, the parking meter was running. She got the picture. Why didn't Bob just let her go?

"But I wanted my partner to meet you."

The door cracked open. Another faded-jeans-wearing young man slumped in, nodded, then sort of threw his body into a chair at the table.

Why didn't they just let her go?

Bob smiled at Puddin, then looked at the other young man. "See what I mean, Lyle? What do you think?"

Lyle pulled at his spiky blonde hair. "Yeah, I see what you mean." They looked back and forth at each other. "Why not?" He tilted his head and pushed his glasses down to the tip of his nose. "You're married, right?"

"Yes."

"For how long?"

"Around thirty years."

Lyle looked at Bob and then back at Puddin. "Sounds good to me."

Bob cleared his throat. "We've got a section of the paper that we think you'd be perfect for. We're trying to give our personal ads a more personal touch, sort of a mother's touch. Well, not so much a mother . . ."

Lyle grinned. "More of a funky cyberspace godmother kind of thing, you know? Or godmother to the hip-hop generation. Kind of a favorite aunt-matchmaker kind of thing, you know? Do you think you'd be interested?"

Puddin reminded herself to breathe when she spoke. "Personals? Like *dating* personals?"

Lyle's hair was almost yellow, like the background of one of the pictures on the wall. "Yes, like dating. Mostly it would be just keeping an eye on things. Keeping things organized."

Bob leaned forward. "Yeah. But sometimes you could reach out and give that personal touch. You know, some personal advice to the lovelorn. You could send emails from time to time. You know what I mean? We don't want people to feel like they're just dealing with an impersonal computer database, you know?"

Puddin felt lightheaded. "Personal ads?"

Bob raked his hand through his hair. "You could just try it out. If you don't like it, no sweat. No hard feelings. It's done. Over."

Lyle shrugged. "You'll have your own section. You can do it all from your home. Set your own hours. Who knows? You might do some people some good. Think about it."

Puddin blinked her eyes a few times just to make sure it was all real. She looked into her eyes in the mirror. What was there to think about? Without some change, there was nothing but more chicken in her future, and Joe was still spending all his time in the reading room; she might as well take the plunge. She looked from the mirror back at Lyle and Bob. "I think it'll do just fine."

18

Mary

Mary checked her makeup in the mirror. She still had not been able to get used to the contacts and the hair. "I don't know about this, Latrice. He didn't sound like my type when we talked on the phone." Mary walked through the house holding the cordless phone while she hunted down her shoes. She paused in front of her dresser and reached in the drawer for the perfume. She lifted the lid and inhaled deeply, then rubbed the scent on her skin and replaced the jar. "He sounded   older." Any excuse would do to get out of it. Maybe blind dating wasn't such a good idea.

She found one shoe, slipped it on, then hopped on one foot until she found the other.

Latrice laughed—no, she brayed. "You're just having opening-gate jitters, baby. Trust Latrice; you gonna be all right." Every snicker made Mary want to block the door, turn off the lights, and pretend she wasn't home. She was not ready.

Latrice mocked her. "'He didn't sound like my type.' Girl, long as it's been, you don't have a type. But trust me, girl, you ready. Hair done, feet done, but most of all, girl, your nails are tight! Just go with the flow, sugar. It's gone be all right. I wouldn't steer you wrong; I'm your girl! You know that. I wouldn't put you in harm's way. If nothing else, you'll get a good, free meal."

He held the door open for her. There was a large circle on top of his head—a clear brown bald spot, except for dark color smudges that indicated a recent dye job. The smudges were almost the color of his dark maroon suit. "You just ease your pretty self on in that seat." Something about the way he said *your pretty self* reminded Mary of slug juice, of a slippery, slimy trail. She shuddered.

"You cold, baby?" Floyd scrunched his book-shaped figure into the driver's seat next to her. His shoulders were broad, which was a good thing if you liked the guy, Mary thought. But it wasn't a good thing if you were trying to think of fifty ways to get away from him. He was sweating—a good thing, maybe, if it's nectar from the one you love, but not in this case—the dampness touching her shoulder made her feel uncomfortable. Exactly why had she agreed to do this?

"I been living in Baltimore all my life, except for the time when I was a cop in another city." Mary looked at him and tried to imagine what city. "I'm surprised I never saw a sweet, lovely thing like you." Why couldn't men you love say things like that, so that it would feel like sweet kisses behind the ear? Instead, it was always men that made her want to run screaming into the night—men whose words felt like some creepy thing crawling up her neck.

He pulled out into the traffic, and based on his driving technique, Mary was pretty certain that *in another city* must have been someplace where they drove on the wrong side of the road and ran red lights.

"So, who did you say your people were?" Now Floyd had the nerve to be doing the Baltimore pedigree thing. Or maybe it was a Southern thing—where you had to tell your relatives' names, where they'd gone to school, where they worked, or who they were married to—anything to help the other person make a connection, to give them something that gave you legitimacy and standing.

She told him as little as possible, hoping he might be put off. Instead, he raised his eyebrows up and down several times. He looked her over. "I love a woman with a little mystery." His lips made a slurping sound, and Mary thought seriously about how badly she might be injured if she dived from a speeding car traveling down Interstate 395. No, it wasn't worth it. She might die. And if she died, she wouldn't be able to kill Latrice when she saw her again.

"You like ribs, don't you?" Floyd licked his lips and looked her up and down again. "I know you do. You a healthy girl—a plump girl. And I know you didn't get that way without exercising your elbow."

There you go, Floyd-baby. Just flatter your way right on into my heart. She was going to order the most expensive thing on the menu.

Only there was no menu.

When they pulled into the bumpy parking lot of the Rib Shack, the sign outside announced that it was *all-you-can-eat night.* Everything that was available to eat was posted, bulletin-board style, on a poster behind the counter clerk. There was nothing available more expensive than the ribs deluxe special—which included ribs, tips, and extra barbecue sauce—for $9.99.

Floyd's eyebrows did their fluttering thing as he leaned in close. "I'm gone get you good and full tonight." He chuckled. "Um hmm!"

They moved from the doorway and began to wind their way through the plastic tables bolted to the floor. The lighting was dim and the décor was early dingy.

Maybe the apostle Paul was right: at the moment, she couldn't think of a single thing wrong with being single and celibate. In fact, being cloistered was beginning to have a certain appeal. Mary imagined herself in a nun's habit.

"Hey, Floyd!" the counter clerk yelled. "We surprised to see you," he joshed. "This must be all-you-can-eat rib night!"

A group of older men sitting at one of the tables near a plate glass window began to whistle and laugh as they pointed at the two of them. *"All right there, now, Floyd." "You cutting the mustard, now, brother!"* They looked from Mary to a group of women sitting at a table just ahead of where she walked with Floyd. *"Show 'em what you working with!"* one of the old men yelled as he ducked his head, giggled, and rolled his eyes at Floyd. Mary wanted to run.

Floyd took her arm and directed her to the table of women. He pointed to a woman with her head covered by a shocking pink pre-formed turban. Little tufts of gray hair peeked around the edges. "This here is my ex-wife." He lifted an eyebrow and looked at his ex-wife. "Lootie Belle, this here is my date." He looked Mary up and down and nodded his head. "We here to eat ribs!"

The old men across the room leaned forward, their ears having grown seven sizes so as to catch every word. Lootie Belle jerked the tropical green polyester jacket she wore over her matching dress. The large pink flowers on the dress matched the turban, her dangling earrings, and the four coats of lipstick on her large, pouty lips. "Shoot, Floyd! Don't nobody care! Do what you want to. You make your own bed; you gone have to lay in it." She turned her back. "You better leave me alone!" The other women at the table nodded. "And don't try to come over tonight, either," she added. "The chain will be on the door!"

One of the other old women at the table gave Floyd the talk-to-the-hand-move. "That's what you get, Floyd." She frowned at Mary. "Bringing that young girl up in here. You crazy or something?"

"That's all right, Floyd!" one of the old men yelled. "Don't worry about it! You got it, baby! You got it! Go on with your bad self!"

Mary took several deep, cleansing breaths to clear her head, so she could think of some creative ways to kill Latrice, and ways to escape the Rib Shack in case Lootie Belle got hostile.

Finally, Mary and Floyd made it to the counter. The clerk, giving Mary the once-over, reached across the counter to shake Floyd's hand and pat him on the shoulder. The clerk kept staring at Mary as he spoke. "I didn't know you had it in you. Where you get her from?" he asked as though Mary was not standing there—it was becoming a regular thing. She tried to rethink the bus routes, wondering if she would be able to get to Latrice and kill her before she had to be at church in the morning.

Floyd licked his lips. "I still got my ways," he said mysteriously.

The clerk kept staring at Mary. She lifted her wrist to her nose and inhaled briefly. She needed the perfume to carry her to New Orleans worse than ever. "So, what are you two lovebirds going to have?" the clerk asked.

Floyd beamed. "We gone have ribs!"

"No, I'm going to have steak. The ribeye." She didn't even like ribeye, but she couldn't see herself sitting at a table slurping sauce with Floyd. The image was so ghastly she was almost overcome. She pressed her wrist, momentarily, back to her nose and tried to summon images of horse-drawn carriages and handsome men sauntering down hot, sultry streets.

"I thought we were gone have ribs. It's all you can eat." Floyd sounded confused, he sounded wounded.

Mary held firm. She forced a smile on her face and sniffed her wrist again. "I'm going to have the ribeye." She was getting desperate. *Come on, New Orleans!*

Floyd threw his hands up in the air. "All right, if that's what you want. Have the ribeye. You missing the all you can eat." He muttered to himself. "The sauce is good."

The clerk still had his eyes on Mary. "You two can sit down. I'll bring your trays out to you."

Floyd tipped an imaginary cap. "Well, that's mighty nice of you to give us that extra service. I'm gone remember that. . . . Right this way, my lady." Floyd bowed and extended his arm to direct her to a table almost midway across the room—it was a little closer to the men and a little farther away from Lootie Belle and her girls.

Once they were seated, Floyd leaned across the table. "You sure are a pretty woman. I love a woman with green eyes."

Mary wondered if she could manage popping the contact lenses out right there at the table.

He sat back and looked out of the corner of his eye across the room at his ex-wife. "I don't know why she keep coming here. She know I don't want her." He did the eyebrow thing again. "Why would I want her when I got a pretty young thing like you on my arm?"

Mary switched wrists. The scent seemed to be all sucked off the one she had been using. She prayed for her ribeye to come.

"Here it is," the counter clerk said as he leaned over her shoulder.

"That was mighty fast," Floyd said. "And it sure looks mighty good." He looked at the food, and then winked at Mary. "Did you bring my bags?" he asked the clerk.

"You bet I did, Floyd. And you just come on up whenever you ready for some more ribs!"

Mary picked up her knife and fork, and then closed her eyes to say grace. By the time she opened them again, Floyd was already shoveling ribs into a to-go bag. "Are you ready to go?" she hoped.

Floyd waved a saucy hand at her. "No, girl. You just take your time. This is all you can eat!" He looked at her steak. "At least the ribs are all you can eat. You take your time and eat that all up. While you eating, I can be bagging. Every week I come in here and I bag up enough of these ribs and tips to eat off of for three or four days. That's what makes it all worthwhile."

Mary began to make methodical, perpendicular cuts in her steak, hoping that the repetitive motion would somehow hypnotize her so that she could sleep through the date. She kept cutting and Floyd kept stuffing, in between lumbering back and forth to the counter for meaty refills. When the tray in front of him was piled high full of bags, he pointed at Mary's plate. "You ain't ate nothing."

"For some reason, I'm not very hungry." She stabbed a large glob of fat and moved it up and down on the plate through and between the small brown rectangles of meat.

"You want a bag for that?"

"No, I'm just not very hungry."

"You can bag it up and eat it later. That potato will be good heated up—just add some butter."

"No. No thank you."

Floyd looked piqued. "I don't believe in wasting food. See, if you had listened to me and got the ribs, I could have just bagged up your ribs and took them on with me. But you got that steak, and now you done messed it up." His voice had taken on a disapproving tone. "I don't believe in wasting food or money." He gave her the if-you-want-to-be-my-woman-you'll-straighten-up look.

Mary laid down her fork and took a deep drag from her wrist. *New Orleans, please!* "I'm not hungry, and I don't want to take it with me." She smiled, but she knew her expression and the tone of her voice were a warning, a warning that she was really close—about one more comment about the food away—to giving Lootie Belle something to laugh at him about if he didn't just let the ribeye die.

"All right. All right. We having a good time."

In what universe? On what planet?

"Ain't no need to get worked up over a little steak." He began to gather his bags. "Come on, let's go." He waved to the men and the clerk, and nodded his head at Lootie Belle and the girls.

When she had settled in the car, and Floyd had his bags of ribs and tips all nestled in the back seat, he got in and started the car. "I got a couple of runs to make."

They drove through Baltimore's south side, winding through neighborhoods and down streets Mary had never seen. They stopped on Hearn Street in front of a brown brick home with evergreen shrubs. "I got a buddy here. I'm working on his car, and I need to check in with him about it."

It was ten-thirty at night. Floyd wedged himself out of the car, then leapt, as on hind's feet, up the stairs to the door of the semi-detached brick home. All the lights were out inside, but came on soon after Floyd began to beat on the door. "Hey! Hey, Ray!"

A man in a robe appeared at the door and turned on the porch light. She couldn't hear, but could see the two men talking. Floyd's head nodded toward the car. The other man ducked back inside, then came out wearing an oil-stained green dungaree work jacket and a pair of matching pants. He walked with Floyd to the car.

"So, you think you'll have my car done tomorrow." The man enunciated clearly and distinctly, as though he were in a play.

"Yes. That should be fine. No problem." Floyd's speech pattern had changed, his words sounded as loud and as contrived as his friend's. "Thanks for walking me to the car," he said.

The man stooped and looked inside. "No problem," he said, looking at Mary even though he was still talking to Floyd, who was still standing outside the car.

Floyd bent over, too. "Oh, I'm sorry. I forgot my manners. Ray this is Mary. Mary, Ray." Mary nodded and tried to find a place on her arm that still held the perfume's scent. It had never been so difficult to summon New Orleans.

Ray and Floyd walked to the front of the car and stood in the yellow circle of the headlights. They shook hands. Ray laughed and pounded Floyd on the back. Hunched over against the night cold, he hurried back up the steps, only stopping to turn around and wave to Mary. The man giggled and then rushed into the house.

Floyd checked on his ribs and tips and then got back in the car. Mary cleared her throat.

"We just got one more stop. I got to see a guy about—"

"Let's just get it over with."

Floyd nodded. "It won't be too long. I don't want the ribs to get too cold." The lights were on at the next house when they pulled in front, and there just happened to be three or four guys sitting outside waiting. "Hey, Floyd!" they yelled.

Mary stared straight ahead. She could see it now. She would cast Latrice's body from a low-flying plane into a quicksand pit—with a vine just out of reach—surrounded by a ring of angry fire ants. No, that still wasn't a cruel enough death for her. After all this she deserved something much worse.

Just before she climbed into bed, Mary checked her email. There was a message from Charm City News, a message about the free online dating service she'd joined. Mary pushed the off button.

She'd had her fill of dating tonight, thank you. She didn't care if she never dated again. She turned off the light, climbed into bed, and adjusted her pillow. "God, what is going on in my life?" She exhaled, and the night's trauma put her quickly to sleep.

19

Moor

G*ive me grace* to run this race alone, until you lead me to the doorway of the perfect wife, my heavenly Father. You and I have a good time talking and studying together, and I have a lot of work to do—so I'm not rushing you. You take your time. I know that you know the perfect woman for me. Today, though I do not know her, I pray that you will make her burdens light. I pray that you will give her peace and reassure her that you are sending her the mate that is a perfect fit for her. Wipe the worry off of her forehead and relax her shoulders for me. Command her to enjoy the day. Rub her feet for me, until I am able to do so myself. Tell her that I am preparing myself to love her sacrificially and wholly as you have taught me to love. Tell her not to worry— I will be looking for her when the time is right. And in the right time and at the right place, I will find her. In Jesus' name. Amen." Moor rose, and then dropped back to his knees. "Oh, by the way, wise Father, please do not let her get any silly American ideas like to diet or exercise too much. You know I don't want a skinny wife. Amen."

He sat in the chair where he always sat at the table, studying by lamplight until the sun rose.

Brighty scratched his stomach as he walked into the corner market. *"You make sure you put on a clean undershirt,"* Blue had told him. *"You want to make a good impression while you searching for a woman for the prince."* He looked around and decided he would try the frozen food aisle first.

This was his second store and he still wasn't quite sure about the details of how you did this. Did you just walk up to any woman hoping to get lucky? Or did you wait until you saw exactly what it was that Moor wanted? He walked by the glass doors, staring at the brightly colored prepackaged entrees. If he waited until he found what Moor wanted, they were going to have to wrap him up and stuff him in one of the cases. Besides, it was cold on this aisle, and he could hear *Authur-itis* beginning to grind his teeth. Brighty moved on to the produce section.

The light shining on the vegetables was especially bright. Every few minutes there was a sound like thunder, then water sprayed over the lettuce and red tomatoes, making them look shiny and fresh. Brighty ducked his head underneath the overhang hoping to see the gizmo that made it all work—the thing that made the thunder sound and the water spout. When he couldn't figure it out, he went back to business. While he strolled, he fingered the potatoes and fondled the green grapes. He lifted a fresh pineapple to his nose.

When he spotted a brown woman leaning over the green leafy cabbage, he made a beeline. "Excuse me, ma'am."

The woman straightened up, turned to face him, and Brighty realized she was a little older than he had thought. But no matter. He would take what he could get.

"Yes?" she said. "Can I help you?"

"You married, ma'am?"

The woman's expression flickered between confusion and amusement. "I beg your pardon?"

Brighty spoke louder and paused after each word. Maybe she couldn't hear that well. "I said, are you married, ma'am?"

She looked around as though she was checking for cameras. "No," she said quizzically.

"Would you like to be?" He scratched his stomach.

"I'm not sure what you mean."

Maybe she could *hear*. Maybe she just wasn't that *bright*. "I said, would you like to be married?"

The woman stepped behind her buggy and began to slowly push it away from Brighty.

"Wait a minute, now. See I'm trying to find a wife for the prince." The woman began to pick up speed with her cart. Brighty jogged after her, waving one hand in the air. "Wait a minute now!"

"Get away from me, right now! I'm going to call the security guard. I'm going to call right now, if you don't leave me alone!"

Brighty stopped jogging and bent to catch his breath. He waved his hand at her. *Good riddance!* Let her go. She was crazy anyway!

He looked over at the meat in the deli counter. All this was making him tired, a little hungry, and he hoped that the prince appreciated all that he was doing on his behalf. In fact, he was feeling a little parched. He began to walk toward the front of the store where the bakery was. They had tables up there where a fella could cop a squat and maybe have a cup of coffee or something. Besides that, there was a hostess there sometimes. He smiled. She might be able to help him out, if she was in. He had been trying to think of a reason to spend some time talking to her. This might just be the perfect reason. Who knew? She might have a granddaughter just right for the prince.

Brighty beamed when he saw her standing there holding a pot of coffee and wearing her little pink apron. She was the prettiest ivory-colored thing he had seen in years. "Hello, miss," he said when he got in earshot.

"Well, hello, yourself," she said. And Brighty was pretty sure she was batting her eyes at him on purpose.

"It's kind of cold in here. I think I'm gone get me some coffee today."

"Well, I sure wish you would, handsome," she said and pulled out a chair for Brighty to sit down. He had never noticed before that she had such a cute little mole on her top lip. "You want something else? A donut? A roll?"

Brighty felt sweat breaking out under his arms and was glad he had doubled up on the deodorant this morning. "I know you're busy." He could feel his face getting warm. He lowered his head. "You don't have to take up all your time on me."

"Time with you is good time," she said and winked. "I see you in this store all the time and I been wondering when you were gone come over here and talk to me." She smiled.

Brighty felt his toes curling up in his shoes. If he'd been wearing a hat, it probably would have blown off his head. He felt like he was floating through the air on her gaze. He sighed.

Then he sat up straight. He was here on business. He was here to look out for the prince. "You got a granddaughter?"

The woman shook her head. "I'm a widow." She let the word drift in the air with all its meaning wafting behind it. "I never had children." She smiled. "You married?"

Brighty was sure his face was red. "Me? No."

She grabbed a cup from the counter and sat across from Brighty. "Glad to meet you. I'm Mabel."

Brighty scratched his head. What was he supposed to do now? Nobody could blame him, could they? He had tried for the prince. He had. He tried to talk to the crazy woman. He looked in Mabel's eyes, then looked down at his hands. Blue would have better luck. And Ali . . . Ali was working on it. They would find somebody for the prince. They were better at this kind of thing. He didn't know what he was doing. Anybody could see that. He might as well sit and keep Mabel company.

Mabel poured black coffee from the pitcher into the cup. Brighty sighed when the bittersweet aroma reached his nose. He had done all he could do. He looked back into Mabel's eyes and let the sight and the smell carry him away.

Ali checked his watch. He didn't have time. He didn't have time, and Moor wasn't interested. Besides, he was sure that Brighty and Blue would drum up more business for Moor than he could handle. Ali walked through the door of his nine-o'clock class and slid in the last seat in the last row just in the nick of time.

Blue stood at the bus stop, his teeth chattering. The mornings were starting to get colder, and he didn't know how he ended up the one at the bus stop looking for women for the prince. The bus thing was Brighty's idea—at least that was the way he remembered it. Instead, though, that trickster had wangled his way into the grocery store while he stood here outside in the cold. The wind wasn't biting, but it was announcing pretty clearly that the seasons weren't changing; they were changed. All the summer clothes were gone. Women were wearing sweaters and light coats. Sitting in the backyard all the time, he had forgotten how pretty they could be and how alive they sounded, even on the way to jobs they hated. Their voices sparkled like frosty pastel colors bouncing on the chilly breeze.

Blue adjusted his black tie. He knew he looked like he was going to a funeral, but it was the only suit he had, and he felt it was important to properly represent the prince. He shook his head. He sure hoped that Brighty had remembered to wear a clean undershirt.

Blue had been standing outside for a couple of hours now, about the time when women go to work, watching the bus lines form. There were lots of brown-skinned women, many of them pretty. But most of them wore wedding rings. Of the ones not wearing rings, most were too thin, or there was too much on top with too little on the bottom. He never would have thought that it would be so difficult to find a woman suitable to be the prince's wife. If they were the right shape or size, then they were not brown. Things weren't going well. And he was not a patient man . . . his wife had always said that about him. Besides, it was too chilly to be patient.

Blue was not a praying man, not unless things got really tight. It wasn't that he didn't believe in God, he just didn't have much to say. But he was getting cold, and he was not a man to refuse help. So he began to pray a silent deal. *Okay, Lord, I'm about to get on this next bus that comes. If you can do all the things the prince say you can do, this ought to be easy for you. You're the God of Abraham and Isaac and that other guy—men like the prince that just got to have a certain kind of woman. I'm getting tired and it's cold out here. Now, I'm gone get on this bus. I'm gone take my seat and close my eyes. When I open my eyes, I want you to make the prince's wife be coming up the aisle. If you do, then I will know for sure that you are real and I will go to church . . . some Sunday. At least for the wedding. Amen.*

When the Number Fourteen bus came, Blue boarded, paid the exact fair, sat down, and closed his eyes. When he opened them again, he saw a pair of brown legs coming up the aisle. His eyes followed from the ankles to the knees, then followed the hem of the skirt to the curve of the hip. So far, so good. With his hand guarding his eyes, so he wouldn't be too obvious as he looked, Blue's eyes drifted discreetly to the woman's collar. Things were looking up.

He felt that exhilaration that people feel when it looks like God is about to do something they had thought impossible. His heart began to flutter and he was momentarily light-headed. It is a strange feeling to feel infinite-sized attention; it is infinitely flattering—like the reaction brought on by fawning attention from a love interest you thought had never noticed you—only exponentially so. It is overwhelming, it is too much to hope for that the God of the whole universe has been listening, and is responding, especially to a silly prayer. It is too much to hope for, and one teeters between giddy belief and relief, and the fear of daring to hope. Blue held his breath and willed his gaze upward. It was too good to be true. Her mouth looked sweet. There were none of the lines that were the dead give-away of a mean, pouting woman. Her nose was like a cute little button. And her eyes, her eyes were . . . green.

Green! Blue groaned and slumped back in his seat. To get so far, only to be disappointed—it was cruel. He stared out the window and shook his head. And it wasn't just the eyes; her hair was blonde. There was no way in the world the prince was going to go for a woman like that. No way in the world.

Well, God, you had your chance.

Fighting disappointment, Blue rode in silence. *Maybe it's her?* No, the prince had been clear—no funny eyes, no fake hair. She was so, so close. Until she got off, Blue looked at the back of the young woman's head and shook his own. When she got off the bus, he took off his tie. He rode to the end of the line and back, and then went inside his home and shut the door. Maybe some warm breakfast would make him feel better.

20

Mary

Glass and silverware clinked together. The room was crowded, and the constant conversation crested and fell gently, almost as though it was orchestrated. Waiters and waitresses in black pants, white shirts, with white aprons tied about their waists scurried quietly among the tables, taking orders and delivering food. Despite its size and the crowd, the restaurant was cozy. The aromas of coffee and fresh baked bread were comforting. Though the room was actually elegant, it reminded Mary of a country kitchen. There was also something golden about the atmosphere, and all the activity made her wonder what it must be like inside of a beehive.

Latrice inspected her fingernails while she laughed. "Oh, come on, girl. It couldn't have been that bad." As Mary told her story, Latrice, Naomi, and Thelma took turns clapping their hands together, shaking their heads, and covering their mouths to muffle their laughter.

"Floyd ain't that bad. He's a good old guy," said Latrice.

Mary looked around the table. "Well, let's just say he's making me think twice—no, forty times—about this dating and romance thing. Maybe I haven't been looking to see just how green the grass is on this side—Floyd helped me understand what it is to be single and satisfied. Or, maybe I'm learning to appreciate the water in the well I already have." It was good to be able to joke now with her friends about what had made her want to jump from a speeding car.

"If I could have gotten to you that night, Latrice, I would have killed you. I mean it. . . . Stop laughing, you all. It was a disaster, and he was showing me off like a new car . . . and to his ex-wife, too. How tacky is that?" She took a drink of her half-and-half. It was one of her favorite things about this restaurant—she loved the sweetness of the tea and the sugary tartness of the lemonade mixed together. Half-and-half was a Baltimore delicacy like crab cakes and turkey with seasoned sauerkraut. "I don't think I'm cut out for dating."

Naomi tossed her good, quality purchased hair. "Oh, girl, you are just getting started. You can't judge all men by that one man. Besides, me and Thelma could have told you not to go out with any of Latrice's hand-me-downs."

Mary began to cough, choking on her drink. "A hand-me-down? No you didn't!" she managed to sputter. She shook her head. Latrice was unbelievable!

"Of course, girl. You know how Latrice is."

Latrice nudged Naomi. "Hush, girl. Mind your business." Latrice looked like she was fighting to hold back the huge smile that was spreading across her face.

Naomi ignored the shushing and continued talking and laughing. "Now, you know Latrice. She is not about to let a man get by her without trying him out. She is so trifling." Latrice played at reaching to cover Naomi's mouth. Naomi dodged and continued her teasing counsel. "I don't know why you went out with him in the first place. If Latrice didn't want him, you know he had to be a reject." While chuckling, she high-fived Thelma across the table. Soon the four of them were convulsed in laughter that interrupted the symphony of sound in the room, so much that some of the other players stared. Mary was sorry about disturbing them, but not sorry enough to stop laughing. It felt good to laugh way down deep.

Naomi wiped a tear from her eye. "I love her, but, Mary, you know Latrice is a trip!"

"I know that's right." Thelma raised one eyebrow, trying to catch her breath. "Me and Naomi were both trying to figure out why you would even take dating advice from Latrice anyway."

Mary looked at Latrice, who was pretending to pout, then back at Naomi and Thelma. "You all didn't say that when you were talking me into getting a makeover."

Thelma raised both eyebrows, laughing, and then pointed across the table at Latrice's hands. "Beauty tips, yes. Dating tips, no. You were always a smart girl, Mary. We figured you would know better than to listen to Latrice." She turned on the booth seat to face Mary. The pleather seat squeaked as she turned. "So, was there anything good about your date? Did he compliment you?"

You could only take this kind of teasing from good friends. Mary played along and put on a poker face. "He liked my eyes."

Thelma shook her shoulders like she was dancing. She looked at Mary, Naomi, and Latrice. "See, I told you—the eyes have it every time."

"They had it, all right. He told me he liked green eyes, and I was tempted to pop them out right there at the table and give them to him." The four women laughed. "I don't think I'll ever look at another rib the same way again. I just wanted to get home."

Latrice, who had been quiet and feigning offense during most of the teasing, smirked. "Okay, so the date might not have been so hot, but it's better than that sad computer dating service you were talking about joining."

"Oh, no, not computer dating!" Naomi shook her head and looked at Latrice. "Girl, you are right. I have to give you some credit for that save." She brushed the hair out of her face and looked across the table. "Come on, now, Mary. Things aren't that bad. Not yet, anyway."

"I don't know, I'm just not sure I'm cut out for all of this." Mary could hear the pleading in her voice. Almost as though she was hoping, once they heard how bad things were, they would let her off the dating hook. "And then, on the way over here, there was an old man checking me out on the bus." She shivered. "It gave me the creeps, you all. Especially after the Floyd episode. The old man was dressed like a mortician or something, and he just kept staring at me." Mary looked at the place setting in front of her, and then back at her friends. "The one day I play hooky from work and decide to meet with you all for brunch—it was like the principal or the crypt keeper had caught me or something. I just had this strange feeling looking at him. He kept looking at me like I was disappointing him. I still feel guilty." Maybe she had paid enough dating dues and they would give her a reprieve.

Thelma winked at Mary. She tried not to stare. She had seen Thelma's eyes many times now, but the blue still distracted her. She had to focus hard to follow the conversation. "Don't worry, Mary. You're just suffering from TDD—traumatic date disorder. And the only way to overcome it is to date again, quickly. Only don't date any more of Latrice's scrubs." She giggled. "So was the old crypt keeper cute?"

Before she could think of an answer, the waiter arrived with their food. She turned all her attention to the plate in front of her. Mary added salt and pepper to her eggs, buttered her biscuit, and closed her eyes when she took a bite. At least for a moment, she didn't have to think about dating. She could feel her breathing become slower and deeper.

The snapping sound of Latrice's fingers startled her eyes open. "Girl, this is a public place, okay? The way you are eating that biscuit is sinful."

Thelma laughed. "Let her eat. While she's relaxed, Naomi and I will tell her about the dates that we have planned for her."

"After that bad experience with Floyd, you'll feel better if you meet the guy first."

Mary's eyes narrowed in on Thelma. Of course, the look didn't stop her. Thelma was the queen of looks, and she just kept talking.

"He's really a nice guy. Honestly," Thelma tried to convince her, throwing her hand up in testimony like she was swearing on the Bible in court. "I met him at a college recruiting function. He's in the military and he's a cutie!" Her eyes rolled up in her head. Then she touched Mary's arm to reassure her. "But not so cute you'll be intimidated. He has a booth set up at the Convention Center. Just go on by the center, take a walk by his booth. See if you like him, and if you do, you can say hello and the date will be on. He's expecting you. No pressure!"

Reggie was cute. Medium height, with dark curly hair, dark eyes, and freckles. He wasn't her normal type. But, then again, as Latrice had said, she didn't really have a type, did she?

So she introduced herself. He didn't have two heads. He had a nice smile. "Why don't you drive your car to my place, so you won't feel stranded, and we'll take it from there. Dinner, okay?" He only had one dimple. *How did that happen? Just one dimple.* "Then we'll see how it goes. No pressure. We'll play it by ear." He patted her hand. "Don't worry, it will be okay. I'm not an ax murderer." That was when she relaxed . . . a little.

The night had cooled. She stood underneath a streetlight. *It will be okay.* Mary tried to ignore the run in her stockings. If she didn't call attention to it, he would never notice it. Men didn't notice those kinds of things, did they? And if they noticed, they didn't care. Only women obsessed over runs and tiny spots. She held her shoulder wrap with one hand and held the bottom of her skirt together with the other so that it would not blow over her head while she climbed the hill to his apartment building. She hadn't bothered to tell him she didn't have a car. If she'd known the bus stop was at the bottom of such a steep hill, she would have opted for flats instead of heels . . . or maybe a cab.

Mary laid a hand over her heart to calm herself. It was all going to be okay. He wasn't an ax murderer.

As soon as she pushed the buzzer, he answered the door. "Come on in." He looked like he had been waiting for her.

She could see from the doorway that his place was clean and well lit. It was painted that off-white color that all apartments are painted so that the renters won't know they have white walls.

She was overdressed. He was wearing white jeans and a T-shirt. "Wow! You look nice." Maybe he was going to change. "Come on in." She was still standing outside, looking this way and that. "Come in, okay?"

He took her wrap. "I hope you don't mind. I decided to cook myself." Mary froze in the foyer. His smile melted her. "It's okay, remember? I'm not an ax murderer."

He's not an ax murderer. And I'm an adult. So I'm going to calm myself down. Breathe slowly, Mary. One breath at a time.

He walked her into the kitchen. On the stove there were pots boiling. He lifted a lid. "See? No bunnies," he quipped. Instead, there was red sauce that smelled of garlic and Italian sausages, and green peppers and onions that tumbled through the sauce as it simmered. "It's been cooking most of the day. I wanted to impress you." He lifted a long-handled fork from the counter and stirred the linguini noodles. He lifted one from the pot, then let it fall back into the water. "Two more minutes." It was working; she was impressed. Her face felt flushed.

He pointed to a small table with two chairs. "Why don't you have a seat?" He pulled the chair out for her. *A gentleman.* "You look lovely. You smell lovely." He folded his hands over his heart. "If I could sing opera for you, I would." He sighed and smiled, and then looked down at her feet. "Since we're eating here, why don't you get comfortable? You can pull off your shoes, if you like." He smiled. "They look lovely on you, though. Keep them on if you like. Whatever suits you." He turned back to the stove and back to fussing over the pots. He was so positive, so accommodating, so attentive. *And he cooks!*

"Have you been to Europe?" Using blue and white potholders, he lifted the pot of pasta from the stove and carried it to the sink to drain. The muscles in his arms rippled, and Mary could feel a goofy smile on her face. She looked away, hoping he wouldn't catch her staring.

Mary shook her head. She was overwhelmed by it all—by the smells, by his attentiveness. She didn't know whether to grab her wrap and run out the door, or run to the bathroom like a giggling schoolgirl and call Thelma to report her good fortune over the phone. *"Girl, you won't believe this man!"*

"They would love you in Europe. Especially the German men, they would eat you up." He nodded. "The Italians, too." His eyes seemed to be full of stars. "They are particularly fascinated by beautiful black women."

They are particularly fascinated by beautiful black women. Reggie was certainly no Floyd. He was almost too good to be true. But here she was, seeing it with her own eyes, hearing it with her own ears. Mary held back a sigh.

After draining the pasta, he pulled a covered salad from the refrigerator along with a bottle of dressing. "I hope you don't mind vinegar and oil—it's all I have."

He took plates and glasses from the cabinets. "Would you mind looking in that drawer for silverware?" He nodded to indicate which drawer. "Beneath it are napkins." *Napkins? Real cloth napkins? Who is this guy, and where has he been hiding?*

They sat down to dinner, and instead of being in Baltimore, it felt as though she were feasting some place far away and romantic. The flavors from the sauce curled around her tongue, and she suddenly was dining along the Mediterranean, or perhaps near a canal in Venice. As they talked, she could see strings of lights twinkling and hear men singing as they played mandolins.

Reggie looked at her and smiled. "*Bella!*" And the one word sent her drifting through clouds of perfumed flowers, riding at night in a gondola through water that gently sprayed the sides of the boat, her dangling hands, her face, and her hair.

When they were finished, he gathered the plates. Mary rose to help. "No, you sit down. I wanted to do something special for you. You relax." Mary sat down, finally relaxing enough to take off her shoes, and curled her feet underneath her. She watched while he scraped and cleaned, making sure that each item, before it was put away, looked just like new. It felt so comfortable and inviting. "I hope it was a pleasant experience for you. I'm not much of a chef."

"Oh, yes."

Reggie extended his hand. "I'd like to spend some more time with you, if you don't mind."

"Oh, yes." Mary took his hand and rose to her feet. Maybe they would dance or take a walk under the stars.

"Maybe a little television."

"Oh, yes." Television was good.

He led her from the kitchen into the living room. It was empty. He explained, "I haven't been here long. I'm still getting things together. I see lots of possibilities for this room. I've never been very good at decorating. Maybe you have some ideas."

"Oh, yes." She could imagine impressionist paintings on the wall, maybe a mural. A grand sofa with lots and lots of pillows.

He continued holding her hand. Her shoes dangled from her other one. He led her through a doorway and turned on the light switch. A floor lamp lit. "We'll have to watch in here. I don't have a sofa yet."

The large bed was covered with a green plaid bedspread. "Sit down," Reggie said indicating a side of the bed. As she looked around the room, Mary reminded herself of the lovely dinner they had just shared and that he was not an ax murderer. *He's attentive. He's romantic. He's charming.* He lifted the remote from the long mirrored dresser and turned on the television. There was also a dresser that faced the side of the bed on which Mary sat. Reggie walked to the other side of the bed, removed his watch, and laid it on the nightstand. He kicked off his shoes, sat down, and then swung his feet up on the bed.

He is not an ax murderer.

"Relax," he said. "I got all this stuff today—the table and chairs, this bedroom furniture. They were having a special at the rent-to-own place." The boat they had been riding through Venetian waters came to a screeching halt, and the mandolins stopped playing. "The deal was, you could choose two rooms of furniture for almost the price of one." The perfumed flowers wilted, and Mary tried not to crumple with them. *He hasn't really done anything wrong . . . yet.*

"I figured if I cooked, I could afford the furniture, so I knew we needed the kitchen set." He sighed and rubbed his hand over the comforter. "I figured the bed was more important than a living room couch, don't you think?" He winked. *He is not an ax murderer. He is not an ax murderer.* "They threw in this bedspread and this cool lamp." He clapped twice and the lamp went out, just before the twinkling lights went out along the Mediterranean. And then Reggie, who had been a handsome exotic in her European fantasy, became a monstrous, drooling octopus crawling from the canal trying to entangle her in its arms. He was no longer a man with one dimple, but a beast with one eye. Mary slugged him, kicked him, grabbed her shoes, and grabbed her wrap on the way out the door, with Reggie close on her heels.

"Hey! What's the matter with you? Are you crazy? Yeah, you're crazy, and your perfume stinks!" She could hear him yelling behind her as she ran down the hill in the dark. She didn't look back. There was enough anger in his voice to tell her to keep going, to keep moving or she was going to be in hot water. "I paid a lot of money for this furniture!" Mary kicked off her shoes and ran, looking to hail the first taxi she saw.

21

Puddin

If *she didn't get* her hands out of the hot dishwater soon, they were going to be ready for some melted butter. The palms of her brown hands looked like red lobsters.

Puddin stood at the sink looking out through the yellow curtains that framed the window that looked out on the backyard. *"Honey, I think the flowers are gone be in bloom, and everything's gone be just fine for our friends and family get-together."* Joe had been talking about it constantly, especially since they'd come back from Texas, coming in and out with cranberry bushes, fall-colored mums, black-eyed Susans, blooms, gourds, bags of soil, and all kinds of gardening tools. *"I want the yard to be just right!"* He was excited about it, and he was excited that the family had asked him to speak. She wondered how thrilled his Aunt Evangelina, the one everybody called Meemaw, would feel about him speaking if she knew he had been doing more than just cultivating the soil in his own backyard.

"Precious Lord, take my hand, lead me on, let me stand." She half hummed, half sang and wondered how long it was going to take Joe to get himself out of the house. She had been waiting for what seemed like an hour.

It was Wednesday evening, and she knew he would be rushing out the door soon—just like every Wednesday. But the last few weeks, Joe had first gotten a telephone call and then rushed out the door early. It wasn't unusual for him to get calls; the brothers were always calling. It wasn't unusual for him to go out on Wednesday evenings; Wednesday night was the night he met with the men's group for Bible study.

What was unusual was how he grabbed for the phone when these new calls came in—grabbed so he could reach it first, even if she was closer. What was unusual was how big his eyes got and how he ran to another room to whisper. What was unusual was how much care he took getting ready, including wearing cologne. What was unusual was how excited he was. What was unusual was that he rushed to leave nearly two hours before Bible study began. *Can't we eat a little earlier on Wednesdays so I won't be late for my meeting? I hate to be late.* What was even more unusual was that though he was never late *before* he began leaving earlier, now he was late all the time. One of the brothers had called to check on him, that's how she knew. *We were just worried. Brother Joe is always so reliable. Well, I'm sure he's on his way.* What was even more unusual was that she had stopped caring.

Let him go. When he left, she went. It was much easier for her to go down the hall and check on her files. There were a couple hundred of them—profiles of men and women, most of them younger. All hers. When he was gone, she pored over them, doted on them. She worried for them and prayed for them that they would find the perfect mate, the perfect match. To someone else they might just be computer files, but to her they were children she had never had. They were her babies. Some of them were the age her baby would have been.

For a moment, she let herself think, daydream about her baby . . . how he could have been. Today, in her imagination, he was a curly-haired boy. And just when her heart was about to break, Puddin shut off the dream and thought about her files, about her living children.

They were hers. She didn't have to share them with anyone. Not with Joe, not even with the doctor. These children wouldn't be stripped from her arms before their first breath. They were already here, healthy and perfect. She wouldn't have to give them up to be taken away. She could love them, and they would never hurt her. And she could help them be happy, she could help them find the person to help make their lives more full and more complete. They needed her.

Joe kissed her behind her right ear. She hadn't heard him walk up behind her. When he hugged her, she tried not to flinch. "Is everything okay?"

"Of course, Joe. Why wouldn't everything be okay?" She kept looking out the window. Joe laid his head on her shoulder. She wanted to nudge him away.

"You just seem distant. You hardly ever smile anymore. When I try to touch you . . . you never want me to touch you anymore. . . . Are you mad at me about something?"

She turned her head and kissed him on the cheek—whatever it took to get him out of the house, to get his hands off of her. "That's silly. Why would I be mad, Joe? You're the perfect husband. It's probably just the change . . . you know how we women are." Yes, he knew about her and many other women, but she wasn't going to worry about that. Not anymore. He wasn't going to hurt her anymore.

He pulled one of her hands from the water and kissed the palm. "Look how shriveled they are. What are you doing, baby? We don't have that many dishes, do we? I brought in carryout."

Puddin looked in his eyes and hoped, for a second, to see that there was still some humiliation in him. That his eyes would blink, something, anything that would tell her that he was embarrassed or at least uncomfortable about lying to her. But there was nothing, just a veneer of sincerity—a thin covering that fooled everyone— that would have fooled her if she hadn't seen him with her own eyes.

He kissed her forehead. "Let's talk tonight. When I get back, okay? Tonight."

"Sure, Joe. Sure." Then he was out the door. He was out the door; she was out of the water, down the hall, and into her files.

Men seeking women. Women seeking men. There were different ages, races, and religious affiliations. Some indicated preferences about their fantasy mate's hair color, eye color, height, shape, and weight. Some gave few details about themselves, and others gave so many she could have almost painted a picture. They gave themselves names to be used on the computer, secret identities. Assigned to their names were all the bits of information—a number of her babies even provided pictures of themselves—that Puddin imagined as dots of color. And if she moved the dots about and arranged them just right—pairing them perfectly—she would create a mosaic of her making. So far, she had let the computer do all the matching, but soon she would be ready. She was waiting for the right moment, the right couple.

She poured through the women. Name after name, she memorized bits of information so that in addition to the computer sorting their preferences, she could become familiar with them. She was systematic; no more than fifty from each category per night—that was all the time she could steal away from Joe. Not that he cared, but it was easier, she was freer when he was gone. When he was gone, she could sit for hours and hours, and it was as if no time had passed.

Puddin stretched her arms over her head, then looked to check the time. She still had an hour. She closed the women's files. With a few keystrokes, the men's files lay open before her. She smiled and breathed deeply. Her eyelids lowered. She ran her hand over the screen as she looked at the information, the dots that made up hundreds of men. Somehow she felt closest to them . . . maybe it was the baby she lost. . . . She imagined what they looked like, what their voices sounded like. She looked to see what kinds of women each one preferred.

"Puddin, what are you doing, honey?"

The dream broke apart around her and gave way under her feet so that she scrambled for a perch.

It was Joe.

In her panic she looked at the clock—*wrong move, a dead giveaway*—and pushed at the power button. *Another wrong move.*

He was back early.

If she were calmer, sneakier, and more experienced, she would have smiled. She would have turned around and kissed him. She would have been prepared and known to hit the minimize key. She would have had an explanation ready. "Joe, you're home early!"

"What are you doing, Puddin?"

She hoped that he could not hear her heart. Funny how the mind works in crisis, because all the while he spoke she was in junior high school. She could hear her teacher's voice reading famous Baltimore poet Edgar Allan Poe's "The Tell-Tale Heart." As the heartbeat of Poe's story played in her ears, providing background to Joe's spoken words, she tried to pick out words to say, to string them together like beads on necklaces. "Nothing, Joe. I was just using the computer. I was just sending some email."

He kneeled next to her. "That wasn't email, Puddin." His eyes were wet, and none of it made sense. "I knew something was going on . . . I could feel it. Is this what it's all been about, Puddin? I never thought this could happen to you . . . to us. We can talk about it. We can get help." He looked like he had been betrayed. He looked shamed. More than that, he looked hurt. "I know there's somebody . . . somebody at the church will help us."

"Everything is fine, Joe." It was happening too quickly for her to process the information.

"What's going on, Puddin? I can feel things are different. Why can't we talk about it? Why can't you tell me the truth?"

"There's nothing going on, Joe." Things were happening too quickly for her to sort it all out, too quickly to correct him. *You've got the problem, Joe. Not me.*

"We can work it out, Puddin." He grabbed her from the chair and into his arms. He sounded so wounded and so determined. "I swear we can. Don't worry, baby, we're gone work it out." He squeezed her to him, and she thought she felt one of his tears on her cheek. Soon she realized she was crying with him.

22

Moor

Moor *breathed deeply* so that the tears would not come. The letter in his hands had traveled a long way. He ran a finger over the postage markings. He imagined his grandmother walking and walking to find someone to write the letter, and then walking and walking to mail it.

My dear grandson, mzuri mwana,

Most days I am happy here with my mountains, but I am an old woman and sometimes I cannot help but to miss you. I think of you, and when my heart is about to break, I think of you as a boy. Then I begin to say the praise for you, to thank God for you. "God, I thank you for this grandson," I say. "He is a very wise man because he is your man and because he comes from a long line of men so wise that people walk for many, many days to talk to them about their troubles and their dreams. He is a very strong man because he is your man and because he comes from a long line of men who have been warriors and providers. Even when there was no food in the village, these fathers walked many miles to hunt the dangerous valleys to feed their people. Thank you for my grandson, this tall and beautiful man. Tall and beautiful because he is your man, and because he comes from a line of fathers so beautiful in form that women from lands far away pay them bride price and beg these men to marry them. Of course, it helps also, Father, that these men come from mothers so beautiful the sun sometimes weeps with shame because it cannot outshine their beauty. I am proud of this man, my grandson, dear God. Please keep him safe until he returns. Don't let him be lonely far away. Lonely can make a man crazy, God. You know. So don't listen to him, though he is a wise grandson, when he tells you how and when to send a wife. You listen to yourself, God. Who knows such things but you?

My grandson, your family is fine. Be a good man. Say your prayers. Study diligently to show yourself approved of God. Do your job. Do not try to tell God how to do His job.

Moor stopped reading for a moment and laughed. The words were truly his grandmother's words. He sighed when he thought of the words of praise . . . *a very wise man . . . a very strong man . . . a very beautiful man . . . .* He missed the phrases, the jewels. She had repeated those words to him every day of his life since he could remember. She and all the other grandmothers had spoken his destiny to him and to their grandchildren. He lifted the letter and began to read again.

Listen and obey when He calls to you, for only God can know when your season of separation is over. I have been thinking that this thing you are doing—"I do not need a wife!"—is no longer obedience, but maybe now an issue of pride. You are saying to yourself, "I am a strong man. I can be alone." You are a strong man, but do not force God to show you the limits of your strength. It is not you keeping you celibate, but the grace of God. Do not confuse His strength with your own. Do not become one of those wicked people who think their self-righteousness makes them better than other people.

You have needed time to heal and to be made whole—time alone with God. That time is over. Now, I am afraid that you are hiding—afraid to see if you are really healed—and calling it virtue. Disobedience is not a virtue.

You have proved you are a strong man. Now, you must prove that you are a wise man—for to do even a good thing longer than the Lord intends is not wise.

I have been praying for you, and even here, far away, I feel that what was once peace for you has now become loneliness. Search your heart and see if what I am saying is true. I think you are ready for a wife. You are a great man, but do not be foolish and think that even a great man can tell the Lord God when He

*is ready for that great man's heart to turn to love. Trust God, and
do not try to fight Him on this thing—your arms are too short.*
Love,
Your grandmother

Moor folded the letter and held it to his nose, hoping for some
scent of his grandmother, some scent of home. He slipped it back
inside the envelope, and slid the letter into the shirt pocket nearest
his heart. *Now, you must prove that you are a wise man.* "Yes, Grandmother," he said.

Ali bounded up the steps and into the library. The paper that
was due was pressing at his temples and making it hard to think of
anything else. He looked around the library. He didn't have time to
scout for girls for Moor. Not that there were many women here that
fit Moor's specifications, anyway. There was one brown-skinned sister stooped over a pile of books, but Ali knew her and knew that
she was married. There was better hunting in the 'hood. Blue and
Brighty would have better luck. They knew the people, and the
odds were considerably better there of contacting a brown-skinned
sister than they were here. Besides, Moor had made it pretty clear
that he wasn't interested in anything casual and he didn't have time
to marry. The prince wasn't ready—period, dot, end. He'd made
that very clear.

Ali stretched his arms over his head and exhaled his frustration.
He had so much work to do, so many papers to write, and so much
studying. He was going to have to let this thing with Moor go and
get down to business. It wasn't his responsibility. He didn't know
why it had even been on his mind.

He looked around the library again. It would take something
God-sized, Allah-sized, for him to find a woman here. He loved the
two funny old guys and enjoyed being a part of their back-street
antics, but they were on their own on this one. Ali found an open
workstation and plugged in his laptop.

Though he looked at the computer screen, he could see

Brighty's face and hear his words. *"What kind of black man are you? We talking about a brother in need of your help, and all you can do is whine. I'm going to the grocery store. Why can't you help out? I guess since you got a woman, you don't care about nobody else."* Ali knew it was Brighty's way of saying that he fit in, that he was one of them. Half joking, half serious in what he said, Brighty was including him not only in the search for Moor's woman, but also in the game of dozens that had been running between Brighty and Blue for decades. Blue only joked with him about his color because it wasn't an issue between them.

He could see Brighty's earnest expression as the old man sat at the table in the alley with Blue holding court. Ali pressed his hand to his mouth so he wouldn't laugh out loud. They were taking it seriously about finding Moor a wife. The two old guys would be crushed if he didn't at least do something. It would be like breaking trust. Whenever Moor was not around, the two old guys mourned about how they had failed—how they'd blown it at the grocery stores and on the bus—about how the prince was never going to find a wife, and how his life would come to ruin. They had not been able to stop talking about it for the last week or so.

"You got to come through for us, Ali," Blue had said during one of their conversations. "Yeah! Or we gone end up going to church for sure!" Brighty had wailed.

The library was quiet, but Ali always felt the ghosts of many minds—many intellects pushing at him to move and make use of the time he still had. He checked his watch. He took a deep breath. He would have to move quickly. Ali pulled up the Charm City News personals site and quickly entered everything he knew about Moor. He couldn't let Brighty and Blue down. It would take only a few minutes, and then he could get on with what was important. His paper.

Once Moor left the lighted streets, the alley was so black that it was difficult to make out shapes. He stopped to let his sight adjust to the darkness. It was cooler now, and night was coming sooner. The summertime sounds of children playing outside at nine were gone. It was the time of night in his village at home when men would have retired to their own homes. If the men met, it would normally be friends—three or four meeting in a home, sharing conversation, a drink, a small something to eat.

He should be home, but he was restless. It was a weeknight and he had work tomorrow. It wasn't safe, but he was restless. He needed company, so he came to see if his friends were still awake. Ahead he could see orange firelight and shadows moving at the meeting place. As he approached, he could see light on Blue's face, cut with dark shadows. Brighty, standing a few feet away from the flames, was almost invisible in the darkness. He could not see it, but from the shape of his outline, he knew that Ali was sitting on a concrete block. They sat in view of the fire, a handsome street city council— even keeping watch over the city by night. As he drew closer, the flames from the iron can revealed more while they jumped and flickered in the drum. The firelight and the shadows were like orange vertical waves that multiplied in size on the house behind the men. The waves flickered and gave off heat as he got closer.

Blue pointed first. "Look who it is creeping up here now." He smiled.

Ali and Brighty turned to look. Brighty scratched at the wool on his face. "What's got you out so late, Prince?" he asked.

Moor didn't have an answer, so he didn't speak. He grabbed another cinder block so that he could sit in the warmth and light. A musty smell met him as he moved the cement square.

Blue nodded. "We was just talking about you. What you doing out here so late at night?"

Again, Moor had no answer. There was no problem; no memory pulled him, there was no face that would not let his mind rest. He had no words of his own, but in an attempt to be polite, in an attempt to explain, he read the letter from his grandmother.

Brighty rubbed his stomach and smiled. "That's beautiful the way she talk about you, Prince. Your grandmother sure must love you. You know, the way she say all that stuff about you and about your relatives."

Moor fingered the words on the paper. "It is our tradition. All mothers and grandmothers say such things to their children. It makes us grow up straight. We know the path behind us, and the one that lies ahead of us, and that it is a good path." He sighed. "My grandmother is a wise woman. She knows the seasons of things." Moor sighed again. He had hidden his loneliness, even from himself. Now his grandmother's words had unveiled it. At first, he was sure, he had chosen to be alone out of obedience, then out of discipline and strength. But as he searched his heart, he had to confess that pride in his ability to be strong was what now kept him alone . . . that, and perhaps, a small bit of fear. *Now you must prove that you are a wise man.* He sighed again. He had come to be with his friends, to hear their wise counsel, to let them know of his confession and surrender.

Blue nodded. "Nothing to say about it. It's just time." He appeared to be writing with his finger on the surface of the table. "Me and Brighty didn't have much luck finding you a woman. We kind of got sidetracked." He pointed a wrinkled finger. "But Ali, there, got something for you. We was just talking about it."

Ali held up a white sheet of paper. "Here's to new beginnings."

23

Mary

Mary shook her head. "It started out so well. It was the perfect beginning." She shook her finger and mocked Reggie's voice. *"I paid a lot of money for this furniture!"* She pressed her hand to her face. "That's what he actually was yelling. There I was flying down the hill like Batman and he's yelling crazy stuff at me like he's the Riddler. And what did he mean by the crack about my perfume?" It had been more than two weeks since the date, and she was still offended.

"About your perfume?" Naomi's voice trailed off. "Who knows? Who cares?" Naomi had her arm around Mary's shoulder. "It's like that sometimes, you know? You just can't tell." The yellow-orange color of the sofa almost matched her hair.

"What was that supposed to mean? The other? He rented furniture, so that meant I was supposed to give him some?"

"Well, that's how some men think." Naomi tossed her head. "And to tell you the truth, that's how it is now. People don't think it's such a big deal anymore. You probably *were* acting crazy to him. Most of us women have gotten over thinking that we're giving a man something special when we give ourselves to him. Men used to think they had to marry you, or at least take you out—wine you and dine you."

She shrugged her shoulders. "Not anymore. We don't think much of ourselves, so they don't think much of us." She took her arm from around Mary's shoulders and poured tea from the pot into the cups on the tray in front of them. Naomi crossed her legs. "Sometimes I get confused by all of it. Am I supposed to be liberated? So I can do whatever I want with whomever I want, whenever I want?" Naomi took a sip from the delicate, elegant cup in her hand. "Sometimes liberation is a good feeling, a powerful feeling. Then something like the Reggie thing happens, or . . . surprise! Even worse, you start having feelings. You know, those love or attachment feelings for someone when it was supposed to be casual, no strings attached." She shuddered and shook her head. The two of them laughed. "And you're right back to feeling like the guy got away with something and you got left with nothing." Naomi sipped her tea. "It can be confusing sometimes. And to be fair, the men are confused, too. But then they always were."

They giggled, and then Naomi continued. "They don't know what's up or down. They don't know what to expect. All the signals they get are telling them they're not men if they don't make a move on us. And we think there's something wrong with them if they don't."

Mary sighed. All of it was too confusing, too much drama. That's why she didn't want to get involved . . . well, she didn't want to be alone . . . but she didn't . . . she didn't know what she wanted.

Naomi kept talking. "It's rare for a man to run across a woman who thinks like you, Mary. How are they supposed to know how to behave?" Naomi lifted her cup, took a sip, then set it back down. "And we forget that it hasn't been that long. Younger women, young girls, today don't know anything about it . . . and even we forget there was a day not long ago when women weren't casual about sex. We saw the change happen, but young girls don't know anything about it, or how it has changed men. They don't know how men used to enjoy women, how they liked us, how they delighted in us."

Mary suddenly felt old. She had been around long enough to see a social norm change, and to have the feeling that she might have liked the old way better.

Naomi felt around in her pocket, pulled out a folded piece of paper and tossed it in the trash. "That, my dear, was the name and telephone number of the guy that was going to be my contribution to the resurrection of your dating life." She laughed. "After what you've been through, I think I'm going to let it alone. Just let that thing die!" She threw back her head and laughed.

Mary felt relieved. Finally, some dating mercy.

Naomi tilted her head and giggled. "Have you thought more about computer dating?"

Mary spoke quickly before Naomi could withdraw her pardon. "I don't think so. I'm kind of thinking I've had enough." Mary picked up her cup and held it in both hands to warm them. "The date with Reggie started out so well. Then . . . poof! Fantasy Island was no more!" She shook her head and sighed. "I don't want to be treated like that. Maybe I'm old fashioned. Or maybe I've been celibate by choice after all. But I don't like the feeling that a man thinks he's paid for me with dinner or with buying furniture. The way he was yelling was like it was not even my choice, but like it was normal, like I was doing him wrong." She took a sip from her cup. "I don't like being alone. I don't like being lonely. But I guess I've gotten so wrapped up in God that I'm spoiled."

Naomi tilted her head and raised an eyebrow. "Spoiled how?"

"At first, when my grandmother died, I was so lonely."

Naomi nodded. "I remember."

"The first night at the house, after the funeral, after everyone was gone, I thought I was going to lose it, you know?" As she spoke, Mary could remember how empty the house seemed, and how cold and abandoned she felt on the inside. "I tried everything I knew. I turned both of the televisions up really loud. I had the radio going. I cut myself a piece of cake and got a huge scoop of ice cream." She giggled briefly to relieve some of the tension she was feeling.

"Oh, girl." Naomi put her arm around Mary again and pushed her head to her shoulder. "Why didn't you call one of us? We would have stayed with you. I would have. I know that feeling. I know how it is to be alone, to lose your family. To be suddenly alone."

Mary nuzzled her head on Naomi's shoulder. It was comforting to have girlfriends like Naomi, Latrice, and Thelma. For all their teasing, she knew when things got hard, they were on her side. For all their teasing, she knew that they accepted who she was at heart.

Naomi sighed. "Believe me, I understand. When my husband left . . . I fought so hard for the marriage . . . and to lose my kids in the divorce, too . . . I can't even talk about them . . . or any kids. . . ." She waved her hand. "I don't want to go into all of that. We're talking about you."

Mary looked at her friend. Naomi was still heartbroken, and it was difficult to get her to talk about it. Instead of pressing, Mary went on with her own story. "I guess in my heart I knew at some point I was going to have to face it alone. All that cake, the pies and stuff leftover, I dived into it—" she laughed—"I guess I was trying to make me a party." She patted Naomi's hand and then sat up. "None of it worked, though. I was so brokenhearted. Lonely and sad. Finally, late in the night when I couldn't sleep—I guess I was afraid to sleep—I got out of bed and got on my knees and prayed. That's what my grandmother would have done."

"Yes, she would have. You had a praying grandmother."

Mary could see her grandmother on her knees, her hands pressed together in prayer. "At first, Naomi, I was just going through the motions . . . saying words I've said over and over. Then all of a sudden I felt this presence—that's the only way I know to describe it."

"I know what you mean, girl. It's like this warmth enfolds you, not like warm to the touch, but warm to the heart."

Mary set her cup down. "That's what I mean. It was like I knew somebody was there watching over me, loving me, and caring for me. And somehow I knew . . ." She looked in Naomi's eyes. She didn't know whether to say it or not. She didn't want to sound hysterical or crazy. "I knew it was the Lord."

Naomi touched her shoulder to reassure her. "I've experienced the same thing."

"Then Bible verses just kind of popped in my mind out of nowhere. Some of them I had memorized at Sunday school and stuff, but others seemed to just drop in my spirit. I ran and got my grandmother's Bible." Mary began to pantomime her memory movements. "I opened the pages and Scriptures just seemed to come alive." She could still feel the excitement she felt that night. "Words that didn't make sense to me before began to speak to my heart." She began to recite snippets of text as though she were reading, flipping through pages. "*'Let not your heart be troubled.' 'For ye shall go out with joy and be led forth with peace.' '. . . to comfort all that mourn . . . beauty for ashes, the oil of joy for mourning, the garment of praise for the spirit of heaviness.'* I knew it was the Lord, Naomi."

She paused to study Naomi's face, to look into her eyes and see if she understood. Mary thought she recognized kindness and understanding there, so she went on. "And then I read, *'He will not suffer thy foot to be moved: he that keepeth thee will not slumber. Behold, he that keepeth Israel shall neither slumber nor sleep.'*"

Mary looked down at the imaginary Bible in her hands and then back up at Naomi. "And I knew it was the Lord speaking to me through His Word, telling me I could rest, because He was on guard to keep me and watch over me."

Mary settled back in her seat and picked up her cup, feeling like she needed a sip to replenish her. It was funny how much it took out of you to risk sharing your heart, to risk sharing your spiritual feelings with even your closest friends. Maybe, she thought, it's even harder to share who you are with those you love. "I had to do it every day, to keep myself sane, you know? I had to pray and read. For a moment I thought, 'you are just using this as a crutch.' Then I thought, so what if I am? People are using pills, food, sex as crutches all the time. If prayer and taking comfort in God's presence is a crutch, it helped me." She laughed. "And it was free."

Naomi chuckled and nodded, and Mary felt even freer to speak her mind. It felt good to be talking about it. She hadn't realized how much she had been keeping inside . . . how much it needed to get out. She was probably talking too much, but she couldn't stop herself. "After a while, even after I was better, I had grown to love it so much, to enjoy the time I spent with the Lord. I found out you could talk to Him, and He talks back to our spirits."

Naomi sipped her tea and smiled. "Yes, He does."

"He teaches us. You know?"

Naomi laughed. "Yeah, if we'll listen."

"He taught me so much about who He is, how much He loves us, how kind He is. He was always there. Always caring for me. The more I read, the more I realized that He was the perfect Father and that I was His daughter, His little girl. That's what I mean about being spoiled. I got spoiled, Naomi!" Mary set her cup down and turned to fully face Naomi. "One thing about girls that are spoiled, whatever man comes along, he has to be like Daddy. He has to be able to love and provide for her like Daddy. And that's what I mean by I've been spoiled. I don't want to be lonely, but I'd rather be alone than have just any kind of man. I want a man like my heavenly Daddy, with a heart like my heavenly Daddy. God has a good heart, so I want a man with a good heart. I want a man that cares for me and prays for me. I want someone who delights in me, who sees me as a precious jewel in his crown. Not somebody that treats me like I can be bought or sold, or thrown away when he gets ready."

Naomi nodded in agreement. "I know that's right."

Mary smiled. "You know, actually, I'm grateful for Floyd and Reggie. They helped me see something in myself. You know, Naomi, I'm not perfect."

Naomi touched a hand to her heart. "I'm shocked, sugar. I thought you were," she teased.

Mary smiled at the teasing, but kept talking. "I'm not looking down my nose at anyone else, or telling them how to live their lives." Her smiled broadened. "But I'm spoiled! If I'm going to give up time that I now have to spend with my Daddy, I want to give it up for someone who is like my Daddy. The only man that's going to appreciate me is someone like my Daddy, and the only way a man can be that is to have my Daddy's Spirit inside him."

Naomi nodded. "Amen." She poured more tea in her cup, added some honey, and then lifted her spoon to stir. "What you're saying makes sense, Mary. The same thoughts have come to me." Naomi looked at her cup as she spoke. "And I tell myself, that's what I'm going to do." She looked at Mary briefly, laughed softly, then looked down again. "Then a fine man comes by, and I think, 'This is the right one! He's sweet, he's this, he's that.' I don't know. I guess I get to thinking how old I am, that time is running out." Naomi's voice was low and calm, but her words reflected pain. "And I guess sometimes I feel sorry for myself. I feel entitled. . . . I didn't cause the breakup of my marriage. I tried to do everything right—why should I be the one to suffer? Why do I have to be alone? Why do I have to feel bad? I was serving God and living right. I want someone to love me. . . . I want to feel better." She looked at Mary, lifted the cup, and then set it back down without drinking.

Mary thought what she saw in Naomi's eyes was her own need to be understood and accepted. Naomi's voice was more hesitant, more cautious. "Then, of course, when it doesn't work out, *then* I feel stupid and *then* think I should have waited." She looked doubtful, like she was waiting to be rejected, like she was waiting for Mary to shake her finger or say, *I told you so!* "I just don't think I'm strong like you, Mary. I'm still trying to figure it out."

Mary laughed. "Girl, I don't have it figured out, either. And it can't have too much to do with being strong willed or I'd still be there with Reggie clapping his lamp on and off."

Naomi looked back at her laughing, though her eyes were full of doubt. "You think?"

"The man was fine, the food was good, and it's been a long time. *A lonnnngggg time!* Look at me and know that what has happened to me has been grace. It wasn't because I was thinking about it. Or smart enough to figure it out. Girl, God keeps babies and fools, and you know which one I am."

Naomi patted her hand. "Oh, Mary, you're no fool. You don't have to say that to try to make me feel better."

"I want you to feel better, but I'm being honest. All this time I've been celibate, it hasn't been me being strong." She smiled. "And I don't think it was just my hairdo or hair-don't!" When Naomi returned her smile, she continued talking. "When I've been weak, God's been strong for me. I think, if anything, it's about trying to have the courage to trust that what God says to me is good for me. And there's a Scripture that says that if we love Jesus, we will keep His commandments—that verse comes to me all the time. And I try. I do.

"But what happened with Reggie might be that my attitude is changing, and I can't take credit for that . . . so it's back to God's grace." She looked at Naomi, hoping that she wasn't talking too much, that she wasn't sounding superior or too preachy. "I just think God showed up strong in my stupidity and weakness. That's not me being strong—that's God being good." Mary shook her head. "I'm *still* struggling. And you know, Naomi, if we even have *thoughts* that we might like to live another way, I believe those thoughts are God showing up in our lives. That's God showing us that He cares about us, that He hasn't given up on us. His timing is perfect and He knows when we're ready to surrender. Like when he came to me after my granny died."

Naomi looked at her. There was so much vulnerability in her eyes. "I feel like I've surrendered. I feel like I'm trying to do it right."

Mary shrugged. "Who knows, girl? What I do know is that God loves us."

"I believe that."

"He loves us and He's patient with us while we try to figure it all out. People may not be patient. They may judge us and forget that God has been patient with them, but I know God is patient. If He was patient enough to wait for the woman at the well, the Samaritan woman—to wait until she knew who He was, until she finally understood—then I'm sure that He'll be patient with us while we learn. If He forgave the woman caught in adultery, then He'll forgive us. He hasn't changed."

Naomi nodded. "The Word says He is patient, kind, forgiving, and not quick to anger. That's what I want to believe . . . that's what I need to believe."

"We get afraid that He's like people. Shoot, people think He's like them!" Mary laughed. "But thank God He's not!"

"I know that's right."

"There are a whole lot of junior Holy Ghosts running around!" Mary fanned herself with an imaginary fan. "And sometimes, Naomi, don't you think it's hard to figure it all out—"

"I always think it's hard to figure out!"

Mary nodded, relieved to have someone like-minded to talk with about it. "Part of what scares me is that most of the people that are telling me what I should and should not do don't look like they have any joy in their lives. They don't look like Christianity—their kind of Christianity—has brought them any joy. And how they treat me sure doesn't look like God's love."

Naomi shook her head vehemently. "Exactly!"

"It's like they have followed all the rules, but doing that doesn't bring them any joy or peace. It's almost like they're mad because they have to follow the rules and they want to make you follow them, too."

Naomi pressed her hands together like she was praying, but moved them back and forth rapidly. "Girl, that's exactly what I have thought so many times. If they're doing it right, why aren't they happy? If they've got it right, why don't they spend their time rejoicing, instead of spending it trying to beat the joy out of me? I enjoy my life. I love God, but I also have joy—some little bit of joy—and I don't want to lose that. And the truth is, I don't feel that because I make a mistake, God stops loving me. I like knowing that He loves me that much. That's something I know about Him that maybe the rule followers don't know—that He loves us all the time. I know He doesn't approve, I know He hates the sin, but He still loves me." She sighed. "I don't see any love in them. Just anger. Just meanness. And the Bible says that people will know Christians by their love. It confuses me."

"I know what you mean, Naomi. It's like they're so busy *working* at being good—kind of like the prodigal son's brother—that they don't take time to enjoy anything. I don't want to be like them. I don't want them to try to make me like them. I don't want to see life like they do, I just want to be a better me—a me that God is more pleased with."

Naomi clapped her hands together. "You just said a mouthful, sister-girl! That one could preach! You could make a sermon out of that point."

"Sometimes, since I've been studying for my classes with the girls, I kind of think of it like the Corinthians and the Galatians in the Bible. We're kind of like the Corinthians."

Naomi laughed. "What you mean, girl? Not the crazy Corinthians, girl! I don't know if I want to be like them. They were a wild bunch!"

"Yeah, they were, but they loved God . . . as messed up as they were, they loved God. And it was pretty clear with all the gifts they had, that God loved them. And as wild as they were, they were still part of the body of Christ. Even Paul, the ultimate rule-follower, had to acknowledge that. Maybe God loved them because He knew how they came to be Corinthian in the first place. Anyway, nobody could kick them out of the church—God had put His approval on them."

"I never thought of it that way." Naomi touched a hand to her lips.

As they talked, Mary could see the printed words on the pages of the Bible. She imagined what the Corinthian church must have looked like to the apostle Paul. He was human like her. She wondered if he struggled to understand. He knew the rules so well, he followed the rules so well. How confused he must have been to see so many people who appeared not to be people that God would want to be with—party people, wine drinkers, lustful people, people with little modesty. She imagined how confused Paul, like the scribes and Pharisees before him, must have felt to see God's Spirit moving among and in those same people. She imagined how confused he must have been when he was Saul looking at the Christians, and she wondered if some of that confusion lingered when he was converted. Did he change overnight and become more understanding, or was it a day-by-day process?

Mary imagined Paul with the Galatians—those that she thought of as the "rule followers." Was the apostle just as horrified, as confused, and as amazed that God worked among them and loved them, though they seemed to have no revelation of God's grace? Did he think that one was better than the other?

Mary imagined the Corinthians laughing, shouting, and dancing—full of God's joy! Full of God's power! She tried to imagine a place where people were freely healing, freely teaching, freely prophesying, freely speaking in tongues—so much so that they were out of order. It must have been a horrible place for Paul, who knew all the rules and followed all the rules. It must have been a mysterious place to Paul. Why would God choose the Corinthians when there were so many other people committed to following the rules? Paul must have wondered, as she wondered now, why God would bless people who didn't seem to be following the rules. Why would He bless her? Why would He shower gifts on the prodigals and not on those who worked so hard to be good? Or did He shower gifts on all of us? It must have been a *wonderful* place for Paul, perhaps the only place where he could gain a complete revelation of the depth of God's love.

Naomi's face was glowing. "People may not approve of us, but we're still part of the body of Christ." She nodded, a smile spreading across her face. "God still loves us, even though we don't have it together—just like the Corinthians."

Mary nodded and repeated, "Just like the Corinthians. And He'll get the truth to us, He'll teach us—not so we can be Galatians—"

Naomi nodded like she was catching on, "The rule-followers, who were trying to find the perfect thing to do so that God would approve of them. And who were . . ."

Mary joined with her, ". . . also part of the church." They looked at each other, still nodding. Then Mary continued. "Not so we can become Galatians—who also play their part in the body of Christ—but so we can become better, more mature Corinthians."

"That's right! We like being who we are!"

"God is patient. He has centuries and eons of patience. He sent Paul at just the right time in his life to teach the rules. Too soon and the Corinthians wouldn't have loved God enough to want to do the right thing. Too soon and Paul would have been ready to kill them rather than loving them enough to tell the truth. Too soon and Paul couldn't have even seen that God loved them and had chosen them. He would have done them like he did the first Christians. He would have missed what the Corinthians had to offer him . . . and the student always has something to teach the teacher."

"And who else would show the rule followers how to party in Jesus and get their praise on!" Her laugh sounded full of relief. "Um-um-ummm!" Naomi took a deep breath and sighed. "Girl! That was deep! There's room for all of us at the table." She shook her head again. "I wish everybody thought like you."

"They mean well. I think we all mean well. That's part of love—believing the best of each other. I just think we forget to trust God. I think we get so caught up in teaching and trying to help that we forget to love and to trust God. We forget that the Lord doesn't always chide—I forget it too, sometimes."

Naomi sighed and smiled. "I might have to rethink what I said about working with those girls. Maybe I need to get some girls to mentor. It's clear that you have been studying, not just memorizing, but actually thinking about the Scriptures and trying to figure out what they mean. It's like you've had a makeover from the inside."

She didn't know what to say. Mary looked out the window and then at her watch. The days were getting shorter, and it was hard to

judge the time based on nightfall. "Speaking of the girls and studying, I do need to go. We've got class. We've been trying something
different." She told Naomi that now the girls were studying and
teaching the class, teaching her. "It's been a little rocky the last
couple of weeks. Now that they have more responsibility—since
they get to determine the direction—I guess they're not quite sure
what to do with it. They promised that this week, they were going
to get it together, but I still better prepare something just in case."

Not wanting to leave each other's company, they hugged, drank
more tea, talked, laughed, and made plans for shopping.

Finally, Mary rose from the couch. Naomi got her coat and
walked her to the door. In the vestibule, Naomi hugged her again.
"You know, Mary, I was thinking. Your grandmother would be so
proud of you."

Mary tilted her head. The glow she felt warmed her cheeks.
"You think so?"

"I know so." Naomi held the door in her hand. "We had some
strong grandmothers, you know? They taught us how to survive,
how to serve the Lord, how to raise families."

"Yes, they did."

"They taught us how to cook. They taught us how to be ladies."

Mary laughed. "They sure did. There were just certain things
you wouldn't even think about doing in front of your grandmother.
They set the standard."

Naomi nodded. "I was just thinking. I just wonder if we're
doing the same thing, if our daughters and granddaughters look at
us the same way. . . . When they look at us, I wonder what kind of
standard we're setting for them."

24

Mary and Puddin

M*ary stepped in the door* of Room Thirty-One. Something was different. It wasn't the lighting, or the tables—it was the girls. Cat and Pamela sat at the table, their Bibles open in front of them.

Agnes was standing at the board ready to teach. "We talked about it. We called each other over the weekend. We're ready, and I'm first."

Agnes first? The girl was never first at anything. She seemed brighter, more awake.

"I found myself," she said. Eagerness made her breathe shallowly—she was almost panting. "I'm like the Canaanite woman I read about." She shifted from foot to foot. "Can we start now?" After a short prayer and hardly any greeting, Agnes insisted that they begin.

She pointed to the Scripture. "It's from Matthew and it's about this woman who is a Canaanite. In another book, I believe it's Mark, there's the same story, but it says the woman is Greek or something." Agnes was so excited she was hardly pausing to breathe.

Mary had never heard her speak so much; she had never heard the other girls—Cat and Pamela—being quieter. There was a light in her eyes that had never been there before. "What's pretty clear is that the woman was foreign. She didn't fit in. She wasn't one of them—she wasn't one of the chosen people. It made sense to me. This is a big church, you know?" She shrugged.

Mary tried to keep her mouth from falling open. She couldn't believe it was Agnes. The girl looked like Agnes, dressed like Agnes, but after that . . .

Agnes was still talking. "I could see two different people describing me differently, like the writers in Matthew and Mark describe the woman, but definitely being clear that I'm an outsider."

Agnes brushed the hair out of her face. She told the story of the woman's pleas to Jesus for help, help to heal her daughter who had an evil spirit. It was strange to hear the girl string so many words together, but she told of how upset the disciples were that a foreigner would dare ask for Jesus' help. "And I've felt like that, that people would rather that I would just go away, that I would just go be with my own kind . . . whatever that kind is. You know, like they would tell the pastor, or even God, to make me go away." She looked at the floor for the first time that day, and then back at Mary.

"Go on." Mary was trying not to beam like a mother at her child's first recital. She looked at Pamela and then at Cat. If nothing more happened, she was satisfied. She had heard grownups read the same passage over and over and never connect with the racial and ethical implications of the story. She had heard grownups read it and never apply the truth of the Bible story to their own lives.

Agnes stopped for a second as though she was suddenly self-conscious, as though she was seeing herself—seeing herself out of place. She looked at her feet and bit her bottom lip.

"You can do it, Agnes." Pamela spoke and nodded to encourage Agnes.

Agnes sighed and then looked up at Pamela. This time, Pamela and Cat both nodded. Agnes took a deep breath, looked at Mary, and began to speak again. "So, instead of sending her—the woman—away, Jesus starts talking to her." She took another deep breath. "And they—the disciples—didn't like it, because first of all, she's a woman. And then on top of that, she's an outsider, you know? So, Jesus tells her that the blessings He has are for the Jews and not for the dogs. I mean He is basically calling her a dog, which is pretty . . . pretty bad, you know?"

Cat pursed her lips and frowned. "Things must have been different back then, because if somebody talked to somebody else like that now, somebody would be dead or on their way to the hospital. You know what I mean?"

Pamela nodded. "People fight now or shoot each other for just looking at each other the wrong way."

Agnes looked at Pamela and Cat. "But see when I read it, I didn't see what happened in the Bible story as so different than today. It was way back then, but that lady could have gone off just like we do now. They were fighting wars over that kind of stuff back then just like now."

Mary looked at the three girls. They were actually having a discussion, and she didn't have to lead it. They were making the passage their own. Agnes had lost her momentary discomfort and was now speaking freely again. "What I see is that Jesus had something the woman needed, and she knew that He was the only one that could help her. She knew He had the power to do it. So, she had a choice. She could have been mad and cussed Him out, which to me it seems to me she had every right to do." She looked apologetically at Mary. "I'm sorry, but I know how she felt. I've been called names—whitey, cracker, swirl—stuff like that. I've had people try to beat me up just because—" she looked at her skin—"of my color or whatever."

She looked at Mary, including Cat and Pamela in her gaze. "It makes me mad! It hurts!" Her shoulders hunched and her voice lowered. "Sometimes I don't want to go to school, I don't want to go to church, and sometimes I want to be mad at God because I think, 'Why didn't you just make me like everybody else?'" Agnes took a deep breath. "But I think she had a choice—the woman in the story—to be mad and offended and stuff, or she could choose to be blessed. Her faith that Jesus could help her daughter was stronger than her need to get back at Him for saying something mean. And that's real faith."

Agnes stopped talking and turned to erase the board. When she finished, she turned back to the others and began to speak again. "When I read this story, it made me feel better, man. I knew I wasn't the only one this happened to . . . that this stuff has been going on for years. And I knew that I'm choosing *not* to fight back not because I'm scared or alone. I'm making a choice. I'm choosing to be blessed. And I believe that God sees the choices that I'm making."

She lifted her head. "And other people may be standing around watching, they may be making fun of me, they may be saying I ain't no good. But God is going to bless me because He sees I got the faith to keep coming to hear the Word, to keep trying. And I'm going to keep coming and coming, until like Martin Luther King says, I overcome!"

Mary and Pamela were clapping. Cat was on her feet and hugging Agnes. "Girl, look at you! You showed off, with your bad self! Girl, I can't believe it! It's about time!"

Mary shook her head. "This was unbelievable! I am so proud!" She didn't know what to do. "Agnes!" Mary stood to her feet, nodded, and looked at the girl for what seemed like forever. She didn't know what to say. She said her name again. "Agnes." She couldn't just keep standing there. She had to do something. She looked at her watch. "Look, how do you all want to do this? We can keep talking about Agnes's lesson—and there's a lot to talk about—or we can press on so that each one of you—"

Cat raised her hand. "I got mine."

Mary dropped to her seat. Cat raising her hand? What was going on?

Puddin sat in front of the computer screen. How long could all this go on? What was she going to do about Joe . . . and about the job? Nothing had changed. He looked sadder, he tried to hold her more often. But he was still going out, still getting tapes, still going to the reading room—though the visits were shorter. When he came out, he had taken to sitting with her in the kitchen or the living room and holding her hand—protecting her from what he imagined to be her addiction while protecting his own.

And he watched her like a hawk. It was more difficult to get the computer room because he was always watching. She couldn't steal much more than sixty minutes or ninety minutes and then only on the nights he had men's group.

He was guarding so closely. He still had it in his mind that she had the problem. Of course he did. That was easier than facing his own problem. Joe kept watching and then telling her he loved her.

Right!

He loved her enough to want her not to leave, maybe. But he didn't love her enough to stop creeping to his hideaway. He loved her. More likely it really was that he was comfortable with the sameness of things, of her. Maybe she put up with him because she was afraid to do something different—afraid to change, to face things alone.

Love is patient and . . . bears all things. The words of 1 Corinthians 13 came to her often when she thought about Joe.

It was hard to suffer long, to be patient, when what he was doing hurt so badly. When he wouldn't even admit that he had a problem. The truth was, she wasn't sure she could bear it; she wasn't sure she wanted to bear it.

Love is patient and . . . hopes all things.

She wanted to believe that something miraculous was going to happen. And maybe something had. Maybe his catching her on the computer—even if he did have the wrong idea—was an opportunity for things to get better. He looked so sincere—she knew he was sincere. Puddin looked toward the kitchen. She could go fix him a nice dinner. They could sit down and talk. She could clear things up about her computer job . . . she could even quit; the guys had said it would be no big deal.

But she couldn't get past the reading room. The door to the room lay between her and the kitchen—really even between her and Joe making it work. She got up from the computer and began to walk toward the door. She didn't have to be so passive. She didn't have to wait for him to change. She could go in—she put her hand on the doorknob—and clean things out. She could gather up the tapes and just throw the whole mess out of their lives!

The doorknob began to turn in her hands.

She stopped.

If she went inside . . . if she went inside, there was no going back. She would have the images, the pictures in her mind, and whenever she looked at Joe, they would be there. If she went inside, what she saw might make her not love him anymore. If she went inside, his reaction—his anger—might prove to her that he didn't love her anymore—that he loved the tapes more.

Puddin dropped her hand from the knob. She slapped the door with her hand and walked back to the computer room.

Cat's spike heels clicked and her hair bounced as she stood in front of Mary, Agnes, and Pamela. She shifted from foot to foot, first jutting out one hip, then another. "You all know I have been through a lot of things in my life, right? I have told you all about that. So, at first, when I started reading, when I started going through the list you gave us, Miss Mary, I thought about the woman at the well in Samaria, because she had had so many husbands, which said she had been with a lot of men."

The words were flying out of her mouth almost too fast to comprehend, but she stopped to let the last few sink in. She changed her stance. "Then I thought about this woman on the list named Gomer. The Bible said she was a whore."

Cat put her hand on her hip. "I didn't even know they called people that in the Bible, you know? But, anyway, God told her husband, who was this prophet, to find a whore, to find Gomer and marry her. And I thought about that. It would be like God telling one of the ministers in our pulpit to marry a whore. You know the whole church and town would go crazy." She waved her hand in the air. "The way people talk about whores and stuff, or even about people who are not married and having sex, is like God does not love them at all." She flipped the paperback Bible she was holding back and forth.

Mary tried not to frown, tried to remember not to judge Cat, but to listen. At least the concentration and effort she was expending on her presentation was cutting down on the girl's wisecracks. Mary looked at Agnes and then at Pamela. She was trying to give Cat the benefit of the doubt, but right now it was hard to see where she was headed.

Cat was still going nonstop. "But this book in the Bible says it's not true. When we do wrong, it breaks His heart, but He still keeps on loving us and wants us to come back to Him. So that is what I was going to talk about. I had studied it and everything." She was quiet for a moment. She looked at Mary. "I was ready."

She sighed. Her breathing slowed and she flipped to pages in the front of the Bible. For a moment, Cat looked as uncertain as Agnes normally did. Then she nodded, as though she were encouraging herself, and plunged. "And then this morning, before I went to school, I picked up the Bible and it just fell open to this passage in Genesis. It was about Sodom and Gomorrah." She looked up from the words. "I know it wasn't on the list you gave us . . . but see, there were these two angels that came to Sodom at night, and this man named Lot talked the angels into spending the night in his house. Well, before the angels could go to bed, the men of the city—all of them, the young ones and the old ones—came to Lot's house and said to send the men—the angels—out so they could have sex with them."

Cat shook her head. She put her hand over her heart. "I almost had a heart attack! Stuff is crazy now. But whole cities ain't going to nobody's house saying send out your company so we can rape them." Her hand slid from her heart to her hip. "I didn't never think I could see nothing that would freak me out. But this? It was crazy. Men wantin' to have sex with angels? That's nasty."

She looked disgusted. Cat was usually so unaffected by anything—she had seen it all. But Mary could tell the story was getting to her.

The girl shook her head again. "So then, I kept reading. This man named Lot was acting all brave and stuff, and he went to the front door and told the people not to do it." She cleared her throat and tapped the book cover with her long, curved nails. "This was the part that tripped me out. He told the men, all of these men, that he had two daughters and if they—the people in the town—would leave the angels alone, he would give his daughters to them. And I couldn't believe my eyes, Miss Mary. He was gone give his daughters to all those men to do whatever they felt like doing!"

Cat frowned and her chest heaved three times. She opened and closed her mouth several times like she was trying to find words—acceptable words. She sputtered and then spoke. "How could some body treat their own children like that? They didn't even know anything about men. How could their own father say that? Just out of the blue?" She snapped her fingers and tossed her hair. "Just like that. He told those men they could do anything to those girls they wanted to do. *Anything!* What kind of father is that?" Cat's face softened, but her eyes reddened and filled with tears. "How could somebody treat you that way? Why would somebody's father or mother think that it was okay? He didn't even think about how his daughters would feel. And that wasn't because it was the olden days . . . it was because he was a jerk!"

She was quiet then. Cat looked away from the group toward the wall. Mary could see that she was trying to compose herself. Hard-as-nails Cat. The girl turned away, and for a second Mary thought she saw her shoulders shake. Cat curved her back, as though she wanted to hide, just as Mary had seen Agnes do so often. Something about the story was so true, so honest that it seemed to have cut through all the hardness.

Cat straightened herself slowly and turned back to face the group. She looked at each of them, closed her eyes, and a tear slid down her cheek. She took a deep breath. Mary thought she could hear a slight tremor in her voice. "But I knew how they felt. I knew how it felt. I know how it feels to have your own parent give you away or sell you just so they can get out of trouble." She opened her eyes. "And I ain't the only kid that knows how it feels to be treated like you don't matter. The streets are filled with them. It makes you hard on the inside, Miss Mary."

Cat's chin was trembling. She stumbled over her words. "You feel like you can't trust nobody. That nobody loves you. Who can you believe in if your own mother, or your own father, would turn you out like that? If your own mother would put you out to hustle or sell drugs. Sometimes people looking at you, they don't know what you been through."

The girl was rocking side to side, trying to comfort herself. A moan slipped from her lips.

Mary was stunned. She knew the girl had lived a fast life, but she wasn't prepared for this. "Cat, you don't have to go on."

Pam stood to try to comfort Cat, but Cat held up her hand. "No, Pam. I just got to get it out! I got to get it off my chest, now." She grabbed her head, but continued. "It breaks your heart. It will make you go crazy! Trying to figure out what's wrong with you, what you did wrong, why don't they love you, why don't they care about you!" Cat clutched her hands to her chest. "It makes you feel like nobody loves you. Like nobody is *ever* gone love you. What's the point in trying to do anything with your life? Nobody's gone love you. Not even your own mother or your own father could love you!" She tried to wipe the tears from her face, but they kept flowing.

She bit her lower lip, trying to stop it from trembling. Trying, for a second, to regain control. "But God cares. God cares! He heard. He wiped the whole city out. Sodom and Gomorrah was punished. He cares about us!"

She was silent for a few moments, except for her chest heaving. Cat still held her hand up to keep anyone else from comforting her. "And that's what I was thinking. That all these young people running around here that have been hurt . . . that God will burn down the whole city if He has to, to rescue us."

She rubbed tears from her face with the back of her hand, and met Mary's gaze. Her voice was calmer, softer; the usual edge was gone. "So that's all I was gone talk about. Then when I was riding the bus, I remembered about Gomer. That God even told a man of God to marry her, after all she had been through. And who knows—Gomer could have been in a situation just like Lot's daughters. And it was like God was speaking to me not to give up, not to throw myself away. That He loves me, and that there is someone for me. And I may not have a home with my mother, but I always have a home with God."

All four of them were crying. Hugging and crying. In the midst of their tears, Agnes looked up and pointed at the makeup smeared and running down Cat's face. "Girl, now who's looking like a swirl? You should see your face!"

The room was quiet.

Then suddenly they found themselves laughing. Maybe it was relief, just a valve that needed to be turned because seeing Cat's heart had been too much, too painful.

Mary shook her head. "What is going on in here?" She wiped her face. "What happened? Last week . . . all these months . . . it's been so hard. Now . . ." It was more than enough. It was more than she had ever hoped for. "You all have no idea. . . ." She stopped before she began to cry again.

People who hadn't experienced moments like this—moments of outpouring, moments of transformation—never believed things like this could happen. Because they didn't have the experience, because they avoided the experience, they felt happenings like this were melodrama.

Mary looked at the girls' faces. She had seen this kind of glow and the tears at women's conferences and, many times, at church. She knew that's why people flocked to churches where the Spirit was moving, why women drove and flew miles to conferences.

Moves of God—Mary had experienced them before. But she never expected to experience the Spirit moving in her classroom with these girls. *Thank you, God! Thank you, God!*

She touched the girls' cheeks, and then she shook her head. "Look, you all, I can't take any more of this. We're going to have to finish next week—"

Pam shook her head. "No, please. Please. Mine won't make you cry." She smiled at Cat and at Agnes and hugged them. "No more tears. And I'll make it short."

"All right, Pam." Mary shook her finger. "But I'm warning you, no more tears."

Puddin stared at the screen and forced herself, at first, not to think about Joe. It didn't take long, though, and she was no longer in the chair at her desk, but she was dancing among her children. She was dancing among their words. She was in a world she liked better, a world where she was loved, a world where she was needed. A world that she controlled.

Daddiesgirl@charmcitynews.com: I think I'm through with dating. The last date was worse than the one before!

Daddiesgirl had twice picked dates from the choices the computer suggested. When the young woman chose dates the first two times, Puddin had wanted to caution her *He's not really your kind,* but she had stayed out of it.

Now, she hit the button to respond to the young woman—her daughter. Puddin sent a reply using her screen name: *HipHop-GodMama.* It had come from the conversation she had with Bob and Lyle when they hired her. *"A funky cyberspace godmother kind of thing, you know? Or godmother to the hip-hop generation. Kind of a favorite aunt-matchmaker."*

HipHopGodMama@charmcitynews.com: One bad apple don't spoil the whole bunch, girl—not even two. Mama's

been watching. Why don't you try Misterwrite@charmcity
news.com? Drop him an email. I'm sure he's more your
type.

She scanned the others and was soon lost in the screen colors—
the vivid blues, the electric greens, the brilliant reds. It was a beautiful world. And she could help them, her babies. She could make
it perfect for them and take away the pain.

Moody1@charmcitynews.com: I think I've met my match.

HipHopGodMama@charmcitynews.com: There's nothing
Mama likes to hear more!

She couldn't figure it all out about Joe. She would worry about
him later. Right now, she would enjoy herself. There was nothing
wrong with that. Watching the clock, Puddin smiled and petted and
consoled and orchestrated the lives of her children for each second
that was hers.

Mary hoped that Pamela was going to keep her promise about
the tears.

The girl stood. She looked acceptable, accepted, and calm.
"There were so many women on the list. When I tried to pick
somebody I could relate to, I just chose Mary, Lazarus's sister,
because she came from a family where everything looked perfect.
You know, people were always coming to their house to visit. Jesus
would come over to their house and hang out with the other disciples. They weren't poor. You know, they had enough food to feed
everybody." She looked like a high school student from an ad campaign, a bright future, no worries. "But then here is Martha, Mary's
sister, criticizing her to Jesus, you know. Like Mary's lazy and stuff.
Like she's not responsible and she's just not good enough. It's like
she didn't like the way Mary showed her feelings, and the way she
wasn't afraid to let the Lord know He was the most important person in the world to her."

Pamela shrugged her shoulders and twisted her fingers together and her ankles together. "And I know how that feels, you know? When your family is trying to keep up appearances and they're comparing you and you're never good enough. But Jesus, he basically tells Martha to get off of Mary's back. And like that never happens—one adult telling another to give you a break—but I thought that was so cool. I wondered what that would feel like."

Pamela untwisted her fingers and began to loop locks of her hair around one of her index fingers. "Sometimes I get sick of all of it, of not being good enough. You know, my parents don't have to worry about me on drugs or me not getting good grades. They don't have to fight with me to get me to go to church. But it's never good enough. It's okay for them to yell at each other, or get divorced, and nobody says anything. But if I'm not perfect, the whole world comes to an end. They're always nagging. They don't have to be perfect, but I have to be perfect so they won't look bad. Sometimes it makes me want to do something crazy, just because I'm sick of them." She laughed. "But it was cool that Jesus did that for Mary. So I started thinking, okay, Jesus, where are you when my mom is freaking out?"

They all laughed.

Cat nodded. "I know that's right."

"Then I started thinking about all the other stuff Jesus did for that family, you know? Just about how blessed they were. But there's Martha still complaining." Pamela nodded as though she was envisioning the scene. "And that one thing—Jesus standing up for her—I bet it made it easier for Mary so she didn't care so much what people thought about her. If He hadn't stood up for her, I wonder if she would have had the courage to pour that perfume on the Lord's feet and rub it with her hair. You know what I mean?"

Pamela began to pantomime the movements of the girl pouring oil on Jesus and rubbing it with her hair. "Because the people were talking about how she was wasting money pouring out the perfume. True, the perfume was expensive. But you know what they had to really be upset about was how she was willing to show the Lord how she felt about Him. And she didn't care what anybody else thought. She didn't let them stop her. And I wondered just how it felt to feel that free, you know?" Pamela lifted her hands over her head and stretched them wide. "To just run in a room in front of your family and everybody you know and just be that free." She stopped talking, untwisted her legs, and stood up straight. "That's all."

"Wow!" Mary leaned forward to rest her chin in her hand. "Stick me with a fork—I'm done. It was great, Pam." She touched her face. "And you kept your promise—no tears."

Mary was moved. She looked at each of the girls. "I guess you all were right." She touched Agnes's hand, and then looked at Pamela and Cat. "I should have been listening all along. You all have taught me. You could probably teach the whole congregation something."

She looked at her watch. She was moved, but they had to go. "We're going to have to wrap this up until next time. I've got to get you guys out of here."

Cat nodded. "Just one last thing, Miss Mary. What's really up with the hair, the eyes, and the nails? What's up with you?"

Mary tried to think of a way to avoid answering the question. *We don't have time. We're not here to talk about me.* Then she decided to just answer. "Really, it's about the thing that we most don't want to talk about with you all. We're afraid that if we mention it, we'll lead you down the path to sin. Sometimes—probably most of the time—we don't want to talk about it with you all because we didn't get it right ourselves."

Cat had replaced her shades, but now she lowered them. "By *it,* you mean sex, Miss Mary?"

"Yes, Cat, sex. But really it's more than that. I'm single."

Cat nodded. "We know."

"Thanks for the support, Cat." Cat bowed and Mary bowed in return. "And I've been trying to decide what kind of life I wanted to live myself. I've also been trying to decide if I wanted to talk to you all about those choices, if I was even willing or fit to have that conversation with you. I wanted to wait and come in here and talk with you all when I had my own life together, maybe even after I was married, if that ever comes.

"I know you all hear churches talking about single this and single that. When I was growing up, no one was really talking about it. No one was really having any deep conversations about how you live your life—your sexual life—if you're saved. No one was having big conferences about it."

As she spoke, Mary wondered if she should be having the conversation with the girls. More honestly, she worried that other people, if they found out, would object to her honesty and frankness. "First, I sort of stumbled into it—it was not something that I planned. One day I was a girl, then I was a woman, then I was saved, then someone said I was a 'single.' And now that you all are growing up, you all have some hard choices before you. Hopefully, your parents are beginning to have those discussions with you now."

Mary spoke from her heart even as she wrestled with her own doubts and insecurities. There were words she wanted to speak, experiences she wanted to share with the girls. She thought them, but did not speak them. *Who am I to be talking to you about this? First, I stumbled into it—it was not something I planned. It was not something I did because I was righteous. Like God calls people to prayer, or to fasting, or to giving, I felt God calling me to live without sexual intimacy. Celibacy wasn't something I had been thinking about. I looked and all of a sudden, I was there. It was difficult at first, and I had to take everything out of my life that tempted me—certain music, certain movies, certain social situations—from the place God wanted me to be, to be His alone.*

Then, there was a period when it was not so hard, when I began to think it was easy—I had perfected being single. I had, in this modern-day world, successfully cloistered myself, so that no outsider— men who might tempt me, or women whose lives reminded me of the joy and pleasure of what I had forsaken—could enter in. Or, at least, I tried to separate myself . . . but my friends, what about them . . . I wrestled with that. I didn't want to struggle, I wanted to hide away, so it would be easy. But what good is it to reach perfection and then drown in pride? What good is the obedience I offer if there is no element of sacrifice, if it has no cost?

She wanted to share so much more with them, to pour freely from her heart. She wanted to tell the girls what she had learned. But she could imagine the disapproving fingers pointing, so she fought letting the words flow from her lips. *And so, the ease went out of my singleness again. Before I talked to you about it, I wanted to be at the end of my journey. I wanted to be able to tell you that if you are good little girls, if you don't sleep with anyone before you are married— or if you have, but you stop now, that your lives will be perfect. That if you fast, if you pray, if you keep your legs closed, that someday your prince will come bounding over the hill on a white stallion. I wanted to be able to tell you—after it had already happened in my own life— that if you are good, you will never be hurt and your prince will come. I wanted to be able to tell you that it's an easy choice to make, that you just say, no.*

I wanted to talk to you at the end of this journey—because I needed to believe that there would be an end to the journey—so I could tell you that it isn't permanent. Or I at least wanted to be able to tell you that if your prince doesn't come, at least you will be perfectly safe. The truth is, celibate or not, your feelings still get hurt.

It's not easy. Some days I feel like I cannot bear it another minute longer. No matter what anyone says, it's not easy. If it's easy, that's just because I'm in a period of grace, and I shouldn't be proud, I should be thankful.

Mary wanted to share with the girls, to make it easier for them, to tell them all she'd learned. Instead she only spoke what she thought was allowed. "I got this makeover, because I wanted to try something different. Maybe if I changed, my prince would come. Or the truth may be that I got the makeover because I was tired of being alone, because it was getting too hard being a nun." The girls laughed. "But I went on a couple of dates and I learned something. I learned that I have made this choice to be celibate because I love God. I'm single and celibate because it's what He wants from me— because He wants me to himself for this season, and it is my reasonable service."

She couldn't speak all that she wanted, so she prayed that some-how—looking in her eyes, or by spirit speaking to spirit—the girls would hear it anyway. She prayed that they would hear and avoid the traps and pitfalls. *But don't make the mistake that a lot of us make—putting ourselves on a pedestal, or putting our purity on a pedestal as though celibacy or virginity is more important than God. Because sometimes I have felt God telling me to walk my pure self to Nineveh like Jonah, or to Samaria like the disciples—you know, where the people are wild and doing all kinds of crazy stuff. Like He's calling me to a place where it is not easy to be pure. And, mostly, I don't go— not because the people are out of control, but because I'm still struggling, and I don't trust myself. Maybe I'm not in control. What if I lose my purity? What if I damage my reputation?*

It's not about our reputations. Like it says in Philippians, we have to be willing to sacrifice our reputations. "Let this mind be in you, which was also in Christ Jesus: who, being in the form of God, thought it not robbery to be equal with God: but made himself of no reputation, and took upon him the form of a servant, and was made in the likeness of men: And being found in fashion as a man, he humbled himself, and became obedient unto death, even the death of the cross. Wherefore God also hath highly exalted him, and given him a name which is above every name."

What good purpose is there in God calling us to lives of prayer if He can only call us to pray in pure and simple places? What good are we to the kingdom if He cannot call us to pray and serve in difficult places? What good purpose is there in God calling us to lives of fasting if we will only respond if He promises that we will never be hungry when we fast? What good purpose is there in God calling us to lives of purity if we can no longer be called into dark or threatening places, if we can no longer be used in places where our purity will shine even though it is threatened? What good is it if we exalt protecting our purity above service?

Like Romans says, it's all about the service—sacrificial service. "I beseech you therefore, brethren, by the mercies of God, that ye present your bodies a living sacrifice, holy, acceptable unto God, which is your reasonable service."

I believe He wants us to be pure, to be prayerful, but the end goal is neither of those; the end is love and service to Him and my fellow man.

Mary hoped that what she did speak to them would be enough. "The truth is, when you are celibate you are still subject to being attracted to the wrong people. If you are a good little girl, your heart may still be broken. If you are a good little girl, your prince still may never come. The truth is that sometimes you are lonely and people treat you like a freak because you're single, even if you are celibate."

Cat laughed. "Oh, wow! A freak!"

She wanted to tell the girls how they had moved her. How what they shared had touched her and challenged her. But maybe sharing her confession with the girls would be going too far. *After listening to you all, I realize the truth is that I have kept myself hidden away like the perfume, like the alabaster jar in my dresser drawer. And I guess that's what most of us do—hide the best parts of ourselves away. If we are kind, we try to hide it so people won't know. We're afraid they may take advantage of us. If we're generous, we hide it. We don't want to be tainted.*

And we hide so our jars won't be broken, so we won't be damaged. Black people hide from white people—or drive them away so they won't be hurt anymore—or so they don't have to be put to the test like the Canaanite woman to see if their faith is stronger than their need to react to offense. White people hide away, pushing away black people, red people, brown people—because as long as they only move in white circles, they're safe, they're never tested. They don't have to worry whether they'll react with prejudice like the disciples, or show compassion like the Lord when a Canaanite comes to their door, their office, their church. Women push men away because it's safer; there are no emotional risks, there is no fear, and because it's more important to never risk who they are—to hide away who they are—to hide away their womanhood—than to trust the Lord and pour all of who they are on the Master. We push our children away—we don't tell them the stories of our own struggles. We don't show them the scars of our own pasts.

We've got to stop being afraid. I've got to stop being afraid.

I'm fine hidden away in a safe place with a perfect image. But who knows, if I follow God's call to Sodom, whether I will prove to be like Lot instead of like Abram. Who knows that if tested, I will not be like Gomer or like the woman from Samaria instead of like Esther. If tested, who knows whether I will be like Mary or like Martha.

I've got to trust God and try. We've got to trust God and try.

We don't want to pour ourselves out. We don't want our precious gifts to be tested. Our reputations, our safety, our titles are more important to us than our callings. We don't want to be tested, because we forget that we are weak and it is always God who keeps us, who gifts us with self-control, whose strength is made perfect in our weakness.

She didn't feel free to share with them all that was in her heart, so she prayed that the little she spoke would be enough. "Each one of us, like the women you talked about, has stories, but it takes all of our stories to build the kingdom. God needs all of us out of hiding, all of us—single and married, young and old, all colors and nations—shining and trusting Him to keep us.

"The good news about the call to discipline is that you will learn to trust God. You will learn obedience, even when it doesn't make sense—obedience just because God is God. And you will learn to have the courage to not choose a meaningless relationship or live a lie just so you can be with someone. You will learn to know God for yourself. And you will learn that God loves you—just you all by yourself. That He will speak to you, and that He can use you, no matter who you are, no matter whether your call to service makes sense to anyone else or anybody's rules or not. Though you may not meet the man of your dreams—and though you may still go on some very, very bad dates—you will learn to trust God." Mary looked at the girls, hoping what she had said—though it was not everything she had thought—would be enough.

Cat sat back in her seat and crossed her legs. "So, Miss Mary, have you tried computer dating?"

25

Puddin

Puddin *was glad about* the special meeting of the Comfort Circle. She was going to take the opportunity to clear everything up about Joe and her computer-dating job. She was tired of flip-flopping about how she felt about Joe. And lately she had been thinking she might have been too hard on him, that maybe she hadn't been patient enough with him. *"Love is patient and . . . endures all things."* She needed to talk about it, she needed to get it all off her chest and get it settled.

So when the Comfort Circle met in Room Seventeen, Puddin didn't wait for the call for new business—even though Sister—now Deaconess—Othella looked like she was just full of new business. Puddin knew that Othella probably wanted to discuss her promotion, and of course, she had every right to be excited.

Othella had done a lot for the church. Some people said she was a busybody. Some people said lots of things, but when times got hard, when it snowed and no one else would go, Othella was the one who would show up with whatever a family needed. When some people couldn't be found, Othella was the one that would be at the hospital praying for the sick and their families. When some people wouldn't even give a dollar, Othella was the one who would give when she and her husband didn't have any more to give. Some people said Othella gossiped too much, and some people thought the pastor should have made some other people a deaconess instead of Othella, but Puddin knew that Othella deserved every bit of recognition she got.

She knew it was Othella's time to shine, but what she needed to say couldn't wait. Puddin felt bad about taking the time away from Deaconess Othella's announcement, but she had to speak her mind. So before the meeting got started good, she began to talk about Joe. She'd been coaching herself, telling herself not to get emotional. "I don't know if I'm doing the right thing." But before she could get going good, she was already crying, and she wasn't sure why.

Puddin put her hand over her mouth so she wouldn't holler, so the tears would flow noiselessly. She told them about Joe and what he had said about the two of them working things out. "I'm so confused. He looked so sincere."

Deaconess Othella's neck jerked, but Sister Minnie spoke first. "What are you talking about, Sister Puddin?"

"I'm talking about Joe, and I'm talking about my job. He has been looking so sad, you all. Really."

Sister Minnie's face said she wanted to sympathize. "Is he doing any better? Has Joe stopped playing the tapes?"

Deaconess Othella didn't say anything, but her face said she wasn't having any of it.

Both of the women knew everything. Puddin had told them everything there was to know about the troubles she and Joe were having. She couldn't pretend, and even though she wanted to cover for Joe, right now there wasn't any way she could. "No, he's still watching them." Sister Minnie was shaking her head. "I know, Sister Minnie. I know, I'm probably being foolish, but if you could have seen him. He was down on his knees. And I've never seen him cry like that." She told them the story of how Joe caught her on the computer going through the files over a week earlier. "He thinks I'm the one having the trouble . . . I'm the one being unfaithful on the computer. He said we could work it out. That he would stick by me." Puddin grabbed a tissue. "I thought about what I have been saying about him here, and about me sneaking and starting this new job. Maybe it was just the shock of him catching me, but I felt so guilty." She blew her nose. "And I still haven't told him . . . haven't cleared it up about me having a job."

Deaconess Othella began tapping on the table with the nail of her right index finger. "Don't you know nothing, Sister Puddin? Don't you know that's the oldest trick in the world? Don't you know that men do that whenever they get caught?"

Do what? Look sincere? Shift the blame? Puddin had lots of unspoken questions, but Deaconess Othella went right on talking.

She cleared her throat and frowned like there was something bitter on her tongue. "Anyway, I called this emergency meeting to talk about that young woman that's teaching that mentoring class with the young girls. All that blonde hair, those nails, and those green contacts! It's not bad enough that she's looking like a harlot, but now she's got the girls reading about them and idolizing the bad women in the Bible instead of picking out the good ones. She's talking to them about sex, and nobody asked her to do that. Nobody approved her to do that. I know because one of the girls was talking to another girl who told her mother. And thank goodness her mother had sense enough to complain to me. Just a Jezebel sitting in the church pews. She needs to just cool her hot self down! What she needs to do is get married, or just go sit down somewhere.

"That's what I came here to talk about—about that woman. I was gone try to keep this other to myself. But since you brought it up! Since you brought Joe up . . ."

That's when Deaconess Othella let out the storm that swelled inside her. "This past Wednesday night, Sister Puddin, the night your husband was supposed to be at men's Bible study—*supposed* to be, because who knows if he ever got there or not. I was driving through downtown minding my own business when I saw the last thing I ever wanted to see. There was your husband sitting in a Starbucks huddled up with a bunch of white women!" Deaconess Othella let the words hang in the air.

The deaconess waited, Puddin felt certain, until Othella was sure pain and shock had both slapped Puddin's face. Then Othella continued talking. "There were a couple of black women, but mostly they were white women, and they were sitting there giggling.

Giggling!" Deaconess Othella's thin lips were twisted with disgust. "I pulled my car over to the curb. I want you to know I was going to march in there, slap his big, red, laughing face on your behalf, and then take a few of the others out along with him before the police got there to get me." Deaconess Othella laid one hand over her heart and one hand on Puddin's arm. "I am a deaconess, but I'm your Comfort Circle sister first, and I made up my mind in that instant that I was willing to suffer the indignity of arrest—and maybe my picture in the newspaper—to stand up for you."

Deaconess Othella's voice was shaking like it was about to break. "Now, I hate to tell any woman to leave her husband, but I saw it with my own two eyes." She made the two fingers of her right hand into a *V* and pointed them at her eyes, then dropped them back to the table in front of her. "I hate to talk this way, but sometimes we have to take our hats off and get real, if you know what I mean. So, I'm just gone say it plain. I just got to tell it like it T-I 'tis. That red man of yours was sitting there giggling with white women and he can't deny it." Her frown deepened. "Of course, when he was making you feel guilty, making you feel like you were the one with the problem, he didn't tell you all this, did he?" Deaconess Othella answered her own question by shaking her head. "So you cry as much as you need to, Sister Puddin. I can only imagine the shame you are feeling right now."

Puddin didn't know whether to run from the room or scream. It wasn't like Joe. It couldn't be. It wasn't the Joe she knew. He said he loved her; she had just held him while he cried, held and comforted him until he fell asleep. She had come to get things clear, not to have things fall apart. It was getting hard to breathe and even harder to concentrate. It couldn't be. God wouldn't let it be. "Are you sure it was him? I just . . ." *"Love is patient, love is kind. . . . It is not easily angered . . . always trusts, always hopes."*

There were so many voices, so many thoughts competing. She didn't know where to focus or what to believe. Othella's voice, however, was loudest, so Puddin grabbed on to the sound and forced herself to concentrate. "Are you sure?"

"Of course I'm sure." Deaconess Othella shook her finger. "I told you, after all these years, you know I'd know that red man of yours anywhere. Puddin, you and that soft heart of yours . . . Wake up! Don't be no fool, Sister Puddin!"

Sister Minnie's brows were all scrunched together. Her hands were wringing. Her mouth was a wiggly line like a cartoon character. "Great God from Zion!" she yelled. "I can't believe it!" She hopped up from the table and began to run back and forth across the room. "I can't hardly sit still!"

Deaconess Othella's mood had changed. She was still an angry storm, but she was quieter. "That's right, Sister Puddin. First, it was video pornography. Then, the Negro had nerve enough to be calling them—the nasty women—on the telephone so he could sneak around and meet them. You said so yourself."

Other thoughts tried to force their way through. *"Love is patient, love is kind. . . . It keeps no record of wrongs . . . always trusts, always hopes."* But Puddin held on to Othella's words, she held on to the safe thing.

The deaconess tapped her finger on the table for emphasis. "Pornography in your home. But that ain't good enough. That wasn't good enough for Joe. No, no, no. See how evil is? Now, he's meeting them in public places and trying to make you think you're crazy to boot! It's bad enough for him to betray you with any woman, but one woman ain't good enough. He's got to have more than one. And he can't just stick to his own color; he's got to be in public with white women. And he don't care who sees him. Joe has lost his mind, turned reprobate, or Satan has hardened his heart . . . or all three. And if you not careful, he's gone drag you down with him." She was finally quiet, but her temples and her jaws continued moving back and forth and in and out. "I'm so mad I could spit! If a woman could lynch a man, I swear I'd buy you a rope and say, 'Sister, go find you a tall tree!'"

Sister Minnie, still overwhelmed, grabbed a wad of tissues and pressed them to her face. "Mercy, mercy me!"

Deaconess Othella's face settled in a firm, no-nonsense look. "You know I believe in the Bible and I believe in God. But you got to be realistic, Sister Puddin. You can't keep being a tenderhearted fool sitting around waiting for a miracle to come. You gone have to check that man and get him to admit it. The Lord hates divorce, but you gone have to leave him!"

"Are you sure? Are you sure it was Joe? My Joe?" *Of course it was Joe.*

"I'm telling you I saw what I saw."

Puddin didn't know whether to be angry or just embarrassed. Her eyes had dried; she could feel one of them twitching. He had made a fool of her again, but it would be the last time! Deaconess Othella was right, she was going to have to get free of the millstone around her neck. A coldness that was almost like peace washed over her.

When Sister Minnie and Deaconess Othella told the story later—when they were interviewed by *The Baltimore Sun* and the Charm City News—that was the moment, they said, when Sister Puddin lost it. "She went crazy!" one of them said.

26

Moor

Who would have ever thought that something so insignificant as a piece of paper would lead to all this?

It was crazy. There was no place to park. For some reason, he didn't count on the museum being so crowded on a Saturday afternoon—maybe that's what was illogical. Buses full of students, tourists, and family members wearing reunion T-shirts filled the street. The lively crowds looked more like those bustling at an amusement park than what he expected at a museum. It was the perfect day, too, for an amusement park, for rides and popcorn. This Saturday was one of those fall days when the weather dips back and forth from cool to surprisingly warm, when the sunlight feels much more like spring—and only crisp brown leaves blowing by remind you of the time of year.

The piece of paper that Ali had given him in the alley had led him to this place. Actually, it had led him to a nickname—*Mookie*—and an opportunity to meet its owner at the museum.

After finding a paid parking space further up North Avenue, Moor stepped from his car looking at the paper and thinking of the meeting in the alley.

"I told them everything I knew about you, everything you had told us, and your preferences—you know, the kind of woman you want. So, this should be a match. It's based on computer logic. How can you go wrong? If you don't like her, you just walk away." Ali was convincing in the alley in the dark, with Blue and Brighty cheering like two of his grandmother's old friends. The dramatic fire, his grandmother's note in his pocket, his friends' enthusiasm—anyone might have got-

ten caught up in the moment and said yes.

But here in the light of day, none of it made great sense. He didn't feel so lonely today, and it was probably the sentimental letter from his grandmother that caused him to feel lonely, anyway. He covered his eyes and looked toward the Great Blacks in Wax Museum. Moor held his head down so that the sun would not blind him. Homesickness was a dangerous thing. This was not such a good idea.

What was a *Mookie,* anyway? She said that she was a teacher, that she was thirty-two, but who knew? She could be anything. She could be crazier than—

"Oh!" she said. And that was the first Moor saw of her. He hadn't noticed her. He hadn't noticed the bus. His mind had been on Mookie and the piece of paper. Homesickness was a terrible thing.

He grabbed the woman's arm to keep her from stumbling. "I am very sorry. I was not paying attention."

"That's okay." Her eyes—green eyes—never really looked at him; they were fixed on the open bus door.

"Can I help? . . . Are you all right?" He was still holding her arm. Her perfume was exotic, extraordinary, hypnotic. But he could not think about her; his afternoon was already planned. Besides, she wasn't his type—though there was something attractive about her. "I was on my way to meet . . . to introduce myself to—" There was no need to look foolish twice, telling her about his blind computer date.

She looked down at his hand on her arm, up at his face, and then at the bus. "I'm trying to make the bus."

"I'm sorry." Moor dropped her arm and watched her walk away and then step up on the bus. He held his position until the bus pulled away. Then he turned back in the direction of the museum. He already had enough on his mind.

What was a *Mookie,* anyway? What if she was crazy? How could he believe that information on a piece of paper could add up to anything good? Who but someone desperate would send in his or her personal information to some computerized lonely-hearts operation? He should never have agreed. Computers understood numbers and science—not people.

He stopped and looked back in the direction of the bus. She—the green-eyed woman—seemed like a woman of good disposition. She hadn't cursed at him, after all—which was showing an exceptional amount of restraint for a city dweller trying to catch a bus. Except for her eyes and her yellow hair, she might be someone he might have introduced himself to, maybe offered to buy her a cup of coffee to make up for the collision. He turned and continued walking to the museum. As he walked he lifted his hand and sniffed. He could still smell the scent she wore.

Perhaps a random encounter—or what appeared to be a chance encounter, like bumping into the green-eyed woman—was actually a much more logical way to meet. Given that there were billions of people on the planet—or just considering the seven hundred thousand people in Baltimore—a chance encounter with a person that attracted him really could not be a *chance* encounter. More likely, such an encounter was the result of the subtle workings of God to move him to the right place at precisely the right time.

Who could tell about such things? It could be that their meeting was providential, not contrived like this, this date, this disaster toward which he was headed. This *Mookie* was probably not even the kind of woman that the men in his family liked.

The wind blew the paper in Moor's hand and reminded him of where he was going. He reined in his imagination and his thoughts. He was being foolish. There was no point in going through the mental exertion. Thinking irrational thoughts was not going to save him from what lay ahead. There was no point in creating distractions. He was committed to the date—he looked at the door of the museum—and he was going in.

When he stepped into the lobby, out of all the people milling there, he knew her instantly. Her eyes were bright, and her big smile made all his worries disappear. She sat on a chair at the back wall, almost directly in front of the main door, and underneath a plaque.

He waved the paper and mouthed her name just to be sure. She nodded and blushed, and he crossed the space between them and took her hand to help her stand. He could not help smiling. In fact, he was certain that he was looking like a fool, grinning from ear to ear. "It is very nice to meet you," he said. Each inch of her was a delight. The men in his family would have been pleased.

"Behold, thou art fair, my love; behold, thou art fair; thou hast doves' eyes." Verses from the Song of Solomon popped into his head.

"It's very nice to meet you." Her voice was soft and pleasant; it had a sweetness to it like ripe apples. She laid a lovely hand on her chest; each finger was perfect and long. "Actually, I'm relieved." Her laugh was somewhere between pleasure and embarrassment. "I almost cancelled at the last minute. I was imagining the worst things, you know?"

He nodded. "And so was I." When he looked into her eyes, he felt comfort; it was almost as though he was home. If only his uncles could see her. The men of his family would be pleased. "I am glad I did not allow my imagination to carry me away."

"Well," she said. "I guess we should look around."

"My beloved spake, and said unto me, Rise up, my love, my fair one, and come away."

He held his breath so that he would not sigh. "Let us see, eh?" He led her from the lobby into an exhibit. The lighting inside was more subdued, but somehow her hair and her eyes seemed to sparkle. Moor pointed to the different figures, hoping to appear somewhat interested in them, while stealing side glances at her. "So, your name is Mookie?"

Her smile seemed to get brighter and brighter. She even walked gracefully. She laughed. "Oh, I forgot all about names. No, my name is Gail. Mookie is just my screen name—the name I use on the computer. It was my nickname that my family called me when I was a little girl." She pointed out several interesting wax figures and then looked back at him. "Your screen name is Africa?"

"No, I don't have a . . ." He thought better of telling her the whole story, of explaining to her about Brighty, Blue, and Ali. "No, my name is Moor."

"That's a nice name."

He nodded. "So is Gail. You make it nice."

When she smiled and looked away, Moor counseled himself. He would have to be careful not to be too eager. He would have to be careful not to frighten her away with too many compliments. It was a computer date after all, and he must already be working against a doubt in her mind—a suspicion that he was desperate. He pretended to be interested in an Old West exhibit. He pointed at one of the cowboys. "Where are these black cowboys? We did not see them in the movies that we saw in my country." As he spoke, he hoped his joke, his satire, would not be too much.

"We didn't see them, either," she laughed. "Not in school. Not in the history books. None of the cowboys looked like us . . . and none of the saloon girls or pioneers. None of the books or stories showed us driving covered wagons or staking out land. There were black people there, though." She shook her head, as though trying to make light of the situation. "I guess we were all absent on picture day."

"Picture day?" While she explained to him that picture day was the day when photographers came to school to take pictures of all the children as a remembrance of what they looked like and who their classmates were, Moor tried to look as though he was interested in what she said and not focused on her smile. "Oh, picture day. I see."

"My senior year in high school, we took this trip. It was to Utah—to Promontory. Do you know about Promontory?"

He shook his head to keep her talking, to keep hearing the sound of her voice.

"Well, in the 1860s in the United States, they built the first railroad that stretched across the whole country, and the point where they finished the railroad, where they connected the points going east and west was Promontory. They drove a golden spike in the ground—well, actually they drove several golden spikes—at that place. There is a park and a museum there now. When we went there, the person that gave us the tour told us about all the men that worked—about the Irishmen and even the Chinese. He said there were a good number of African-Americans that worked the rails and that helped build the railroad. Historians knew it, but they just didn't have pictures of them, and the men didn't show up in the movies made at the time."

Gail laughed again. "The poor guy, he looked so confused—like he wanted to apologize when he looked at us. Like he just couldn't figure it out, why there weren't images of the black people on the railroads." Her smile and expression were bittersweet. "'They must have missed picture day.' That's what we told the man. It felt funny, it felt bad, but we tried to cover it up with a wisecrack." She shrugged. "You know how kids are."

Her smile was fading, and her pace slowed. "I guess this is not good first-date talk."

"Do you have a car? Is your car here?" He didn't want to talk any more about cowboys or the problems of the world.

She looked mildly confused by the sudden twist in the conversation. "I do have a car, but I caught the bus. You know . . . traffic."

"It is the city way, is it not? Buy a car, but catch the bus or train." He bent close to her ear. "Come away with me." He felt his smile broadening. "Come away with me so we can talk. We have time. We will get a bite to eat."

27

Mary

Thelma *looked at her watch.* "I can't be out late, you all." She poked at the salad in front of her. "It's Wednesday night. I don't know why we can't just do this on the weekends. I've got papers to grade."

Mary smiled and rubbed Thelma's shoulder. Thelma, who was ready for fun on the weekends, was usually like she was now—tired, stressed, and worried over the work she had to do. "Come on, girl, loosen up. We're not going to be out that long. It's been a few weeks, and I just have something I needed to talk to you all about."

She looked around the restaurant. The place was almost empty. The pizza—sausage, pepperoni, and mushrooms—should be coming soon. "Wait a minute."

She slid from the booth, almost floated to the jukebox, and looked over the selections. From her pocket she pulled four quarters. She made three selections and then walked back to the table and slid back into her space. She looked briefly out at the window's neon lights, then turned back to her friends. "Okay, now, I'm ready."

Soul singer Patti LaBelle began to wail in the background.

Latrice nudged Naomi. "Look at sister-girl." She smiled across the table at Mary. "She is beaming." Latrice waved her fingers. "Girl, what's up?"

Thelma's blue eyes sparkled. "Did you do the do?" She leaned back and raised an eyebrow. A smile cracked Thelma's face. "No, you didn't!" Thelma said as though she really thought Mary had. "You found a man and worked the plan! Yes, you did. You did the do!" She stamped her feet up and down underneath the table. "I can't believe it! Hallelujah!" She stood and briefly did the shimmy. "All our hard work paid off! Free at last! Free at last!" She slumped back into her seat, as if overcome, and began to fan herself with a menu.

Naomi was quiet. She just smiled tentatively as she brushed her hair out of her face. But Latrice began to do a dance, a seated dance that starred her elaborately manicured nails. "All right, girl! You got it! You got it! You got it going on!" she half sang. "So, who is the brother? Spill the beans!"

Mary tried not to participate, but she couldn't keep the smile off her face. Soon she was laughing. "Come on, you all." She gasped for breath. "Give me a break, okay?"

Thelma opened her eyes wide. "Give you a break? It seems like you already got a break, Miss Mary. And by the expression on your face, it was a good break indeed!" Thelma clapped her hands together. "I haven't seen you glowing like this in a long time."

Latrice leaned forward and cradled her chin on her hands. "Okay, girl, give us all the details."

Mary was still trying to stop laughing. "There's nothing to tell," she said as she gasped for breath. "Really!"

Latrice laughed. "Girl, who you think you kidding? Something is up with you. You giggling about something. And trust me . . . I'm pretty sure what that something is."

Mary got her breathing back to normal and looked around the table at her friends. "It's not that, you all. Honestly. Something has happened, but it's not that. . . . It's about the museum. I was at the Great Blacks in Wax Museum . . . well, it's not exactly about the museum."

Latrice looked at Mary like she had two seconds to explain before she made the mental health call to 9-1-1. "What are you talking about, Mary? I know you are not trying to tell me a museum statue has you giggling like this. I know better."

Thelma nodded. "Your face is all flushed and you're breathing heavy. The museum's good, but it's not that good. So, go ahead. Just 'fess up, girl. It's okay. We'll let you keep your wings and halo. We're all adults, here. Confess it—you bit the apple!"

Mary laughed. "I didn't bite any apple. I'm not married. I'm not even in love . . . not yet, so you *know* I didn't bite any apple."

Thelma laughed and poked at her salad again. "What's love got to do with it?"

Mary smiled at her. "Love has everything to do with it. That's why—"

"I don't believe in love." Thelma said it matter-of-factly. "I don't mean to rain on your parade . . . on your pizza party." Her smile was fading. The tired, stressed Thelma was reappearing.

She was not going to let Thelma's mood spoil her own. She looked across the table at Latrice and Naomi. "Something wonderful has happened and I wanted to share it with you all, because it couldn't have happened without you all."

Thelma looked at her watch again. Her teacher's expression had returned. "Well, like I said, Mary, we need to get this over with, soon." She touched the side of her mouth with her napkin, then returned it to her lap. "I hope you didn't have me come down here to tell me some schoolgirl story about love. Because if you did, I don't have time."

Latrice looked at Mary and then at Thelma. "Come on, girl. Don't be such a party pooper."

"I'm not pooping anybody's party. I'm just saying I don't believe in love." Thelma reached into her purse and put on her glasses. "There is no such thing as love."

Latrice shook her head. "Thelma, what bee is up your butt?"

"Look, I don't have time for this on a school night. I'm tired. I've been chasing kids all day. I'm just telling the truth—there is no such thing as love. It's just one person with a predisposition to be attracted to a certain set of physical characteristics that meets another compatible person. Or a person with a certain psychological makeup that meets another person with a compatible psychological makeup, a person with a weakness or need that meets another person with a complementary weakness or need. It's a biological imperative that keeps the species alive. Nothing more. Nothing less."

Latrice sat back in her seat. "Come on, Thelma. You don't believe that."

"Yes I do. We have romanticized a biological need, and set up social systems around that need. That's exactly what I believe. Having schoolgirl crushes is fun when you're a girl. Now we're adults—educated adults—and it's time for us to grow up."

Latrice waved her hand in the air. "I don't believe you, Thelma. You are just trying to pull somebody's leg. Of course you believe in love. We may not be getting any, but we all believe in love. I mean we make do with what we got, but we all believe in love."

"*We* may, but *I* don't. I just don't talk about it because people freak out when I say it, just like you're doing, Latrice. You're starting to sound like Mary." She frowned. "That's why I don't follow the rules." She pantomimed quotation marks with her fingers. "They're antiquated and pointless. I live the life I want to live." She put on a forced tight smile. "Love is not the star of most of our relationships, not even relationships that last a lifetime. That's the honest medicine without the sugar-coating. So shoot me."

Latrice was quiet. Naomi stirred her drink with her straw. Mary searched for the right words to say and tried to catch her breath. She wanted to say nothing, but she couldn't—there was too much hanging in the air. "I think love has everything to do with it. The Bible says God is love, and if love doesn't exist, then there is no—"

"Why do you have to drag God into everything, Mary? You know what, I'm sorry to be short with you, but I'm tired. I've got work to do tomorrow . . . and tonight before I can go to bed." She looked at her watch and yawned to mask her agitation. "I'm not telling *you* how to feel. I'm just telling you how *I* feel, what *I* believe. Why isn't that good enough? Why do you and everybody else that believes something different think it's your duty to try to convince me that I'm wrong? Why do you always have to be looking to recruit people to what you believe? Like you're so sure you're right."

Thelma wiped her mouth and threw her napkin on the table. "I just don't feel like it tonight, okay?"

None of this was happening the way Mary had planned. It was supposed to just be a good time among friends. A moment when she could tell them that something wonderful had happened to her. What was supposed to put smiles on all their faces was making knots in her stomach. Mary sighed. "Don't be upset with me, Thelma. You're right."

She looked around the table. "You get to think what you want to think." Mary pointed at her green eyes and then at Thelma's own blue ones. "But the truth is, we're all recruiting backup. Nobody wants to be alone in her own opinion, not even people that believe they do."

While Patti sang "You Are My Friend," the waitress delivered the hot, cheesy pizza and put a single steaming, gooey slice on each of their plates. When the waitress left, Mary continued. "I just don't want to be with a man unless I do it the right way, unless I'm in a marriage that God has blessed. You don't have to believe that, but that's what I believe . . . that's what I've learned to believe. That's what you all helped me to understand that I believe. You don't have to believe it—"

"Mary, really, I hope you didn't call us here for more preaching. Really, I—"

"When did it become preaching, Thelma? I'm just giving my opinion, just like you—"

"Since my divorce, the in-crowd has turned me out." Latrice turned, her mouth open, to look at Naomi. Naomi tossed her hair. It was just about the first thing she had said all evening. "At first, I didn't even realize it. It took me years before I realized that they weren't—as much as I went to church, as much as I served—no one was asking me to be a deaconess, or appointing me as head of any committees. My church family abandoned me. What kind of love is that?" She stirred her drink again. "I believe in love. I want love. I just think people are more interested in reputation and show than they are in love. As long as I had the right credentials, I was lovable."

She looked across the table at Mary. "I believe you, Mary. I respect what you believe. But it wasn't right what happened to me. I know I go back and forth about it, but the truth is, it hurts, and I'm not over it, you know? I try to be, but I'm not." Naomi tilted her head. "It's like I was good enough to be there and serve and tithe. With a husband—even if we weren't getting along, as long as we had a sham marriage and played the game—then I could be 'in.'"

What was happening? Mary looked at Naomi and Thelma. She hadn't asked them to meet so that they could argue. She wasn't sure what to say.

Naomi continued speaking. "Being divorced makes you a deviant, no matter who you were in the past. That's what I found out. Somehow, being single makes you dangerous. Especially women— we're a necessary but dangerous burden to the church." She put on a forced smile. "But, hey, I'm not bitter. I don't have to be where I'm not wanted. But I tell you this much; they may reject me, but no one's going to separate me from the love of God. They can't keep me from Him because I'm single. I just do my own thing. I'm not proud of it. I want something different. I do. I'm just not there." She looked down at the table, and then back at Mary. "I go where I'm wanted, where I feel loved. I'm sorry, Mary." She dropped her head.

Mary thought of the conversation that she and Naomi had sitting in her place, sipping tea. This didn't sound like the same Naomi. This Naomi was more wounded. "Naomi, you don't have anything to be sorry to me about."

Naomi went on as though she hadn't heard. "I didn't want the divorce. He cheated on me. Shoot, he cheated on me so many times. . . . And I prayed about it to God, but He let it happen. I try not to let it get to me, but sometimes it still does. God let it happen, and I don't understand that."

Naomi poked her pizza with her fork. "And when we went to divorce court, the judge gave my ex the kids. Took my babies, took everything from me. I didn't do that to myself. I tried to hold on, but I could see the church didn't want me there, nobody wanted me around. My presence made them have to choose sides. So, I . . . let . . . go. *We love you, Naomi. Don't go.*' That's what they said when I was leaving. Hypocrites! They couldn't wait until I got out the door."

She frowned and tossed her head. "Now, I'm not looking for love from anyone. I'm not bitter. I guess I'm not bitter. But at least I'm being real. I just do my own thing. I tried to be the good guy and I got kicked in the teeth. Now, I play a little hit and miss when I've been lonely too long. When I have an itch, I scratch it. So what? God knows my heart . . . and He knows what happened to me." Naomi stopped talking and stabbed her straw, several times, into her glass of fruit punch.

Latrice laid her hand on Naomi's shoulder. "Girl, I feel your pain—"

Naomi pushed Latrice's hand away. "I'm not in pain!"

"Take it easy, okay?" Latrice patted Naomi's hand. "I'm on your side, okay?" Latrice pursed her lips and looked at Mary. "Nothing really bad happened to me. No tragedy. I just like doing what I like to do." She laughed.

Mary looked at her friends. What was going on? This was just a friendly get-together. How had it turned into true confessions? This was not why they were here.

Latrice shook one of her manicured fingers. "No heartbreak for this girl. So what if I have a little fun? Life is short, baby. I don't have to get in some relationship where I'm going through a lot of changes—" she nodded at Naomi —"where I end up getting divorced, where I end up getting hurt, just to prove something to other people. Other people don't keep me warm at night or pay my bills. I'm just being real about it. I'm a good consumer, okay? I take what I need and leave the rest behind for whoever wants to buy the goods."

Latrice wagged a finger and smiled. "What difference does it make? I'm still saved. If people can lie, cheat, and steal . . . if they can be mean as sin . . . killing other saints with their tongues . . . and they're still saved . . . and nobody puts them out of the church—" Latrice snapped her fingers —"then, baby, I know I'm saved! Sin is sin and they can't convince me mine is bigger than theirs. It's like this: if Strom Thurmond went to heaven—and I believe he did—so is Lil' Kim. That's my theological take on the whole thing. Sex ain't the worst thing in the world."

Mary sighed. She didn't want to talk about this. It was not what she had planned. She knew there were so many raw emotions, because it was much more than a conversation about sex. It was a conversation about their hearts and about their vulnerabilities. Underneath the words, they were talking about the loss of little-girl dreams and little-girl hopes. Underneath the words, they were whispering about disappointments and hurts that made them want to give up ever hoping for the best. They were discussing risk—risking hurt and heartbreak to trust God in the face of what looked to be insurmountable odds.

Mary knew what they were really discussing was whether they were willing to drop all their disguises, all their defenses, their walls of protection—all the years of patterns and thoughts built one on top of the other. They were discussing tearing down those substantial walls to trust God's promises, to trust God's words: *"I will never leave you nor forsake you."* They were being asked to trust in something they could not touch: *"We do not look at the things which are seen, but at the things which are not seen. . . ."* *"For we walk by faith, not by sight."* They were really being asked to trust that if they would believe and make themselves vulnerable— *"Do not fear, for you will not be ashamed"*—in a world where no one cares or keeps their promises, they were being asked to believe that the unseen God would always love them and keep His promises.

They were being asked to give up what they knew, to trust that God's words were sure. *"For as the rain comes down, and the snow from heaven, and do not return there, but water the earth, and make it bring forth and bud, that it may give seed to the sower and bread to the eater, so shall My word be that goes forth from My mouth; it shall not return to Me void. But it shall accomplish what I please, and it shall prosper in the thing for which I sent it. For you shall go out with joy, and be led out with peace; the mountains and the hills shall break forth into singing before you, and all the trees of the fields shall clap their hands."*

Mary knew the scariness of surrendering something you love, something that makes you feel better, in hopes of a better promise. "You know what, Latrice? I'm not qualified to have this conversation. I'm not some super saint. I don't even want to *have* this conversation. This is not what I came here to talk about. And like you've told me before, you've been saved longer than I have."

She reached across the table to touch Latrice's hand. "I look in your eyes. You're my friend, and I know your heart. I know you love the other saints and that you would do anything you could for anybody. I don't know anybody with a more generous heart, and that's the truth, Latrice. The fruit of the Spirit, the tell-tale signs of love—I see them in you."

Mary could see Latrice's expression softening as she spoke. "God has given you the best that He has. Other people may not like it. It may make them uncomfortable. Just like some saints in the early church in Jerusalem might have been uncomfortable that God had given His Spirit and spiritual gifts to the Corinthians. But because God gave them the gifts, that didn't mean that they weren't doing God wrong, that they weren't breaking His heart." She took a deep breath. "You know, Latrice, I don't know why God is involved with us. Because for all our doing wrong, for all our pretending that we don't know what God really wants from us, we really do know the truth. And even though we know what He wants, and He knows that we're not doing it, He keeps loving us. And we say that means we're justified."

Latrice held up one hand. "Mary, we don't have to talk about this."

"No. No. I let you have your say. You brought it up, so I get to talk, too." Mary shook her head. "I don't understand how we can think we're okay just because God doesn't destroy us—just because He's merciful, just because He gives us grace.

"It's just like being greedy, or just like being prejudiced . . . people doing it know they're wrong. They don't need anyone else to preach another sermon to them to tell them they're wrong." She lifted her purse and tugged at her ear to illustrate. "How can you have money coming out your ears, more than you will ever need, and not give when you see homeless people everywhere?" She shook her head. "How can anybody make up lame excuses? *They did it to themselves.' 'Jesus said the poor we will have with us always.' 'If you give to a man, you just help him stay down.'* Who are we kidding? We know we're cheap. God knows we're stingy. But He keeps loving us anyway."

She touched the skin on her arm. "And prejudice—we all know the story. All the games, all the justifications, and we all know they're lies. Girl, in this day and age, how can anybody sit in an office, a big office full of white people, with no blacks, no Asians, no Hispanics? How can they justify not having any 'ethnic' employees, no people that make them uncomfortable in their office families? Especially when they're trying to get *ethnic* money. Girl, God is not fooled!"

Latrice held up a hand. "Amen! Hallelujah to that, sister!"

Mary nodded. "And just because God continues to be with them, to bless them, they use God's mercy and grace to justify to themselves that they couldn't be doing anything wrong. They tell themselves, if they were wrong God would strike them down. We know Him giving them a break doesn't mean they're right."

Naomi tossed her hair. "We know that. Nobody here is arguing that, Mary."

Mary continued. "The point is that *we* can see that, but they don't. We see the dot in their eyes but not the log in our own. They look at us and shake their heads, because they see the dot in our eyes and not the log in their own. When we're doing what we want to do, when they're greedy or prejudiced, we're all forcing God's Spirit inside of us to participate in the wrong that we're doing."

Thelma shook her head. "Maybe I'm just tired, but I don't see that my making choices about my own personal sexuality compares in *any* way with someone lying, or stealing, or being greedy or prejudiced."

Mary turned in her seat to face Thelma. "We don't see it, because we don't want to see. We wish that God would take His love away from people that are prejudiced . . . unless we're the ones being prejudiced. People want God to take His love away from people who are fornicating, or getting divorced, or having abortions, or doing whatever else it is they think shouldn't be happening, because that's not their sin." She shrugged. "We want Him to forgive our sins, but not theirs. We want Him to show *us* mercy, but we don't want Him to show mercy to others that are doing stuff that makes our lives uncomfortable. We get mad because of how strong God's love is. . . .We get mad because His love endures all things. And we want to act like we have to take control of the situation and punish other people because God is too tenderhearted and just doesn't know any better."

Mary sighed, looked out the window, and then took a drink of her soda. She really didn't know how she had gotten into all of this.

She turned back to the group. She didn't want to have the conversation, but it was a conversation they all needed to have. She needed to talk through it herself. "God doesn't hate sex."

Naomi, Latrice, and Thelma stared at her in silence. Then they began to laugh. Thelma shrugged her shoulders and lifted her hands. "Mary, girl, what are you talking about? Who said He did? Nobody here at *this* table!"

"Nobody said it out loud, but lots of people think He does. That's partly why we're having this discussion. Our thinking is out of order. God created it. He wants us to enjoy it. But just like all our other desires, He wants us to bring our sensual desires captive to His Spirit, so that we do them the way He wants us to."

She pointed at the pizza on the plate in front of her. "God is not against us enjoying food, but He wants that desire to be in order, you know what I mean? The same way with sex. We just want to *overeat*, if you know what I mean." Latrice smirked, but Mary ignored her. "And what God says is order, is His blessing on the union—anything else is unclean. To tell you the truth, I even sometimes think that getting married with a piece of paper is not sufficient."

Naomi scratched her head. "Wait a minute, Mary."

Latrice waved her hand and then pointed. "Girl, you are tripping! You sure you don't have a little *sumthin-sumthin* in that cup?"

Naomi looked at Latrice, nodded, and then looked back at Mary. "Girl, what are you talking about now? You've just been sitting here arguing with us about marriage. Now, what are you talking about?"

"Look, you all, I'm not a pastor, I'm not the pope. But think about it. Most of the people I know don't ever ask God, 'Is this the woman or man you have for me?' How many people do you know, saying, 'Lord, send me the person you have for me'? I don't know. I just think there a lot of couples walking down the aisle together that God never intended to unite."

Mary poked her pizza. "We're asking for His blessings on something He never ordained. We're like Sarai in the Bible, just trying to make something happen. Then we're confused when it doesn't work out. . . . Then we're mad at God." She shrugged. "I just wonder about it sometimes when I hear pastors say that God's not responsible for blessing anything He didn't start—"

"Mary—" Latrice objected.

"No really. While I'm on a roll, I just need to finish. We bring shame unions, guilt unions, I'm-just-tired-of-being-single unions, manipulation unions, greed unions, lust unions, revenge unions, trying-to-please-my-parents unions—all those relationships that we're in for the wrong reasons—to the altar. We put on white, whisper some magic words, and try to pretend that the ceremony makes it holy. But if our prayers and fasts stink in God's nose when we do them for the wrong reason, why do we think marriages are excluded? Then we're trying to hold together, and praying like He's responsible for its survival. But you know what? I'm not a pastor—I'm just thinking out loud, and that's a conversation for another day."

Latrice drummed her nails on the table. "Girl, you think too much."

"What I am trying to say is that God says that sex is for a union that He has blessed . . . for marriage . . . to bind a couple, to seal the union. Anything else is sin, it's unclean."

Latrice, laughing, waved one of her hands in the air. "It may be unclean, but, girl, you know it's fun! Let's just tell the truth about it!"

Mary nodded and smiled. "I'm not denying that. But it still binds us to people we're not supposed to be connected to. We get tied up to a lot of fools that way."

Latrice put a hand over her mouth and laughed. "Girl, you sound like Prophetess Juanita Bynum."

Mary nodded. "She was telling the truth. We know it. And the thing is, it's not just women. There are lots of men sitting on couches with their heads in their hands wondering how they got there. They were just getting their groove on, having a good time with the temporary woman. But before they know it, girlfriend is setting up house. They don't even like her, and next thing they are walking down the aisle, swearing out a lie. When the *right* one comes along, it's too late. They're caught up."

Naomi laughed. "Yeah, girl, I have to admit it. I've seen it for myself." She smiled. "It's not fun going to sleep with Denzel and waking up next to Bozo."

Latrice laughed out loud. "Girl, you know you right! I got a whole bunch of men I can't shake loose. They just stuck to a sister!" She shook her hands like she was trying to get something to *un*stick. "They won't let go!"

Mary smiled, happy that the mood was changing. She pulled a string of cheese from her slice of pizza. "I don't know. I don't know all the answers. I can't tell you all what to do. I love you too much to even try. I'm not God. And if God gives us free will, then who am I to try to take it away. I just think it's important enough to think about. It's important for our children—not just the ones we give birth to, but to all the children that are looking at us trying to figure out how to live life. It's important so we don't end up marrying Bozo, or training our children to marry Bozo."

Even Thelma yawned and laughed. "That's nasty. Just the thought . . . married to Bozo. That's like being married to Ronald McDonald."

Latrice snapped her fingers. "Girl, don't hate. Even Ronald needs love."

Naomi groaned.

They all laughed. Mary pressed it further. "And then we end up crying and our children crying because we end up married and having Bozo's kids. Or Bozo-etta's kids for that matter."

Thelma spit the tea she was drinking out of her mouth. "Girl, you are crazy!"

Latrice feigned a sympathetic glance. "I don't see why you all getting down so hard on Bozo, anyway. I like that red nose, okay? And he's got a good sense of humor."

Thelma grunted. "Is there a man you don't like?"

"Well . . ."

Mary shook her head and smiled. What was happening now was what made the three women precious to her. "We ought to be able to talk about this kind of stuff. If we're friends, we ought to be able to. have frank conversations about things. We shouldn't have to be shallow all the time. If we can play—and we know we can—we should be able to talk about difficult things too." She wiped her mouth with her napkin. "We don't have to keep treating God like a chump because He keeps loving us and taking us back. We can grow up and realize how good He is. We can decide to honor Him with everything we have because He loves us enough to keep taking us back even when we do wrong. That's all I'm saying."

Mary picked up her slice. "The bottom line is that I love you all. Whatever choices you make, I love you. I hope you love me the same way. My job is to be your friend and love you, and if I learn something good, something that works for me, I should share it. If I learn about a good stain remover, I should tell it. It's your choice whether you want to buy it or not. I don't have any business getting mad either way. All I'm trying to do is give you my testimony as your friend. I'm not judging how you keep house. I've got some of the same stains in my *own* house. In fact, I had the same stain I'm talking to you about. I'm not being proud. I'm just telling you what worked for me, and what I have learned. The choice is up to you." She nibbled at the tip of the slice, then took it away from her mouth. "Besides, you all brought this conversation up. This is really not what I asked you here to talk about, anyway."

Thelma swallowed a mouth full of pizza. "Well, if it's not, then you better start talking, sister." She looked at her watch. "You got fifteen minutes."

28

Puddin

The talk was all over town.

The trees had surrendered their leaves and the mornings were cooler. It wasn't so much the weather that had people talking. The old folks said that you couldn't tell from one minute to the next whether it would be hot or cold, raining or dry—you couldn't much use the weather to judge the seasons anymore. Instead, they just used the weather as background for people, to give the story—the real story—flesh and detail.

Yes, there was lots of talk. People were talking about the sniper trial. *"Who would have thought that two black men would do something like that? Killing all those people, even shooting that boy. Terrifying the whole area." "It makes you sick on the inside, don't it? Maybe integration wasn't such a good idea after all." "Now, I wouldn't go that far." "I don't know."*

They talked about whether the mayor was going to run for governor. They even talked about music. *"Remember when Ronald Isley sang sweet love ballads? You know, before he became a dirty old man?"* They talked about the Ravens and whether there would be another Super Bowl win.

There were lots of stories, lots of things to talk about. But what people talked about most was Puddin. *Eleanore "Puddin" Jenkins,* the newspapers called her.

Anyone who wanted to know the truth would most likely have had to try to find Sister Puddin or Brother Joe, or at least go to Old Frederick Road and try to question some Sunday churchgoer.

There were so many ludicrous speculations. Some people said

there were weapons involved; some people said it almost tore the church and the whole city apart. Most people exaggerated, as people will do, and said they were sure some hot grease was thrown or hot grits were involved. *"No, that wasn't Sister Puddin. That was somebody else."* What they all agreed on, however, is that there was chicken involved. Lots of it.

Sister Minnie and Deaconess Othella tried to resist, they really did. But finally after getting their arms twisted, they talked to the newspapers. *"I had never seen her act like that. The Negro . . . excuse me, Brother Joe drove her to it. First she was okay, then she was crying and screaming. We closed the door, but people could still hear her outside. It was a sin and shame."* They said after they told her about Joe and about the Starbucks, Puddin paced back and forth yelling over and over again. *"What am I going to do now?"* Contrary to what others witnessed as they saw her leaving the church, Deaconess Othella said, *"She wasn't calm at all. She was a mess. We witnessed it with our own eyes, and we knew everything was going to fall apart."*

Puddin slumped onto a dining room chair. She looked down the hall at the reading room and thought about going in there, about breaking in there. It was Wednesday evening, and while Joe was out she would tear up all the tapes—unthread the tape, stretch it, and tear it from the holders. Maybe she would overturn the video player and watch it crash to the floor at her feet. Then she would unplug the television and hurl it out the window onto the yard and laugh as it rolled down the slope of the front yard and out onto Old Frederick.

If Joe wanted to leave then—after he saw it—then let him leave. She didn't need him.

For better or for worse . . . for richer or for poorer . . . in sickness and in health . . .

She wanted to stop thinking about it. She wanted to stop caring. She wanted it to be over. Maybe destroying it all would do that. The sad truth, though, was that she wasn't sure she wanted it to be over. She wasn't even sure she wanted to hurt him. And what was the point of going in the room? What was it going to solve? What was behind the door could be even worse than she imagined. Maybe it was better that she didn't know.

There were other ways. She didn't have to wreck everything. It was all going to be hers anyway. What was certain was that she wasn't going to cry anymore. She wasn't going to let Joe walk all over her anymore. She didn't have to figure it all out . . . not right now.

The house was silent, almost mournful. There wasn't even the sound of a ticking clock. Most days she hated that Deaconess Othella had told her about Joe. Maybe she didn't hate it. But she wanted it over and out of her mind. It had been weeks, and still she couldn't get it out of her mind; she couldn't stop worrying about what she should do.

She didn't have to work it out right now. Puddin laid both of her hands flat on the table and pushed herself to a standing position. She had other things she could think about.

She turned and walked down the hall to her computer. When it was on, she opened her files, and began to sort through the names, through the stories of her babies.

There were no lights on in the room and no windows. She touched the glowing screen and their words; they comforted her. She felt warm, almost, toward the words, toward the names. They trusted her, they needed her. She could trust them. And if she didn't have Joe's love anymore, at least she could give her love to them. She could show them how to find it . . . how to find true love.

Some of them had gone on dates and she read the feedback they posted, both good and bad.

Fussygrl@charmcitynews.com: No chemistry, but we might get to be good friends.

Babycakes@charmcitynews.com: It was a disaster.

Africa@charmcitynews.com: I think she might be the one . . .

After only one date, Africa had posted the words, and she weighed cautioning him to be careful, to not surrender his heart too easily. She touched his name and his description. He lived in the city but was originally from Lesotho. "Be careful, my son," she said to the screen, then moved on. She stopped four more names down the list, went back up, and sent him an email.

HipHopGodMama@charmcitynews.com: Africa, don't move too quickly. See what change the new season brings.

Puddin continued combing through the names of men and women, looking for new faces, new entries, or new information. Most of them were the same—names and faces that had been there all along. She moved quickly over the name Praline-@charmcitynews.com and had gone down twenty or so, before she came back to it. *Praline*. She opened up the new picture next to the name. Praline was a blonde with green eyes, though her description listed her with brown eyes and black hair. It was more than that, though. Praline looked familiar. She lived in the city, so maybe she recognized her from the store or the library.

Puddin rubbed her eyes and looked at the picture again. She was tired . . . but of course she knew her. *Oh my!* It was Mary. Mary from her church, the one that ran the mentoring group with the young girls. Mary who lived down the street.

The young woman had been the other topic of conversation the day she learned about Joe. "*She needs to just cool her hot self down. What she needs to do is get married.*" Maybe Deaconess Othella would be happy to know that Mary was trying.

Puddin looked at the picture, at her baby. "I'm watching out for you. It's going to be all right." Here, now, was a new favorite—not that she didn't love all her children. Now, Mary was one of her babies—she felt her concern and affection for the young woman growing. She had seen Mary first toddling, then skipping, then walking down the street holding her grandmother's hand for years—until finally the roles reversed, and it was the grandmother who held on to the girl for support.

Puddin knew Mary and her grandmother well enough to wave and know their names and faces. They were church nodding acquaintances, not talk-over-the-fence friends or sit-down-to-coffee friends. Now, this way, she and Mary—*Praline*—would become closer. She would watch over her. Without the girl knowing, she would look out for her—make sure she ended up with a good man, an honest man, the kind of man her grandmother would have wanted for her.

Puddin touched a finger to the young woman's picture on the screen again and then closed the record. She sorted through the rest of the files—she didn't want to leave them. Her babies were her only joy. But finally, she shut down the computer and then dragged herself to the kitchen.

Opening the deep freeze, she reached in for a bag of chicken, popped it in the microwave to thaw, then went to the cabinets and took out a large frying pan and cooking oil. When the microwave beeped, she removed the chicken and transferred it to the sink to wash. She patted each piece dry with a paper towel, seasoned it, floured it, and then dropped it in the hot oil.

She was a fool. She'd been a fool. Who knew how long Joe had been meeting with the women? Maybe all the years she thought that everything was so wonderful, maybe he'd been cheating all those years, too. She poked at the chicken in the pan with a long-handled fork.

"Now, I hate to tell any woman to leave her husband, but I saw it with my own two eyes."

Of course it would be Deaconess Othella that saw him. Probably the whole church had seen him at one time or another for all she knew. And, of course, Othella's advice was right. Joe wasn't going to get any better. His habits weren't going to change. She should leave him. Ninety-eight out of a hundred women would tell her to leave him. *"Leave him and take everything he's got. Take him to the cleaners and just leave the dirty dog with the empty plastic bags."*

The only problem was that forty percent of that ninety-eight didn't have a man—had never had one—and would probably be praying that they could date Joe as soon as she left him. Of those that remained, probably fifty percent had already left their own men, but didn't bother to tell her that they still cried every night about them being gone. Maybe one or two out of that ninety-eight didn't like men anyway. So that left only a few that gave the advice to leave without carrying some ugly business in their hip pockets. Leaving was a scary thing.

Then that left the two out of the hundred that would say *stay.* One of them was crazy and the other was just a merciful saint, and Puddin wasn't feeling like she could identify with either of the two.

She flipped the chicken over. He was probably cheating all along. She was at home pinching pennies. *"No wife of mine is going to be working while I sit at home."* She was home cooking chicken every day. She could have had a career, or at least a worthwhile job, but she was home penniless while he was hanging out blowing money they couldn't afford at Starbucks.

She looked at the ceiling. "See, I told you, God. I told you he was going to make a fool of me." The part she left unsaid was, "And you let him do it."

Puddin grabbed a green platter from the cabinet and covered it with paper towel. She took the hot chicken from the oil, laid it on the platter, then took the platter to the dining room and set it on the table.

He was at Starbucks drinking coffee. Drinking with white women. "White women! If you're going to cheat, Joe, couldn't you cheat with your own kind?"

She stormed back into the kitchen, yanked the freezer open, grabbed another bag of chicken, and popped it into the microwave. She stared at the window on the microwave door and watched the chicken turn. White women. *"There was your husband sitting in a Starbucks huddled up with a bunch of white women! . . . There were a couple of black women. . . ."*

She should have asked Deaconess Othella for more details. Were they young? What did they look like? Were they thin? Of course they were thin. Of course they were. Joe was probably buying drinks for them. *"Here, young lady, let me take care of that for you."* She could hear his voice. She could hear him being smooth. If those women knew what she knew, they would have thrown the coffee back at him.

Joe was spending every penny they had at Starbucks, while she stayed at home cooking chicken. And who knew? Who knew? Maybe without his coffee habit, without the videotapes, without the women, there might have been money for her to have something other than chicken.

The microwave beeped and she took the chicken to the sink to wash it. When it was washed, she patted it dry with paper towel. She seasoned it, floured it, and dropped each piece into the hot oil to fry. She poked at the chicken with the long-handled fork.

Maybe there might have been enough money for her to have beef sometimes. Instead of Joe guzzling Starbucks, she could have had a nice, thick, juicy homemade burger . . . or maybe a steak. She flipped the frying chicken. Instead of those videotapes, she could have had some ribs, or a pork loin or pork chops . . . or some lamb.

When the chicken was done frying, she reached into the cabinet for a white platter, covered the platter with paper towel, and placed the pieces of fried chicken on the platter. When the phone rang, she set the platter on top of the microwave and answered it.

"Hello, Puddin?" It was Joe.

"Hello."

"Is everything okay, Puddin?"

"Yeah, everything's okay. Why shouldn't everything be okay, Joe?"

"You just sound funny. You sure everything is okay?"

"It's fine, Joe."

"Okay, then. Well, I was just calling to let you know I won't be home for dinner. I've got something . . . I've got something I have to take care of." Puddin could hear people talking and laughing in the background. She knew where he was. "When I finish, I'm gone go head straight to the church for men's group, okay?"

"Okay, Joe."

"You sure? I was trying to call before you got dinner started. Have you started cooking yet?"

Of course she had. "Yeah."

"I'm sorry, Puddin. Really."

"Don't worry about it, Joe. I'll figure out something to do with it."

"See you later. I love you, Puddin."

"Yeah."

"You sure you're okay?"

"Yeah, Joe. I've got to go. The chicken's burning." She hung up the phone. *The chicken's burning now, and you're going to be burning later.* She laughed to herself and got a bag of wings from the freezer.

She poked at the frying wings. Some lamb would have been nice. Shish kabobs—that would have been a tasty change. It would have been nice to have something different.

When the chicken was finished, she grabbed a blue platter and placed the wings on it. She set them on the counter.

She should leave him. She *would* leave him. Let the Starbucks girls come fry his chicken for him. She grabbed another bag of wings from the freezer. Better yet, maybe she would stay and make him miserable.

When Puddin had finished frying chicken, when it was dark, when there was only one bag left in the freezer, she turned off the stove. She went to the closet and got her coat. After she put her coat on, she dumped all the chicken from the platters into doubled plastic grocery store bags, grabbed her keys, and left the house with all the bird in tow.

29

Moor

Blue bit into the hot chicken leg. Juice dripped down his chin and he wiped it with his hand. "I don't care what nobody says, Tyrone's makes the best chicken in town." Without the firelight, in the darkening evening, they wouldn't have been able to see the steam rising from the food.

Brighty was gnawing on a piece of gristle. "That's what you say, but I say Simone's will give them a run for the money." He dropped the bone on the ground and grabbed another piece from the box on the table in front of them. "And this Wednesday special—a bucket of legs and thighs for $7.99—is something to write home about."

"It don't matter what I say, does it, Brighty? If I say grass is green, you got to disagree. If I say the sky is blue, you got to say something different." Blue pointed at the ground. "And pick up that bone you dropped."

Brighty nodded with his head. "That bone is for the dogs. They got to eat, too." He smacked his lips together. "Anyway, what good does it do just to agree, when sometimes the grass *is* brown, or sometimes the sky *is* orange or gray. I know you think you know everything, Blue. But here's some news for you: I know some things, too." He took a big bite of chicken and kept talking. "You need to get over that—thinking you the only one that know anything."

"You know there's nothing better than sitting around—just the guys—chewing the fat and eating some chicken." Ali sat on his concrete block while holding a hot piece of chicken in a paper napkin, chuckling in between bites.

Blue shook his head at Brighty. "I ain't got no time to fool with you. Look at you, talking with your mouth full. It's a wonder that woman at the store will have anything to do with you." Truth be told, he was happy for his friend. Blue's own marriage had been good, had been good for him. As much as he teased his friend, he hoped that joy would find him, too.

Brighty shook his head. "You can't get my goat. And you leave her out of this, you jealous old buzzard."

Blue waved his hand at Brighty. "I'm through talking to you. I'm through trying to help you. Who's going to stay with an old fool that chews with his mouth open? You watch, that woman is gone drop you like a hotcake. Besides, I don't want to talk to you." He looked at Ali. "I want to hear about the date."

Ali swallowed. "Well, Moor said it went perfect. It's been a week or so, and they're still . . . you know. I wish he were here to tell you. But here's what he told me. . . ."

Moor looked into her eyes and loved it that she blushed when he did, though she did not look away. He ordered crab cakes and she ordered a salad.

"So, you are from Lesotho?" Her eyes misted over when he described the mountains, the wild flowers, and when he told her about his family. "I've always wanted to visit Africa," she said. She looked down, then looked up, batting her eyes. "Sometimes I've wondered what it would be like to live there."

"Oh, you would love it, my sister. And the people would love you, especially my family, my uncles. We would make a big feast for you. My grandmother would cook."

Her sigh trembled with contentment. "I would love that. It seems like a dream too good to be true."

Her skin was smooth like brown satin. It was all he could do not to touch it. Before he fell too deeply, he would ask her the question that would settle it all—the deal breaker, as Americans said. "Do you go to church here in Baltimore?"

She nodded and told him where. "What about you?"

He could feel relief settling in his shoulders. He could hear it in his voice. "I go to New Worshipper," he told her. "Maybe you will visit some time. Maybe you will visit . . . with me."

"I would love to."

"Do you like children?"

"Of course." She giggled. "I'm a teacher."

"Of course, you're a teacher." He smiled and laid his napkin across his lap. A teacher could find rewarding, exciting work in Lesotho.

He frowned. "There is something I must tell you." He cleared his throat. "I will only be in Baltimore a little while longer, then I am on to California. I don't know how you feel about that."

"How do *you* feel about it?"

He shrugged. He should never have come. There was no time to marry. "It could get complicated," he acknowledged.

She reached across the table and patted his hand. "Where you're going in California, they have telephones? They deliver mail?"

"Yes."

"And airplanes? An airport within driving distance?"

"Yes! Yes! Of course!" He smiled.

"Then I think we can work it out." She lowered her eyes and her lashes touched her cheeks.

Just before his heart burst, before he prematurely dropped to his knee, the waiter came with the food. Moor said grace.

When he had finished, she daintily placed a forkful of salad in her mouth. "Don't worry. Everything will be okay."

Blue and Brighty sighed together in the moonlight. "It sound just like a fairy tale," Brighty whispered.

Blue nudged him. "Oh, you just saying that 'cause you all puffed up yourself." He shook his head, but he couldn't stop himself from sighing again. "It does sound good, though. It sounds like you did a good job, Ali. I'm happy to know the prince is satisfied."

Ali scratched his head. "He sounds like he's floating on a cloud. The only bad thing he could come up with was that she talked with her mouth full." He shrugged then tore at the piece of chicken in his hand.

Brighty belched. "That can be irritating."

Blue frowned at him and shook his head. "You ain't kidding, brother." That woman from the store was going to have something on her hands getting his friend straightened out.

Brighty grabbed another piece of chicken. "But for true love, ain't nothing that can't be overcome."

30

Mary

Mary opened her mouth wide and took a big bite of pizza. She looked at her watch and hummed as she looked around the restaurant. "Wednesday nights are a good night to eat out. It's quiet, not many people. . . ."

Thelma grunted and nudged her. "Girl, if you don't hurry up and spill the beans," she picked up her knife, "I'm going to cut you wide, cut you deep, and spill them myself!"

Latrice laughed, "And I'm going to help her!"

Naomi looked at Latrice. "I don't know if I'm going to be able to help you, sister-girl," Naomi said. She fluffed her hair. "You all might want to fight, but I got to think about my 'do."

Mary giggled, pleased that her friends were playing along. But it *was* getting late, it was a weeknight, and she knew she was going to have to say something soon—or she might never be able to speak again.

"Come on, girl." Thelma nudged Mary again. "What about the *museum* could have you out here glowing and willing to be sacrificed, all for the name of love?"

Mary swallowed. "Okay. Okay." She wiped her mouth. "Well, first of all, I've had a breakthrough with the girls. Things are much better. We're talking about a *real* breakthrough—and talking about real things, things that matter. Some of the women at church are offended, but I figure they'll forgive me for offending them if I'm able to do something real for their children."

Thelma was groaning. "Mary, you are killing me. Really! I know you didn't call us here to talk about the kids."

"Okay! Well . . . you all know how crazy my dates have been."

Latrice raised her hands. "Hey, that's not my fault! Floyd said if you had just ordered the rib special, everything would have been all right."

Thelma clicked her tongue. "And Reggie was a catch, girl. He's got a stable job. He's good looking. I wouldn't have thrown that fish away so soon, if I was you. And the man can cook." She pursed her lips and then took another bite of pizza.

"You're right. He *can* cook. Really well." Mary took a small bite and started humming again.

Naomi looked across the table at Thelma and laughed. "Forget about messing up my hair. You hold her, and I will beat her down my own self!"

Latrice tapped on the table with the nail of her index finger. "Girl, if you don't swallow that stuff and start talking . . ."

Mary covered her mouth with her hand while she laughed. "Okay. Wait a minute." She took a drink and then wiped her mouth. "I got a call the other day." She looked around the table. "From Reggie." She let the news sink in. "He apologized. He asked me to give him another chance."

She looked at Naomi. "I thought about our conversation. Maybe I didn't give him a chance, you know? Maybe I was scared. Maybe he was confused." Naomi, Latrice, and Thelma were staring at her. Their mouths were open so wide, their chins were almost touching the table. "He asked me out. Again. But I told him it had to be a public place. And that there were no promises, we would just talk. We would see." She took another drink and waited for some response.

Latrice answered first. "You would see? You would see what?" She wrung her hands together. "Girl, I'm gone kill you!"

Thelma narrowed her eyes to slits. "Okay, and what did the museum have to do with all this?"

"That's where we met. I caught the bus to the museum, and we met there. He apologized again. He told me he respected what I believe in." Mary couldn't help smiling. "He said he would be patient and take it slow. He didn't even ask me to go anywhere after that. He said we should take it one step at a time. He even said he would go to church with me sometime."

Naomi brushed the hair out of her face. "Girl, look at you! Look at you!"

"We've gone out on a couple of short dates. You know, in public places like at the movies, bookstore, at the Inner Harbor. He's been a gentleman. He says I'm worth taking his time."

The three other women looked shell-shocked. No one said a word.

Mary took another bite of pizza and swallowed it. When she looked at Thelma again, it looked like she had tears in her eyes.

"Well," Thelma said. She closed her mouth tight. She looked down and then looked back up in Mary's eyes. "Well." Thelma blinked several times.

Latrice clapped her hands and hummed the theme song to *An Officer and a Gentleman.* "Way to go, Paula! Way to go, Paula!" She stopped clapping. "Oh, wrong girl! I mean, way to go, Mary!"

Naomi shook her head at Latrice. "Girl, you are a fool!"

Thelma looked like she was blinking back tears. Suddenly, she reached to hug Mary. "Girl, I think you're going to marry that man." She hugged so tightly, Mary could hear her heart, so tightly, Mary was having difficulty breathing. "My friend is getting married!" She whispered into Mary's ear. "I'm happy for you, Mary. You be happy. You deserve every bit of it."

Mary tried to talk through Thelma's hug. When Thelma released her, Mary looked closely at her friend. There were definitely tears in Thelma's eyes. Mary smiled at her. Maybe her friend's cynicism was an act to guard her heart. Deep inside, they were all hoping for evidence—looking for proposals, confessions of love, marriages—that would tell them something in the world was true. "We're just taking one day at a time, okay? Nobody's proposed to anybody."

Naomi was beaming. "A woman knows these things. We can see it on you." She shook her head and whispered, squealed. "I'm going to be a bridesmaid! I think your colors ought to be cream and peach."

Latrice clapped again. "And I'm going to be the maid of honor!" She began to snap her fingers and dance the snake in her seat.

Thelma broke the hug. "I don't think so, sweetheart!" She grinned across the table at Latrice. "Not if she wants it to be a tasteful affair. Leave it to you and instead of making sure she's coming down the aisle holding flowers, you'll have her marching with an armful of ribs!"

"That ain't fair, girl. Floyd was okay. She should have gave him another chance."

Mary looked from Thelma to Naomi to Latrice. *Give them joy, Lord. Give them their true hearts' desires.*

Thelma raised an eyebrow, a mock frown on her face. "Right. Well, we see she's not marrying Floyd, is she? And maid of honor? It seems like to me that honor ought to definitely go to the one who brought the man in the first place! And that means me, not you." Thelma bucked her eyes and shook her head.

Naomi pinched Latrice. "You two hush! You're going to get us kicked out of here."

By the time they finished laughing and teasing each other, they were well beyond their fifteen-minute limit. What was a little sleep compared to good friends? Riding home in Thelma's car, Mary looked up at the moon. It was full and clear and shining brightly.

31

Puddin

I t's *Wednesday night* in B-more! Do you know where your loved ones are?" The radio announcer's voice was too chipper, so Puddin clicked it off and rode in silence.

The moon was too bright, and Puddin wished a cloud would cover it. When she pulled into the church parking lot, she drove around until she found Joe's car. Leaving her car running, she slipped the engine into park and turned out the lights. She looked around to make sure no one was watching and then grabbed a bag of chicken.

Just like usual, he left his driver's side window cracked. She lifted the bag and began to force chicken wings through the hole. Puddin shoved the pieces of chicken through the space one at a time until the first bag was empty.

"I love chicken, baby." Well, if Joe didn't love it before, he was going to have to learn to love it now. He was going to be riding home with chicken. She looked around again then moved quietly to her car and got in and closed the door. He didn't have time to come get the chicken? Well, the chicken had come to him. She laughed to herself. Joe's chicken had come home to roost . . . right in the driver's seat of his car.

Puddin put the car in gear and drove to a dark, secluded space on the church lot. She walked quietly in the back door of the church and climbed the steps until she reached the balcony. She ducked low and hid behind a pew. She was out of sight, but not out of earshot. The acoustics were good and she could hear every word. She could hear Joe's voice.

"Brother, we are happy to have you here with us. Yes sir." It sounded like Joe was pounding someone on the back. "You got a minute?" The men's meeting must have ended. "I'd like to talk with you."

"Of course." Puddin thought she detected an accent. She crawled on her knees to the wooden, fabric-paneled, enclosed rail of the balcony.

"So, you from Africa?"

"Yes, sir. My country is called Lesotho."

She peeked over the rail. Joe had his arm around the young man's shoulders. "I've been meaning to talk to you for a while, now. You a long, long way from home. You must be lonesome."

The young man nodded. "Yes. It is a long way from my home, from my family."

Joe laughed. "Well, there's no need for you to be lonesome here. There are plenty of pretty women in this church." Joe laughed again. "Yes, sir. Plenty of good-looking women."

Puddin shook her head, stuck out her tongue, and made a face at Joe. He didn't see any of it, but it still felt good to do it anyway. If anyone knew where the good-looking women would be, it would be Joe, wouldn't it? And if the church harvest of women wasn't good enough, she was sure Joe could direct the young man to a promising crop at Starbucks.

Joe continued talking. "Have you dated any since you been here?"

The young man laughed. "I have been on just one date—what you call a blind date. A computer date."

Joe laughed so loudly he doubled over. "A *computer* date?" He snorted trying to stop himself from laughing.

Puddin frowned. Everything was a joke to Joe. Nothing was beyond his ridicule.

The young man nodded. "That's what I thought, too. 'It's foolishness,' I told myself." He paused. "A friend of mine put my information online, gave me a name—Africa—and then *bam*! There it was." He shrugged again. "The surprise is that I like her—my date."

Africa? Africa? Puddin lifted her head higher to get a better look. It was her son—one of her babies! And there was Joe with his cheating arm wrapped around him!

"Well, listen to me, son. Do you mind if I give you some advice?" It should have been her, but instead it was Joe—Joe the coffee-guzzling liar giving her son advice.

The young man, her Africa, nodded. "Of course, my father."

Joe waved his hand and shook his head. "First of all, forget all about that computer dating thing. It's for kooks!"

Puddin snorted.

"Is somebody up there?"

She ducked down just before she was seen.

"Is somebody up there?"

Yeah, you should *be afraid that somebody's watching. I've got my eye on you! But even more, you need to know the Lord's got His eye on you, you cheating chicken-eater. You ought to be feeling some heat around your feet any day now.* Puddin held her breath hoping he wouldn't find her out.

Joe continued talking. "I guess it's just the floor settling or something."

When she thought it was safe, she again looked over the railing.

"Like I was saying, forget that computer dating stuff. If you like the girl, that's fine. Just take it slow. You been away from home a long time. That can impair a man's judgment, if you know what I mean." Both men laughed. "Take it slow."

Africa nodded his head.

They began to move in opposite directions, then Joe turned back. "Hey, why don't you come to the singles dance that's coming up here at the church. You can meet lots of nice people—"

Puddin backed away from the railing. How dare he? He had taken her whole life. She had spent her whole life serving him, letting him make a fool of her in front of the whole church, in front of the whole city. Puddin crawled from the front of the balcony to the doors at the back. She inched them open, quietly left the church, and ran in the dark to her car. He had humiliated her. Wasn't that enough? Did he have to ruin Africa's life, too?

She started her car, then drove it and parked, again, next to Joe's car. She took a piece of chicken from one of the bags, reached for the floor lever, and after popping the trunk, dug inside until she found the tire iron.

Joe had done enough damage. Now, he was trying to take her son! Well, he wouldn't get away with it. She walked to Joe's car and lifted the tire iron in the air. He wouldn't take one more thing from her, and he wouldn't get a chance to contaminate Africa! She hit the windshield on the driver's side and watched the crack travel across the window. Puddin laid a fried chicken breast on the lower corner of the windshield where the crack began. Joe's free ride was over. The war would now begin!

Puddin lay in bed, half asleep and half awake. She was on alert and heard every sound in the house. She was ready for him.

Joe came home later than usual. She heard the back door crack open slowly. He had probably run to the arms of one of his chippies for consolation, drowned his sorrows over a cup of joe. She snickered to herself. Joe drowning over joe? Left up to her, it was about to become a regular thing.

"Puddin? Puddin?" He sounded uncertain. He had every right to be. She lay still. She could hear his footsteps coming up the hall. "Puddin? Puddin?" He cracked the bedroom door open. "I'm late. . . . Something crazy happened. . . ." He fumbled over his words. "Puddin?" He stepped through the doorway.

That's when she let him have it!

She threw a chicken breast at his head like it was opening day at Camden Yards! *Batter up!*

"Puddin!"

Before he could get out another word, she had swung her legs

over the side of the bed, reached in the chicken bag on the nightstand, and pelted him again.

"Puddin?" He turned and the next piece caught him on the
shoulder blade. He raised his hands to defend himself, to block the
chicken fire. "Puddin, what's wrong with you?"

He was running down the hall. She followed after him with the
bag of chicken slung over her shoulder. "Honey, what's wrong?
Ouch!" She was throwing too slowly. He was getting too many
words out.

He tried to duck, but her pitches were too good. If she hadn't
wasted her time with him, who knew? She could have played
women's baseball. She kept pounding him.

"Ow! Puddin! Stop! This ain't funny!"

She hit him right up over the left eye.

"Puddin, stop playing. You're going to put my eye out!"

She kept throwing. "No, not your eye—I'm putting you out,
Negro!" She grabbed another bag of reinforcements. They were
mostly breasts, fried hard. "You get out of here, Joe! Right now!"

"Puddin? What—" He ducked and a breast went through the
glass of the china cabinet door. It was just one of the casualties of
war. "Can't we talk?" He was panting.

"No, we cannot talk! I'm through talking! It's over!"

"Puddin!" He ducked and a breast skidded across the dining
room table and dropped to the floor. He took a step forward; it
looked like he was thinking of making a frontal attack.

She hurled a thigh that hit him right smack-dab in the middle
of his forehead. He stumbled backward and then turned to continue
his retreat.

He was hollering over his shoulder, "It's about the chicken, ain't
it? We don't have to eat chicken anymore, baby! We can eat whatever you want, okay? We can have pizza!" She hurled two pieces
that hit him on the shoulder. Another piece hit the wall near his
head and slid to the floor.

She had him on the run, forcing him toward the back door.

"Don't baby me! It's too late to negotiate now, buddy! You are out of here! And don't call!" She threw another piece as he ran out the door. "Don't try to use your key to get back in here." She threw another piece at him. He dodged it, and it hit the sidewalk. "We are over! We are through! And we are bye-bye!" She threw another piece.

Joe was looking frantic. "Where am I gone stay, Puddin? It's cold outside!" His chest was swelling and deflating rapidly. His eyes were large, round, and his eyelashes were fluttering. He was wringing his hands.

"They got hot coffee at Starbucks!" She threw a piece—a chicken leg that clipped his ear.

"Ow!" He touched his ear like he was checking for blood. "Starbucks?"

No, he wasn't trying to play *stupid!* She dug in the bag for a neck and hit him in the chest. "Don't play with me, Joe!" Her fingers found another drumstick and hit him on the hand. "And stay away from Africa!"

"Africa?"

She began to close the door; her work was done.

"Puddin, wait! What about . . .? What about . . .?" He looked around desperately for anything he could pitch. "What about the friends and family get-together?"

Puddin laughed and slammed the door.

32

Moor

Moor *opened the door* to the New Worshippers fellowship hall and stuck his head inside. There was a large banner hanging from the ceiling: *Singles Night Out*. Each letter was painted a different color, and he could not decide if the sign was festive and cheerful, or graphically trying just a bit too hard. No doubt about it, he was in the right place—the singles social.

He looked around the room. There were lots of friendly faces, not many of them familiar. Well, that wasn't true. Many of them were familiar from Sunday church service . . . familiar and attractive, but none were the face he had invited. Gail had promised to come. He looked at the clock. *"Eightish, okay?"* she had said. He looked at the clock, again. Eight-fifteen still surely qualified.

Gail was beautiful. When he thought of her, he knew a stupid smile appeared on his face. But he could not help it! He could not help himself! He was smitten. She was the kind of woman the men in his family liked.

Moor wandered by the food table and selected a few items: some cheese, some crackers, some carrots, and two hot wings. At the end of the table, he saw his new friend. "Brother Joe!"

Brother Joe smiled broadly and waved him over. When he got closer, the smile disappeared from Brother Joe's face. Brother Joe looked at Moor's plate and then touched his fingers to a bruised spot on his head.

Moor looked at the man. "Is something wrong?"

Joe looked across the room, then back at the plate. "The chicken."

"The chicken?"

Brother Joe shook his head. "Never mind. It's too hard to explain. I can't figure it out myself," he muttered.

"Eh?"

Brother Joe shook his head as though he were clearing it. "Don't worry about me. You have a good time." He smiled. "There's lots of nice women here." He pointed around the room. He looked at the plate again, and a shadow crossed his face. "There's nothing sweeter than a good woman. 'Whoso findeth a wife findeth a good thing.'" He sighed. "Just be careful, son. Be careful." Brother Joe touched his hand to his head again, looked across the room, and then walked away.

Moor looked after him. Sometimes American behavior still confused him. He wandered around the large room, moving among the tables. He stopped and inhaled.

It was the green-eyed woman—the woman from the museum, from the bus. He remembered her and the scent of her perfume. She looked around the room like she was alone, like she was waiting for someone. There was no one sitting at her table.

He looked at the clock. Eight-thirty.

At least he could say hello. "Hello," he said. "I am sorry. Please forgive me."

She looked up and smiled. "You didn't do anything. There's no need to apologize." She stuck out her hand. "Hello, I'm Mary."

Her hand was very soft. "Mary," he said. "Do you mind if I sit down?"

"I'm waiting for someone." She looked at the clock.

"Me, too."

"But I guess it will be all right."

She was even prettier than he remembered, except for the green eyes . . . and the yellow hair.

"That's what we're here for, right? To meet people?" Her smile was warm. It was not—her smile, or her voice—what he would have imagined from their encounter, their collision outside of the museum. She was sweet—a little plump, and sweet.

"You do not remember me, do you?"

She tilted her head. "I'm sorry." She blushed. "There are so many people in the church. I try to remember. . . . Do you go to eleven-thirty service?" She smiled apologetically. "Your accent is so beautiful . . . you would think I would have remembered." She shrugged her shoulders.

He sat down. "No, I go to nine-thirty. It was not here that we met, though. It was at the museum."

She looked perplexed. "The museum?"

"I ran into you outside of the museum. You were running for the bus." He smiled. "I grabbed your arm. I almost knocked you down."

Realization came into her eyes. "I don't know if I want you sitting at the table with me or not! You almost killed me!" She laughed.

"That was not my intention. I apologize."

"No apology necessary." She touched his hand. "I'm just kidding. I should have been looking where I was going." She nodded, looked around the room, and then back at him. "I was going to meet a date."

"Oh."

"The same one I'm meeting here tonight."

Her skin was lovely, but the yellow hair was so distracting. "Actually, I was leaving the date when I met you . . . when we ran into each other." Her laugh was very pleasant and natural. It gurgled like stream water.

"You will not believe this." He leaned toward her so that he would not have to keep yelling to be heard.

She leaned forward, too. "What? What won't I believe?"

"It must have been some strange kind of fate."

"What do you mean?"

"I was at the museum . . . I was on my way to meet a date, also. A first date. A blind date. A *computer* date." He smiled and hoped that she would not think he was desperate.

"A computer date? Isn't that funny?" She giggled.

She thinks I am a fool. He looked at his plate and tried to think of a way he could leave gracefully.

"I signed up with a computer dating service, too," she whispered conspiratorially. "I haven't had the courage to respond to a date. Actually, my friends won't let me. They think I'll run into an ax murderer."

"My friends thought it was a good thing at first. Now they are not so sure." He told her about Brighty and Blue and Ali. "But that's how I met Gail." He nodded. "She's the woman I'm meeting tonight." He looked at the clock. "If she comes."

"If *he* comes," she added. She pointed at the chicken. "Good wings. They're really good."

"Have one?"

She patted her stomach. "No, I've had enough. I've been here awhile. If I eat any more, they're going to ask me to leave."

This Mary was funny. And smart. If only her eyes weren't green.

She winked at him. "Maybe this is some crazy, divine plan. Maybe God has been orchestrating all this trying to get us together. What do you think?"

"Oh, yes. He caused us to run into each other at the museum, caused us to come here, and then made our dates stand us up." They both laughed.

"Well," she said. "We'll know for sure if our dates don't come."

"Mine—Gail—said she would be here before nine."

Mary looked at the clock. They were both giggling, but the noise of the crowd covered them. "Okay, I'll tell you what." She paused. "By the way, what's your name?"

"Moor."

She repeated it. "That's a powerful name. Lots of history hangs on that name."

"Yes." She was very smart. "Your perfume—"

"Yes?" She looked nervous.

He was surprised that he could smell it. His sinuses had been especially stuffy lately. "It smells lovely. When I smelled it tonight, I remembered it had made an impression on me outside of the museum."

"Thank you." Her smile relaxed. "Okay, Moor, here's the deal. If our dates don't show by nine, we exchange numbers, okay?"

"Yes, we will consider it a divine meeting, a divinely appointed encounter."

She pointed at his plate. "Okay, enough talking. Eat your chicken, and when you've finished, you can tell me about my competition."

And when nine came, they exchanged numbers, as they had promised.

33

Mary

Mary *kicked the covers off* and pressed the phone closer to her ear. "So, nine o'clock came and we exchanged numbers like we had agreed."

Latrice laughed so hard Mary had to move the phone away. "No you didn't, girl? No you didn't? Look at you! I thought you were headed down the aisle, but you turning into a playa! We have created a playa! Well, at least *I* have—a dating machine! Girl, I'm gone have to watch out for you! If I'm not careful, you'll be catching up with me."

"I don't think you have to worry about that," Mary quipped.

"I know, honey." Latrice laughed. "I'm just trying to make you feel good. Trying to keep you encouraged. That's how the mama eagle teaches the little babies to fly."

"No, I think what eagles do is push the babies out of the nest."

"You know what, Mary? The trouble with you is you are always taking things to the textbooks and ruining the moment. That's your problem. That's the next thing Mama Latrice is gone have to work on."

"Anyway, Latrice, like I said, we exchanged numbers." She sighed. "What a beautiful man, so black, and what a sexy accent."

"No, you didn't use the *s* word. Girl, what is coming over you?"

"Latrice, let me finish the story. Oh, and he liked my perfume."

"He did?"

"Yes, he did. Why do you say it like that?"

"Never mind. Go on with the story."

"So, anyway, we exchanged numbers, then things got crazy."

"What?" Mary could hear Latrice moving, like she was settling in to hear the story.

"Well, just as I put Moor's number away, in walks Reggie."

"Uh-oh! The brothers didn't go to fist-city in the church, did they? I'm gone have to school you on what to do when the brothers run into each other . . . how to play it off. . . . It's an art form. Did the brothers get to swingin' up in the church?"

"No, Latrice. Nothing like that. It was no biggie. Reggie didn't see the number, and I mean Moor and I really weren't serious. But it would be nice to be church friends, you know?"

"Church friends? *Church friends?* What you talking about, girl?"

"Just church friends. A guy you can go places with and you don't have to worry about anything. . . . You know, there's no attraction."

"Excuse me, sugar, but you weren't talking like there was no attraction."

"He is handsome. He is intelligent. He has a way, you know? Kind of noble and exotic and everything . . . but I'm seeing Reggie."

"Girl, I'm gone have to put you in remedial training."

Mary laughed. There was no one more fun to talk to on the phone than Latrice. She was non-stop entertainment. It was easy to see why all the men were charmed. "No, really, Latrice. And besides that, he has a girlfriend. She showed up right after Reggie."

"Oh, man. Ain't that nothin'! I thought this was gone be some story." It sounded like Latrice might be punching her pillows, settling in, getting really comfortable.

"Well, you know. It was fun." Mary looked at the piece of paper lying on her dresser. "It was a small rush."

"So, then what happened? You all just left?"

"Well, not quite yet. That's just when things got weird." Mary sat up and took a drink of the water sitting on her nightstand. "Reggie and Gail came in, like I said. They got some food and the four of us sat there talking." She giggled, remembering. "Moor and I kept this private joke going, stealing sorrowful glances like star-crossed lovers. You know, playing."

"Right. Playing."

"Well, then this man that lives down the street from me comes up to us. I know he goes to the church. I just know he and his wife in passing. Mr. Joe, and his wife's name is Miss Puddin. Anyway, he starts talking to the four of us, laughing and having a good time." She took another sip. "And I started thinking to myself, 'Hey, maybe this singles stuff is not as bad as I thought.'

"Anyway, Mr. Joe and Moor are really hitting it off. He's patting Moor on the back. And he says, 'See wasn't I right? Isn't this better than that other thing?' And he winks at him and then says, 'But I do think you've made a wise choice.'"

"What?"

"Who knows what they're talking about. Just some man-speak going on between them. Anyway, while they're talking, I try to make small talk with Gail. She seems like a nice woman. She's pretty. She seems intelligent."

"But?" Latrice giggled with anticipation. "Come on, girl, I can hear you got something you need to say to Mama Latrice."

"But . . . but . . . she talks while she's chewing."

"Oo-oo! Yuck!"

"I know it's silly. It's not even a big deal. But that's what the lady—what Miss Puddin said to him."

"That's what the lady said to who, Mary? What kind of pudding? Girl, you are confusing me! Do I need to book you a spot at Betty Ford?"

"Very funny! I'm trying to tell you the story, but you keep interrupting me."

"Well, tell on, sister. I'll keep my mouth closed."

"So, like I said, Mr. Joe is standing there talking to Moor and kind of to Reggie, and I'm trying to make small talk with Gail while she chews. Well, all of a sudden Miss Puddin walks up out of nowhere. She waves this piece of chicken in front of Mr. Joe—I think it was a breast—like she was waving a blade in a napkin. Then she hands the chicken to him. Well, actually she slaps it onto his chest. 'Puddin!' Mr. Joe hollers, and he jumps about fifteen feet in the air.

"Then she says, 'I told you to leave my son alone. I told you to stop messing with Africa!'" Mary scratched her head. "I don't know them well, but I never knew them to have any kids." She shrugged her shoulders one time. "Then Mr. Joe starts backing away holding the chicken to his chest like he's been stabbed by a butcher knife. 'Okay, Puddin, he says. 'Whatever you say.'"

"What? I don't understand. That sounds crazy."

"Well, that's what I was thinking. 'This is crazy!' But that's just part of it. Right there, right in front of Gail, Miss Puddin—that's the lady's name—she says to Moor, 'I saw you looking at her. I've been watching you since you came in the room from that corner over there. You know it's not going to get any better. What's a little pebble in your shoe is going to be a boulder in thirty years. Believe me. I know.'"

"What?"

"Then she starts making this chewing motion with her mouth and points to it. 'You know what I mean,' she says to Moor. 'I'm just trying to look out for you. Something better is coming. Just keep your eyes open.'"

"What do you think she was talking about?"

"Well, I think she was talking about Gail chewing . . . but, she was crazy, so—" Mary could still see the scene in her mind.

"Then what happened? Did they throw her out?"

"No." Mary took a deep breath. "She was crazy! I've never seen her that way before. Not that I really know her." She laughed. "Then she said something to me."

"What?"

"She pointed at Reggie. 'Don't let him fool you. This dog ain't no good. And believe me, I know a no-good, dirty dog when I see one. He's been looking around the room for prospects since he got here. Any bone will do. Don't fool with him. He's up to no good and he'll break your heart. Keep your eyes open. Something good is right in front of you.'"

Latrice huffed on the other line. "That was it?"

"That was it. It creeped me out. . . . It creeped everybody out. Pretty soon after that, everybody started leaving."

"That was strange."

"I know."

"What do you think she meant?"

"You know, I don't know." Her laugh sounded nervous to her own ears. "She was crazy. All I know is that when we got outside, that guy Mr. Joe was hollering and jumping around saying there was chicken all over his car."

When Latrice hung up, Mary's phone rang again. "Hello."

"Hello, Mary? It's me, Garvin."

Mary kicked the covers. Why didn't she check her caller ID? She just wasn't in the mood for the intercourse inquisition.

"Mary, I'm running. I'm not going to bother you long. I just wanted to say I love you."

"I love you, too." Mary held her breath waiting for the other shoe to drop.

"Enjoy yourself, okay? That's what I've been praying for you— that you would enjoy yourself."

Surprise made Mary sit up further in the bed. "Well. Well, that's nice, Garvin. Thanks. That's a nice prayer."

"A nice prayer for a nice person."

She wasn't sure what to say. "Thanks. You too."

"Well, I've got to run."

"Okay. Well, talk to you later, Garvin."

"You too, Mary."

"Okay, then."

"Mary?"

"Yes." *Here it comes.* She knew Garvin could not resist.

"I almost forgot."

Here it came. Here at last was the lecture and the grilling. Mary hunched over and held her breath, waiting for the tongue-lashing.

"I'm going to be in the area soon. I'll try to call. Maybe we can see each other, have a cup of coffee, if you're not busy."

The air went out of Mary. "Sure. Sure. That would be nice."

"Okay. I'll talk to you later."

"Later." Mary decided to lie down again since she was pretty certain that she already had to be dreaming.

34

Puddin

When *Puddin stepped through* the door of the Starbucks it was as if she was stepping into a dream. She drifted on the warm, bittersweet aroma past the tables and chairs, past the coffee displays, and stepped up to the counter.

"May I help you?" the man behind the counter asked.

"Yes, I'm sure you can."

She lifted the food storage container she had brought with her and placed it on the counter. It was over between her and Joe, but she wasn't heartless. She couldn't stand to see Joe starving. When she saw him at the Singles Night Out, she knew he wasn't eating. He couldn't live with her anymore, but she wouldn't watch him starve to death and not feed him.

"Yes?" The clerk smiled, but looked uncertain.

"It's chicken."

"We don't sell chicken at Starbucks. Only Starbucks products mostly. A few confections. A few books." He pushed the container toward her. "We definitely don't sell perishable food on consignment."

"I'm not selling. This is for Joe. He comes in here all the time. He's my husband. My ex-husband. Well, we're not divorced yet."

"Well, Joe can't sell chicken here, either."

"This is not for sale. This is for him to eat. Anyway, just tell him Puddin was here. No, better yet, don't tell him anything. He'll know who it was." She turned and started out the door.

"You can't leave this here!" the clerk shouted after her. Puddin continued walking to the car and then drove away.

Pretty soon, it was all over the church that Puddin had had a breakdown. Of course, it was the consensus of the women of the church that Joe had driven her to it. *"Poor thing. She was a good woman."*

Puddin was still functioning, still coming to church, still grocery shopping, but you could tell that she just wasn't herself, people said. Puddin heard whispering that she just wasn't the woman she used to be.

As happens in times of crisis, the gulfs that separated the groups of women within the church narrowed. There was a bigger fight to fight, a bigger fish—or in this case—chicken to fry. So Mary lost her status as the church poster child for sin. *"She isn't so bad. Maybe a little misguided. But her heart is in the right place."* That honor was transferred to Joe. It didn't matter anymore if they were married or single, young or old—the women blamed Joe, and by association, they blamed all the other men, too.

The women did more than just give lip service to their solidarity. It became a regular thing for Puddin to find a pink rose on her porch . . . or several pink roses. And attached to each rose was a Starbucks coupon. *We're with you, Sister Puddin,* one note card read. *Just so you know, you can go to Starbucks, too.*

When she walked into meetings, or even to her regular seating area in the sanctuary, the women near her stood to their feet as a show of respect and togetherness. Word spread beyond New Worshippers to churches all over Baltimore—Bethel, United, St. James, New Psalmist, Pleasant Grove, Empowerment Temple, New Shiloh, Bethany, Mt. Olive, First Church, Rock—size and denomination didn't matter. The women stood with Puddin.

Of course, there were also some callous villains who took advantage of the situation. Copycat crimes. They all involved chicken being left as a calling card. At first, Puddin was blamed for all of them. Then the copycats began to get careless—too many crimes in too many areas. She had enough to worry about; she shouldn't have to shoulder blame for imitators, too, people said to her.

Women all over Baltimore were sympathetic and they whispered to the other women they knew. Pretty soon, word of Puddin's plight had slipped over racial and geographic barriers. Women from churches in Ellicott City, Glen Burnie, Columbia, Prince George's County, and even Montgomery County responded. What socially, geographically, and economically divided them paled compared to the crisis at hand. They were at war, unified against a common enemy. (Now, this might have been the perfect time to discuss and come to agreement about the things that normally kept them apart. But they were busy lobbing words at the enemy, and didn't have time or, maybe, courage for such sidebar issues.) And after Puddin's story was reported in the papers, there was a groundswell of sympathy, and chicken and chicken incidents began popping up everywhere.

Pretty soon men throughout the area began to wonder, when they saw chicken on their plates, if it was just dinner or if it was a sign—a political statement. When it showed up on plates at the mayor's fundraiser—wielded on trays by tens of tuxedoed women—people said he was afraid to eat it.

"Girl, you should have seen him," Puddin heard someone say. *"Shaking like a leaf!"*

That's what brought things to a head, people whispered. According to reliable sources, the mayor made a few calls. Those callers made a few calls.

The bottom line was, something had to be done.

Shortly thereafter—after the mayor's dinner—Puddin received a phone call from a well-known councilman. "You and Joe are tearing up the city. Women won't cook, and when they do, the men are afraid to eat. Marylanders are at risk! Families are in crisis! For goodness' sakes, for the good of the churches, for the good of the city—you have to talk!"

Puddin looked out the window as she listened to the caller. It was, indeed, getting colder, but she was still alive and walking at too high an altitude for anyone to think she was going to be talking to Joe.

35

Moor

S*aturday morning in the alley* with his friends, Moor shook his head. Everywhere he went for the last couple of days, men and women were talking about the same thing. It was in all the papers. *Chickengate*. That's what they were calling it.

Brighty held the hamburger away from him and shook it. "See, that's why I don't go to church, just because of crazy stuff like that. A crazy woman scaring people with chicken. What about the economy? The chicken people are gone go out of business."

Blue nodded. "It's getting cold out here and this ain't enough. Hamburgers! We need hot food like chicken. The whole city been turned upside down by one crazy woman."

"I saw her for myself." Moor shuddered. "I didn't know it at the time. Who would have suspected such a woman would be in the church? She was like a witch doctor or something. I do not understand you Americans sometimes!"

Brighty shook his burger in the air. "Witch doctor? Well, that shouldn't scare you. You people should be prepared for that kind of thing. Everybody know you all got those witch doctors over there in Africa. It ain't nothing new to you. We the ones scared. The onliest way we can buy chicken now, is you got to check and make sure it's a man back there behind the counter cooking. Anything else, you could be taking your life into your own hands."

Moor wrapped the rest of his sandwich and threw it in the trash can. "My father, you are wrong. Like you, I have never seen a witch doctor, except the ones on television. My father went to church; his father before him and his father before him were all Christian men.

My family has also raised me to know the Lord, and I have never seen such a thing in our church. Only here in America!" He shook his head. "And in Africa, it is safe for a man to eat anywhere! No woman would do such a thing to a man! It is so . . . so . . . primitive!"

Blue looked from man to man. "Now ain't no time for us to be fighting with one another. We men got to stick together to survive."

Ali bit into a kosher dill pickle. "No doubt." He held up a bean pie. "Man, we are gonna have to try some other things."

Moor sat back down on his cinder block. "Maybe we are being overly cautious, my fathers. No bad chicken, no poisonous chicken has been found or reported."

Blue rubbed his chin. "Well, now, son, I wouldn't do any experimenting if I was you. I wouldn't want to be the test case." Blue poured some hot coffee from a thermos sitting on the table in front of him. "Now, Prince, tell us again exactly what happened and what she said."

"Well, as I said before, my fathers, I was sitting at the table at the dance." Moor began to think about Mary and would have sworn that he could smell her perfume. "I was sitting with a beautiful girl—"

"I thought you said your date didn't get there until late."

"It was not my date, my fathers. The beautiful girl was not my date. I mean, it was another beautiful girl, but she was not the kind of girl the men in my family like. She was beautiful, she was brown, and she was fat." He fluffed his hands around his head, as though indicating an imaginary cloud. "But she had yellow hair and green eyes."

Blue jerked forward, spilling some of his coffee. "Green eyes and yellow hair?"

"Not my kind at all, but she was . . ."

"I saw a woman just like that the other day on the bus. A pretty girl, but with green eyes and blonde hair—"

"She was not my type. . . . She was attractive nonetheless."

Brighty smacked his lips. "Sound all right to me."

Blue turned to his old friend. "Who asked you? Don't nobody care what you like. We know what you like is at the grocery store bakery. Now, hush and let the boy talk." He turned back to Moor. "All right, now, you go on, Prince."

Moor almost didn't want to tell the story, to remember how close he had come to the chicken lady. "So, the beautiful woman and I were sitting at the table conversing. After a while, our dates came."

Ali smirked. "That was *after* you and this woman that *wasn't* your type had already *exchanged* the digits, right?"

Moor didn't know why Ali was smirking, why he kept making such a big deal about the telephone number exchange. "Yes, we had already exchanged telephone numbers and our dates had arrived, when this kind man I know came to speak with us. While he was talking, this crazy woman came from out of the shadows, from out of nowhere. I did not know who she was."

"That was a close call!"

Moor nodded emphatically. "She was no more than two feet away from me." His eyebrows were raised, as was the pitch of his voice. "I had no idea how much danger was confronting me."

Brighty shook his head. "Like I said, like I said, that's why I ain't eager about going to church."

Blue waved Brighty's comment back to him. "That ain't why you ain't going to church, you old heathen."

Moor's heart was beating faster as he got closer to the climax of his tale. "So while the four of us sat, the nice gentleman came to speak with us. He scoffed at my computer dating, but said that my date was very nice. Everything was fine, then this woman came out of nowhere. She pointed at my date and gave me a warning."

Ali bit a plug out of his pickle. "Oh, man!"

Blue eyes grew large and he leaned forward. "What kind of warning?"

"A warning that this woman would get to be a burden. That I

would grow weary of her habits . . . of her talking with her mouth full."

Brighty took a big bite of his burger. "Well, you got to be careful of a woman. Something like that, talking with your mouth full, year after year will get on your nerves in a way you can't explain." He swallowed.

Blue shook his head. "You can say that again."

Ali snickered. "You guys kill me!"

"It was horrible!" Moor laid his head in his hands, then lowered them and looked up. "Of course, the crazy woman was wrong. Gail and I like each other very much. But it has made me wonder, my fathers."

Brighty shook a finger at Moor. "Wonder? Your mind wandering? Who knows what kind of spell, what kind of roots she might have tried to work on you."

"I do not believe such things. I am a man. I am God's man. I make my own choices."

Brighty raised an eyebrow. "I've heard lots of men say that before."

36

Mary

As soon as she stepped through the door of Room Thirty-One, Agnes, Pamela, and Cat were all over her. "Miss Mary got a date! Miss Mary got a date!"

"What are you all talking about?"

Pamela grinned. "We know all about it!" Agnes nodded her agreement.

Pamela reached for the bag on Mary's shoulder and set it on the table. "Besides that, the truth is all over your face. You are glowing."

Cat raised an eyebrow and smiled. "It does pay off then?"

"What pays off?"

"You know." Cat purred and ran a hand up her arm. "Being pure."

"Yeah, Prince Charming did come." Mary felt silly talking to them, almost like she was sixteen herself. "Well, I think he's special." She blushed. "But I've been thinking about it." She began to unload her bag. "And I've been thinking that the time I was alone was really about me. It was about getting me healed from all my issues." She scrunched up her face.

Pamela danced around the table and flopped down in her seat. "So you're saying that now you don't have any more issues?"

Mary began explaining. "No, I've still got issues. But I think I can say that I have less than I had, at least as far as men are concerned. Having a man is not life or death to me anymore. And because it's not life or death, it's easier for me to be more forgiving and more patient." She looked the girls in their eyes. "I know more about what real love looks like, so I can recognize it better in someone else, I think." Mary sat down in her seat. "I don't think that being celibate is what brings Prince Charming." She smiled at Pamela, Cat, and Agnes. It was worth it, she knew now, to go through the rough times with them. Now, they trusted her. Now, they knew she cared, and that her heart was invested in them. Now, it was good to walk in the door. "I think that because I feel better, because some of my baggage is out of the way and my vision is clearer, I'm able to recognize a prince when he comes."

Cat pulled down her shades and looked at Mary thoughtfully. "Okay, Miss Mary, you're going to have to make it plain."

"I think this time alone with Him was getting me prepared so I would be ready if God chose to bring someone into my life—or so I would be ready for however He wants to use me. I've been thinking that to heal some wounds, we have to get really close to God. He knows that, so He moves things out of the way so He can be alone with us. We don't understand it when it's happening—we just feel alone. But now, I'm pretty sure it's part of God's plan."

Cat pushed her glasses back on her nose and put her feet up on a chair. Everything hadn't changed. "So are you trying to make me believe that you were happy to be alone?"

"No, I wasn't happy." She thought of Floyd. "Well, maybe some of the time." She thought of the long conversations with her friends. "Definitely some of the time." She smiled. "And during that time, I learned that God loves me, that He delights in me so much that He wants to be alone with me." She opened her Bible and read from the Song of Solomon.

> *Rise up, my love, my fair one,*
> *And come away.*
> *For lo, the winter is past,*
> *The rain is over and gone.*
> *The flowers appear on the earth;*
> *The time of singing has come,*
> *And the voice of the turtledove*
> *Is heard in our land.*

The fig tree puts forth her green figs,
And the vines with the tender grapes
Give a good smell.
Rise up, my love, my fair one,
And come away!

Mary closed her Bible and could not help but sigh. "And that love, that's how God feels about all of us. It was like a season of healing."

Cat wasn't letting her off the hook. "'*It was . . .*' You say it like it's over."

Mary could feel herself blushing again. "I think it *might* be over. I feel more at peace with who I am . . . with who I choose to be." She touched her hair. "As a matter of fact, I've been thinking that I would let the hair go . . . and the contacts." Mary looked at the girls, each one of them so different, each one of them so precious. "I wasn't doing what I wanted to do, or what made me comfortable. I was doing what my friends wanted me to do." She smiled at Cat. "Besides, one bombshell in this little space is enough, don't you think?"

Cat stretched. "Maybe for now." She purred. "But who knows who I'm going to be at the end of my season?"

"Hmmm. Well, Cat, if you choose it, I pray that your season alone with God will be beautiful. I pray that it will transform you— to make you not like me or anybody else, but a better you. The you that God wants you to be." Mary risked touching Cat's hand. The girl did not pull away. Mary squeezed her hand, then sat back in her seat. "Like I said, I learned that God loves us just for who we are—not our hair, or our skin, or our jobs. He just loves us. And He wants us to love Him back, He wants us to sit with Him, to finally have our time alone with Him be our choice."

She smiled at Agnes and lifted the girl's chin. "That's when He knows that we love Him first and best, when He is our One desire, our choice. That's when, I think, He begins lavishing His love upon us, to make gifts to us of our lesser desires. I surrendered to God's love . . . and probably the greatest thing I learned was that surrender is always my choice."

On the bus ride to Sibanye's, Mary kept touching her hair. Her head felt lighter. There were fewer stares without the hair and the contacts. Men didn't stop as often to open doors.

She smiled at a little girl playing a radio across the aisle from her. *You're listening to the heartbeat of gospel music!* the announcer said.

There was less attention, but somehow she seemed to be breathing more deeply. And, after all, it wasn't about the men, it was about her.

She stepped off the bus at the corner of Reisterstown and Rogers Roads and walked the half block to the store. When she looked through the window, she saw Reggie inside wandering among the paintings, statues, and African clothing. She looked up at the dark blue sky. Clouds rolled by, covering and uncovering the stars. It felt perfect. It felt right. "Thank you, God." And the steam of her words curled from her mouth and dissipated in the cold night air. She opened the door and stepped inside the shop. A few people had already gathered for the local author's book signing.

Robin Green and Felicia Polk, the bookstore owners, were behind the counter laughing. "Hey, girl!" they said when they saw Mary and reached over the counter to give her hug.

Reggie looked at her, then looked back at the statue he was admiring.

She squeezed the proprietors' hands and then made her way to Reggie's side. "Hi," she said.

He barely looked. "Hello." He moved away from her to another piece of artwork farther down the aisle.

She laughed, walked down the aisle, and stood closer to him. "You don't know who I am, do you?"

He looked at Mary, blinked, smiled, frowned, and blinked

again. "Mary?" He looked at her hair "Wow!" And then at her eyes. "Wow!" He frowned and then smiled again. "This is a new look." He laughed shortly. "I didn't know who you were."

Mary slipped out of her coat. The shop was intimate and warm. It suited her mood. It was good to see Reggie, to hear his voice. "Do you like it?" She touched her chin-length hair. "I just felt like being more of me."

Reggie walked to the next piece of art. "I thought I kept hearing your voice. I just thought it was in my head." He laughed again. He looked at her and then back at a piece of artwork. "So, you think you are going to keep this look?" He smiled.

"Maybe. But I think I'm keeping the nails." She flashed them. "I kind of like the nails."

"Nice." Reggie nodded, then he pointed toward the chairs. "Maybe we should take our seats."

Mary took his hand, as usual, to walk to the seats. They settled onto two together on the back row. He let go of her hand and stood to remove his coat. "It's kind of hot in here, don't you think?" Reggie seemed self-conscious. When he sat down, he scooted his chair a foot or so to the right. "Whew!" he said. "For some reason . . . I'm feeling a little warm."

It seemed silly to try to hold his hand with so much space in between them.

They left early. "We can get ahead of the crowd." Reggie seemed distracted during the ride to the restaurant and no better after they were there.

"Is everything okay?"

He lifted her hand from the table, kissed it, and smiled. "Sure, baby. Everything's fine. It's just something at work."

"Something you need to talk about?" She smiled. "My ears are yours if you need me to listen."

He rubbed the soft place between her index finger and thumb with his own. "No, it's nothing important. Nothing out of the ordinary. I just have a new project I'm working on, and I really need to be spending some time on it." He tilted his head down, and then looked up at her through his eyelashes. "You wouldn't mind if we . . . ?" He shook his head. "Never mind. That wouldn't be fair."

"What, Reggie?" She touched his hand in return.

He pulled his hand away and stretched. "Never mind. I'm just a little tired."

When dinner came, they ate quietly. "Are you sure you're okay, Reggie?"

He put down his fork. "You know what? This isn't fair to you, is it?"

"What? I don't mind. I—"

"I'm not very good company tonight. My mind is on my new project." He shook his head. He leaned forward and took her hand. "Would you mind . . . would you mind if we made it an early evening? The project is on my mind, and I don't feel like I'm being fair to you." Reggie called for the waitress and stood to put on his coat as he was speaking.

When she opened her front door, the warmth rushed out to greet her. She stepped inside, turned to face Reggie, and the cool night air blew across her face.

He leaned against the doorjamb so that his nose touched hers. "You aren't mad at me, are you?" He gave her a warm, short, moist kiss.

Mary closed her eyes. "For cutting short the evening?" She opened them and fumbled for the light switch.

Reggie pushed her hand away. "We don't need that." He let go of her arm and his hand moved to touch her hair. His fingers ran up the back of her neck to caress her scalp. "This was quite a change." He spoke quietly, and his laugh was husky.

"I hope it wasn't too much of a surprise."

He slid an arm underneath her coat, around her waist. "I'll get over it." Reggie pulled her to him.

Mary heard a nervous giggle escape from her chest. She closed her eyes again.

He put his other arm around her and kissed her. He breathed in her ear. "Can I come inside?"

She stood on the step teetering between yes and no, and took a deep breath. She opened her eyes. "I don't think it's such a good idea. You know?"

He pulled away from her. "Yeah, I know, Saint Mary." He stepped close to her again and kissed her neck. "Are you sure?"

She backed away before she surrendered. "You know what I believe." She closed her coat about her. "I'm just not ready."

Reggie stepped back. "Yeah, right." He stepped farther away. "And I said I was going to work on my new project anyway." He walked down the steps, turned at the bottom, and blew her a kiss. Mary blew one back and then closed the door.

37

Puddin

P*uddin walked out* the door of Room Seventeen after the Comfort Circle meeting. Deaconess Othella and Sister Minnie, in addition to giving her loads of advice, were still treating her with kid gloves. They acted as though she had a sack full of chicken strapped to her back, ready to do battle with anyone that got in her way. That's how they acted, and they seemed determined to remind her just who the enemy was.

"Don't give him nothing! Let him crawl and beg, and then don't give him nothing!" they said.

"I don't intend to talk to him at all."

"We don't blame you." Deaconess Othella and Sister Minnie looked at each other.

"I wouldn't want to talk to the no-good dirty dog, either." Sister Minnie shook her head.

Deaconess Othella spoke with authority, as though she were chairman of the Joint Chiefs of Staff. "But just in case you happen to run into him . . . somewhere, remember what you been through, honey. I ain't saying you will run into him . . . not anytime soon. But just in case, you be ready. Be ready at all times. And remember this ain't just about you and that man—" he was no longer Joe, but *that man*—"remember, this is about women and men everywhere."

When Puddin stepped out of the back door of the church, the wind was blowing, and she ducked her head. When she reached the car, she stuck her key in the lock and turned.

"Hello, Puddin."

It was Joe!

She was trapped!

Her coat flapped. The wind was blowing, and she smelled conspiracy in the air.

Before she looked up, Puddin tried to think of some way to escape. She looked inside the car, hoping against hope there was a forgotten bag of chicken there, or that suddenly the magical bag of bird that Deaconess Othella and Sister Minnie seemed to believe she carried around with her would suddenly appear on her shoulder.

In about three seconds, her brain ran out of plausible alternatives, and Sister Puddin began to run. With Joe following close behind and calling out her name, she ran behind, around, and in between parked cars. They looked like elementary school kids playing tag—only this was not a friendly game.

Puddin's body betrayed her—it jiggled and flapped around her as she ran. Or maybe she had betrayed it, and it was doing the best it could. She could feel Joe almost upon her. She wheezed as she made a diving roll, just out of his grasp, over the bumper of a car onto a grassy median in the parking lot. She would feel that in the morning. She hopped to her feet and kept running. "Leave me alone, Joe!"

"What makes you think I'm gone leave you alone?" He didn't sound as winded. "What makes you think I'm gone stop chasing you now?" He was coming faster. He sounded determined.

Puddin was running out of options. It was time for a desperation play. She ran toward the Dumpsters, hoping she could squeeze between them and the wall, hoping it would take Joe a little longer to get through—and hoping the extra time might allow her to make a getaway. She lost a shoe running, but poured on everything she had left. She had gained a lead by the time she made it behind a Dumpster.

But she hadn't calculated well enough. She was cornered.

Joe walked into the trap just close enough to keep her from escaping. His chest was heaving. His hands were on his hips, and he kept bending forward. He was frowning trying to breathe. He pointed at her with one hand. "Puddin, stop running!"

If she had had enough breath, she would have told him that he didn't own her, he didn't run her life. She would have told him to kiss her where the sun didn't shine. But since she didn't have the wind, she just said, "No!" and stood still trying not to look like she was wheezing, trying not to look like she was having as hard a time catching her breath as he was catching his.

"I mean it, Puddin!" Joe stamped his foot and pointed at the ground. "We are gone be here until we get this settled. Until you tell me what this is all about."

Her diaphragm began to relax and a little more air seeped into her lungs. "Well, you better call for room service! I am not talking to you, Joe Jenkins!"

"Puddin, I mean it, now. I'm not kidding." He took a step closer. His face was still red and now there was water in his eyes. "I mean it, Puddin." His voice was cracking. "Okay! Okay! I get it! You don't like chicken. But that's nothing to bust up a marriage about." He took another step closer.

"Don't you come near me, Joe! I mean it!"

"We been in love since we were kids, Puddin."

"Don't call me Puddin anymore. My name is Eleanore."

The water in his eyes was coming down his face. "You're my sweet chocolate Puddin." He took another step.

"Don't you come near me, Joe." She backed further into the corner. "And don't act like I'm crazy, like this is just about chicken." She shook her finger at him while she scrunched in tighter. "I know about everything. About the tapes—"

Joe froze. "You know about the tapes?"

"I know everything, Joe. You were watching those things day after day. How did you think that made me feel? How did you think I was supposed to feel?"

Joe stepped closer. He reached for her. "Puddin, I didn't know. I didn't know it would make you feel so bad. I guess I was wrong. I shouldn't have tried to keep a secret."

She used her hand to knock his away and tried to push herself farther into the corner. She could feel tears on her own face now. They surprised her. "How could you not think I would feel that way? You spent all your time in there. I knew you weren't reading." She heard her voice break. "Why wasn't I enough, Joe? Why wasn't I good enough?"

"I was trying to make you happy. I'm sorry, okay? We can work it out. I'll get rid of the tapes. Or we could watch them together."

She shook her hands at him. "Are you crazy? After all this time? It's too late, Joe. And what am I supposed to do? Just forget about Starbucks?"

"Here you go with Starbucks again! What are you talking about?"

"Are you trying to tell me you never go to Starbucks?"

"I go there for coffee."

"Coffee? Coffee?" She turned and took a step toward him. "You mean cream, don't you?"

"Puddin, what—?"

"Don't insult me, Joe! Don't lie! I know you go there, Joe! I know you go there to meet women. People have seen you, Joe!"

His arms dropped to his sides. "Puddin."

"Don't Puddin me! I know you go there to meet white women. White women, Joe? White women! I mean really."

Joe sighed. "Puddin."

"And out in public. You know how people talk. You should have known it would get back to me."

He sighed again and nodded his head. "I should have known."

She heard herself yelling; she could hear the torment in her own voice. Her chest was heaving. She knew anyone outside could hear her, but she didn't care. "How much did you expect me to take, Joe? First the pornography, then the calls, then your meeting them in public." She shook her head. "And you're supposed to be . . . you're almost a deacon! . . . You're supposed to set the tone for the other men."

He shook his head and wiped the tears from his face. "Puddin," he said. "Puddin? Is that what you think of me?"

"Yes, Joe, that's how I feel."

He stepped toward her and lifted his arms as though he was going to embrace her. When she saw daylight under his arms, she dived through the opening. He pitched forward and she scrambled to her car, flung the door open, gunned the engine, and sped off the lot before he could get his footing.

Joe was on foot, his car parked in front of their house. So she was down the street, parked, and inside—probably before he even got to his feet.

She locked and latched the back door and propped a chair under the knob. She could feel him coming. Panicked, she looked around for a weapon. She walked to the freezer and pulled out the last pack of chicken—she'd been eating tuna and burgers since he'd been gone—and shoved it in the microwave. It was a long shot, but maybe she could get it done before he forced his way in. "God, please!" She looked at the ceiling. "Please help me!" She had to keep moving. She opened the cabinet door and reached for flour. She shook her head. She had to get hold of herself. It didn't need to be seasoned. She wasn't feeding anyone.

"Puddin?"

She turned and half the sack of flour hit Joe's shoulder and powdered his face and hair. The front door! She had forgotten to block the door!

"Stay away from me, Joe!" The microwave hummed behind him; she couldn't reach the chicken. She brandished what was left of the flour at him. "I mean it, Joe! Stay away!"

He spit and coughed a cloud of flour. "For goodness' sakes, Puddin! Will you cut it out!" He raised his hands in the air. They were full of videotapes. "Will you look at these?"

She was as insulted as she was frightened. "No, I will not look at them with you! What kind of woman do you think I am? I am not going to look at that pornography, that filth!"

He shook the tapes at her. "What pornography? What filth? And you got a lot of nerve—you and your computer!"

"My computer? That's nothing compared to you, Mr. Starbucks! Mr. Pornography!"

"It's okay for you to do your dirt on the computer?"

"It's nothing compared to what you're doing, Joe!"

He shook the tapes again. "I'm not doing anything bad . . . nothing so bad. Puddin, my goodness, it's Luke and Laura!"

"I don't care who's on that filth!"

"It's not filth—it's Luke and Laura. You know, from the soap opera . . . *General Hospital* . . . Luke and Laura!"

She hit him with the flour. "You pervert!" She ran past him to the dining room. She turned on him. "Luke and Laura? On porno? That's disgusting!"

He followed her around the table. "No, Puddin, you don't understand. I like watching them."

"I know you like watching them, and that's disgusting! It's filthy!" She clamped her hands over her ears.

"No, I mean I like watching soap operas. See?" He reached with one arm and grabbed her from behind about her waist. "See!" He held them up in front of her. "I like soap operas! Okay? I like soap operas!"

"Soap operas! Is that what you expect me to believe, Joe? Do I look like a fool to you, Joe?"

"It's true! Honest!" He leaned his forehead on the back of her head. "Puddin, is that what you think about me? Is that what you've been thinking about me all this time?" He raised his head, took one of her hands down from her ears, and pressed the tapes into her hands. "I like soap operas, okay? After I retired, I don't know, I just got hooked on them. I didn't want you to know. You were hounding me about getting a job, and I just thought you'd really lay into me if you knew what I was doing . . . and, well, you know, most men . . . most men don't watch the soaps. Not real men."

She turned around to face him. They might as well have it out toe to toe. "Right, Joe. So what about the brown paper bags? How do you explain them?"

"Bootleg tapes."

"I know they're bootleg. But what are you talking about, Joe?"

"I was watching the soap operas and they kept showing Luke and Laura, *now,* but they kept talking about Luke and Laura, the way they used to be. I wanted to see it."

"Joe, do you expect me to buy this?"

"It's the truth. I was at church, and I overheard these two women talking about bootleg videotapes, that there was a woman you could call who had personally archived all the old shows, and if you called her, you could make arrangements to buy copies. But it all had to be done on the QT."

"Joe, you've got to be kidding?" What kind of fool did he think she was? She wanted to slug him.

"At first, I was calling her, the source. Then after awhile, after she got to trust me, she would call me when she had new tapes available." Joe clamped his hands to the side of his head. "I don't know. I guess I just got caught up. I never thought anything like this would happen. I didn't want you to be ashamed of me." He raised his shoulders and hands. "The *new* story lines, they're okay, but the *old* ones . . . that's real love. . . . I just got hooked. And then, I got an idea." He motioned toward the reading room. "Come let me show you."

"Joe, I am not going in there!"

"Please, Puddin? Let me show you? I can prove it all." He took her down the hall, only half tugging at her, because she only half resisted. It was crazy. All of it was too crazy to believe, but her heart wanted to believe, and she followed. Everything in the room was just as he'd left it. She had not been inside.

There was a large leather recliner, with the footrest still up, that faced the television and VCR. On the back of the chair was a green comforter and Joe's blue robe. He swept them off with one hand. "Here, sit down, okay?"

Up under the television there was a cabinet. Joe knelt down and opened the doors. Inside the cabinet were black boxes, like stationery paper boxes with lids on them. He slid the boxes from the cabinet and brought them to her. His face lit like a little boy showing his box of treasure. Joe lifted the lid. Inside were steno pads. He lifted the covers, and the notebooks were filled with Joe's handwriting. He smiled shyly. "I've been writing a book. I'm trying to, anyway."

He curled up at her feet with notebooks cradled in his arms. He handed them to her one by one. "I knew you were sick of chicken. I knew it. But I just couldn't think about going to work. Then I got an idea." He lifted one of the tapes scattered on the floor. "I was watching one of these, and it came to me. I'm always talking about love . . . about real love. So I figured I could write a book. I could write a romance novel—a real romance with everything about love, complete love. I was watching the tapes and trying to figure out how to write a novel. I told my Luke-and-Laura source, and then she told me about this group of romance writers that meets in Baltimore."

Shame began to creep into her cheeks and make them warm. "Joe? Romance writers? No?"

He nodded. "Yep. That's where they meet, at Starbucks." He shook his head. "I should have known somebody would tell you. But I wanted it to be a secret." He flipped through the steno pads. "I've been working on it for a long time. It's probably not any good, but my dream was to get it published and maybe get you something other than chicken." He kept looking at the box. "Some of the women are professional writers, and they've been helping me." He dropped the pads back in the box. "But it isn't worth losing you over, Puddin." He put the lids on them. "Nothing's worth losing you." His eyes were full of water again. "How am I supposed to live my life without you?"

"Joe," she said and leaned forward and kissed him. The flour on his lips was dry and dusty. She kissed him again anyway.

He bowed his head. "I never dreamed you would think anything like that about me, Puddin. Is that what you really think of
me?"

She didn't know what to answer. Puddin tried to come up with
an explanation that would fit. She couldn't.

Joe filled the silence. "I kept trying to figure it out. I told myself
that maybe you were so ashamed about me catching you with the
computer, that the shame just overwhelmed you." He kissed her
hand. "But you know there's nothing you can do that would separate us, Puddin. We can work it out. I found out there are lots of
women hooked on written pornography on the computer and in
books. I guess if it's words and not pictures, it's easier for women to
tell themselves it's okay. But I don't fault you, Puddin. Maybe I
haven't been paying you as much attention as you need."

"Come on, Joe." Puddin tried to keep a straight face. "I've got
something I need to show you." She stood up and reached for his
hand.

He shook his head. "No, Puddin. I don't want to see it. Let's
just put it behind us."

She held out her hand. "I need you to see it, Joe."

Puddin took Joe to the computer room and showed him the
emails and the personal files from Charm City News. "I call them
my babies." She touched his face with her hand. "I've got a part-
time job, Joe. It's not pornography." She batted her eyes and looked
at him earnestly. "Is that what you think of me, Joe?"

He grabbed her in a bear hug. "Shut up, girl!" They tussled and
giggled on the floor like school kids who have finally, after what
feels like forever, made up. "You're my chocolate Puddin!" He kissed
the tip of her nose.

"I figured if you were sneaking, Joe, that I could, too. And I
was trying to do something good. You know matchmaking . . . well,
the computer does most of the matching. But I can reach out
and . . . you know." She smiled. "Like you know that young man
at church? The African?"

He nuzzled her ear. "Yes."

"Well, he's on here. He's one of my babies. And that girl from church, the one with the green eyes and blonde hair?"

"You mean Mary from down the street?"

"That's the one. Well, I've decided to try to get the two of them together."

"Puddin! Puddin, just leave well enough alone. If they're supposed to be together they'll be together." Joe shifted her so that she was sitting on his lap. "No matchmaking, Puddin. I mean it. You stay out of it. He's got a girlfriend and she's got a boyfriend. Just stay out of it, now."

She kissed his cheek. "I know, Joe. But you saw Mary's boyfriend. Come on, now. You know he's no good. He was looking at everything in the room that had on a skirt. And Africa's girlfriend . . . oo-oo, it was so nasty seeing her chew with her mouth open!"

He returned her kiss. "All that may be true, Puddin. His name is Moor, by the way, not Africa. But you stay out of it. I'm back now, and you've more than got your hands full." He nuzzled her neck. "And I'm hungry. Real hungry!"

She moaned as he kissed her. "Luke and Laura, Joe? I mean, *really!*"

She woke, in the middle of the night, to Joe's snoring. His mouth was open and drool leaked from the side of his mouth. He was beautiful. She leaned and whispered in his ear. " 'Whither thou goest, I will go. Whither thou lodgest, I will lodge. Thy people shall be my people, and your God my God.' " She rolled back to her side, slid from the bed, and tiptoed to the computer room. She gently closed the door and then turned on the computer. She turned in the darkness and whispered toward the closed door, "And I will doeth what thou sayest, my beloved husband, as soonest as I sendest these email invitations to Moor and Mary to come as dates to the family and friends get-together."

38

Moor

oor! *Moor!*" It was Ali across the street from the bus stop
with Brighty and Blue. They were yelling like three tru-
ant schoolboys. Ali was waving a sheet of white paper.

They needed jobs, each one of them. It was too early in the
morning. Moor waved his hand. "Go away! Go away! I don't have
time." It was embarrassing.

Moor watched as the three of them conversed for a moment.
Then Ali, blonde dreadlocks flying, dashed across the street zigzag-
ging between cars. "Whew!"

"You are a crazy white boy!"

Ali waved the paper. "It's from Charm City!"

Moor shook his head with disgust. They were like children, his
three friends. They needed a dose of his grandmother's medicine. "I
already have a woman."

Ali nodded. "I know, but this one is special. It's a special invitation. It's not computer generated. It's to meet a woman named—"

Moor waved his hand to cut off Ali's foolishness. People at the
bus stop were looking at them. "I don't want to know her name. I
told you, I have a woman and I am perfectly happy."

Ali kept waving the paper. "But it's for some kind of family and
friends thing in this lady's backyard—"

The bus was only a block away, and Moor prayed for it to come
quickly. "I am not interested, Ali. Go home. You embarrass yourself." Ali didn't look the least bit embarrassed. "Run across the street,
now, and play with the other little boys. I like my woman fine. She
is the kind of woman that the men in my family like. She is fat!"

Some of the people at the bus stop laughed. "And I like her just fine. Go away, now!" The bus stopped, the door opened, and Moor stepped onboard.

"But she talks with her mouth full!" Ali yelled as the door was closing.

When Moor was seated, after paying his fare, he dropped his head into his hands and shook his head with embarrassment. Ali stood outside the bus waving the paper and yelling until the bus pulled away.

39

Mary

Mary got off the bus and rushed to her house. She checked her watch. She had just enough time to check her email and get ready before Reggie arrived. He was taking her to have dinner and play video games at a place at the Inner Harbor.

She turned on her computer. There wasn't much mail. Just someone connected with Charm City News Personals, someone named *HipHopGodMama* inviting her to a friends and family gathering over the weekend. The address was on Old Frederick Road, just down the street, and the invitation listed her date's name as Moor.

Moor?

Mary looked at the piece of paper on her dresser. It couldn't be. But how many men were there named Moor in Baltimore? Probably *more* than she could imagine. Mary laughed at the play on words. She read further in the note. The person's screen name was Africa. She shook her head. It had to be. She looked at the scrap of paper again and remembered. *"Maybe this is some crazy divine plan. Maybe God has been orchestrating all this trying to get us together. What do you think?"* Her own words came back to her.

She wrote a response with a negative reply.

Reggie was sweet. She looked at the crumpled piece of paper again. If it was a divine plan, the timing was anything but good. Maybe if they'd met sooner. She reread her response. Her finger played over the send button. She looked at the piece of paper. *"Maybe this is some crazy divine plan."* Maybe not. She pushed the button and sent the response on its way.

Mary looked at the clock. She had showered and dressed long ago. Reggie was more than an hour late, and she was beginning to worry. Had something happened to him? Had he had car trouble? She called his home, but there was no response. He didn't answer his cell phone, either. Should she call the police? She got up from the chair where she'd been sitting near the front window and went to the kitchen to get the telephone book.

The phone rang and she answered, afraid to hope he was okay, and feeling foolish for worrying. "Hello?"

"Mary, it's me, Reggie."

"Reggie, thank God you're all right! I was worried."

"Nah. Everything's cool." Mary could hear noises in the background and people's voices. "I got off a little early and I decided to come down to the game room ahead of time by myself."

Mary exhaled with relief. "You want me to just come there? I can get a cab. Why didn't you call me?"

Reggie cleared his throat. "Nah. You don't have to take a cab. It's too late for you to be out trying to catch a cab."

"I can call one."

Mary thought she heard a voice in the background. A feminine voice. "Wait just a minute." She could hear Reggie whispering.

"Reggie?"

"Just a minute." Mary could hear more whispering.

"What's going on?"

Reggie laughed and then cleared his throat. "Look, Mary, I don't think it's going to work out between us. I appreciate all the attention and everything, but I don't think I can give you what you need. You deserve somebody better than me. Plus, I don't have a lot of time right now. You know I got that new project I was telling you about."

She had been so stupid. Mary felt like she had been alternately punched in the gut and slapped across the face. "Is that the new project I hear giggling in the background?"

Reggie gave a short burst of laughter and then quieted. "Yeah, something like that."

"What happened?" She hated the way she sounded, like she was begging. "I thought everything was going so well."

"You know, you believe what you believe, and that's not going to change. . . . I don't want it to change. I respect your beliefs. I give you your props for that. We're just not each other's types, you know?"

"Was it the hair?"

"What?"

"I said, was it the hair?"

"Well, it was a surprise, you know? But, nah, you just deserve somebody better than me. You do your hair the way you want to. I just can't give you what you want, what you need, or what you really deserve."

"You're right," she said and hung up the phone before he could hear her cry. "Oh, God!"

Mary pulled off her clothes, stumbling through the house, and dropped them as she walked to the bedroom. She laid down across the bed and cried herself to sleep.

The phone wakened her. First the sun, then the clock, told her that she had been sleeping too long.

It was Garvin. "Mary? Hi, Mary? It's me. Garvin. I would love to see you. You awake?"

Mary yawned. She didn't feel like seeing anyone. She didn't feel like feeling.

"I'm in Baltimore. I would love to see you."

She would be polite. She would ask her cousin where she was. She would be too far away; she would tell her that was too bad. She would give her regrets, and that would be that. She wanted to sit with her misery alone for just a little while. She deserved that.

"Mary, are you there?"

"Yeah, sure, Garvin. I just had a long night."

"A hot date, huh? Was he a nice guy?"

"Yeah, real nice."

"Well, I would love to see you. I don't know where this is in relation to you." Coming now was the information that was going to take her off the hook. "Funny. We talk all the time, but I don't know your address. Anyway, I'm on Frederick Road . . . on Old Frederick Road. Do you know where that is, Mary?"

Mary sat up in bed. "Old Frederick Road?"

"Yes, it's a sort of friends and family get-together. It's a beautiful day . . . it's warm enough that we're outside." Garvin giggled. "You never can tell how the weather will be. I wish you could come. I would love to see you."

"Old Frederick Road?"

"My Meemaw, my grandmother," Garvin began to whisper, "is kin to this guy, to the husband here. I don't know. I guess he's my distant relative, too, some kind of way. Meemaw asked me to come with her. So I came hoping I would see you." She stopped whispering. "He and his wife are really sweet. I told them my cousin lived in Baltimore. They told me to call and invite you. There's tons of food. They said they would even come and get you."

Old Frederick Road? It couldn't be. *"Maybe this is some crazy divine plan."* It couldn't be. "Are you sure? Old Frederick Road?"

"Yes, that's about the only thing I'm sure of. Come on and you can meet Meemaw and see me. My husband, GoGo, is at home babysitting. He gave me a breather; he's so sweet. So you won't be able to see him or meet the baby. But at least we can see each other for a few hours."

It couldn't be. *"Maybe this is some crazy divine plan."* She had to stop saying no. "I live right down the street. Give me the address."

Mary showered and dressed quickly. She looked at the piece of paper on her dresser. Who would have *thunk* it? She left the house, walking down the street and soon found herself running.

What had she been thinking? Why had it taken her so long to see, so long to believe? She glanced at the house numbers as she ran. It's funny how you could live on a street and never pay attention to the addresses. She stopped in front of Sister Puddin and Brother Joe's house. *The chicken lady?* She scratched her head, looked down at the paper, at the numbers on the house, shrugged her shoulders, and began to climb the stairs.

40

Puddin

P*uddin walked out* the back door and down the steps balancing a bowl of potato salad on one hand and a platter of deviled eggs on the other. Mary was sitting at a picnic table with her cousin Garvin. She was obviously happy to see her, but Puddin watched the way she kept scanning the yard, the way she looked hopeful each time the door opened or the gate swung wide.

Mary was looking for Moor. Puddin was sure of it, and she wished she'd listened to Joe. *"Just stay out of it, Puddin."* Now it was too late. She didn't know any good way to tell her to stop looking—Moor wasn't going to come. She had gotten his negative response before she'd gotten Mary's. But unlike Mary, it looked as though he really wasn't going to come.

Moor wasn't there, but the yard was full of people: cousins, uncles, and friends—even some people from the church—Deaconess Othella, Sister Minnie, and some others. Joe was especially glad to see his Aunt Evangelina—Meemaw is what Garvin called her. He was fawning all over her.

He was proud of the backyard—everyone was commenting on the flowers and on the bales of hay he had brought in for seats. He was proud of the cooking. There was some chicken, but mostly beef—beef ribs, beef steak, hamburgers, meatballs in barbecue sauce. But he was most proud that the family had asked him to say a few words, to bless the gathering before they ate.

It was perfect. The only thing that would have made it more perfect was Moor. If only she'd listened to Joe and left well enough alone.

Joe cleared his throat. He was ready to start. "I don't know much of anything that could make me happier than having you all here. Love between friends and family is important. And we got family and friends all the way from North Carolina." He nodded at Garvin, Aunt Evangelina, and Aunt Evangelina's friend, Mr. Green. "Love is important to me." He looked at Puddin. A shiver went up her spine. "I think about it all the time. I think about all kinds of love—spiritual love, romantic love, brotherly love.

"I'm just fascinated by it. I'm not an expert at it, but since it's my house, and you all invited me to speak—" Joe laughed—"I'm gone tell you what I know."

He nodded. "Take spiritual love—God's love for us and our love for Him. What I figured out, which has taken me most of my life, and the prayers of my sweet wife to learn it, is that God wants to be in each one of our lives. Not just to have us going to church because our mother or our grandmother went . . . or because we want someone influential to see us there in hopes of getting us a job. He doesn't want us to go to church, or not to drink, just so we can get a position on the deacon board. He doesn't want us to pray just to impress other people, or even fast so the church leaders will approve of us."

Puddin was so proud of her husband. She watched as he looked around at the people gathered while he spoke. "Whatever we do or don't do, God wants us to do it because we love Him and His Son Jesus Christ. See, God already proved His love for us. He gave up His only begotten Son and let Him die for our sins in our place so that we could have eternal life. He let His Son die. He gave up His Son. That's love."

"That's love!" Meemaw echoed, nodding.

"So God has already proved His love. He did it first. If we do any of those things—going to church, praying, fasting, or whatever—God wants us to do it because we really love Him. Not to impress people, to fit in, or to be part of some social group. I'm not telling you how to live your life, what to do or what not to do. But just sometime take a moment and ask yourself are you living your life—are you doing anything in your life that says to God, 'Father,

I love You,' that says, 'Jesus, I love you'?"

Puddin smiled at him when he looked at her.

He quickly turned back to the group. "Family love? Ain't nothing sweeter, and ain't much that can break your heart quicker. We love times like this, don't we? You know, where we get together, eat, laugh, and talk about good times.

"The hard part, though, is the bad times. But that's as much a part of family as anything. We set ourselves up for heartache if we tell ourselves all we're going to have is good times. Bad times is part of it. Confusion is part of it. It takes all of that together for us to bond and to make us strong. And I tell you the truth, as tough as it is sometimes, still most of us at one time or another still thank God for the family He put us in. Amen?"

The people in the yard answered, "Amen."

Joe cleared his throat again. "Finally—and I ain't gone take too long, 'cause those ribs are smelling mighty nice—I want to say something to my pretty wife in front of you all."

Puddin could feel her face warming. She had been in the news enough lately. She wasn't sure she wanted any more attention.

"I know there have been rumors and stories flying around. I know everybody knows we have been going through some tough times."

Joe turned so that he was fully facing Puddin. It was hard to believe that she ever thought she might want to live without him. "But right here, in front of everybody, I want you to know that I love you. I always have, and I always will.

"Now, you may put me out again. I sure hope not though! And I sure hope you don't throw no more chicken." Joe touched his forehead, and people chuckled.

"Whatever you do, Puddin, I want you to know I'm not going anywhere. Like that song I'm always singing to you, 'Ain't No Mountain High Enough' . . ." Joe looked like he was fighting back tears. "You see, baby, I already made my choice a long time ago. I'm not with you because I'm scared of divorce." He cleared his throat. "I figure if God forgave the apostle Paul murder, then He will forgive me divorce. Staying together like that ain't love. That's fear, and fear don't honor God.

"I ain't with you because the church won't make me a deacon if I leave you. That would be living a lie, and a lie can't honor God."

He smiled and when she looked at him, her heart broke with love. "I'm with you because every day I think of life with you and I think of life without you, and every day, I choose you over and over again.

"I know you're suspicious and you're probably going to be that way for the rest of our lives." Puddin laughed through her tears. "I know you listen too much to other people."

Deaconess Othella and Sister Minnie looked at each other and then stared straight ahead.

"Most of the time, it's the wrong people. And you're scared to trust your heart because you're afraid you'll end up looking like a fool." His grin broadened. "And I know you're probably thinking I got my faults, too."

Puddin laughed. "No, not you, baby." Their friends and family laughed with them.

"I'm stubborn. I get my mind fixed on one thing and I can't hardly see nothing else. I think I'm right all the time." He smiled. "Anything else?"

She shook her head. "That will do . . . for right now." There was more laughter.

"We got some spots on us, ain't no doubt about it. But Puddin—" he walked across the yard and put his arms around her—"nobody else makes me feel like you do. That's why I keep saying yes. Even when you get on my nerves, I can't help but love you. And I love that even when you're feeling scared, somewhere deep inside you can't help loving me—even if you sometimes have got a funny way of showing it." He squeezed her tight, and Puddin laid her head on his shoulder. "Our love is for real, baby. God knows our names. He knows us together as one." Joe kissed her forehead. "So you can throw all the chicken you want, that's not gone stop my love. Ain't no mountain, baby. Ain't no mountain."

Puddin stood at the window washing dishes and looking out at Joe still putting food on people's plates. Aunt Evangelina was standing next to her, a dish towel in her hands. "You should be sitting down resting. You're company. You don't have to help me."

Aunt Evangelina laughed. "Yes, I do! That's what company does—good company, anyway. Besides, it gives me a reason to hear your sweet voice. That's one of the things Joe told me about you. 'She has the sweetest voice.'"

Puddin tried to stop herself from blushing. "Joe is always talking about you. 'Aunt Evangelina this and Aunt Evangelina that.' He was so happy to see you when we were in Texas."

She began to dry the plate that Puddin handed her, wiping in circular motion. "Well, I love him, too."

"There's a nickname I've heard him call you. Your granddaughter calls you—"

"Meemaw." She laughed. "And that girl means it, too. Me maw. I'm *her* grandma. As loving as she can be, but I'm her grandmother. Sometime I'll have to tell you the story of how she was ready to kill her husband 'cause she thought—"

"Meemaw, are you in here telling stories on me?" It was Garvin coming in the back door with Mary.

Meemaw chuckled. "Chile, please! Would I do something like that?" She winked at Puddin.

Puddin laughed. "Well, let me change the subject then. That gentleman you're with . . ."

Meemaw's eyes were shining and she raised one eyebrow. "You mean Mr. Green?"

"Is he significant?"

Garvin groaned. "You don't want to get her going on this one."

Meemaw swatted at her granddaughter with the towel. "Significant?" she said to Puddin. "Is that modern for is he my beau or my gentleman caller?"

"I don't mean to be nosy."

Meemaw smiled. "Oh, you're not being nosy . . . just curious."

She held the plate she was drying up for inspection, and then set it down. "Is he significant? Well, there's lots of ways of looking at a thing." She picked up a glass bowl. "Oh, he's significant, all right. There's lots of stories I could tell you."

Garvin grabbed a dish towel and a wet plate. "See, I told you."

Meemaw looked at Garvin and laughed. "I thought I told you to hush."

It was fun to watch the grandmother and granddaughter enjoying each other's company. "I'm sorry, I shouldn't have butted in. But, you know . . ."

Meemaw wasn't smiling, she was grinning from ear to ear. "What? Know he's white? That ain't half of it. Mr. Green is Jewish!" She laughed. "So you can imagine the gossip we have caused since my husband died and then his wife died. We been the subject of a whole lot of talk." She set the bowl she was drying on the counter and reached for a plate. "I guess I could put it all to rest." She wagged her head as she laughed again. "But I'm an old woman and I deserve a little fun. Plus, I provide opportunity for the Lord to test people's proclivity to gossip!"

"I shouldn't have asked."

Garvin nodded. "I told you so."

Meemaw nodded to her and went on talking. "Oh, honey, you have no idea how much a little color difference can stir things up. We got a long way to go before Jesus comes. There's still a lot of wrinkles and stains on the body over race."

Puddin winced inwardly and hoped it didn't show outwardly. *White women! White women!* She was glad that Meemaw hadn't heard her, hadn't heard her and her Comfort Circle sisters. Embarrassment over her past anger burned her face.

Meemaw spoke as though she were reading Puddin's mind. "We all are struggling with it, and most of the times pretending we don't. It's the other person being sensitive. We still haven't learned how to love."

Puddin looked back out the window at Joe. What was the problem with her anyway? Where did those thoughts even come from? Was it about her thinking she wasn't good enough? Having society tell her she wasn't good enough, could never be pretty enough, could never be valuable enough?

Was it unfinished business? A rivalry that both sides hated, but sometimes enjoyed? Was it not being willing to let go of past hurts, wounds, and slights? Was it rage against misguided notions of superiority that fed one's ego, while debasing another?

Let's see. I'll give you five hundred for the one with golden hair and a thousand for the one with blue eyes. A bonus for the one with large breasts, and a grand prize for the one that is a size two!

No one forced her—or anyone else—to participate in the judging, in the competition, in the auction. No one could make her feel insecure unless she allowed it.

Meemaw's laughter brought her attention back to the conversation. "The truth about me and Mr. Green is we're good friends—longtime and good friends. Any other mountain people want to make out of the molehill, why, they're free to do so." She set down the bowl she was drying and grabbed another. She winked at Puddin. "We're just good friends. *Very* good friends!"

Garvin nudged her grandmother with her shoulder. "Meemaw, you are always keeping stuff going." She looked at Puddin. "I'm sorry. I try to keep my eye on her."

Meemaw giggled like a schoolgirl. "You didn't think I was gone come to town and not have nothing to say, did you?"

Puddin smiled. "Well, I'm happy you're here."

Garvin clamped her hands to her head, pretending to be worried. "Now, you've done it. You're egging her on."

Meemaw giggled again. "What? You can't stand the thought of me and a little romance."

Garvin looked at Mary and shook her head. "See what I have to put up with? She just loves trying to shock me."

Meemaw looked at Mary. "You want to come join in? Here, take my towel, and I'll take your seat."

Mary smiled, took the towel, and began to dry.

Meemaw pulled the large shoulder bag she had brought with her near to where she was sitting. "So tell me about you." She looked at Mary. "Are you married?"

Puddin groaned inwardly.

"No, ma'am," Mary answered.

"Do you want to be?"

"Meemaw? Stop it now. It's getting so I can't take you anywhere."

Meemaw's face looked like an innocent baby. "What? What's wrong with that, Garvina?"

"She's single."

"Why you bugging your eyes at me, Garvina? Is it something you don't want me to say? You don't want me to talk about the woman being single? What, you think she's gone do something bad?"

Garvin put the towel up to her face.

"Being single is not a disease, you know? Wanting to be married, wanting to be loved by a man ain't a disease, either." She shook her head. "Sometimes I think we've gone too far with this modern stuff, making people feel shame. God ain't mad at us for being attracted to another person. He's not condemning us. He's a passionate God."

Puddin watched Mary and noticed that her face and shoulders relaxed as the older woman spoke. "All this silliness, teaching that relationships between a man and a woman is spiritual failure on their parts . . . well, we can see the fruit of that. Look at people that's been practicing that for years . . . all confused and frustrated. My goodness—and uptight!"

Garvin wrung her hands and laughed nervously. "Meemaw!" Puddin could see that this was part of their love, part of their play with each other.

Meemaw began to dig in her bag. "I didn't come here to teach, but since I'm here . . ." She retrieved her Bible and began to read from Song of Solomon.

> *"Many waters cannot quench love,*
> *Nor can the floods drown it.*
> *If a man would give for love*
> *All the wealth of his house,*
> *It would be utterly despised."*

Meemaw looked up. "That's in the Good Book. And listen to this from Proverbs:

> *Let your fountain be blessed,*
> *And rejoice with the wife of your youth.*
> *As a loving deer and a graceful doe,*
> *Let her breasts satisfy you at all times;*
> *And always be enraptured with her love."*

Garvin threw her towel in the air. "Meemaw, good grief!"

"What, Garvin? I'm not making it up." She pointed at her Bible. "It's right here in the book." She nodded at Mary. "See, sometimes the people that are the most worried about what other people are doing are people that were out of control doing lots of wrong themselves!" She raised an eyebrow in Garvin's direction.

Garvin laughed. "Okay, Meemaw. You got me. I confess."

Meemaw settled herself onto her seat. "Mm hmm. I know I'm right. Those people don't want to show their scars or tell where they came from. And the Lord wants us to do both of those things, so people who are wounded will know they can be healed, and people who are lost will know they can be found."

The old woman nodded at Mary. "Now, I'm not arguing—some people are meant to be alone. But not everybody. We get confused sometimes, but God never said He didn't want men and women to love. In fact, He said it wasn't good for man to be alone. And while we're at it, the original sin wasn't sex. Read Genesis. The original sins was fear, disobedience, unbelief, and lying—pretty much some of the same sins mentioned at the end in Revelation."

Garvin laid her head on the counter. "Other people worry about their teenagers! I have to worry about my grandmother!"

"Hush, girl!" Meemaw waved a hand at Garvin, then looked back at Mary. "We mean well, but we want to rush and put on a bandage that will fix everybody and keep chaos out of our lives . . . messy relationships out of the church. While we try to fix it up, we mess it up."

Meemaw looked at Mary like she was her own grandchild. "God ain't mad at you, baby, if you don't want to be alone. But like any other desire, that desire shouldn't consume you."

Mary nodded. "Yes, ma'am." Her eyes filled with tears.

"It shouldn't be the only thing you think about in the morning and at night. God should be first, whether you're married or not."

"Yes, ma'am."

"And contrary to what people might tell you, He don't kick you out of heaven if you don't get it right the first time. I ain't telling you to do wrong. I'm saying God will teach you how to do right, and that He'll be patient with you, just like He was patient with the rest of us . . . like He *still is* patient with the all the rest of us while we're learning." Meemaw nodded. "We want to forget about that, because waiting on people to learn is a messy business. But God still loves us, and He is patient while we learn."

Puddin watched it all. She was going to take this conversation back to the Comfort Circle.

Mary's face glowed with peace. "Yes, ma'am. Thank you, ma'am."

Meemaw looked at Garvin. "I'm finished now."

Garvin sighed. "You sure, Meemaw?"

"Yes, sugar. I've done everything I came here to do."

41

Puddin and Mary

Before the nine-thirty service began, people crowded around the pews talking about the friends and family get-together. *"It was beautiful!" "It did my heart good to see the two of you back together!" "There was enough food there to feed three hundred people— and nobody threw any!"* Of course, there were also some busybodies. *"What was Joe's aunt's name?"*

"Aunt Evangelina."

"Such a pretty name. And who was that white man with her?"

"Mr. Green."

"Yes, that's right—Mr. Green. And, now, he's her husband, her boy-friend, or something? I know somebody told me, but I forgot."

"They're just friends."

"Friends, huh? Well, she sure does look good for a woman her age. I guess some friends are close like that. You sure they're just friends?"

A few pews in front of Puddin, Deaconess Othella sat with the other deaconesses, her broad-brimmed hat bobbing up and down. "Brother Joe is outstanding. Yes, he is! I told Sister Puddin she should have listened to her husband! I tried to tell her all along!"

As the church began to fill, people moved to their seats. Puddin held Joe's hand and leaned to whisper in his ear. "I should have listened to you, Joe. I feel so bad about Mary. I know she was there hoping to see Moor."

"The man said he had a woman already. You saw her at the singles thing with your own two eyes. I told you to leave it alone, baby, to let God be God."

"I know, Joe, but the woman he's dating—she talks when she chews!"

The praise team began to sing. "Our God is an Awesome God . . ." and the congregation joined in—singing, clapping, and moving with the rhythm of the song. By the time they had begun to sing "Hallelujah in the Sanctuary!" the miracle of worship and uninhibited praise had begun. Young people danced. Old people on canes forgot them and joined in the celebration. People that didn't know each other became joined in musical union and laid their burdens down.

The crowd got excited and stood to their feet when they saw the reverend come through the door.

Pastor Howard stepped into the pulpit wearing a long white robe with maroon velvet trim. He smiled at the congregation and nodded. "I don't want to hold you long. So if you don't mind, I'm going to jump right in today."

Joe called his assent. "That's all right, Rev!"

"Amen," someone else said.

Pastor Howard smiled and began. "The great teacher and philosopher Socrates said, 'The unexamined life is not worth living.' Sometimes some of my brothers of the cloth get a little nervous, and sometimes the leaders get a little angry when people begin to ask questions."

He smiled and gathered up his robe around him, pretending to be afraid. "Truth be told, sometimes questions make me uncomfortable. 'Are you doubting my leadership? Are you questioning my authority?' Thank God for the Holy Ghost, because at moments like that He reminds me that the Lord asked us all to examine ourselves"—he pointed to his chest—"to make sure we were praying for the right reason. That we were fasting for the right reason. That we were eating or not eating for the right reason. Even that we were giving for the right reason."

The pulpit was raised ten steps from the floor where the congregation sat. The pastor looked down and nodded at the deacons and the trustees that sat nearest the front. "What I'm about to say, these fellas here may want to shoot me." He waved his hand in their direction as he spoke to the congregation. "See, we want you to give all the time—we got light, heat, mortgage to pay. We got people to feed and clothe. That's church business. God wants you to give because that desire is in your heart—the desire to please Him and to do good for the body. He wants a cheerful giver. He wants an obedient giver." He grinned and moved away from them. "Let me get off of that before I get called into a church meeting."

He exchanged smiles with the deacons. "To get to the heart of the matter, to examine this heart stuff, you got to ask yourself a lot of hard questions—hard questions about the choices you are making in your life, hard questions about why you do what you do."

"Listen! Listen!" a man called out from the balcony.

Pastor Howard nodded. "And I tell you, examining the heart is tricky business. You know some people do things—go to church, get married, dress a certain way—because everybody else does, all the people in their family do it, and they don't want to take the time to think about it. I think that's called laziness, and I think that's numbered as a sin. Today, we're not going to commit that sin. Amen?"

"Amen!" a woman called to him.

"We're going to examine ourselves. We're going to examine the state of our hearts." The pastor rubbed one hand across his bald head. "Socrates said the unexamined life is not a life worth living. I say, the unexamined life is not a life that can please God. So this is the examination I put to you today—what is the condition of the church? And I'm not just talking about New Worshippers, I'm talking about the body, about all of us who are called by God's name."

He picked up his Bible. "The question before us is are we alive? If we don't love one another, then we are dead. It's simple. Love equals life. John says, 'We know that we have passed from death to life, because we love the brethren.' We know, if we're talking about our family members, we love sometimes—when it's not too hard."

Puddin turned to look at Joe's profile. She squeezed his hand. *God, forgive me. Joe, forgive me.*

The pastor walked as he talked. "If we're talking about our neighbors or other people in the church—it's getting kind of tight up in here. We love as long as they don't offend us, aren't too different, don't step on our toes."

Puddin thought about Mary and the Comfort Circle meetings. She sighed. They were going to have to do better.

"And let's not even talk about how we treat those we are supposed to be introducing to the kingdom. We shun them; we don't show them love." He waved his hand. "Let's move on, let's examine our hearts. And the best way I know to examine a heart is with the Word of God.

"Read with me. First Corinthians chapter thirteen." He opened the pages of his Bible. "If you're reading the King James Version, every time you see the word *charity*, I want you to translate what you read as *love*.

> *"Though I speak with the tongues of men and of angels, and have not charity, I am become as sounding brass, or a tinkling cymbal. And though I have the gift of prophecy, and understand all mysteries, and all knowledge; and though I have all faith, so that I could remove mountains, and have not charity, I am nothing.*
>
> *And though I bestow all my goods to feed the poor, and though I give my body to be burned, and have not charity, it profiteth me nothing.*

"Beautiful words, aren't they? There's no more beautiful poetry, I think, than in the Word of God. But don't let's get caught up in the poetry. Remember, now, we're examining the body. So let's go back to those characteristics, those gifts that Paul lists for us, and let's look at them from a body perspective. When you read the gifts, those characteristics, I want you to think what that looks like in the body today, the body as we know it. Think who that characteristic describes. You might substitute the name of a certain group that comes to your mind, a certain ministry, maybe even a certain denomination."

Puddin listened closely. She had heard and read the passage over and over again. Usually, she thought of it in terms of individuals— one person needing to be patient or kind. It was a new thing to begin to think of the passage applying to groups of people.

"I told you I wouldn't be before you long, so let's get down to business. We're examining our hearts, examining the body for signs of life. I'm going to ask you to take a leap with me. Consider that the apostle Paul who penned these words, at the time he spoke, was speaking to the body, the body joined together. Let us consider this morning that if Paul was going to address the body, he might be talking to many different administrations or denominations within the body."

"Teach, Rev!" Someone shouted to the right of where Joe and Puddin were sitting.

"And I believe what God is saying to us now is that yes, we are blessed within our individual denominations with gifts, but if we don't have love, those gifts mean nothing.

"Come on and read with me:

> *Charity suffereth long, and is kind; charity envieth not; charity vaunteth not itself, is not puffed up, doth not behave itself unseemly, seeketh not her own, is not easily provoked, thinketh no evil; rejoiceth not in iniquity, but rejoiceth in the truth; beareth all things, believeth all things, hopeth all things, endureth all things."*

Puddin looked at Joe again. Through this whole ordeal—Chickengate, for goodness' sakes—the words the pastor was reading had been in her heart. They were the words that had held her and her husband together. If what the pastor was saying was true, couldn't the words hold the body of Christ together?

Pastor Howard picked up a handkerchief from the podium, as

he replaced his Bible, and wiped his face. "Let's stop there. We don't need to go through all of them to get a reckoning of our spiritual health." He walked to the edge of the speaking area. "The people with the gift of tongues, are they patient with the people who don't share their gift? The people with wisdom and knowledge, do they believe the ones who speak in tongues when they talk about their gift? Do they think they're better than the ones who operate in faith? Do they envy the ones who have the most money to give? And let's don't add color or ethnicity into the equation. If we do, we know this body is stinking." He shook his head. "Somebody call for the life support!" He smiled. "Oh, I know it's tight, but it's right!"

He moved back toward the podium. "'Love believeth all things.' Do we believe each other? When we discuss our individual or denominational experiences and the mysteries of God, do we speak kindly with one another? Do we speak patiently with one another? Are we even civil? Do we trust one another? Is the language of our hearts love?"

Learning to love, learning to trust, was going to be as difficult for the body as it had been for her and Joe. But it could be done—if you wanted it bad enough, if you were willing to fight for it. Puddin held his hand tighter. Their love proved that.

"The Lord says that people will recognize us by the love we have for one another. Are we as Christians still recognizable?"

"Lord, help us!" One of the deaconesses waved a hand in the air.

He laughed. "You all are looking at me like you don't understand."

Someone in the congregation yelled to him. "Preach, Rev!"

He waved his hand. "I told you I wouldn't be long."

"Take your time, Rev!" one of the deacons called out in response.

"I'm finished." He began to walk away.

Mary nodded as she listened to the pastor. Loving was a difficult thing. Difficult for the church . . . and definitely hard for her. After Reggie, after all she'd been through, it was hard to believe that love was ever going to find her again. And it was difficult to believe that if it did find her, she would be willing to surrender, to try again.

She'd been excited, even hopeful, as she climbed the stairs to the friends and family gathering at Sister Puddin and Brother Joe's. But that was yesterday. When she got there, Moor wasn't there. She didn't want to be disappointed, but she was. She looked down from the balcony at Pastor Howard walking away. That's what she wanted to do—to just give up, to walk away from it all.

Suddenly, he turned dramatically. Something in his movements made her sit forward and listen.

"I believe God put a little bit of truth about the kingdom in each of us. It's like a piece of a mosaic, or a piece of a puzzle. Each of us, each one of those areas Paul mentions, only has a piece of the puzzle. That's why he says, 'We know in part, and we prophesy in part.' Working separately we don't get all the picture. That, I believe, is why Paul says, 'We see through a glass, darkly.' As long as we're immature, as long as our love is immature and not perfected, our vision will be cloudy. The only way to get clearer vision is for all of the gifts—all of the body to work together. The only way for us to work together is to work at perfecting our love."

"Hallelujah!" a man sitting in one of the pews beneath the balcony shouted.

"Perfected love is what God wants to bring out of us. Perfected love—love that is patient, kind, not self-seeking, gentle . . . you know the rest. It's right there in the Bible. The other gifts—except for love, faith, and hope—are temporary—just a means to an end. When perfection comes, when perfect love comes—which is Jesus Christ, which is God's love abiding in all of us, which is life in all of us—then prophecy, tongues, knowledge, they'll pass away. We won't need them anymore."

"I'm waiting for a word that will change my life." Mary thought of the girls she mentored, how different they were, but how beau-

tiful they were when they came together. Like a mosaic. Then, something Agnes said came back to her. *"I keep coming, hoping to hear one more sentence to keep me alive."* Mary nodded. That's what she needed, a word to give her hope. A word to keep her heart alive.

Pastor Howard shook his head. "Right now, at best we're like children. We love immaturely, so we have to rely on our immature gifts to help us see. Our perfect gift, the more excellent way . . ." He shook his head. "I don't believe we're there."

He picked up his Bible and turned again to leave. "So are we alive? Maybe? Just barely? We've got a little love—we haven't flat-lined yet. But if life equals love, then we're just barely breathing. If we've passed from death to life, we love one another. Do we love one another?

"My brothers and sisters, I'd say we're just barely breathing." He stood still. "And I'd be worried, except, like Ezekiel, I hear the Spirit asking, 'Can this body live?'" Pastor Howard began to slowly raise his arms.

Mary looked toward the ceiling. *Lord, let him say something that will make my heart want to live!*

He continued to raise his arms. "I hear the Spirit saying prophesy to these dry bones—to the faith bone, to the knowledge bone, to the charity bone, to the wisdom bone, to the tongue-talking bone—to all of us separated—O ye dry bones, O body of Christ, you will live. We will love again! God is going to breathe new life into us! He is going to bind us together. He's going to get us on one accord and strengthen us! He's going to breathe life into us, and we shall live! He's going to breathe love back into us—love that will not die, love that will not fail! We will love again!"

He began to walk again. "Amen?"

The congregation said, "Amen!" The choir began to sing.

42

Moor

When the nine-thirty service was over, Moor waited in front, hoping to see Mary among the thousands of people flowing in and out. The truth was he could not get her off his mind.

What was also true was that Gail had very easily gotten him off of hers. "I know I said I wasn't dating anyone, and really I wasn't—we weren't committed. But he's asked me to marry him and I said yes." The rest of the conversation he didn't hear. He'd just stayed on the telephone to be polite. It surprised him that he wasn't hurt.

What was even truer was that he couldn't stop thinking about Mary. The green eyes, the yellow hair . . . he would have to live with them—if she would have him. If that was what was meant to be. *"Maybe this is some crazy divine plan. Maybe God has been orchestrating all this trying to get us together."* Her words kept haunting him. He couldn't stop thinking of her. And who was He to tell the Potter what kind of vessel was best for him? So what if she was not the kind of woman that men in his family liked? They would all have to live with it.

This was it. This was his last try. He was running out of time here in Baltimore. If he didn't see her, if he didn't see the woman with green eyes and blonde hair, he would say it was the Lord's will and let it be done. He would keep looking. He would give it a chance elsewhere.

"Hello." A hand tapped him on the shoulder.

Moor turned to say hello, then turned back quickly to watch for Mary's green eyes and yellow hair. He had to pay attention. Even with blonde hair and green eyes it would be hard to find her among the thousands of people pouring from the church, not to mention those on their way inside.

The hand tapped him again. "I said hello." And as he turned, the person that belonged to the hand kept talking. "This is no way to treat your divine destiny!"

He only recognized her voice after he smelled her perfume.

It was Mary. No yellow hair. No green eyes. But it was Mary. It was funny, intelligent, kind, beautiful Mary—looking like the kind of woman the men in his family liked! "Oh" was all he said.

"You didn't recognize me." She smiled shyly. "Well, this is the real me. Take it or leave it."

"I've been looking for you. I was standing here looking for you. Amongst all these people, you are just who I wanted to see."

She reached her hand toward his. "Shall we try?"

He took her hand. "Oh my!" was all he said.

Puddin

P*uddin rubbed scented cream* on her arms, hands, and elbows as she listened to Joe read from the last pages of his manuscript.

"It was all more lovely than any of them could ever have imagined. The African prince, in traditional attire, walked down the aisle on the arm of his beautiful beloved. Waiting for them at the altar were three wise men by his left side and three beautiful young virgins on her right.

"And so after months and months of worry, years and years of heartbreak, the two of them were finally joined in wedded bliss. The choir began to sing, and the church bells rang the moment they said, 'I do.'"

Joe closed the book that held pages of his manuscript and pulled off his eyeglasses.

"Oh, Joe. That was beautiful, honey. Who would have ever thought?"

"It wasn't so hard. I did what the romance writers taught me. I borrowed a lot from real life." He was grinning, obviously pleased with himself.

Puddin opened the drawer of her nightstand to put the jar of cream inside. The bottom was littered with Starbucks coupons. She took one out and held it up. "Joe, what am I going to do with all of these?" She waved it. "I don't even drink coffee."

Joe laughed. "Another thing I learned at Starbucks is that it's kind of like life."

Puddin closed her eyes for a second. She could feel one coming.

"Oh, Joe. Please?" He grinned, and she knew he was going to drop one of his nuggets anyway.

"In life, there are always choices, and that's how it is at Starbucks. If you don't like coffee, they make a mean cup of tea!"

"Oh, Joe!" Puddin began to giggle and couldn't stop, even when Joe put one arm around her and used the other to reach over and turn off the light.

Readers' Discussion Questions

As you read the questions, pray to God to open your heart, to reveal the answers inside of you, and to show you the answer in His Word.

If you've never prayed before, or if you're not sure you believe in God, ask Him to help you. My experience is that He will respond. You'll be amazed! He's been waiting to talk to you.

1. Do you have relationships in which you are waiting for the other person to love you before you love him or her? Describe those relationships. Why don't you love first? Will you be able to continue loving if they don't love you in return?

2. What are your flaws? Because you are flawed, do you worry that God doesn't love you? Do you try to hide your flaws? Could God use your flaws? How? Can you find people in the Bible with similar flaws? How did God use them?

3. Have you failed to offer God's love, or your love, to someone because you thought they weren't good enough, weren't right? Have you failed to serve someone, or love someone, because he or she was different? Why? Can you behave differently? Will you behave differently?

4. Are you afraid to love? Are you afraid to show love?

5. Are you showing love before you discipline your children? Have you established a loving relationship before you begin to correct

your stepchildren? Are you showing love before you punish employees?

6. Do you love God? Do you show Him that you love Him? Do you love Him the way He wants to be loved?

7. Are you afraid to get close to God because you think you're too wrong or too flawed? What does God say about that?

8. Are you enjoying your life? Why? Why not?

9. If you are a minister, do you spend more time serving or trying to make sure people think you've got it all together? Why?

10. Have you been on any really bad dates?